Journey
to the
Bone Tree

JAN THACKER

ISBN 978-1-68197-805-5 (Paperback)
ISBN 978-1-68197-806-2 (Digital)

Christian Faith Publishing, Inc.
296 Chestnut Street
Meadville, PA 16335
www.christianfaithpublishing.com

Printed in the United States of America

For Troy, my kind and caring husband of 50-plus years
who has given me a life of adventure and always encouraged
my dreams and ambitions. You are wonderful.
You are God's gift to me.

Also, for my children who are so very much loved:

For Janelle, who continues to astound me with her ambition,
zeal, love for life and the beauty she brings to others through
her Morningsong Flower Farm. And for Casey, our beloved
son-in-law who is right there beside her.

For Lisa, who I so admire for her compassion for foster children
and for what she brings to the lives of others and for her
dedication to community and family. And for Rick, our
treasured son-in-law, who is the glue that holds
his sprawling family together.

And, as always, for our dear Scott, who was always so proud of
"my mom the writer" and is waiting for us in Heaven.
Dear Scott, when we see you again- what a day that will be!

Grandchildren, what a blessing they are.
For Christopher, Kiana, Amanda, Keenan, Cody, Troy, Alex,
and Scooter - our older grandchildren. I am so proud of the
strong, independent, successful, and fine-looking men
and women you have become.

And, finally, for "the babies," our youngest grandchildren
and great-grandkids: Gianna, Andra, Benjamin, Owen,
Max, Quinn, Kevin and Klaire. May you always see the
world with such inquisitive and joyful natures.

Acknowledgements

While *Journey to the Bone Tree* is fiction with made-up characters and scenes, there are nuggets of truth in this story. My fictitious "Danford" is actually my hometown, Whitefish, Montana, in disguise. There truly is a bone tree there, just as there is a Rice's Hill. And there were once two little girls who played and dreamed on that hill. I was Sacajawea and Lynn Hetrick was Pocahontas. Our bone tree, alas, held nothing more than old bones and rocks and pine cones - none of the treasures that Marcy and Anna placed inside. But we did fix up the pole barn and we did create a white rock-lined "graveyard" and we did play with pop beads and dream of horse ranches. There were real horses in our lives and, just like Sharon Peterman in this tale, I went through a time of great despair when I came home from school one day and discovered the owner had taken away my beloved Cindy, the gentle mare I had loved for many years.

We are all old now, the neighborhood gang that played endlessly at Cow Creek and on Rice's Hill and in the glorious fields and woods surrounding our neighborhood east of town. Our members were few: Ted Tveidt, Doug and Lynn Hetrick, Vicki Barnes, I and my sister Judy Wood, and sometimes our very young siblings, but our exploits and adventures were worthy of multitudes of novels!

Just like we have all grown up and changed, so has Whitefish changed. It is no longer the tiny modest jewel of a town nestled in some of the most gorgeous country in the world. Flathead Valley has been discovered by outsiders. Whitefish is now a town of wealth and pompousness, of gated communities, and boutiques. A lot of the pasturelands and simple storefronts we grew up with are gone. Fields have given way to subdivisions and downtown traffic is endless as it slithers through streets that are now lined with buildings stunning in beauty and extravagance.

Where is my dear and precious Whitefish? This town where my maternal and paternal great-grandparents settled in the 1800s? This town where decades of us dwelled and thrived? It's all still there -- etched deep in memories and tales handed down.

To me, Whitefish will always be as it was in the 1950s - a little town with little crime where people looked after one another and where kids could play from morning until nightfall without worrying about anything more than getting home before dinner hit the table. A town where if a stranger was seen on the street everyone within fives miles knew within five minutes. A town where wives wore house-dresses; where newspapers were sometimes delivered by horse; where females wore hats and gloves to church; where logging trucks were as common as farm trucks: where twenty-five cents would get you in the Saturday matinee at the Orpheum Theater with enough left over for pop, popcorn and a candy bar; where John Bartlett at City Pharmacy would bandage a scrape if you fell off your bike; where you could go to Penney's and take home clothes "on approval;" and where you could "charge" a quarter or fifty cents at the pharmacy if you needed fast cash.

It was where, as a teenager, you lolled at City Beach or paid fifty cents for a lift ticket to race down the slopes at Big Mountain; where you drove endlessly around and around and around the town on Friday and Saturday nights, honking and waving and switching from car to car at intersections and finally ending up at Gordy's Drive In. It was a little town that was pretty much heaven on earth.

Today's generation will never know what Whitefish was - what an amazing childhood we had back then. They will never know the freedom we had, the joy, the camaraderie, the spirit that made Whitefish what it was. We were family. All of us. One big, happy, sometimes quirky, but always loved, family. I graduated in 1964 with the same kids I started kindergarten with. It was that kind of town.

And so, I want to acknowledge all of the Whitefish kids of the '50s and '60s (cheers to you, class of '64!), and especially, to the beloved members of our neighborhood gang. We were so much more than friends. We grew up together and our mothers and fathers were parents to us all. We were siblings. Finally, this tale is dedicated to Ted Tveidt, the oldest of our ragtag bunch who died a few months ago, the first of us to go. What a wealth of memories he left behind.

To all of you who were such a part of my life, thank you. You are loved.

To my readers

I started Journey to the Bone Tree many years ago. It is so odd--
and wonderful -- how God works, how he prepares us for life. As
you know, *Journey to the Bone Tree* deals with the death of a child.
God enabled me to envision the emotions and the stages of grief that
such a situation would bring about. I shed an abundance of tears
over what Marcy went through when losing her friend, and what the
Millers went through when losing their only daughter.

I had already finished writing *Journey* when our wonderful son,
Scott, died unexpectedly in a tragic accident. After years of struggle
Scott had just gotten his life together and was at peace and abun-
dantly joyful when God chose to bring him home. Later, when I
reread *Journey to the Bone Tree* I was able to see how God prepared
me. Through this book, he had already walked me through all the
emotions and stages of grief. He gave me a great understanding of
how to cope with Scott's death and this allowed me to help my husband and Scott's siblings and children get through it.

God, through *Journey to the Bone Tree*, had already given me the
end of my own story of dealing with the death of a child. I knew that
despite the darkness of our sorrow we always have hope and that God
never leaves us. He is with us steadfastly through all of our trials and
tribulations. I pray that if you don't know him, that you will seek him
out. Life eternal is a free gift from him and all you have to do is just
grab it and hang on!

Chapter 1

* * *

No one knows why they call it Rice's Hill. Maybe it's some pioneer name from long ago. There is a log here on this hill not far from the Bone Tree. The wind probably blew it over decades before. One time, Anna wrapped her arms around the big end and, keeping them in a circle, walked to the Bone Tree. Yup, she declared, the log had broken off—had snapped right off and maybe fallen on a rabbit. Poor thing. Then it crashed to the ground, taking its innards and leaving behind the hollowed-out mother stump—our Bone Tree—sitting jagged and bereft. The log was part of our play, and we had carefully carved our names, Marcy and Anna, on the smooth wood. Later, we added Pocahontas and Sacajawea, our Indian names. We ran along its length in our moccasins, imagining we were crossing deadly waters and trying to escape the enemy. The log was also our table and, when straddled, our place to sit when we talked about serious things. Girl things. Oftentimes, during the endless days of summer, we nestled in the grass and leaned our backs against it. Then we gazed down the hill and imagined the future.

* * *

Twelve-year-old Marcy Peterman could feel her steps falter as she got closer to the house at the end of the block. The September sun fell on her face and arms in a sheet of enveloping warmth, but she felt cold inside. A shudder started in her innards and snaked upward. Her arms clenched her sides and hugged the sales packet she carried.

"Why're you walking like such a pokey?" Ben asked when his sister slowed to a shuffle. In answer, Marcy came to an abrupt stop. Her feet felt as firmly rooted to the sidewalk as the nearby knots of wood that gnarled and twined out of the earth beneath a shading oak.

"You don't have to walk with me," Marcy said without looking at him. "There's no law that says you have to."

"Maybe I won't," Ben said. "Maybe I'll run all the way home and eat all the cookies."

"Do that," Marcy said. "I don't care."

"I don't know why you passed our house anyways," Ben said, turning around and pointing. "It's right back there, and you just walked by like you forgot."

Marcy knew what she would see if she looked behind her—a street lined on both sides with houses built in the 1940s and 50s. Sturdy houses, with wide front porches and surrounded by thick-trunked maples and elms and beds of perennials. Some had flag-poles standing at attention on the front porch. Others had gazebos or swings with the lawn underneath worn down to circles of brown dirt from decades of barefooted children.

Window shades would be pulled this time of day to try and get ahead of the late afternoon heat. It was unseasonably warm, even for an Indian summer. It was hard for residents of the small town of Danford, Montana, to comprehend that winter was the season beyond this one. Gold, red, and orange leaves stuck to trees as if clinging to life itself, as if knowing that when they dropped to the ground, their months of glory would come to an end.

Home was back there too, behind her. The only home she had ever known. This house, the one she shared with her parents and nine-year-old Ben, was sprawling and elegant, with lots of fancy gingerbread and a front porch with enough old wicker furniture to seat ten people. The house, with arched front windows with stained-glass panes at the top, had been the fanciful dream of her great-grandmother.

She wished she was there now, at home, with her mother hugging her close.

But she wasn't headed home. She was going from house to house selling items to raise money for her school. She dreaded every knock on every door because it brought her closer and closer to the one house that would be mighty hard to approach.

This house was different from the rest. Set back on a corner banked lot with a set of rock stairs leading upwards through a notch in the four-foot wall, it was quiet and still and lifeless. The draperies drooped, and one panel had been askew, resting on the back of a sofa for at least two months. Sun-rotted newspapers nestled in dying knee-deep grass, and a rake remained where it had been thrust on a day so tragic, so heartbreaking, that its user never returned to put it away, let alone finish the job. Now weeds twined around the metal spokes, and most of the handle was obscured by seeded grass.

The day before, Marcy had looked at the rake curiously as she rode by on her bike. Had it been that long? It seemed so strange that the world hadn't stopped and life was continuing, speeding by as if nothing had ever happened.

The yard was a constant reminder to everyone in the neighborhood. It was like a marker in a book. Oh, this is where we left off. Before it are pages of the past, and ahead of it are pages of the future.

But the marked page never changes, and there is no going back or forward until it is dealt with.

After the tragedy with Anna, an assortment of friends and neighbors had asked to take over outside chores, but they were turned down. "Just leave things as they are," they were told. In time, the lawn would be watered and raked and mowed. In time, the page with the marker would be turned.

But deep in the night, old Mrs. Franklin snaked her hose through the hedge between her house and the Miller's house and watered the roses and flower beds and sprayed a bit on the lawn. That, she thought, was the very least she could do for these poor people.

"Maybe you should go home," Marcy said to Ben. "I'll be right behind you. And you'd better save me some cookies."

Chapter 2

* * *

In the springtime, water trickled down the ditches on either side of Second Avenue, the road that linked us to Danford and ran along the south side of Rice's Hill. The snowmelt tumbled downward until it flowed into Slate Creek, which ran north to south at the bottom of the hill. Spring was the time to find beautiful rocks washed by rushing water until they were glistening clean and shiny. Our pockets would hang heavy, full of treasured stones. Offerings for the Bone Tree. One spring, for two whole days, Anna and I dragged branches and boulders and piled them against the culvert under the road. The next morning, on our way to school, we were gleeful to discover the brown water right to the top of the road, and we sprinted back home certain we would have to miss school because of the unfortunate flooding. Instead, Anna's dad loaded us in the car and drove us up the hill and around the stockyards and through Danford and eventually to school. The next day, the county people came and unblocked the culvert.

* * *

Marcy struggled with herself. She didn't want to go to this house and face these people and their consuming grief. She knew it was there. She could see it when she rode her bike down the street and glanced toward this island of anguish. Shadows of death and heartbreak seemed to pulsate from the windows. They mirrored the shadows deep in her own soul.

She was only twelve years old, but she was wise enough to know that she wasn't mature enough to handle walking up to the door of this house. Anna's house. The house where Anna lived. Used to live. Now she lived in a brass vase called an urn. Odd how that was, Marcy thought. That you could get a whole body into a metal urn. One day you're playing hopscotch and talking dreamy talk about someday... Someday you'll have a horse ranch and you'll go to college to become a teacher and then you'll marry a handsome man and have four children, maybe five, and live in a big house in the country with horses in a pasture. Someday. Dreamy, dreamy somedays.

One day you're there and the next day you aren't. How long would it be, she thought, until she talked about Anna and the person she was talking to asked, "Anna who?"

She didn't want to go to this house. But how could she not? Anna's father and mother hadn't gone back to work since their daughter's death. While Marcy had been roaming past a window, the Millers may have seen Marcy going from door to door, to door, working her way up the street and taking orders for stupid rolls of gift wrap and bags of cheap bows and nonsensical items that didn't make a lick of sense to her.

Why, she thought, would Joe and Barbara Miller want to buy gift wrap when their only child was so recently dead the carnations in her grave flowers were still almost fresh? And why would they want to buy anything from her when she was the one to escape while their daughter had been the one to die?

But how could she not give them the honor of at least a semblance of normality.

Do you want to buy some gift wrap? Or some really nice flowered note cards? If you get two gift bags, you get one free. The money is for playground equipment. So kids can play. Not your kid. She's dead. But other people's kids.

She had been in their house so many times she called them her second mom and dad, so she couldn't just sidestep the house like it wasn't really there. But she couldn't imagine that they would want to buy anything from her. Or from anyone else.

Her steps faltered. Maybe she should just turn around right now and go home.

Lavender, the pudgy poodle with an overbite that belonged to the elderly couple next door to the Millers, barked, and Marcy gave a soft whistle. The ancient dog, its eyes cloudy with cataracts, recognized the sound and wiggled from head to toe before bouncing to Marcy's side. The young girl's silky honey-blond hair fell in long shiny sheets on either side of her face as she knelt to pet the dog.

"Hey there, Lavender. It's me. Your friend, Marcy," she said softly, tossing down the sales book. The book made a gritty sound as it skidded on the sidewalk. She hugged the dog, burying her face in the curly fur. Lavender lived up to her name. She smelled good, like the lavender toilet water her owner, Mrs. Franklin, sprinkled on her wrists and neck morning and night. Toilet water…Marcy and Anna had laughed so often over the phrase. Who'd want to wear toilet water?

"I'll bet you miss her, don't you, baby? She was your friend too, wasn't she, Lavender?"

A car passed by and then another. Whorls of air moved upward and loosened a sifting of maple leaves. They cascaded softly, comfortingly, on the girl and the old dog.

When she stood, Marcy's steps were no longer hesitant. She walked with purpose, perhaps gaining a sort of strength from a wise old canine that seemed to sense her distress.

The house seemed so different now. It had lost its vitality and personality and was now just a bundle of materials that could be bought at any one of a dozen stores in that part of Montana. The bones were there, and the skeleton and even the skin. But the soul was gone. Two people lived in the stately white house, but it was still empty.

Standing at the door, Marcy at first couldn't figure out what to do. She couldn't bear to ring the doorbell since she had done it a thousand times before. Those times, the rings were answered with friendliness and fun. The door would burst open, and Anna would reach out and pull her into her world. She didn't want to ever again hear the chimes.

So she knocked.

Once, twice, five times.

She closed her eyes and waited. She could hear rustling.

The door opened slowly, and she opened her eyes. Just a sliver of gloom could be seen from where she stood.

Joe Miller was just inside the door. His eyes, black holes in a pale and whiskered face, were haunted and filled with something she couldn't fathom.

"Marcy?" His voice was raspy, as if he hadn't talked for a long time and his vocal chords were out of tune. He opened the door wider.

She walked into the room and knew she shouldn't have come. Not to sell trinkets and brightly flowered junk to this man who had just lost his daughter. Her reasons, that they would feel left out if she bypassed the house, were totally skewed. She realized now that the Millers were so drenched in agonizing grief that they wouldn't have comprehended or even noticed if she walked past their house.

Without looking, she could tell the house was not as tidy as it usually was. Drinking glasses, coffee mugs, and plates held down papers that littered tables. It smelled too, like an old book found after decades of living entombed in a box.

"Our class is selling this stuff," she said, holding up the sales packet before letting her hand drop to her side. An order blank fluttered under a hall table. Her eyes filled with tears, and her lips curled downward. She looked through the tears at her new school shoes, so shiny and black. They looked happy. She wanted to kick them off and throw them away.

"I thought maybe I should come here, but I don't know why now," she said, looking up. She used the back of her hand to wipe her eyes.

He stared at her, holding his hand out to her before pulling it back. He was silent.

"I haven't seen you since the funeral," she blurted. Her voice sounded loud and muffled in the gloom. Hollow. She lowered it to a whisper, "I wanted to, but I didn't know how to come here."

He opened his arms, and she walked into them. They both cried, and he rocked her slowly back and forth. Over the years, she had been hugged a hundred times by Joe and Barbara Miller, but those were quick, hard, "I love you, sweetie" hugs. This was one that passed pain from one to the other. Still, it was comforting to both of them.

Finally, he released her and used the knuckle of his forefinger to brush away her tears before using the back of his hand to wipe his own eyes.

"It's okay, Marcy. Don't cry. It's okay. You have to be safe," he said. "Come in the living room and be safe. We have to figure out how to protect you."

Marcy walked deeper inside the room.

They didn't speak. She didn't know what to say. What do you say to a grieving father? Talk about the weather? *It sure is hot, isn't it? A real scorcher for September.*

That was about all she was good for these days—talking about the weather or the new store downtown or the latest movie or school. Shallow subjects in a life that was now so shallow she felt like she was floating.

Joe Miller was agitated, pacing back and forth across the room and muttering to himself and swiping away tears when he noticed them searing his cheeks.

"I'm sorry," he said, quickly coming to a stop before her. He turned and swept away a pile of papers and clothes from the red chair.

She loved the red chair. It was covered in smooth silky fabric and was apple red—not one of those dark ominous reds or insipid faded reds, but a color that was warm, vibrant. She and Anna decided when they were eleven that when they started their periods, they would sit in the red chair during those times, just to be safe in case of accidents.

"Don't move," he warned Marcy as she perched at the edge of the chair. "We have to keep you safe. I'm afraid you'll go toward the water, and you can't be by the water. I have to figure out what to do."

"Mr. Miller, it's okay," she told him. "I'm safe. Nothing's going to happen to me." It was distressing and alarming to see him so agitated.

He seemed to read her mind and tried to put her at ease. "I was doing all right, and today was really quite a good day." He paused, and a frown settled over his face. "Then you came here. I can't let it happen again, Marcy. I couldn't bear it if something happened to you too, and it was my fault."

Her heart ached for him. She knew what he was feeling. It had taken weeks of listening to her parents to finally accept that there was nothing she could have done. Life on earth was transient, and this wasn't really home for a Christian. We were just visitors wearing earth suits and waiting to go home. The simple fact was that God just took Anna home. Could she make him see this?

"But it wasn't your fault. It wasn't anyone's fault. She slipped and fell in the water, and it swept her away. God brought her home," Marcy told him. He shook his head, and his eyes were so sad she looked away.

He started to cry and slumped into a nearby chair and held his head in his hands. "My poor Anna. She was so full of life, and now she's gone. I should have protected her."

Marcy got to her feet and went to him and placed her hand on his shoulder. She had no words. Not one word came from her brain to offer him solace. So many comforting platitudes had been poured over her in the last weeks, and she couldn't remember any of them.

When he spoke again, his voice was a choked raspy whisper, "It could have been both of you."

"You couldn't have done anything," she said. Her voice sounded hollow. "It was an accident."

It killed her to talk about it. Each time she did, or each time she was forced to remember, it killed her, piece by piece. If it didn't stop, soon there would be nothing left but a long scream. And then silence.

The police had forced her, at least four times, to tell the details. Every detail. What were they wearing, what time it was when they entered the pasture, if they were fighting, why Anna was running ahead…

Telling them was remembering out loud, putting words to the day.

Inwardly, she went over the details endlessly. It was the never-ending story. Like the John Jacob Jingleheimer Schmidt song they sang at camp—the never-ending song that infinitely looped until they were laughing too hard to sing it again.

Now the memory swept again through her mind, coming to life with a flutter of black dots, like the eight-millimeter family movies her great-grandfather used to play on his old projector.

Chapter 3

* * *

Nothing ever stayed the same on Rice's Hill. One weekend there would be patches of flowers, delicate white, purple, and pink shooting stars and exotic lady slippers and tiny bluebells, and the next weekend they would be gone. We loved the wild flowers, and at first, we picked them and took them home to our mothers. Then I told Anna we should let them live as long as they could. She agreed, saying "They, oh the poor things, had a hard enough time, what with fighting the springtime cold and the endless nibbling by rabbits and deer and other creatures." The dandelions weren't so revered, and we chained them together until our fingers turned gold. Then we draped the flowery necklaces around our necks where they became hot and moist and wilted droopily. Sometimes, with great ceremony, we carried long ropes of chained dandelions to the graves of our make-believe Indian ancestors. The graves were carefully tended and decorated with white rocks and transplanted wild daisies. The dandelions, Anna said, made them even more beautiful.

* * *

July 21. Would that date always be embossed on her mind? She knew many birthdays, but would this day always hold honor as the first death day? Except for an uncle she barely knew, death had never visited Marcy Peterman's life.

It had been raining hard for nearly three weeks, but then the sun had finally come out and dried out the land and brought back summer. They had been walking in a nearby pasture, the low pasture close to the railroad tracks, along the irrigation ditch. There were signs of course; there were always warning signs around the irrigation ditches.

It wasn't the first time they went to their private sanctuary this way—through the pasture. She didn't know why they decided to on this day. It wasn't any closer than just staying on the road and, midway to the top of Rice's Hill, climbing through a weak spot in the barbed-wire fence to the place where they played. In fact, it was much easier just keeping to the road.

The pasture was at the bottom of the hill. The barbed wire was stretched tighter here and was more difficult to get through. The land was dotted with thistles, and they had to keep watch for the cows that called it home. They didn't think the cows would hurt them, but they did sometimes thunder across the pasture when they spotted outsiders crossing their territory. Going through the pasture also meant, at the edge of it, picking their way through a series of ancient, leaning, paint-faded sheds and hay barns and leftover farm equipment that hadn't seen use in decades. Most importantly, it meant sneaking and hoping that old Mr. Knutson didn't spot them and holler from his side porch to stay away from that ditch if the water was high.

They hadn't discussed going through the pasture, and she guessed it was because they wanted to get away from the cars speeding by and spitting up gravel and dust. The traffic on the road had increased five-fold since the new subdivision had been built further down the road, interrupting any conversation and privacy the walking public might have had.

So they lifted the wire one for the other. Anna snagged her new blue shorts in the process and was worried the small hole would turn into a bigger hole, one of those that frayed and was unfixable.

"Doggone it anyway," she said, stomping her foot. Anna always said "Doggone it it anyway" when she was perturbed.

"It's okay, Anna," Marcy said. "It'll match the big tear in the back of your new shirt."

"What?" She turned in circles, trying to see the back of her shirt while Marcy laughed.

"Just kidding," Marcy finally said.

"You are a brat," Anna said, reaching down and grabbing a handful of weeds and throwing them at her.

Irrigation ditches can be friendly, or unfriendly, depending on the rainfall, the time of year and when water is released upstream. Sometimes, the water is just a happily flowing amble through the land; other times, it is raging and ferocious.

On that day, the brown water was very high, but it didn't look deadly, and they didn't realize that it was moving with incredible speed.

They knew, all the neighborhood kids knew, that irrigation ditch water was different from the water in Slate Creek, where they played in the summer. Slate Creek was low enough they could jump from rock to rock and never get wet. The one place where it was deep enough to swim had banks that were so infested with nettles and cockleburs they didn't go there. Instead, they played on the plank bridge with its spatters of cow pies or dabbled in the water where it was shallow or romped on the grassy banks where they sometimes, when it was staggeringly hot, would get a whiff of wild mint or sweet clover.

Anna was skipping ahead; she was always skipping ahead, as if so anxious to bolt into the world, she couldn't do it at a normal pace. Her hair, as black and curly as her father's, caught the sunlight, and shimmers of light danced on her head.

Marcy envied Anna's beautiful hair and her flawless rosy complexion and deep blue eyes. In comparison, Anna thought herself to be pale, her golden hair too straight and lank. To onlookers, they were night and day—the exotic beauty of darkness and the sunny beauty of daylight. The looks of one complemented the other.

It was a gorgeous midsummer afternoon, and they had packed cheese sandwiches, baggies of chips, and cans of Coke for a lunch. It wasn't traditional Indian fare, but it would do. They could pretend it was pemmican and venison and wild berries and a drink made from the sweet syrup of wild honeysuckle.

On this afternoon, they weren't going to Slate Creek even though it was hot enough from the summer sun to warrant a day spent with feet dangling in cool water.

Instead, they were going to the Bone Tree on Rice's Hill, a hollowed-out scraggy stump over two feet across and not quite four feet tall where they cached hunks of bone they found or interesting rocks and pieces of wood and hidden treasures. Sometimes, they added tinfoil-wrapped bits of wisdom they had written down or a special trinket. Once, while scavenging in the woods on Rice's Hill, they found a shed deer antler and pondered it mightily, wondering at the beast that had sported such a fine antler. It was added to the Bone Tree.

In a small ceremony, they thanked the deer for providing it for them. Someday, they decided, they would take it from the tree and carve on it with their jackknives or maybe use permanent markers to decorate it. First, they needed to copy a design from the book on North American Indians that Joe and Barbara Miller had in their library. Much of what they incorporated into their play came from poring over this book.

Everything in the Bone Tree had meaning, and nothing was dropped into it without thought. A treasure had to measure up to their expectations before being added to the rest of the collection.

At the bottom of the Bone Tree, the very bottom and covered by a square of moss they had cut from a fallen tree with their knives, was an ornate tin box. It was the first item they ever placed in the tree. That was the summer they were nine. They agreed to cement their friendship by writing secrets: a list of life goals, of people they liked and disliked, and declaring they would be friends forever.

The next day, Marcy brought two pens and two sheets of fine linen writing paper pilfered from her mother's desk as well as two sealable plastic bags. Anna brought the tin box that was shaped like a heart and enameled with pink flowers.

"You stay here, and I'll go over there in the sunflowers," Anna had said, and they spent the next half hour writing.

"I'm putting you at the top of my list of people I don't like," Anna called across the grass. Then she fell over with laughter, her legs kicking at the air.

"I have a whole *page* of stuff I've written about why I don't like you," Marcy retorted. "Plus, I'm taking you out of my will. Except for my socks. You can have my dirty socks." Reaching down, she pulled off her shoes and peeled off her socks. "You can have them right now!" she said, tossing them toward Anna.

"Oh, yuck! Not the socks. Please, not the socks!" Anna said, jumping up and grabbing a stick and flinging them back toward her friend.

A few minutes later, they came together and solemnly put their carefully folded papers, unread by the other, into the box.

Marcy carried this offering to the Bone Tree and leaned in and dropped it in the hollow. Then Anna placed a hunk of old plastic tablecloth over it and dropped in the piece of moss. They used a stick to make sure it totally covered the box.

The two friends sat on the ground, and Anna brought out her jackknife. Following her lead, Marcy reached in her pocket and pulled out her knife. Wordlessly, but not without some groaning and high-pitched yelps, they poked holes in the palms of their hands and then, when the blood bubbled, held them together.

Blood sisters.

When they graduated from high school, they vowed they would return to this childhood fairyland and remove, piece by piece, the items of the Bone Tree. They would sit in the summer sunshine and would read and laugh over what they had written so many years before. In the three years since that day when they were nine, they had never once thought of opening the tin box.

Chapter 4

* * *

We didn't play on Rice's Hill in the wintertime, at least not that part of the hill. But we did slide down the road that was notched through it. Every weekend, a lot of us from the neighborhood would gather there with our sleds. On a day when the road was really slick if we started at the very top, we could scream down the hill, fly over the flat area by Mr. Knutson's house, zip down to the gully, cross Slate Creek, and make it halfway up another hill before slowing to a stop. Anna was belly down on her new Christmas sled one Saturday and couldn't get steered away from an oncoming car. We were horrified when she disappeared underneath, but she popped out the other side. She was fine.

Generally, we had two good days of sledding before the state sanded the road. We loved our sleds and the terrifying feeling of flying down sheer ice.

* * *

After the funeral, Marcy sat on the hammock in her backyard and shuffled her feet back and forth. During this time, she thought back to the last words they would ever say to one another. It had been such a happy and joyous day that it was hard to believe it could have ended in such tragedy.

Anna wouldn't tell Marcy what treasure she was adding to the Bone Tree that day, just saying that it was a surprise and it was something so wonderful, so awesome, that Marcy wouldn't believe it. She bounced and hopped in her excitement.

No amount of cajoling or begging could get even a hint of information out of her.

"You won't believe it when you see it. My grandpa gave it to me," she said, lifting her arms and spinning.

"Well, what if I don't want to see your stupid treasure," Marcy had said, feigning nonchalance.

"Oh, you'll want to see this!" Anna had teased. She was ahead of Marcy by now and turned around to walk backwards so she could face Marcy. "I'll give you a clue. It has to do with Indians."

Marcy rolled her eyes. She hated guessing games. Sometimes, she refused to play, and after a time, the other person would just blurt out whatever it was they thought was so important they had to make a game out of it. This time, Marcy was too curious to wait.

"I guess.....a drawing."

"A drawing? From my grandpa? I don't think he could draw a smiley face, let alone an Indian."

"Okay, a keychain with an Indian face."

"Really, Marcy, have you ever in your life seen a keychain with an Indian face?"

"Well, no, but that is what would make it unique and a treasure."

"I'm not going to tell, so even if you did guess, I wouldn't tell you," Anna declared.

"Is it a scalp?"

"Yuck. Gross. Yeah, like I have a scalp in my pocket. My grandfather had it in his dresser drawer. Forgot all about it until the other day when he fished it out and gave it to me."

Marcy didn't tell Anna but she had her own treasure to share. Her mother had given her two ropes of pop beads leftover from when her grandmother used them in the sixties and gave them to her years before. Marcy's mother, Sharon Peterman, had discovered the beads the night before, buried deep in an old sewing box and twining around some rust-pocked crochet hooks.

Pop beads. What a wonderful find. Marcy couldn't wait to show them to Anna. The plastic beads had a hole on one end and a little button knob on the other. They could be taken totally apart and popped back together in any number of ways. She and Anna could spend the whole afternoon playing with the pop beads. She had even wrapped them in an old linen napkin so that she could lay them out on it and display them properly.

Marcy was partial to the bright yellow string, but she would sacrifice it if Anna really wanted it. She would be happy with the multicolored beads. Maybe, she thought, they could just mix them all up, or maybe they could trade off each week. The possibilities were endless.

As Anna dashed ahead along the irrigation ditch, Marcy fingered the beads in her pocket. She smiled to herself in anticipation.

The Bone Tree on Rice's Hill and the area around it was their private place, located in the middle of the hill where the land leveled out a bit and, for some reason, the buck brush didn't grow wild. It was parkland with soft grass, patches of flowers, and towering trees. There was a hushed atmosphere that seemed to keep the rest of the world at bay. Some areas, deep in the trees where little light penetrated, had a ground cover of plush green moss that deadened most sound.

They were Indians on Rice's Hill. Marcy was Sacajawea, and Anna was Pocahontas. They wore fringed and beaded cowhide moccasins bought with babysitting money and wore genuine Indian headbands. Imaginary horses, beautiful horses that they rode with barebacked abandon, were tied to nearby trees where they nickered softly and flicked their glorious tails.

Two years before, the summer they were ten, a beautiful rust-colored mare with a flowing blond mane and tail suddenly appeared on the hill with her foal, evidently, they thought, pastured there by someone who had arranged it with Mr. Knutson. The two horses made that summer the most delightful. They named the horses Kemo and Sabe, a nod to the old *Lone Ranger* series they watched on television. Anna had looked it up on the Internet and learned the word *kemosabe* meant faithful friend or trusted scout. Either way, the names fit perfectly.

In time, they became brave enough to climb on Kemo's back, and the matronly mare didn't seem to mind at all. They didn't have a bridle or anything to use for reins, but the horse quickly learned to move to the left or right by a hand placed on her neck and pushed in the direction they wanted her to go. She learned to stop when they pulled back on her heavy mane.

Sabe the colt, probably no more than a few weeks old when he came to the hill, was boisterous and energetic and quickly learned to head-butt the girls, which was fun at first. By the end of summer, he had gotten so big he could send them sprawling.

The horses were welcome additions to their village, which, in their imaginations, was accessed by going through a secret maze in the rocks. They had burial grounds on this land and areas where tribal members slept and cooked, carved arrowheads, and created buttery-soft doeskin dresses in front of campfires.

The first year, they had cleaned decades of cow dung from an open pole shed that had a sloping roof, eventually reaching clean earth, which they tamped down until it was smooth and hard. Then they tore boughs from trees and, using lengths of baling twine found in the rafters of the shed, covered the sides. They declared it their teepee.

During the summer months, Marcy and Anna balked at haircuts and managed to escape any such plans their mothers may have had for them. The two Indian maidens kept their hair long so that it could be plaited into braids that hung in thick ropes down their backs. Most of the other preteens had shorter hair, which they straightened and rolled and permed and curled. Marcy and Anna thought their peers were extremely silly.

They planned here, Marcy and Anna, and dreamed. The reality of life was never allowed in. Marcy's marginal grades were meaningless in their village, as were Anna's vacillating feelings about her budding breasts. This was a place to tie together poles and gather cedar and spruce branches to make a hut to escape a rain shower. It was a place to put stones in a ring for an imaginary fire.

Sometimes, when the air was damp and they knew it was safe, they built real fires—small fires—with matches smuggled from Marcy's grandparents' cigarette drawer. The terror brought on by such rebellious acts was as delicious as apples stolen from the neighbors' trees.

Rice's Hill was their paradise, a place to share life and share treasures.

Chapter 5

* * *

We were playing in the grass close to the Bone Tree, racing on our imaginary horses. I was Sacajawea, and Anna was Pocahontas. We were wearing our headbands and moccasins and running with the wind up the hill toward the old pole shed. The ground here under the tall ponderosa pines was bare, with just patches of sickly grass. Brown pine needles carpeted most of the area. Suddenly, Anna stopped and stood looking down at the ground. Then she crouched, and I could see her stroking something, moving her right hand gently back and forth. It was a young crow, its blue-black wings glistening with life even though its cloudy eyes told the truth of death. My instinct was to push it around with a stick, but before I could find one, Anna had picked it up and nestled it in her arms. She was crying. Before we buried it in the grave we dug near the Indian burial ground, she carefully pulled out four long black tail feathers to be added to our headbands. The feathers were almost the same color as Anna's raven-black hair.

* * *

Marcy thought that until the day of her death, she would wonder if her moccasins had saved her life that day. She and Anna ran silently across the pasture, carefully traversing patches of thistles and cow pies. Both girls loved their moccasins, the fact that they were so low to the ground they felt they were one with the land and they could move with quiet stealth.

They were racing, running with wild abandon on imaginary horses, feeling the wind on their faces and their hair flying behind. Kemo and Sabe were gone from their lives, having been there just one long summer, but they continued to use their names. In their minds, Sabe had grown to be a sleek black stallion, and Kemo could run as if the devil himself was behind her.

And then it happened. Marcy's moccasin flew off, and her naked foot landed on a thistle. She yelped in pain. Anna slowed and turned around, prancing backward.

"You okay?" she hollered back.

"My moccasin fell off, and I stepped on a thistle," Marcy yelled. "Wait for me."

"I'll meet you by the old tractor," Anna said, running off.

"Aw, c'mon, Anna, just wait a second for me," Marcy yelled. Spotting a clump of grass, she hopped over to it on her good foot and plopped down. Pulling the sole of her foot into her lap, she pulled out the stickers and ran the backs of her fingers over the rest of her foot to make sure she'd gotten them all. Looking up, she spotted Anna, racing alongside the irrigation ditch.

"Don't go close to that ditch or I'll tell on you," Marcy hollered as Anna rushed along the ridge. The high water boiled in swirls and eddies just a few feet away from where her feet nimbly landed.

Anna turned her head and laughed.

"And who are you going to tell?" she yelled back. "No one's here but you and me, and we're Indian maidens galloping along so fast on our wonderful horses that no one can catch us."

By now, Anna was a half a block ahead.

"Anna, I mean it," Marcy yelled as she yanked on her moccasin. "You know those ditches are dangerous. Come back here with me."

The Indian maiden, Pocahontas, raised her arm high in the air and made a wide circular motion as if swinging a lariat. Behind her and still on the ground tying her moccasin, Sacajawea knew she was supposed to interpret the sign to mean she'd better get her imaginary horse moving or she'd be left in the dust. But the fantasy was suddenly gone, giving way to reality. She didn't know why but she was suddenly terrified for her friend. She jumped to her feet and started running. Faster than she ever had before. She thought she screamed Anna's name but later couldn't remember if she did, or if she only thought she did.

The bank gave away.

Anna was there. And then she wasn't.

There was no sound. At first. Just an empty pasture clear to the tree line and, beyond that, the railroad tracks.

Marcy ran. Later, she wouldn't remember that part of it. She wouldn't remember how she got there so fast. Sometimes, she wished she hadn't moved at all, that she had just stood where she was until darkness settled and the stars came out and someone found her there as still as a statue. Maybe frozen into a pillar of salt like Lot's wife.

But somehow, she did get to where the bank had crumbled into a pile of dampened dirt. Later, she thought it was so odd that she remembered Anna's moccasin. It was stuck in the dirt with the toe imbedded and the soft heel thrust upward, like she had been lifted from her shoe while doing a pirouette.

She could see Anna's hair and the blur of her body beneath the brown torrent. Her head was barely above the water, and she frantically tried to swim, but the water held her down. It was moving fast. So fast.

Anna feebly called for help. Or was it just an imagined whispered plea coming through the roar in Marcy's head?

Marcy clambered back up the slope and ran along the bank. Her lungs ached, and she was too terrified to scream, afraid that she would lose some momentum. She tried to keep her eyes on Anna and run. Faster and faster.

She ran until she reached Anna and then ran past so she would be ahead of her when she leaped into the ditch.

Oh god, oh god, oh god. The words were a mantra, a prayer without praying, a hope without hoping. But Marcy knew before she jumped. Anna was totally under water, and she wasn't fighting. Her body traveled swiftly as the water took her downstream, as compliant as a water bug or a spawning salmon that couldn't fight the current and just let the water carry it wherever it wished. She bobbed up and down, her hair rising and falling with the current, her red shirt floating up and revealing her back.

The water must have been cold, but Marcy didn't comprehend it as she hurtled over the bank and dove. She was moving by reaction rather than by planning. She grabbed for Anna, but the water was too fast. She plunged her arm toward a flash of red, and the fabric brushed against her fingers, a whisper of hope, before it floated away.

The water was evil and relentless and pulled Marcy under with such force she had to fight with every ounce of strength to break free of its mighty hold, its determination to pull her under.

Later, she wouldn't remember the water gurgling with terrifying speed through the culvert below the bridge, taking Anna with it.

She wouldn't remember screaming or being trapped in the water or hanging onto the culvert edge for dear life, her legs sucked into it, sticking straight out and pointing the way of the water.

They found Anna's limp and lifeless body a quarter of a mile away, her red shirt caught in a tangle of debris and a bump on her head where she must have banged it on a rock when she tumbled into the water.

Her parents told her about that part the next day. They also named Marcy's rescuers as if the names would be important to her, but they were meaningless. There was only one name that meant anything—Anna.

They told her, endless well-meaning people who paraded through the hospital where she was kept for observation, that she was lucky to be alive. Lucky? How could that be when all she wanted was to be dead? How could she be called lucky when her best friend, white-faced with the blood sucked out of her during death, was entombed in a brass container?

She asked her father to fetch Anna's moccasin from the ditch, and he cleaned off the dirt and gave it to her. She held it close. Even though they knew it should go to the grieving Millers, her parents didn't have the heart to pry it from her bandaged fingers.

The cuts from the culvert were deep. Every finger was slashed, some so deep they required stitches. She relished the pain. She didn't know why but she clung to the pain like it was a living entity. Was it a reminder? Punishment? Or was it simply that her hurting hands allowed her tears to come.

She couldn't hold a fork or spoon with the bandages, so her mother patiently fed her, coercing and pleading with her to eat as if she were an infant.

The funeral was a blur. Then school. Seventh grade, which meant leaving the security and safety of grade school and the comfort of old teachers and being thrust into the trauma of a multitude of classes and queues and throngs of raucous students.

She had never carried a purse and couldn't imagine why a twelve-year-old would ever need one, but she carried one now. She kept the moccasin in it. Nothing else, just this shoe that was worn and scuffed and represented everything good and right and Anna.

Ten dozen times a day, she would surreptitiously finger its softness and run her nail across the soft chatter of beads that decorated the toe in a flower pattern. Sometimes, she felt as if this shoe was the only thing that kept her going.

Chapter 6

* * *

I remember one Saturday when I was so excited to get to Rice's Hill that I could hardly stand it. Mom made me do dishes and clean my room, and then just as I was ready to take off down the driveway on my bike, she had me sweep the back porch. The night before, Dad had been cleaning out the garage and organizing tools. On the wooden work bench were six or eight old jackknives. He gave me, when I pleaded, two of them. We had spent enough time camping and in the woods that I knew knife etiquette. Both knives were small with three blades. Anna declared her yellow knife was the very best present she had ever received, and she gave me a big hug. She studied it carefully, opening and closing the blades and testing their sharpness. Then she declared we needed to make bowls and eating utensils. We carved until we had each created a small, rough, and humble bowl and a spoon. We carved until we had blisters on our fingers.

* * *

Joe Miller sat very still in the chair. His head was still bowed. Marcy wasn't afraid. This man—a teacher who was highly regarded in the community—was warm and loving and kind, and he had been another father to her. He had teased her and braided her hair some mornings when she stayed over, and he made her special pancakes with her initials in them. He said it was a secret when she asked how he did it, but then he showed her. Dipping a spoon into the batter, he dribbled her name backwards—y-c-r-a-M—into the sizzling grease of the frying pan. He let it cook for a few seconds before spooning a puddle of batter over it. When the pancake was done, her name was darker than the rest.

So she sat and waited. She couldn't force herself to just get up and leave.

Finally, he sighed and raised his head.

"Where is Mrs. Miller?" Marcy asked quietly. The words seemed to echo in a room that was filled with furniture and photos and paintings and books but was still totally empty. The life had been sucked out of it. Even the colors seemed muted and faded and dead.

He looked at her. Stared at her. Finally, he started to answer. His voice broke, and he gave a soft cough and started again.

"School," he said. "Went back to her class. Didn't want disruption."

After a long pause, he added, "Second grade," like that would explain his wife's decision to abandon her grief.

"Oh." Marcy didn't know what to say. She settled back into the chair.

The silence lengthened, and she suddenly knew that she was right where she was supposed to be. They taught that in Sunday school, that God will put you in places where you can help others and that you will know when that happens. She knew for certain that this was one of those situations. She didn't know how but she was helping. Not only Joe Miller, but herself.

His eyes brimmed with tears, and she watched in fascination as the pools deepened and finally spilled over his eyelids and tumbled down his cheeks.

She remembered a fanciful conversation with Anna about tears—that they were the juice of a soul that was either so happy or so sad that the emotion couldn't be contained. Tear juice, she called it.

"I couldn't do it," he said, and Marcy knew he was talking about his high school English class.

"It's okay," she said. He nodded.

Marcy could see through the windows that the afternoon was waning. The light had changed. Her mother would be worried. She had been hot in her school clothes when she walked here, but she was cold in this house. A shiver jolted through her body.

She pushed back a strand of hair. "I'd better go," she said.

Startled, Joe got to his feet. "You can't," he said. "You have to stay here where it's safe. I can't trust you not to go back to the water."

"I won't go to the water," she said. "I will never go there again."

He ignored her assurances as if he hadn't heard her words. "I told her about everything, about kidnappers and bad people and what to do if she got lost in the woods when we were fishing. She knew about the irrigation ditches. She *knew*."

Tears welled in Marcy's eyes, and she blinked them back. Her throat ached with grief.

"I knew too," she said. Her voice was tiny. Thin and whispery. He didn't respond. Thankful that he didn't scream at her for not doing more, for not running faster, for not fighting harder to take the road rather than the pasture, she stood and stepped forward. Two steps. Then three.

"My mother will worry if I don't come home."

He started to make a noise she didn't recognize. Couldn't name. Then he responded.

"No!" he hollered, slamming his fist on his knee.

Then he spoke more softly and reached for her hand. His voice conveyed a sense of urgency, of pleading. "Don't you see? You have to stay here. I can't let you leave."

Marcy bent over and picked up her sales packet. She didn't know what to do or say. She was torn. She wanted to stay and help him. She wanted to run home to her family.

"Sit! You have to please just sit there until I figure it out."

Marcy glanced at the door and the chair. She sat back down. Her lip quivered, and she bit back fear and tears. Anna's father was making less and less sense, and she didn't know what to do or how to handle the situation. She was raised to trust and obey her elders. Should she run?

Somehow, she knew she shouldn't, and she let God's peace shove aside any other emotion. The fleeting fear she had felt disappeared.

Reaching behind him, Joe Miller unplugged an extension cord from a lamp and jerked it from the wall. Then he approached her.

"Please don't be afraid. I just have to do this. I am so tired, and I am just so afraid you will be taken away too." He pulled her left arm toward him and tied it, and then he tied the other. The cord was loose, barely staying on her wrists. He patted her bound hands and then turned around and went to the rocking chair where he had been sitting. He pulled it in front of her and sat down. He put his head back and closed his eyes. Marcy slipped her hands out from the twined cord and placed them under it.

He sat back down in the chair. Soon, he was asleep.

Marcy studied his face, and she lowered her head and cried softly. In sleep, his face looked normal even though it was shadowed with beard and the lines around his eyes and mouth looked deep and cavernous. He looked almost peaceful. She wondered if it was the first time since his daughter's death that he had really slept. She knew how awful it was—the way the memories crowded away slumber as it approached.

Would life ever be normal again?

She doubted it.

She wasn't afraid at all, even though Joe Miller had made a sloppy attempt to tie her up. She knew she could trust God. And Joe Miller. She was safe.

She just hoped her mother didn't worry.

* * *

After pacing and fretting and swinging her head to look at the kitchen clock every few minutes, Sharon Peterman decided there was only one description to the tumultuous emotion coursing through her mind. Terror. She was terrified. Marcy should have been home an hour ago. Sharon looked at her fingers curiously as she dialed Jim's cell phone number. They were shaking. She held up her hand and willed it to be steady. When it didn't comply, she tucked it in her armpit and clamped down her arm.

Since the accident, Jim had started having his cell phone more readily accessible. Where he once didn't always carry it with him, he did all the time now. When he was in his office, it was on his desk, just inches from his hand.

He flipped it open on the first ring, knowing it was his wife.

The Petermans owned the Ford dealership in Danford, and she could hear the familiar echo of the showroom and the loudspeaker summoning a salesman. Without waiting for her husband to say anything, she just blurted what was on her mind. "Jim? She isn't home yet. I don't know where she is. She should have been home long ago."

"It's okay, sweetie," he said as he lined up four pens on the top of his desk and then glanced at the clock. "I'm sure she's fine. It's not even five o'clock yet, and any other time, you wouldn't think twice about this. You know she was going to go selling again tonight."

Sharon walked the length of the kitchen and through the dining room and looked out the window. Then she let the curtain drop and walked back to the kitchen.

"I was going to drive and see if I could find her, but I don't remember where she was going. She canvassed our whole neighborhood last night. Was she going into the new subdivision? Oh, Jim, I'm so worried. What if she went back to the ditch?"

"You know she wouldn't go there. Maybe she did go into the new subdivision. I'm sure everything is fine. She's probably just racking up the sales. She is the daughter of a car salesman after all. Tell you what, I'm just leaving work. I'll drive around and look for her. You just don't worry. She's fine."

"Thanks, Jim. I know I'm being really crazy these days, but... well, you know."

"You're right. I *do* know. I love you, Mrs. Peterman."

She started to cry. "I love you too," she said. Hanging up the phone, she wondered how it was that such a tragedy of losing Anna had brought her and Jim closer together. Closer than they had been in a long time.

Hearing Ben laughing upstairs in the game room at a cartoon, she decided to put off making dinner. Instead, she joined him and watched as he played a video game. She had no clue what the goal was other than leaping across alligator-infested ponds, jumping barrels, and climbing ropes. She had the urge to grab her son and hold him close, but she knew that he'd fuss over losing this round of the game.

Through Anna's death, she had also learned to treasure her family more than she ever had.

* * *

Barbara Miller was weary and didn't know how she had made it through a day of teaching. Ten thousand times, her mind had gone to the horror of losing Anna and the emptiness in her soul. Would she ever rid her mind of the image of her drowned daughter, of that little body slumped and lifeless and so pale, so horribly white?

She climbed into her Ford Explorer and put her head on the steering wheel and closed her eyes.

A knock on the side window startled her.

"Are you okay, Barb?" Allison Chambers's pudgy face, normally pleasant and happy, now looked worried and concerned. The palm of her hand rested on the window. On either side of her wedding band, the skin plumped out, a testimony that it had been there for decades. An errant thought raced through Barbara's mind: if Allison was ever held up by bandits, they'd have to cut the finger off to get the ring.

Barbara nodded and waved, and the well-meaning principal turned and walked away.

Why couldn't everyone just leave her alone? She was so sick of being polite and understanding. She was tired of the words and the hugs and the pitying glances. Sackcloth and ashes were favorites in the Old Testament, and now she knew why. Sometimes, she wished she could just go somewhere and scream until she was out of screams. She wanted to beat her chest and wail and moan and tear her hair.

Instead, she pulled the gearshift into Drive and slowly started home. Home. Could it even be called that anymore?

Chapter 7

Pastor Mike put a hand to his back as he straightened from the task at hand. Why on earth, he wondered, had he ever decided to forego the carwash and wash his pickup himself. His jeans and T-shirt, bright yellow and advertising a zoo in Florida, were soaked. His tennis shoes sloshed when he walked. Worst of all, his back hurt, he'd banged his elbow on the door, his head was sweaty under his Montana State University ball cap, and he was only half done.

"From now on, the youth group is going to have a car wash once a month during the summer," he vowed to Midas.

He looked behind him and muttered. That dratted dog had sneaked away again. Honestly, Mike thought, that dog is slipperier than boiled butter.

"Midas! Here!" Looking around, he tried to spot his dog, a half-grown mutt he'd rescued from the pound a few weeks earlier that looked to be part golden retriever, part wrinkled sharpei, and part something that was very furry. The dog's body was a gangly, wrinkled mass of yellow fur. His face was a collection of furrows, which gave him a comical, friendly look, and his brown eyes confirmed the truth that he truly was a clown of a dog.

Because of his thick golden coat, Mike had changed his name from Furry to Midas. It took three dog treats and half a slice of bacon to get him to respond to the new name.

Except for this running away habit, he really was a great dog, Mike thought, trying to reason with himself. It didn't work. Slamming down the hose, which leaped back up from the water pressure and drenched his rear end, he stomped across the lawn.

Midas was in the backyard, happily excavating a new route to China next to the garage. His rear end wobbled in the sunshine as sprays of clawed-up dirt flew out from either side. His head was buried so deep in the hole, Mike realized, that it was no wonder he didn't hear his name being called.

Pastor Mike wasn't married, had never been married, and of course, didn't have children. The members of Danford Worship Center would have frowned mightily if he had children with no wife in his past or present. As it was, he was thirty-two years old and single. Very single. This meant that every person within forty miles who had a spinster sister, sister-in-law, friend, coworker, acquaintance or even non-acquaintance, paraded their proffered females before him in hopes that they, halleluiah, would be the one to go down in history as having introduced him to his future beloved.

Maybe one of the reasons he spoiled Midas was because he didn't have anyone, at least that was the reason he gave himself. He deserved to spoil this dog he'd snatched from the jaws of euthanasia. And so he watched with growing amusement as the dog tore into his petunia bed, flinging dirt and leaves and roots all over creation.

Before long, Midas was hunkered down and stretched into the massive hole, and Pastor Mike could swear he heard bits of Mandarin coming from it. As could be predicted, Midas lost the tenuous hold he had with his hind legs and feet and sprawled headlong into the chasm, his back legs flailing in the air as he tried to right himself.

Mike laughed at the spectacle and leaned over and howled when Midas poked his head out of the pit. One floppy and very dirty ear was turned inside out, and a pink petunia rested above the mutt's left eye. The wrinkles in his face were caked in dirt.

"Come here, boy," Mike said, hunkering down. Mike buried his face in his arms when Midas came before him and shook violently, effectively covering his master with a fine spattering of dirt.

"Let's go turn off the hose and head for the showers, Midas," he said. He was blessed to have a huge double-headed shower stall in the master bathroom, which made it easy for him to shower both himself and his dog in emergencies such as this. No two critters needed a shower more than these two.

Chapter 8

* * *

The best summer we had on Rice's Hill was the summer of the horses, when we were ten. The colt was too young to ride, but Kemo was patient and gentle with us. The first time, Anna was the brave one. "Marcy, you are such a chicken," she teased. Then since Kemo was standing near the log, she just jumped on the log and then onto mare's back. One fluid motion and there she was, as beautiful and proud as any Indian princess with her black hair flowing down her back. Grabbing hanks of the pale golden mane with either hand, she leaned forward and gave Kemo's flanks a little tap with her moccasined foot. They were off, she and Kemo, loping along the hillside. Soon, she was back, her face glowing with excitement and with two bright red circles of joy on her cheeks. Anna explained the hand movements to control Kemo, and I climbed onto the log and slid cautiously onto the horse's back. Has there ever been such a feeling of absolute and total joy?

* * *

Marcy's hands were tired from twisting and turning and playing with the electrical cord. Otherwise, she was faring well from her ordeal. She hadn't panicked or felt the urge to scream at the oddness of it all, and the thought of just getting up and leaving hadn't entered her mind. She knew she had to just quietly stay still and seated.

While Joe slept, Marcy slipped off her shoes and used her big toe to pull her purse toward her other foot. Then she bent down and pulled it into her lap. She slipped a hand out from under the cord and reached in the purse to ferret out Anna's moccasin.

Now she was okay. The comfort of Anna's moccasin was with her.

Joe Miller was still asleep in the chair in front of her, his head at such a severe angle that it looked very painful. He looked peaceful and relaxed, and she wondered how he could sleep with his head flopped to one side like it was. His neck would surely hurt when he awakened, Marcy thought.

The sun had gone down a bit. She could tell from the sounds. With the heat ebbing, the robins were starting to sing, and she could hear mature voices coming from people on the sidewalk. That meant high school was out, and it was past four o'clock. Barbara Miller would be finished straightening up her second grade classroom and would be home soon.

The refrigerator in the kitchen came to life, and she thought it was odd. She had been in this house hundreds of times and had never heard, to her knowledge, the refrigerator. There was always music or television or just talk and laughter. Joe Miller played guitar and sang, and Barbara played piano. Anna played piano and sang beautifully, but she admitted truthfully, she couldn't play the guitar worth a nickel.

Marcy turned to the right and glanced at the instruments now and was saddened to see them covered in dust.

Barbara Miller's car crunched on the driveway that hugged the side of the house until ending at the garage in back. A few seconds later, the car door shut. Joe didn't move but continued to snore softly.

Marcy could hear her coming up the back porch steps and opening the kitchen door. She heard the soft thud of her purse as it hit the counter by the sink and her steps crossing the tile floor. "Joe?" she said quietly, peering into the living room. Her eyes weren't yet used to the lack of light.

She saw him then, sleeping in the chair with his back to her, his head lolled back. Her hand went to her heart, and her face crumpled. As much as her heart broke for herself, it also broke for this gentle man she loved so dearly. Her face emoted compassion and love.

Then she looked beyond him and spotted Marcy, her hands wrapped up in a white cord and sitting in the red chair. She screamed. It wasn't a loud heart-wrenching scream, like the one that was emitted when she learned about Anna, but more of a startled, dismayed, agonized choking sound.

"Oh god, what is happening? What are you doing?" she said as she shook her husband's arm and then pushed him mightily. She fought off the urge to push him so hard he flew across the room and splattered against the wall. There had been too much pain, too much horror, and now he had to add more to the heap?

"Joe! What is happening?" Her voice was high-pitched and strangled, and in her mind, it didn't sound like her at all. Her head was filled with hot buzzing, and the words had to fight their way through the tremendous noise.

A second later, she was kneeling in front of Marcy, untangling the cord from her hands. "I'm so sorry. I'm so sorry," she said over and over, more for the fact that her trembling hands couldn't untangle the knots Marcy had made than the situation as a whole. She couldn't, right now, comprehend the situation as a whole.

Throwing the cord away from her, Barbara pulled the girl into her arms and hugged her as if she would never let go. She crooned and wailed softly.

"Are you all right? Are you hurt, Marcy?" She wondered how many times she said it. Right now, this girl's well-being seemed more important than anything else.

Marcy felt herself go limp in the comforting arms, and she cried. Not big gulping tears and then not even for herself, but tiny hot tears for the Millers. She still knew, deep in her heart, that God was here and that he was a part of this.

Joe looked upon the scene with dismay and puzzlement. He remained in his chair, his eyes filled with a dawning horror.

Barbara Miller scooted into the chair beside Marcy and pulled the young girl into her lap. She pulled Marcy's head against her chest and cuddled her like a newborn.

She looked at Joe imploringly. "Why?" she asked.

Joe simply shook his head. He didn't know. He couldn't explain.

"Joe, you tried to tie her up. This child that we love so dearly and that we have treasured as if she were our very own. Do you know how horrible that looked when I came in here? How ugly that scene was? Why, Joe?"

Her first impulse was to cover Marcy's ears and scream at him and tear into him with all the emotion she had been stuffing inside for the past weeks. She wanted to pick up the cord and whip him with it. She wanted to break something, anything, just to feel the satisfaction of getting rid of some of the inner turmoil that churned relentlessly and continually.

And then her love for him overcame any urge for violence, and she felt her heart melt with understanding and pity. She knew. Deep in her soul, even though she couldn't comprehend or justify his actions, she understood. Since Anna's death, she had been terrified someone else would die. She made twice as many phone calls to her mother now and her sisters. At school, she watched and listened on the playground as if she was the only thing between a child and death. She wanted nothing more than to put everyone she loved into cages so that they would be safe.

Still, even though Marcy wasn't really bound, the intent was there. She couldn't understand the awfulness of what he'd done. She looked at him imploringly, her face a crumpled mask of dismay.

"I was afraid she would leave," he said. His head wagged from side to side, and he raised his hands in surrendered desperation. "The water. I was so afraid she would go to the water."

"But she wouldn't do that, Joe. Do you think, after what happened, she would ever go to that irrigation ditch again?"

His words were edged in agony. "I couldn't bear to lose her too. She's our link to Anna, and I was so afraid we'd lose her."

"That doesn't make sense. You aren't making any sense. Don't you realize? This could be called kidnapping, Joe. The police could come and take you away. We could lose each other too."

She broke down and sobbed, pulling Marcy close. "Oh, dear god, please help us," she said in a choked voice.

Marcy hadn't said a word, but now she knew what she had to say.

"We have to call Pastor Mike," she said. "Right now. And see if he will come over here. Tell him it is an extreme emergency."

Barbara Miller looked at her and nodded in agreement. Then she scooted Marcy off her lap and went to the kitchen phone, grabbing a handful of Kleenexes on her way.

Chapter 9

The pile of wet clothes and wet towels was so deep he had to walk around it to answer the incessantly ringing phone. He had heard it blaring during the shower, upon getting out of the shower, and now that he was dressed, it was going off again. Clearly, someone was highly impatient.

Truth be known, he was hesitant to answer. He'd known this morning that this was going to be a trying day. He thought once he'd passed the dinner hour, he'd be safe. He just had one of those feelings in his gut.

He picked up on the third ring. There was no voice, and he was about to hang up when he heard crying.

"Hello?" he said. "Is someone there?"

"Pastor Mike. Thank God you answered. This is Barbara Miller…" she couldn't go on.

"Barbara, are you all right? What's wrong?"

The crying continued, and the phone dropped. He stayed on the line, listening. He heard comforting words, "It's going to be okay…Please don't cry…Don't worry…God is here with us."

The voice the preacher heard next was young and familiar.

"Pastor Mike, this is Marcy Peterman. I told Mrs. Miller to call you. We need you to come to the Miller's house right now. It's a dire emergency."

"All right, Marcy. Let me put Midas in his kennel, and I'll be there in less than five minutes," he promised. He knew better than to waste valuable time asking questions over the phone. He would discover the "dire emergency" when he got there.

He had to smile at the phrase despite the fact that something was truly very wrong. Anna and Marcy were always using extravagant, sometimes emotional, phrases to describe situations.

Last year, he had asked them to create a sign for the Annual Harvest Dinner. Their sign, which he didn't have the heart to replace, declared the event would be an "exceptionally elegant evening with exorbitantly exquisite cuisine, fine exotic drinks, and breathtakingly bald entertainment." Ham and boiled potatoes and accordion music by Slim Hardesty didn't seem to quite fit the billing. The really humorous part of it, a mistake in the second letter of the word *bold*, which he didn't catch when he read it, was that Slim Hardesty truly was as bald as a spring mushroom.

Somehow, despite Marcy's flowery description, he didn't think the event he was headed to tonight was going to be much fun.

"Midas, come!" he demanded, and the dog, hearing the authority in his master's voice, pranced obediently to his side. Together, they walked to the garage where Mike put him in a spacious chain-link kennel he'd installed the week before.

On his way back through the house, he grabbed his Bible and started praying before he opened the front door. By the time he started his car, he had already pierced the late afternoon sky with a multitude of prayers headed straight to heaven.

In less than five minutes, he had pulled into the Miller's driveway and headed toward the front porch.

Chapter 10

Jim Peterman sat at the kitchen bar and held his head in his hands. He didn't know what to do. There really wasn't anyone else to call. No one had seen her since school let out. She had a multitude of acquaintances, but Anna had been her only true friend—the one whose house she would be in.

They had rounded up Ben, who was nine, and taken both cars and driven up and down the streets, asking people they knew if they'd seen Marcy that afternoon. Jim went into Polsky's Market, and Sharon checked at the Sheer Perfection Beauty Salon to see if Alma had seen her pass by. No one remembered seeing her.

Once home, Sharon admitted to him that she had scrambled over Rice's Hill hollering Marcy's name to no avail.

She looked startled when Jim told her he and Ben had driven to the road along the pasture where the irrigation ditch was. Using binoculars, he had checked to see if Marcy was there.

"We need to call the police," Sharon said.

"Mom, I'm scared," Ben said. "Do you think she's okay?"

She held him close. She hadn't realized that their words could strike terror into his little heart.

"I'm a little scared too," she admitted to him, ruffling his hair. "But I'm sure she's fine. She's probably just taking a walk or still selling stuff from the gift catalog."

"She went past our house to sell junk. Maybe she went to that Mrs. Vietti's house. She talks a lot," Ben said.

"I'll tell you what. You can either stay here in the kitchen with us or you can go play a video game. You choose, okay, buddy?" She knew what he would choose since playing video games was a privilege, not a right.

"Video game. But you come tell me when you find her, okay? Promise?"

"It's a deal," she said, sticking out her hand.

After Ben was safely out of earshot, she turned to Jim. "I really do think we need to call the police."

He didn't know why he was so hesitant. Was it paranoia? Fear?

"Let's look at this rationally before we do that," he said, looking at his watch. Right now, it is a little after five. If this was six months ago, would we be worried?"

Sharon sank into a kitchen chair, ducked her head toward the table, and twined her hands behind her neck. Then she straightened and, flattening her palms on the table, looked at him.

"Maybe not, but mainly because she would have been at Anna's or hanging out in Joe's classroom or maybe helping with some project Barbara had going on. The thing is, without Anna, where would she be?"

She turned her head away from him quickly before he could see, knowing that he was sick and tired of the endless tears not only from her but also from himself. Losing Anna was like losing one of their own.

Jim Peterman's shoulders sagged. "You're right," he admitted. "Hand me the phone."

Chapter 11

* * *

I brought a lighter to Rice's Hill, pilfered from the overflowing junk drawer at home. Anna was horrified at the thought of playing with fire, but the Pocahontas part of her soul welcomed the addition of fire to our village. The next day, she brought an old pan, and I brought sugar and a jug of water. Using a hunk of bone from the Bone Tree that was shaped like a paddle, Anna dug a small pit in the earth, and we ringed it with stones gathered from along the road. I broke off a branch from a ponderosa pine and carefully removed the dead needles and kept only those that were limber and green. After the water was boiling, we put in the needles. The smell was intoxicating, but the pine needle tea was bitter even with generous additions of sugar. Still, it was a gift from the earth, and we treasured it greatly.

* * *

The front door opened before Mike could knock, and he entered quickly, almost surreptitiously, he thought wonderingly, although he had no reason to treat this as a clandestine visit.

He had been in this house many times before for parties and gatherings, and he always felt that it was a cheerful, happy house. It wasn't that way today. It felt chilled and disturbed.

The scene was surreal. After letting him in, Barbara returned to the red chair and perched on the arm, her hand holding Marcy's. Joe was seated in a rocking chair in front of them. On the floor, oddly, was an extension cord.

Pastor Mike hugged Barbara and Marcy and turned to shake Joe's hand. The man clung to his pastor's hand as if he'd never let go. Mike dropped to one knee and hauled him into his arms, holding him close. He knew from the shuddering coming from this church member and friend that Joe was silently crying.

As Mike got back to his feet, Barbara swiped at her eyes and quickly recovered her manners. Crossing the room, she dragged a chair from a corner so that Mike could sit close to the others.

"Would you like coffee or tea, something?" she asked and then thought how stupid that was—to be offering him tea as if this was just a social visit and nothing out of the ordinary was going on.

"No, I'm fine, Barbara." He sat at the edge of the chair and waited quietly, wondering if he should have accepted something to drink if, perhaps, it would have settled her down if she had something to do with her hands. Then he stood up.

"Don't anyone move. I'll be right back," he said. Going into the kitchen, he quickly found the cupboard that held glassware and took out four tall glasses. He filled them with cold water and put them on a tray he spotted on top of the refrigerator. Noticing a napkin holder on the counter, he grabbed a few and tossed them on the tray.

Returning to the living room, he handed out the water and napkins. Joe grasped the glass gratefully, as if he hadn't had a drink of water in days. Barbara took a few sips and gently set her glass on the end table that flanked the red chair. When Marcy handed Barbara her untouched glass, Barbara carefully placed it beside the other. All three of them used the napkins to wipe leaking eyes and to discreetly blow their noses.

"I'm glad you could get here so fast," Barbara said. Her voice was muffled through the napkin. "We have a real problem."

"No matter what the problem, you know that God loves his children, and there is nothing that is too big for him to handle," he assured her before she started.

"I don't know if he can handle this one," she said, grabbing Marcy's hand again. Marcy laid her other small palm over the older woman's. Barbara noticed that the child's hand was cold and damp from holding the glass.

Using the low, unemotional, monotone voice that people sometimes assume when detailing a crime, Barbara reported what she found when she came home from school. If Pastor Joe was shocked, he didn't show it. Instead, he turned to Marcy.

"So he tried to truss you up like a Christmas turkey, did he?" he asked her, smiling.

She gave a small laugh. "Yes, sir," she said quietly, smiling back at him.

"Can you tell me about it? Were you scared?"

Marcy, who had been almost totally silent since Joe tied her up, suddenly came to life. The words tumbled and fell from her heart.

"I came here to sell those stupid packages of wrapping paper and ribbons. It was dumb, I know, because why would Mr. and Mrs. Miller want gift wrap and ribbons anyway after what happened? I just didn't want them to feel left out when I went to everyone else in the neighborhood."

"I think that was very thoughtful," Pastor Mike agreed. "So what happened next?"

Marcy related the story right up to the point where Pastor Mike entered the room.

"And you are sure you are okay?" he asked her. His concern right now centered on this child who had gone through more trauma in less than a month than some people do in a lifetime.

"I'm fine," she said, "Well, except…" Marcy looked down and became silent, and the three adults knew she was struggling with emotion.

"Except for what?" Pastor Mike's voice was encouraging and comforting.

"I'm fine, but I don't think they are fine," she said, lifting her head and looking at Pastor Mike. She knew if she looked at either Joe or Barbara, she would bawl like a silly crybaby.

"Oh, Marcy," Barbara said, lifting Marcy's hand to her cheek and cuddling it there.

A frown passed over Pastor Mike's face before flitting away. "Well, I can see why you called me," he said to Barbara.

Then he scooted his chair over beside Joe's, and the tone of the conversation immediately changed. Mike's voice was soft and full of compassion and understanding. "Joe, can you tell me what happened?"

Up to that point, Joe had barely uttered a word. "I really don't understand why I did it," Joe said. "I was just so tired and so worried about Marcy. None of it makes any sense now but it did at the time. I just was so afraid something would happen to her and I wanted to keep her safe. I just wanted her to be safe."

"I can understand that," Pastor Mike said. "I think if we explained it all to the police, they would be very understanding, con-sidering the pressure you have been under."

"Do you think they'll take him away?" Barbara asked quietly.

"In all my years of counseling, I've seen grief take a strange turn sometimes," Mike said. "They might just recommend he talk to a grief counselor."

"I just can't comprehend that I could do such a thing," Joe blurted. "To tie her up like that?" The last words were choked, and he turned his head away from the others.

"I understand," Marcy said quietly from the red chair. The three adults turned to her. "He hasn't slept. He told me that. He hasn't slept except for a little bit here and there in his recliner since the accident. Anna was lost, and I was almost lost. I don't know why God allowed me to live while she was swept away, but I accept that since God knows everything. He had a reason for wanting me here and for wanting Anna in heaven with him."

She looked at each of them in turn and gathered her courage. Suddenly, she knew that all she really needed to do was to let God do the speaking through her.

"Anna is gone, and she can't be protected now, but I can be protected," she continued. "Mr. Miller just wanted me safe for a little while so that he could sleep. The only way to do that was to do what he did. He didn't want to hurt me. He loves me. He was protecting me. Don't you see?"

She had gone to stand by Joe and had placed her arm around his shoulders. Her eyes implored the other two to accept and agree with her truth.

"Your explanation will be too simple when they know what he did," Barbara said sadly.

Chapter 12

* * *

One Saturday, she didn't show up on the hill. I had telephoned her ahead of time, and she had been vague, saying maybe she would be there but maybe not. I tidied the graveyard, removing bits of wind-blown debris, and I used a branch we kept in the old pole barn to smooth the dirt floor. I fingered some of the treasures in the Bone Tree and then put them back. Finally, when the robins started their end-of-day song, I trudged home. The next day, she was there, acting as if the day before had never happened. I yelled at her, and she yelled back. She had things do to, she said, besides hanging around on Rice's Hill. I cried at that, and she called me a silly willy girl, a crybaby. Then she saw my face as I started to stomp away, and she apologized. The truth, she said, was that she had been invited to a birthday party, and her mother made her go. I hadn't been invited, and she didn't want to hurt my feelings by telling me. She vowed she would always, always until the end of time and with a cross-your-heart promise, be my best friend.

* * *

The Millers knew that Anna and Marcy, while generally docile good girls, could have frightful fights. Now they saw a side of Marcy they didn't know.

Leaving Joe's side, she snatched up the cord. She stomped off and threw it in the kitchen trash can.

"No evidence," she said, coming back into the living room with tears tumbling down her cheeks. "Nothing happened here today except for my best friend's father trying to help me and help himself get over her death. None of us are acting normally. What is normal anyway when your daughter has drowned? When your best friend is gone? What is normal?" Her voice rose to shrillness and then dovetailed to a choked whisper. Pastor Mike stood up and pulled her close.

"As a pastor, I have certain responsibilities," he started.

"And that means you have to tell? Even if it was nothing, and no one else has to know? In that case, let me ask you something. How do you know when you do something that God wants you to do?"

"Well, I just know. It's a feeling. A calmness and a sureness. And he usually has me saying words that are much too brilliant to be coming from my lips."

"God tells you?"

"Sometimes. Sometimes, I just know in my knower what I am supposed to do. Other times, I can almost hear his voice directing me."

"Well, today was a God day for me. Anna and I call them God days…when we do something that we know God wants us to do. That last week we're together, she had five dollars in her pocket from babysitting, and God told her to give it to a poor lady in the grocery store. She went up to the lady and handed her the money and said, 'God wants me to give you this and to tell you that he loves you.' The lady cried. She said she had no money at all and her children needed milk and bread."

"She did that? Anna did that?" Joe asked. Marcy looked at him.

"She did that all the time," she told him. "On the playground, she looked out for the little kids and protected them. Sometimes after school, we'd come in here and make sandwiches, or we'd go to my house and make sandwiches and take them to the park for the homeless people."

She turned to Barbara Miller. "Mrs. Miller, do you remember the tan winter parka she lost and you were upset? She gave it away to a very poor girl on the street who had nothing on but a sweatshirt, and it was cold that day. I gave the girl my mittens and scarf, and my mom about killed me. I told her I lost them."

She looked at Pastor Mike. "Anyway, no one was ever supposed to know. She'd be really mad if she knew I was telling. In Sunday school, they told us if you talk about your good deeds, they won't get recognized in heaven. We called them God days, the days we did these things."

She paused and looked down at her hands and then said quietly, "They were all God days with Anna."

Before they could react, she continued. "Today, God told me that everything was going to be all right. He was healing Mr. Miller, and I was a part of the healing. And while he was healing him, he was healing me too. I was never afraid or worried, except that my mother must be frantic by now. Today was a God day because he was in it through this whole afternoon. I was right where I was supposed to be right at the time I was supposed to be there."

Pastor Mike chuckled. "That sounds like a paraphrase of one of my sermons," he said.

"Could be," she admitted. "I don't want to be mean, but if anyone says anything about a cord or ever again uses the word *kidnapping*, I will say that it wasn't true. I wasn't kidnapped. I was being used by God, and no one can argue with that."

Then she turned to Joe Miller. "Mr. Miller, I hate to be critical and hurt your feelings, but you really need to watch more of those police shows on TV and learn how to do things. I wasn't even tied with that extension cord. Plus, you didn't tie my feet. I could have just walked right out of here."

She looked imploring at Pastor Mike. "But I didn't because I knew I was right in God's will. I've been thinking that if Mr. Miller needs a grief counselor, he can visit you. Three times a week. And he will do that too, won't you, Mr. Miller? Go talk to Pastor Mike, or someone else who can help, three times a week?"

The three adults looked at each other. When Pastor Mike nodded, so did the Millers.

Marcy headed toward the door. "I'm going home now, and I'd like you all to walk with me. At least part of the way," she said. She held out her hand, and Barbara Miller took it.

"Your sales stuff…" Joe said, standing up and reaching for it.

"I never did sell any of it, and I don't want to sell any of it," she declared. "There are more important things in life than selling stupid plastic bows and Christmas paper. Don't tell my dad, but I don't think I'm cut out to be a salesperson."

Chapter 13

The sheriff's deputies had been polite, courteous, and understanding. And also calming. Sharon and Jim Peterman were hopeful now that Marcy had just gone home with a friend and she was safe and sound and would soon be back where she belonged. Still, the deputies said, they would put her description out to the other agencies and the rest of the force. If she wasn't home in two hours, they would more actively pursue finding her.

No one mentioned the Amber Alert, but it was in the back of everyone's mind.

Jim put his arm around Sharon's shoulder as they walked with the two deputies to the front porch. Just then, another patrol car pulled up, its lights flashing. The lone deputy got out of his car, grinned to no one in particular, and sprinted to the group.

Clearing his throat, he declared the latest news in a tumble of words. "We just got a call from Marcy. She's been trying to call here, but I guess the phone was busy. She said she knew you'd call the police since she was so late. She's down the street at the Millers. Her and Pastor Mike from the worship center. She said to tell you she's on her way home."

Sharon's hands flew to her face, and she started to cry. Jim grabbed her and pulled her to his side, and the two of them started down the porch steps to the sidewalk. They could see the foursome coming toward them. Marcy and Barbara Miller holding hands in front and Pastor Mike and Joe in the back. Barbara looked like she was faring well, but Joe looked like he'd been through hell and back.

As dusk continued to push out daylight, the group met in the middle. After hugs and a few perfunctory words with the deputies so they could close out their report, they just shared in the joy that all was well.

"I was so worried. I couldn't imagine where you were," Sharon said, hugging Marcy fiercely. Then she pushed her away and took her by the shoulders and shook her slightly. "Don't you ever do that again. Do you hear me? Don't you ever scare us like that again."

"I'm sorry, Mom. I just needed to spend time with the Millers, and time just sort of got away from me."

"We can talk about it later, but I think you might be grounded, young lady," Jim said. "You really scared us."

"Sorry, Daddy."

Joe Miller started to protest, but Pastor Mike broke in before he could say anything. "You might want to be a little lenient with her," he said. "She was right about needing to spend time with the Millers. In a way, she was doing God's work."

"Well, just don't do it again," Sharon said. "I mean you can do God's work, but you don't have to scare us in the process, okay?"

Sharon Peterman turned to the others. If there was one thing she was good at, it was feeding people. She was a nurturer who had a gift of doing her best nurturing with good food.

"I've got lasagna in the oven, a salad ready in the fridge, and it will take about ten minutes to set the table and make garlic bread. Can you stay and eat with us?" she asked.

"Sounds great to me," said Mike. "I'm starving, and as a bachelor, I never turn down a free meal."

Barbara looked at Joe. "I think that would be good," she said.

"I'd rather go home," he said, careful not to meet her eyes because he didn't know what he would see there. "I'm tired, and… well, it's been a rough day."

"It would be good," she said, cupping her hands around his face and forcing him to look at her. The love he saw was overwhelming, and he could feel those damn tears starting again. "It's time to get back to life. Anna would want that. She'd want us to be with friends."

He nodded. "All right, but let's not be gone very long, okay?"

"Just for a little while, I promise," she said, taking his hand and starting to follow Sharon toward the house.

"I'll be right behind you, okay?" he asked, and she nodded and left him on the sidewalk with Marcy.

Marcy, quiet and waiting, stood with her back to the house. Closing her eyes, she listened to the flurry of steps on the sidewalk and then the more rhythmic clomping up wide wooden stairs to the veranda. When the old ornate screen door finally shut with its familiar squeak and thud, she moved to stand next to Joe, and they both looked heavenward. Marcy's eyes automatically settled on the North Star—the star that always seemed to shine so brightly just at sunset. "We miss you," she whispered into the night sky. "Tell God thank you for this God day."

Then she turned and grabbed Joe Miller's hand. "Come in just for a few minutes. Then if you want to go home, I'll walk with you. But I'll make a bet that once you smell my mom's lasagna, wild horses couldn't drag you away."

Joe hesitated. "I don't know what to say to you, Marcy, except to thank you," he said. "For the first time, I feel like there's hope that I can get through this…that things will be all right."

"You know that saying 'What would Jesus do?' I use that a lot, but sometimes, I think, 'What would Anna want me to do?' It helps. I know Anna would want us to be happy and to be normal."

Joe looked at her and shook his head and smiled briefly. "You're an amazing kid, you know that, Marcy Peterman? You are very wise for a twelve-year-old."

Chapter 14

They were all easing cautiously back into the stream of life. Joe was back to teaching part time, and he and Barbara were talking regularly with Pastor Mike. Marcy was also going in for counseling to try and help her understand what she was going through.

Now Joe and Barbara were taking another step forward and attending a meeting that was designed specifically for grieving parents. It was their second time to attend.

The Danford Baptist Church, not far from Danford Worship Center, which was their home church, was dark, except for the entryway and the bank of lights in the basement. Entering the front foyer, Joe and Barbara could hear voices from downstairs and spotted the humble sign that had been placed on an easel: "The Compassionate Friends meeting downstairs in the Fellowship Hall. Welcome!" They made their way down the stairs to a broad landing where the stairs made a right turn. All along the stairs were posters colored by children declaring God's love, his mercy, his caring, his peace, his grace, and his faith.

"You sure you want to do this again?" Joe asked, stopping on the landing to confront his wife.

"Do you think anyone really *wants* to go to these meetings?" Barbara asked quietly. "I doubt it, but I think we need to, don't you? It's been almost three months since the funeral. We promised we'd go to six. Just six meetings, Joe, and if they don't help, we can quit."

"I just don't know what to say to anyone, either to help myself cope with Anna's death or to help anyone else cope with the loss of their child. For the first time in my life, I don't have any words. They're all just stuck in there somewhere."

As he spoke, she looked at him carefully and thought he looked older. She wondered where he was, that carefree Joe she had married who had been such a crazy wild guy. She wondered where she was too. Whatever happened to cute little Barbara Jean Smith, who married strong and handsome Joe Miller? Was that person gone forever? Were they both gone forever?

Sometimes, she saw glimmers of those other people, that other Barbara Miller and Joe Miller—a burst of laughter between them or a quick teasing or a hug that wasn't one of desperate clinging but a simple sharing of love. Those times were happening more often and gave her hope. Gave them both hope. The "Marcy episode," as they called it, had been a pivotal point in their healing. Now they were going to actively pursue understanding and dealing with grief.

"I know, Joe," she sighed. "I feel the same way. Like a robot. Just going through the motions of life without any feelings other than grief. But there is hope. Someday, we will laugh again and discover ourselves again. Turn around. I want you to look at something."

They turned around on the landing and looked up the stairs. Barbara brushed the hair out of her eyes and pointed. "Read what the posters say about love, mercy, caring, peace, grace, and faith. God is with us through this. We are so much more fortunate than others who don't have God. We aren't doing this alone, Joe."

"I wish I had your faith. You see more than words in the signs. I just see the words and wonder if they mean anything anymore."

"You're having a bad day today, I can tell," she told him. "But I'm having a good day. I think this will be very helpful."

Good days. Bad days. It was odd how that worked. Sometimes, they would sail through a day and that black clump of horror would be so distant it would barely be visible on the horizon. Other days, it would settle on them until they couldn't move from the weight of it. It was a blessing that they more and more frequently shared good days and that in the last month hadn't both been simultaneously stricken with a bad day.

Turning, Joe started down the stairs toward the meeting room.

There were many of them in the room, people like them who had lost a child. They would learn later that the stories varied—cancer, fire, accidents, heart defects—and so did the ages. Two couples had lost newborns; another couple had lost their sixteen-year-old to brain cancer. One couple, the Lincolns, had two children, ages two and five, die in a car accident. One very old woman, a widow, had lost a son in Vietnam, and the war in Iraq had triggered emotions she thought had been buried in the 1960s.

Joe and Barbara were the only ones present who had lost a child by drowning. They were also the newest grievers to walk through the door.

It was Pastor Mike who had suggested that, along with talking to him, they join The Compassionate Friends group. The first session had been traumatic—their grief so raw and horrible that they felt it must be palpable in the room. People were kind and compassionate, but they didn't pity. Best of all, they understood.

It had been difficult telling their story. They paused at times and choked on the words at others. Another person telling about the death of her toddler daughter told her story in a rush—the words, an avalanche of feeling that didn't stop until it had buried all of them.

This was the second meeting, and they had forced themselves to come.

They had gotten to the meeting early, just as Rod and Caroline Lincoln, the couple they learned lost two of their three children in the car accident, were making coffee, placing chocolate-chip cookies on a plate, and setting up chairs. The Lincolns were both tall and slim, well-groomed, and very likeable. Without preamble, the couple explained a bit about the group and said that they attended to put into perspective the deaths of their children and to help others.

"You will discover that this is a very diverse group," Caroline said after the couples reintroduced themselves. The first meeting, a month earlier, the Millers had been so distraught that few of the names caught hold and stayed in their minds.

"Sometimes, there are twenty-five or more of us, and other months, there are less than a dozen. People who come range from teenagers mourning babies who were stillborn to great-grandmothers grieving the loss of adult children. There are also people like Gladys Abrams, who lost a child twenty or thirty years ago and are just coming to grips with that death. Others just buried their child a couple of weeks ago."

She looked at Rod, which he took as a cue to make Joe feel comfortable.

"It's a loose organization," Rod said as he reached into a cupboard to take down a stack of Styrofoam cups. "We all just learn from each other through sharing. Sometimes, there is a short program, and about every six months, we have a ceremony where we release balloons, and last summer, we also released butterflies. That was pretty amazing."

He reached in a drawer for plastic spoons. "Anyway, all of us are trying to rebuild our lives, but we realize that it will never be the same. You will learn that all of us are at different stages in our grief. Some are stunned or resentful, others rage. All of us recognize the emotions. We've all either been there or we're heading there. It is a group of shared sympathy.

"You will learn that grieving sometimes takes years. One fellow here, who lost his fifteen-year-old son to suicide five years ago, is just now able to go into his room and look at his boy's things. You will also learn that all of us have stories of strangers and family members who either didn't know what to say or said the wrong thing."

He looked at Caroline, and she picked up where he left off. She looked at the Millers with love and understanding.

"The last meeting, when you told us about Anna, was probably the hardest thing you will go through here. Actually, you don't have to talk at all if you don't want to," Caroline told Barbara, briefly patting her hand, "except to introduce yourselves. You should know though, that because this is a small town, most people will recognize your names."

Barbara gave a small sad laugh. "Just as I recognized your names," she said to the Lincolns. "I have thought about you often and prayed for you. I couldn't comprehend how you could live through such tragedy, losing two children at once. Isn't life odd that here we are, learning from you how to cope?"

"That's one of the reasons we keep coming," Rod said. "It's a tribute to our two kids that we can help people like you. I've always believed that God sometimes has us endure hardships so that we are better able to help his people."

"That's a tough way to learn a lesson," Joe said, "to lose two children so that you can help us."

"It was a freak accident, and no one was to blame," Rod said. He opened the cupboard to put back extra cups and shut it carefully, thoughtfully. Then he turned around. "Tommy was four, and the baby, Josie, was just two. They were sitting in their car seats, beside each other in the backseat. Michael, who was six—and is eight now—was next to them. We were going less than thirty, way below the speed limit because it was snowing. We hit a patch of ice on the road. There were no other cars around, and we spun around twice and ended up facing the other direction. It was no more scary than a carnival ride." He looked at Caroline, and she picked up the story.

"We were laughing, and Michael was giving a wild whoop, and then he started yelling. Rod and I turned around, and there was blood coming from Tommy's mouth and his eyes…Well, it was obvious he was gone. Josie died a few days later. Their heads had banged together when we skidded, and that was it."

"I am so sorry," Barbara said. "I remember reading about it, but I didn't know what exactly had happened."

"We've told the story so many times you'd think it would get easier," Rod said. "Maybe someday it will."

"And your story will get easier someday too, sweetie," Caroline said to Barbara, pulling her into a quick hug. "I know you are just coming to grips with Anna's death and that your life almost seems to be over, but there is a lot of truth in the saying that time heals all wounds. Rod and I believe that God, though, is the infinite healer."

Joe cleared his throat. "We believe that too. I really don't know what to say except that by looking at you two, I see hope that we might survive this."

"You will, I promise," Rod said, clapping him on the arm, "but right now, we'd better save all this for the meeting. Sit with us, okay?"

Chapter 15

* * *

The railroad tracks were just below Rice's Hill, opposite the roadside. Beyond was the big meadow. A century before, maybe longer, builders of the railroad had carved out the land to lay the tracks. We could hear the trains at night, their mournful whistles as they came close to town, and the endless bumping and crashing of boxcars as railroaders switched them from one train to another. With the trains came the bums—transients riding the rails to greener pastures. In the neighborhood, we would see them sometimes and the cry, Bum! Bum! would travel from kid to kid. For the most part, they were travel-weary men in worn clothing in search of a meal, although one old fellow knocked on our door and asked my mom for a needle and thread. Anna's mother and my mother and the other women in the neighborhood made the bums sack lunches while they waited outside the kitchen door. We didn't tell anyone that sometimes a carefully laid-out bed of newspapers, evidence of a small fire, and usually a whiskey bottle or two let Anna and me know that they were also in our woods. We weren't frightened. We knew they simply spent the night on Rice's Hill and caught the next train out. In a way, we envied their freedom.

* * *

Danford Elementary School, along with Danford Middle School, was housed in a handsome three-story brick building that had been built in the 1930s. Set back on the lot, the front of the school was a massive lawn that rarely saw any student activity. It was as if there was an unspoken code not to walk on the grass. No one ever threw a football there or a snowball or even just sprawled out to bask in the sunshine. It was also unthinkable that anyone would climb the massive birches. Children and teachers kept to the broad sidewalks, pretty much ignoring the park-like setting.

The elementary portion of the school was as familiar to Marcy as her own home. She knew all the teachers, knew where to take the erasers to wash them in the sink in the janitor's room, and knew, along with the rest of the school, that the second floor supply closet was where the principal found Mr. James kissing Ms. Scouville. The school was a cozy and friendly place that was filled with happy children and teachers who cared for them. The halls were kept glistening by young Hadleigh Moore, whose father—aging Hadleigh Moore Senior—took care of the middle school. Young Hadleigh Moore, as he was known by everyone in Danford, was at least forty-five years old and would probably die being known by the preposition in front of his name. Marcy wondered once how many of her classmates thought the fellow's first name was actually "Young."

The classrooms at Danford Elementary were enticing for a child, with tables of crayons and markers, building blocks, and modeling clay. The toilets and sinks were low to the ground and coat hooks in the classroom held rows of tiny jackets and sweaters. It was quiet there for the most part and peaceful and orderly and smelled good—of paste and clay and well-scrubbed children.

In contrast, the west end of the school, which housed the middle school, sixth grade through eighth, was chaos. It was difficult for sixth graders to be tossed out of the familiar grade school setting into a world where classes were changed every forty-five minutes and the halls were clogged with yelling and laughing and rowdy students. The overwhelmed teachers didn't seem as caring, and none of them seemed to be inclined to nurture or coddle their students.

School had been in session for a month, and Marcy was struggling. At first, her peers were compassionate and caring about the loss of Anna. The first day of school, girls huddled in the hallways or in the bathroom and wept for their fellow student. As Anna's best friend, Marcy received a lot of unexpected attention, and she didn't know how to react. She had hoped school would be a refuge from the anger and grieving that tormented her soul.

She had always liked school and felt at home in the halls and classrooms. She befriended the teachers and was known as friendly and fun Marcy Peterman, everyone's buddy. Now she crept through the halls on quiet feet, hugging her books to her chest and keeping her eyes to the ground. In the classroom, she sat quietly and didn't speak unless she was made to do so.

The whispering started one day, and the laughing. Stuck up Marcy. Marcy Peterman, who thought she was too good for the rest of the class.

No one understood. Even the teachers, who implored her to "just get over it and get on with life." Her grades slipped from *A*s to *C*s. She didn't turn in homework because she didn't care. Of what importance to her life as it was right now was knowing about the Louisiana Purchase or how to compute a complicated math problem or knowing who ran the country if the president and vice president and most of Congress died from food poisoning.

She was in the sixth grade. Twelve years old. She felt like she was twenty. Some days. Other days, she felt as young and immature as a first grader. The kids in her grade twittered and giggled, and the girls flirted, and the boys scoffed at them. The most important things in the world to girls her own age were television shows, getting their ears pierced, and any of a hundred other trivialities.

She didn't fit in. She sometimes wondered in amazement that she ever had…that she had been so shallow and clueless. Classmates didn't know what to do with her, and she didn't know what to do with herself.

The day an unthinking girl teased her about seeing her at the cemetery was the day Marcy started to hate school.

"So, like, what do you do, live up there at the cemetery?" the girl had asked. "That's kind of stupid, isn't it? She's been dead for about three months now."

Marcy wondered herself why she went to the cemetery. Anna wasn't there. Her cremated remains were in an urn in the possession of her parents.

However, there was a memorial bench placed in the cemetery for Anna just a few weeks after her death. It was of white granite and an angel, almost life-sized and holding her hands out with her palms up, sat at one end. A black plaque on the front of the bench gave the scripted details of Anna's life. Marcy knew it was just a memorial, that no part of Anna was there. Still, it was a place to go—a centering location she could visit that would provide an alignment with Anna. It was a comfort for her to sit on the bench.

Since that first jab, a few others seemed to have something to say. Usually, the comments were about death or graves or making fun of Marcy if it looked like she had been crying. She had watched once, years before, when a chubby boy in grade school was continually bullied and teased on the playground. Anna had attacked them with a fierceness that startled the tormentors, and they had backed off.

There seemed to be no one to come to Marcy's aid, no one to make them back off. She was too tired to fight. It was much easier to just endure. Besides, maybe she deserved their torment.

Today, instead of going to her locker and perhaps enduring a hurtful remark, Marcy turned around and headed to her classroom. Not going to her locker meant she wouldn't have her math book, but she would plead stupidity. Who cared anyway?

"Marcy! I've been looking for you." The voice behind her was chipper and loud.

Mrs. Erickson. The "get her done or die" teacher who managed to finagle most of the students into helping out with one stupid project after another. The woman, who was tall, thin, had high energy, and was high strung, was never content to just float along through life but always had to be doing more. The problem was that she fixated on massive projects she couldn't put together herself, so she counted on her army of slaves. The year before, Marcy, even though she had just been a fifth grader and not even in middle school, had been at least a colonel in Erickson's army. Now that Marcy was officially in middle school world, Erickson felt she had a firm claim to her talents.

Marcy attempted to side-step the teacher. "Hi, Mrs. Erickson. I'm almost late for class. Can we talk later?"

"Nope! Cleared the class thing with Mr. Morris. Told him you'd be late. I have a project I need your help on. Walk with me to my room. I'll clue you in." She took off down the hall, expecting Marcy to follow.

Marcy stayed rooted in the empty hall. Suddenly, she was overwhelmed with a flood of self-confidence and courage. She shook her head. Mrs. Erickson came back and stood in front of her. "What?" she questioned, throwing her arms wide and shaking her head in exasperation.

Taking a breath and standing her ground, Marcy looked right into the teacher's eyes. She was startled by this newfound boldness that made her voice firm and sure. "No more projects. I can't. You'll have to get someone else."

"Oh, c'mon, Marcy, you've got to get back into life. Besides, I need you to make some posters for me. You and, well, you and Anna, you were my best poster makers, and now, there's no one who can do half as good."

"I'm out of the poster business for now. Ask Jake Simmons. He can draw pretty good."

Mrs. Erickson took a step backward, and her lips pursed together as she considered the refusal. "Humph. Well…" she said a bit snidely. "I am really sorry you're still having a hard time over this. Don't think I don't understand. I lost my cat a few weeks back. Never came home. Maybe hit by a car. But if *that's* how you feel…"

"Truthfully? Right now, I don't really 'feel' anything," Marcy said, turning around and walking away. Then she yelled behind her. "Your *cat?* I can't believe you said that."

Mrs. Erickson stared at Marcy as she stomped off. Then she gave another humph, rolled her eyes, shrugged her shoulders in dismissal, and strode briskly down the hall to find Jake Simmons. Maybe he would be more agreeable than that Marcy Peterman. She had certainly gotten a sour attitude over the summer. Then she looked back. Marcy was almost to the front door that led outside.

"Hey, wait a minute! Just where do you think you're going?" The teacher's voice was so strident she attracted the attention of the principal, who came out of her office to see what was happening.

Marcy just knew she had to leave. She couldn't breathe here, and she felt like she was dying. She needed to escape. "I don't know. I'm just getting out of here," she yelled back calmly, shaking her head.

"You can't just leave. You get back here!" Mrs. Erickson threw her notebook to the floor and prepared to run after the recalcitrant child. Then an arm gently held her back.

"It'll be all right. Just let her go. I'll call her mother. That poor child needs to find her way through this." The school principal, Stella Draper, watched as Marcy sprinted across the lawn, headed toward home. She had known Marcy Peterman since the child was born and knew more about her situation than she was willing to relate. She turned back to Cynthia Erickson.

"We need to be a little more compassionate and understanding with her. The other kids have become frustrated with her, and I've heard they're being cruel. But they're children. We're adults, and we can be a little more sympathetic and maybe set a good example for the students." Then she patted the teacher's arm twice and went out to retrieve the books Marcy had thrown to the sidewalk.

Chapter 16

Setting the table for dinner was still one of the hardest things Barbara Miller did each night. For weeks after Anna's death, she and Joe, without discussion and in silent agreement, had simply not used the dining room table. Since their marriage fifteen years earlier, the Duncan Phyfe mahogany table, which had belonged to Barbara's grandmother, had been a place of refuge from the stresses of the day. It was a place to share, to dream and to plan, and to laugh. After Anna came along, it became a place for the three of them to join together as a family. They had enjoyed such great times at that table.

After three weeks of eating on TV trays in the living room, Barbara decided they needed to go back to the things that were important in keeping them united. She fixed Joe's favorite meal—meatloaf, mashed potatoes, and brown-sugared and buttered carrots—and carefully set two places. But this time, instead of Joe at the head of the table and places for Anna and Barbara on either side, she placed both settings on the sides of the table. Since she felt she was now the stronger of the two, she took Anna's place.

Grace that night was difficult, but Joe got through it. Afterwards, Barbara noticed two glistening tears in the center of his plate. There was a matching tear sliding down her cheek.

It had been nearly three months, and it was easier now, eating meals at the table. They were finding their way, picking their routes carefully through the landmines and traps and cautiously skirting pits of desolation. They were learning to keep to higher ground and choose happiness over despair. A time or two, they even discovered themselves laughing over something silly that happened in either his classroom or hers. Joe had been back to teaching full time for several weeks, and he was finally getting his feet back on the ground.

Now as she set the table, Joe wandered in. He had a book tucked under his arm.

"So who's the extra plate for?" he asked, noticing that she had settings for three stacked up and that she was using a tablecloth rather than the familiar red quilted placemats.

"If you didn't have your nose so deep in that book, you would have heard me tell you," she teased. "I swear I don't know how you can get so immersed in a book about bird nests."

Putting the book down, he reached over for the stack of crystal glasses and put one to the left of each plate. Barbara put down the silverware and napkins.

"Now that's funny, coming from you, considering you have a whole row of bird nests on the window ledge in the garage," Joe said. "It sounds boring, but it really isn't. For instance, you've probably heard of bird's nest soup, but did you know that it was made from bird saliva? The birds build these congealed and glutinous spit nests in caves. The nests are actually controlled by law and are carefully collected to be cooked up by Chinese chefs. They say the soup doesn't taste all that great."

"I did know that, about the bird spit," she said, moving the glasses to the upper right side of the plates. "But I didn't know about the law part or that the soup wasn't all that hot. So how much does it cost?"

"Interesting you should ask, my dear," he said, wagging one eyebrow. "I checked it out online. A bowl is around $60. But wait! That's not all. You also get crackers. There's probably a great joke in there somewhere…you know, instead of the waiter spitting in your soup, the bird does."

"I'm sure you'll share it with me when you come up with it. So tell me more."

"A lot of it you know, about the nests that are in trees or in hollows of trees or the waterfowl nests that are on the ground. But I'll bet you didn't know about bowerbirds."

"I don't know about bowerbirds, but I'll bet you're going to tell me." She loved it when he was this way – excited about something he was reading and wanting to share it. He was a man of a thousand interests and a multitude of things in life seemed to captivate him. It warmed her heart to see him so enthused.

"Make you a deal. I'll tell you about bowerbirds if you'll tell me who's coming for dinner."

"Pastor Mike. He called and left me a message at work asking if he could come over tonight. He said it wasn't anything important, he just wanted to ask us to do him a favor. Since we had leftover pot roast, I told him to just come to dinner."

"He probably just made that up—the favor thing—to snag a free dinner."

"Joe! That's a terrible thing to say."

"Hey, I remember bachelorhood very well. A guy can't very well show up at Mom and Dad's every night, so you learn to be creative. I remember visiting my aunt and uncle once around dinnertime, and I thought they'd never get around to eating. It was about nine o'clock at night, and my stomach was rumbling."

"Why didn't you just go to McDonalds?"

"Aunt May was the best cook this side of the Mississippi, and it was worth the wait."

"That's probably why you married me. Because I'm a good cook."

"Well, plus other things. Besides, I didn't know you could cook until long after I fell in love with you. It was your pretty little face that caught my eye, and that cute little butt."

"Not so little anymore," she said, laughing and taking a swipe at him with the dishtowel she had draped over her shoulder.

"Still little, still cute," he said as he attempted to grab the towel from her.

"So tell me about the bowerbirds," she prompted over her shoulder as she headed back into the kitchen to check on the rolls. The aromatic smells of roast beef, potatoes, and carrots and hot bread were filling the house. An apple pie, which she had in the freezer for such an occasion, was ready to pop in the oven as soon as the rolls were done.

He traipsed after her, grabbing the book off the table.

"Bowerbirds. You won't believe this, Barb," he said, sifting through the pages. "I first heard about them a long time ago on Paul Harvey. I think it was one of his 'rest of the story' things. I don't know what made me think about it the other day, maybe the fact that the leaves are gone and you can spot nests more easily. Anyway, I looked it up on the Internet and then went to the library and picked up this book. It's really very interesting. Look at this."

Barbara turned from the sink where she'd started to wash some of the pots and utensils she'd used for cooking and dried her hands on a dishtowel.

"Oh my, what is that?" she asked, looking at the page he had thrust under her nose. She took the book so she could see it better.

"It's a bowerbird nest. See that little nondescript fellow over there? About the size of a wren? He's the master builder."

The photo showed a huge, at least six-foot tall, edifice made of carefully placed pieces of wood. It was decorated with orchids, berries, and hundreds of colorful items she didn't recognize.

"That little bird made this?" she asked, leaning with her back settled against the kitchen counter. "It's incredible."

"The male bird. There are something like sixteen different types of bowerbirds, and they live in places like Australia, Kenya, and Tanzania. They all have different building styles, but a few of the species didn't inherit the decorating gene."

Joe's excitement made her smile inwardly. Oh, how she loved this man of hers.

"Some of them build nests in a sort of maypole style by building huts nearly five feet high around this pole structure," he continued. "Others, like the golden bowerbird, pile sticks and saplings up to nine feet high and use crossbars to hold it together."

He took the book from her and turned back a few pages. "You'll like this one," he said as his black eyes scanned the page. "'The Archbold's bowerbird,'" he read, "'drapes trails of orchids over their bowers, daily replacing fading flowers with fresh ones.'"

He looked up from the book. "Most of them decorate with anything colorful like lichens and mosses, butterfly wings, beetle skeletons, yellow leaves, and even brightly colored fruits and flowers and berries. Not only that, but they smash berries and flowers and use their beaks to paint sticks and other items different colors."

"That's absolutely amazing," Barbara said, looking at him. "So do they do this to attract a mate?"

"Yup. It's sort of the bird version of a convertible and good cologne, tight jeans, and a good haircut. But get this. The birds that live near humans are thieves and will make off with anything colorful, from ballpoint pens, lost jewelry they find, red shotgun shells, bits of ribbon and tinfoil, anything that is bright and pretty. Plus, they actually decorate with color schemes."

"You're kidding." She was truly finding this subject very fascinating.

"No. Scientists studying these birds did a test where they put out poker chips in a variety of colors. The birds very carefully selected the colors that would match those of their bower. Some removed only the chips of a certain color—like red or yellow—and others, evidently with more discerning taste and deriding cheap plastic, rejected all of them."

"So the little fellow builds this huge beautiful nest and woos the female to come live with him?"

"That's the funny part. She selects the guy with the best nest, but after he has his way with her, she doesn't even live there. She flies off and builds her own humble little abode, lays her eggs, and raises her young all by herself."

Barbara laughed gaily. "And I know there's a joke in there somewhere. Somehow, all this bowerbird stuff must fit society as we know it."

The doorbell rang as they were laughing.

"Saved by the bell from having to go *there*," Joe said, striding toward the front door.

Chapter 17

While he was waiting for the doorbell to be answered, Pastor Mike hunkered down and talked into his dog's ear. "Okay, Midas. This is it. All you have to do is remember your manners. Otherwise, they're never going to agree to babysit you. No jumping up or chewing things, and for crying out loud, don't go peeing on the floor. Just behave, okay?"

Midas looked at him with enormous brown eyes then opened his mouth and used his long pink tongue to give a slurping swipe to his handsome face. Mike was grateful the dog was washing his own face and, for once, hadn't aimed for his master.

"Good boy," Mike said. "It's good to be tidy and clean." He straightened up just as the door opened.

"Mike! Welcome. Come in," Joe said as a streak of yellow whizzed past him and bounded into the kitchen.

"Midas! Get back here!" Mike hollered.

"He's okay," Barbara yelled out, laughing. "Who taught this dog to kiss anyway? He's a very sloppy kisser."

"Darn that dog," Mike said to Joe as he stepped inside and slipped out of his tennis shoes and shed his coat. "We've been working on manners all week just for this occasion, and then he goes and embarrasses me like this."

"Just wait until you get married and have kids," Joe said, laughing as he clapped his friend on the back. "Come in the kitchen and greet the cook."

In the middle of the kitchen floor, the cook and the dog were engaged in mutual admiration. Midas was so happy to see this new friend he was jiggling from side to side and grinning. Barbara was hugging his neck and had her face buried into his fur.

"I think they like each other," Joe said, leaning against the door jamb. Mike shook his head.

"Sometimes, I think I was crazy to pick out this dog at the pound. I mean there were a ton of dogs there—all sizes and colors and breeds. Little tiny poodles that would have fit perfectly in my lap and dogs even bigger than Midas. Good dogs. Probably dogs that had etiquette training. But there was something about his goofy look that got to me. Look at the guy. Have you ever seen a dog that looked that goofy? He really is a clown."

"Oh, are you a clown, Midas?" Barbara crooned, her voice muffled in the thick yellow fur.

Midas wiggled even more heartily and slapped his tongue against her neck.

"No kisses. Bad dog. *No kisses,*" she said firmly, raising her head and wiping her neck with her forearm. "Yuck."

"If you're done spoiling my dog, I'll show you what we've learned this week. At least I'll try and show you. I think he's all befuddled what with the smells coming from this kitchen. What is in the oven anyway?"

"Leftover pot roast and all the trimmings, and apple pie. I just took the rolls out."

"See? Now this is what I think heaven is going to be like," he said to Joe. "Pot roast and apple pie and hot rolls. Man, I love coming over here!"

"You need a wife," Barbara said, getting up from the floor and brushing off the dog hair. "Someone who will cook for you and clean your house, help tend your flock, and iron your shirts." She looked pointedly at his very wrinkled University of Montana sweatshirt and reached out and plucked a hunk of the fabric between her thumb and forefinger and then let it go. She wondered how on earth he managed to wrinkle a sweatshirt to that extent.

"Oh no. Don't tell me you have a stepsister or a maiden aunt hiding in the closet," he groaned.

"That bad?" asked Joe.

"You don't know," he said, shaking his head. "It's an endless parade of eligible females. They range from eighteen to about seventy two. Sometimes, it reminds me of a reversed trip to the pound, except they're all coming to me and checking me out. Remember Alma and George Snorl, who moved from Danford to Missoula a few years back? They called and said they were back in town and wanted to go to lunch. Sure, I said. After all, he was an usher, and they are great people. It would be a nice time, right? They didn't warn me that Cousin Sissy from Bohunk, Alabama, happened to be visiting. I'm not going to say anything against this woman, bless her heart, so you can get that eager look off your face, Little Miss Barbie, but…do you remember that old painting of the sourpuss farmer and his wife standing there and he's got something like a rake in his hand? That's all I'm going to say."

"But can she cook?" asked Joe, laughing. "Did you find that out at least? Can she cook?"

"I'll bet she'd be great in bed," Barbara said, batting her eyelashes seductively. "I've heard about those Southern women."

Then she looked shocked. "I can't believe I said that to my pastor!" she said, feeling her face redden. Both men howled in laughter.

"It's not like he's a priest!" Joe said. "I'll bet he knows all about sex."

"Sex. Yes, I have heard of that," Mike said, feigning somberness. Then he added, "So do I have enough time before dinner to show you how much Midas has improved?"

For the next fifteen minutes, Midas, after getting under control and paying attention to his master, showed that he could sit, stay, lay down, and heel.

"That's amazing," Barbara said. "Three weeks ago, he was just a big ol' cute galoot. How did you do that so fast?"

"Do you remember Bob Markham from church? Big guy? Older? Wears camouflage shirts a lot? He saw me struggling with Midas one day, trying to get the fool dog to just walk down the sidewalk with me, but he was jerking me along like he was Denali the sled dog trying to win that big Iditarod Sled Dog Race in Alaska.

"Bob pulled over in his beat-up pickup and said, 'Ya'll havin' problems with that mutt of yours?' You know how he talks. By that time, Midas had wrapped me around a tree. Old Bob got out of his truck, untangled the leash, and in about three minutes, had Midas heeling and sitting. It was amazing. Since then, we meet every few days. The guy is a dog whisperer, I swear."

"Well, I'm certainly impressed," Joe said. "I have some kids in my classrooms I wish he'd whisper to."

"Actually, Midas is why I'm here," Mike admitted. "I'm wondering if you'd babysit him for three days so I can attend a conference in Victoria, British Columbia. Sort of a conference. Actually a board meeting. I've been asked to sit on the board for Hope Ministries. I could always take him to a kennel but, well…"

Except for the hiss of potatoes in the oven, the nonstop chatter in the kitchen suddenly turned to silence. Joe looked at Barbara, and she stared back. They both turned to stare at Mike and then back at each other. Barbara shrugged her shoulders and gave a slight smile.

"Well, why not?" Joe said. "What do you think, Barb?"

"We can keep him for a whole three days? The clown dog?"

Mike ducked his head and cringed. "Well, it's probably more like four or five, what with travel time…"

"We'll do it!" she declared and dropped to her knees to hug the dog. Then she pushed him away and looked in his eyes and said, "But you have to be a good dog. Hear me? A very good dog."

Inwardly, Mike prayed he would be.

A few minutes later, they were eating dinner, and Midas, as if he had done it all his life, was sprawled out under the table and sleeping soundly.

* * *

It was quiet in the house and dark. The dishes were done, and Mike had long gone, taking his dog with him. Barbara and Joe had settled into bed.

"Are you asleep?" Barbara whispered into the darkness, turning toward him.

"Mmm-hmmm," Joe answered groggily. "You okay?"

"Yes, but I was just thinking," she said softly. "Do you remember that book, *The Perfect Nest*? Your story about the bowerbirds made me think of it."

"*The Perfect Nest*. How could I ever forget *The Perfect Nest*?" he said, now wide awake. "How many times do you think we read that book to her? Probably about a million. If I close my eyes, I can see every page, including the cover where that dingdong mother bird is sitting next to her nest in the tree."

"I hated that book," Barbara admitted, giggling. "I hid it once under the towels in the closet, and I was free of it for about three weeks, and then one day she found it. She said, 'There you are!' as if the book had just wandered off on its own."

"You did that?" Joe said soberly. "I can't believe you'd do that to her. She loved that book."

There was a bit of a silence. "You're right. It wasn't very nice," Barbara said with a sigh.

Then he broke out in laughter. "I hid it in the garage in my toolbox. She found it in less than a week!"

"You! Oh, Joe, that is so funny!" Barbara declared, joining her giggles to his hearty laugh.

It felt so good to laugh; she wanted it to never end. There was something so special about laughing in the dark with the man you love. She reached for him.

Their lovemaking that night was sweet and wholesome, fulfilling and nurturing. It was a sharing and a blending of their souls and a declaration to their future. It was very unlike the first time after Anna's death when the act had been rough and almost violent. It left them both feeling empty and hollow and guilty that they had betrayed their grief in an attempt to grab some meaningless pleasure. Afterwards, she realized she had cried through the whole thing.

Tonight was so different. Later, as he slept with his naked back to her, she was still chuckling inwardly about the bird book when she placed her hand softly on his shoulder and prayed a blessing over him and thanked God for the peace and healing he was bringing to their lives. She thanked him for the friendship of their pastor and for the gift of laughter.

She was just about asleep when he turned over. His voice was so soft she could barely make out the words.

"Barbara?" he whispered. "I just wanted you to know that I could build a beautiful bower for you, but it would be nice if we could build it together."

"I love you, Joe Miller," she said, but she wasn't sure, in her drowsiness, if she said the words aloud or if they just floated through her mind.

Chapter 18

The hand-painted sign hanging from the front porch of the Petermans' house was festooned with colorful flowers and had a blue butterfly in the upper corner. It declared that the dwelling housed Jim, Sharon, Marcy, and Ben. The names were under four flamboyant sunflowers of differing heights.

The house was old and elegant and very large. Built "out in the country" in 1921 by Sharon's great-grandparents, Micah and Rosamond Givens, it had, in its heyday, drawn many a Danford resident out for a Sunday drive. They would drive by slowly in their newfangled cars and gawk at the sprawling house. Of course, it was nothing compared to the two mansions in Danford that were known throughout the northwest for their magnificence. O'Malley House and Whitmore Mansion, both built in the 1890s, were a testimony to the wealth of that age, which came from hard work and a knack for smelling out Montana's path in the future—in other words, cattle, timber, land, the railroad, and mining.

In comparison to the O'Malleys and Whitmores, Micah Givens—who was more or less an accountant who gave business advice—was a flash in the pan, garnering just enough money from investments to build his bride of ten years this sprawling house. A few years later, his finances, due to a long string of dimwitted floundering in the stock market, took a downturn. Except for his banker, few people realized the truth or even saw through the charade. Micah and Rosamond attempted to keep up the soirees and dinners but soon were forced, because of lack of finances, to quit entertaining. This meant incoming invitations also dwindled.

Finally, only a few loyal friends remained. These few attributed the dated clothing, cheap wine, and meager food offerings—plus the fact that the Givenses quit spending money on art or furnishings—to a newfound sense by Micah Givens that he and Rosamond should be more frugal.

It was a quirk of fate that, when the crash of 1929 hit and the Great Depression followed, many of their former friends and acquaintances looked back and thought erringly that Micah Givens was a man of rare insight and astuteness. They declared among themselves that Givens had seen this coming years before. They wondered why they had been too stupid to see it themselves.

Micah's accounting business flourished, and surprisingly, men of great import sought his advice. Being a clever man, Micah skillfully turned conversations around so he would learn where and when these men thought of investing. He would tuck each tidbit of information into his head and also on a notepad. He quickly learned to see trends, and by studying newspapers he had mailed to Danford from cities all over the US, he could see the way things were developing. While all of this helped, it basically boiled down to the fact that, for the most part, people were paying for their own advice.

But it wasn't only the bookkeeping and advice that was keeping them afloat. Rosamond, who had brains equal to her beauty, was kept abreast of things in Micah's business world, and together, they too cautiously invested.

They lived a comfortable life even though millions were suffering, and they were more than charitable in helping others. Rosamond took it upon herself to ferret out those who were most needy and help anonymously.

In time, the couple had two children, Violet and Frederick. Violet died at a young age, and Frederick was Sharon Peterman's grandfather.

As the only child of an only child, Sharon inherited the old place just after she and Jim were married. By then, it had been empty for many years, and most of the elegant furnishings had been sold off by her grandmother, who had a yen for more modern furniture. She thought that decorating with old hand-me-downs just implied you weren't wealthy enough to purchase new items.

Sharon never really thought she'd stay in Danford after finishing high school, but fate had kept her here. Not really fate actually, but love.

Jim Peterman. Even after all these years, when she thought about him as he was in high school—the handsome football star every girl dreamed of—she still got shivers of excitement. Aloof, polite, extremely bright, and on the honor roll, he excelled at every sport the school offered. Except golf. He could barely hit the ball, and it became one of the most frustrating aspects of his adult life. She wondered why he kept trying to conquer such a formidable foe.

Jimmy, as he was known back then, didn't date much, and when he did, it wasn't with the most beautiful girl in the school or the most popular, even though they did everything but salivate and beg for his favor when they were around him. Instead, he chose the most interesting. Many of them were plain girls with not much style but an affinity for laughter and quick wittedness. Most of all, he chose the girls who put God first in their lives.

Interestingly, it was his quiet Christianity that wooed the girls in the school who evidently, at least inwardly, yearned to be with a fellow with good morals and who they knew would treat them properly.

However, he took a great deal of ridicule from his peers in the locker room, who likened him to Billy Graham or even Father Gimball down at St. Pat's. He took their teasing with good cheer, and they soon treated him like anyone else on the team, especially when they realized that he didn't judge. They could talk about their conquests in the backseat of cars or the case of beer they'd consumed the weekend before, and he never commented one way or another. He felt it wasn't up to him to judge. That was God's job. All he could do was to set a good example.

The good example paid off frequently when one of his teammates would seek him out for counsel. He had prayed privately with at least two dozen of his schoolmates, and they, nor he, ever let on. Jim Peterman was usually the first to know about a girlfriend's skipped menstrual periods and subsequent positive pregnancy test, the fighting and beatings at home, the shoplifting charges, and a myriad of other incidents that displayed the weakness and frailty that comes with being a teenager and the innate tendency of mankind to succumb to the darker side of life. Many of the teens he prayed with showed up sooner or later at one church or another in town.

Sharon was a sophomore the year Jim was a senior. She, along with every other female in the school, sighed when she saw him. While he was always nice and kind and offered a cheerful word now and again, he didn't treat her any differently than most of the other girls.

That changed the summer she graduated, when she got a job in the office of Peterman Ford, Lincoln and Mercury—the large dealership started by his grandfather in the 1940s that his father now owned. Jim was in his third year of college studying for a business degree, and he was home working at the dealership for the summer.

She would always remember his first words to her when he saw her sitting behind the desk in the reception area. She was wearing a red shirt over black slacks and had tied a long black-and-white checked scarf around her waist.

"Hey, little girl," he said, laughing in surprise, "what are *you* doing here?"

She couldn't remember what she said back to him, except that it made him laugh, especially when she got so flustered in trying to talk to him and answer the phone at the same time; she sounded like a bumbling fool.

As the two youngest employees, they were naturally drawn to one another, and soon, they were taking breaks together and going out for an occasional lunch.

A parade of leftover girls from high school, who hadn't married or moved out of Danford, traipsed through the dealership that summer—dressed to seduce—and declared they needed to buy a new vehicle. It was obvious that most of them didn't know a tachometer from a transmission, but they would *ooh* and *aah* over the engines and the tires and the cute little seats that moved back and forth.

He always caught her eye during these sessions, his eyes twinkling. From the window in the front office, she would laugh back and shake her head.

She thought he was wonderful, and she knew she had fallen in love.

He loved her too, but he had one year left of school. Maybe after…

The week before he was to leave to go back to University of Washington in Seattle was hard for both of them. He couldn't promise her anything. He was dependent on scholarships, his parents, and a part-time job to get him through college. She declared she'd wait forever. After much thought, she scrapped her plans to attend the University of Montana and decided to stay at the dealership and take night classes at the community college.

Finally, they were down to one day—his last day in Danford, before he started the drive early the next morning back to Seattle. She sniffled throughout the day, and when he showed yet another car to Melody Goodrich and looked toward her window, she didn't smile back or laugh. She simply turned and wept.

It's funny how things in life can change so quickly. One minute you're driving happily down the highway,, and a half hour later, you are in the emergency room where doctors are wading through your blood as they sew you back together. One day you're having lunch with a beloved family member, and the next day, you're planning his funeral.

Sharon happened to be gazing out onto the showroom floor that afternoon when Bob Peterman, Jim's jovial father, who owned the company, walked across the glossy blue tiles. He staggered slightly and reached out toward a Lincoln town car to correct his balance. Then he simply sagged and crumpled to the floor.

Sharon leaped out of her chair and started running, yelling, "Call 911 and find Jim!" at the top of her voice.

She knew he was dead before she ever dropped to his side and did the preliminary checks of pulse and breathing before starting CPR. One of the sales people took over pushing on his chest while she breathed life-giving air into his lungs. The procedure went so smoothly, she thought later, that it was as if they had practiced many times.

Jim came and sat on the floor in stunned silence. Minutes later, the paramedics arrived and took over CPR and whisked him away. Marcy and Jim followed. One of the salesmen called Trisha Peterman to tell her simply that Bob had collapsed and to meet them at the hospital.

It was an aneurism, an exploding vessel in his head that changed all of their lives forever. College was canceled as Jim settled into his dad's office and took over the dealership. His love for Sharon deepened as she helped him cope with his loss, and the next summer, they were married. It was because of her that he took enough correspondence courses to graduate. It took three years, but he finally had his degree.

Now, seventeen years later, she was content, if not happy. She had a great husband and two beautiful children.

If she was honest, however, she'd have to admit that right now, things were starting to unravel. At first, Anna's death had brought them closer, clinging together in desperate support. Now they were isolating, holding back.

Their son, Benjamin, was a typical nine-year-old who was into every and all sports, and he posed no problems, except for an occasional bit of missing homework, and once, he came home with a head of lice.

Ben slept with his baseball glove, and nearly every article of clothing he owned had some sort of team emblem. His room, of course, was decorated in a hockey/baseball/football/soccer/golf theme. A row of logoed baseball caps rimmed the upper walls just below the ceiling.

It was Marcy who was the problem. Since Anna's death, they didn't know how to handle her. She had always been such a good child, mannerly and well-behaved. But now, she frequently skittered out of control, screaming and yelling and crying and spending long periods of time in silent brooding.

"You need to talk to her," Jim implored continually. "Just talk to her."

"Damn it, Jim," she had yelled back tonight in the kitchen after dinner. "I *am* trying to talk to her. We're all trying to talk to her—counselors at school, Mike at church, *you*. You've tried talking to her. You know how it is."

"You don't have to swear," he retorted loudly. He opened the refrigerator door and then slammed it shut. Pages of a calendar hanging nearby fluttered in the air.

"And you don't have to lay all this on my shoulders," she said, stepping away from the sink to confront him. "I am the one who is lying awake all night while you are snoring away. I am the one who has to go to the school and talk to them about yet another scrape or beg their forgiveness because she's simply walked out again."

"Well, what do you want me to do? Quit my job? Sell the dealership?"

The overpowering silence that came from his question settled them both. Then she looked at him sadly and shook her head. "I don't know what I want, Jim," she said quietly. "I guess I just want our lives back. I want our Marcy back." She placed her hand on her cheek and closed her eyes. Then she felt his arms around her as he pulled her close.

"We can't do this, Sharon. We can't keep fighting, and we have to find a way through this helplessness. We have to work together to help Marcy. I know I haven't been much help, so I want you to make a list of what I can do. We can get through this, but it's going to take trusting God. We both know he hasn't abandoned her, or us."

"I know," she said, settling herself into his embrace. "I'm sorry I'm such a shrew."

"You're not a shrew. You're a mother who is desperately worried about her daughter. And right now, I think you need to go upstairs, fill the tub with hot water, add some of that smelly stuff to it, and put on one of those classical CDs you love."

Chapter 19

* * *

Summer was the time of big fluffy cumulous clouds, which were much different from the endless stretch of suffocating gray clouds that covered us during most of the winter. The towering clouds blossomed and swirled and traveled quickly some days. Other days, they moved gently and seemed to linger in content, just happy to be up there and floating quietly by. Anna and I spent Cloud Days on our backs in the grass on the hill, searching out familiar shapes. We could see unicorns and rabbits and elephants. Once Anna said, "Look, there's Bigfoot," and I looked and looked and couldn't see anything that looked like Bigfoot. Then a shadow passed my face, and I saw her naked foot right in front of my nose. We laughed and laughed.

* * *

Upstairs in her bedroom, Marcy heard them fighting. She turned up her radio and then pulled the pillow over her head. When she felt someone touch her foot, she threw off the pillow and jerked to a sitting position.

"What!" she yelled at Ben. "Can't you leave me alone, you little brat!"

He stood before her and didn't move, and her heart melted. "I'm sorry, Benny," she said, reaching for him. "You aren't a brat. I'm the brat. I don't know why I keep acting like this. I'm just so mad, and I miss Anna so much."

"They're fighting," he said, pointing at the floor.

"I know, and it's all my fault. Maybe I should just go live with Grandma or something for a while."

"No! You can't leave, Marcy. 'Sides, that would be awful. You'd have to watch those stupid soap opera things with her and eat fiber. She always makes us eat fiber, and I don't even know what that is. And no Coke or McDonalds. Plus, she'd make you work. Scrubbing floors and stuff."

"Yeah, you're right. Living with Grandma wouldn't be a picnic. She'd make me wear black orthopedic shoes."

"Maybe it'll just get better after a while," he said. "Maybe someday you won't remember Anna or what happened. Like when Uncle Phil died a long time ago. I don't remember him, do you?"

"Sure I remember him. He was funny. But I was a lot older than you. And I really don't want to ever forget Anna. I just don't want it to hurt so much."

"Maybe you should pray more," he said thoughtfully and then added with a grin, "And maybe eat more fiber."

She looked at her brother and smiled a sad smile. "You know, you are one terrific brother," she said as she ruffled his curly blond hair.

Chapter 20

There were already a few cars in the parking lot when Joe and Barbara got to the October Compassionate Friends meeting. Despite having to take time to assure Midas that they indeed would be coming back home later, they were fifteen minutes early and pulled up to the church at the same time Rod and Caroline Lincoln were getting out of their car.

Joe walked over to Rod, and they started to walk toward the church. Behind them, Barbara and Caroline were hugging and happily greeting each other. Both couples rejoiced at their newfound friendship even though it came about through tragedy. Since the first meetings, they had gone to dinner and a movie the weekend before.

Barbara and Caroline had assured their husbands it was not a chick flick, but to their chagrin, they found out differently as the theater filled with women, all of whom sniffled in unison as the movie dragged on. Next time, Rod and Joe declared as they walked out into the lobby, the girls could go to their movie and they'd see something with a little blood and violence.

"Big crowd tonight," Joe said, motioning to all the vehicles already in the parking lot.

"It's because of the balloon launch," Rod said. "We only do them a couple times during the year, and people get a lot of healing out of them. Some of the members have been calling people on the list and telling them about it."

"You've talked about it, but just what is balloon launch," Joe asked as they entered the church and headed downstairs to the fellowship hall. Before Rod could answer, their wives had caught up, and the conversation turned to the unusually warm weather.

Instead of the usual sharing and talking, there was a program during this meeting. A grief counselor from the hospital spoke on practical ways to cope with grief, including dealing with feelings, seeking outside support, helping your marriage and relationships, arming yourself with education on the grieving process, and being kind to yourself.

Everyone in the room seemed to get a lot of helpful information from the presentation. After the speaker finished and the applause died down, Rod and Caroline went to the front of the group and explained the logistics of the balloon launch that would take place on Saturday.

"Some of you have taken part in a balloon launch, but some of you haven't," Rod said. "Basically, before we meet next Saturday— not this Saturday but the next Saturday—you simply write a poem or something you would like to say to your loved one on an index card or piece of paper. Then we meet at the park at two o'clock—the quiet side of the park by the pond and gazebo. We'll have balloons on hand and helium, and we'll attach the cards and letters to the balloons. Once all the balloons are ready, we'll have a prayer, someone may read a poem, and then we will release the balloons all at once.

"You're invited to bring friends or family members, and they can also release a balloon. Of course, we all know the balloons won't actually reach heaven and our loved ones won't actually read the messages, but this is a great way of remembering. I think you'll be surprised at the amount of healing that takes place when you sit down and thoughtfully write something and then when you actually let go of that balloon.

"Also," Rod continued, "please bring a photo of your loved one so that we can put it out for others to see. We'll have a table set up here in the Fellowship Hall for photos. Afterwards, we'll have a sort of a picnic here. Caroline makes awesome potato salad, and some of us tougher guys will go outside and barbecue hotdogs and burgers, and we'll have cookies for dessert. All sorts of cookies." Longtime members of the group, knowing his penchant for cookies, chuckled.

"If you could let us know if you plan to stay for the picnic, that would be great," Caroline offered. Then she pulled her lips into her mouth for a second and glanced at Joe and Barbara before telling the group she hoped they would all participate.

"I know it's hard, and I know it's awful. Death is ugly. But there is something about these balloons—these bright colorful balloons that represent childhood and all things good and happy—that is so wonderful. Watching them as they float away is the most emotional feeling. We had just lost Tommy and Josie a few months earlier when they had a balloon launch at the park in early spring. By letting loose of those strings and watching my prayers and love go heavenward, I was finally able to let go of my babies.

"So," she concluded, shaking off the bit of grief that threatened to settle in, "if you want to bring a dessert or side dish or something, just let me know, but you aren't obligated to bring anything at all. We'll have plenty of food."

"Two o'clock, Saturday after this one," Rod reminded. "I hope we see a ton of people there."

Later, as Rod and Joe put chairs and tables away, clusters of people chatted in the hall and in the parking lot. One young mother whose three-year-old daughter had just died of cancer was sitting in a corner with Caroline and Barbara.

After the distraught mother left, the two couples finished tidying up the kitchen.

"So how are you doing, really," Caroline asked as she folded a dishtowel and put it on the counter. Her back was settled against the stove.

Joe had taken his jacket from a hook behind the door and was sliding his arm into the sleeve. He answered for both of them.

"I think we're doing quite well, considering," he said, "we've had some rough times, but we're making progress. Coming here has really helped. In a way, Barbara and I are closer than we ever were."

"Our faith has really pulled us through, and we know God is walking this very difficult path with us," Barbara added. "And you two are truly a blessing."

"I keep telling Caroline that—that I'm a blessing from God—and she just rolls her eyes," Rod said, and they all laughed.

"Seriously, you have been a lot of help. And I'm looking forward to the balloon launch," Barbara said.

"Speaking of which," Caroline said as she reached behind Joe to grab her sweater, "how is Marcy Peterman doing? Do you think she would want to come and participate? Maybe her whole family?"

Joe and Barbara looked at each other. Of course Marcy should be invited. They were ashamed they hadn't thought of it themselves.

"I think that's a wonderful idea," Barbara said. "She's having a hard time. She seems to be stuck in the anger part of grieving, and Joe and I have both heard she's having a hard time at school—not only her grades, but getting along with the other kids. Maybe this would help, this balloon launch. We can call her mom and dad."

"Do you think we should bring her to the meetings?" Joe asked the Lincolns.

"Of course," Rod said. "It's for everyone, and she might find some help here."

* * *

They were quiet on the ride home through the darkened streets of Danford. Instead of taking the shortcut, Joe drove through the town center—past the old ornate brick buildings, a few that had housed businesses since the 1890s. The Model Café was still there and the hardware store and the Whistle Stop Bar and Hometown Furniture Store. Polsky's Market, now run by members of the fourth generation, held reign on the corner. While there were several chain stores on the outskirts of town where the malls were, old-timers still shopped at Polsky's.

"It's a nice little town, our Danford," Barbara remarked, gazing at the storefronts as they went by. The town fathers had, years before, seen the value in the beautiful old lampposts and the architecture of the buildings and had gone to great lengths to preserve the character and flavor of the town. Now, except for the hardware store and Polsky's, however, it was mostly for tourists—with classy dress shops, antique stores, and gift shops.

"I think, sometimes, what would have happened if I'd accepted the teaching offer in North Dakota," Joe said. "I wouldn't be living here, wouldn't have met and married you, wouldn't have our house or our friends…Yup, it's a pretty great place to live."

But if you'd gone to North Dakota, Barbara thought sadly to herself, *you might have a wonderful wife and a whole houseful of kids*. She had always regretted not being able to give him more children, and the hysterectomy after Anna's birth had made it impossible.

"I wouldn't trade my life for anything in the world," he said as if reading her mind. He reached across the console to grab her hand, and she clung to it tightly and brought it to her lips and then held it to her cheek.

She closed her eyes and basked in the comfort of this big strong rough hand of her husband. She knew his hands as well as her own—

the scar on a middle finger from a childhood fishhook mishap, the lump on a forefinger from where he broke it during a high school basketball game, the ring finger of his left hand, which was white and smooth under the gold band.

"You're a good man, Joe Miller," she said.

Chapter 21

Hope Ministries was a huge and very well-known Christian ministry that had been founded two decades earlier by four pastors of differing denominations. It was a missions-based ministry that also had roots in poverty-stricken areas in big cities in the US, where it provided counseling, clinics, and food programs. Pastor Mike had been astounded when he received a call from the director of the organization, asking if he would consider serving as a board member. He still didn't understand how they even got his name.

Someone less humble would have realized the answer was in the strong congregation he had amassed through his simple preaching of the truth and of his ability to use his God-given sense of humor and common sense to reach people. He was gaining a reputation throughout Montana and into adjoining states and frequently accepted speaking engagements throughout the northwest, as long as they didn't interfere with his ministerial duties.

The board meeting had been heartwarming yet tiring. He had been shocked to learn of the current atrocities against Christians throughout the world, and he had been saddened to learn how desperately people needed the Good News that was spread by Hope Ministries. While he, of course, had bits of knowledge about both subjects, he had never been able to fully grasp the full scope of the need or the hostility toward Christians. What disturbed him even more was the plight of people in his own country.

He had always been a man of prayer. Even as a child, he had prayed and sought God. But now, at this meeting, he was awake most of the night, praying ceaselessly for the needs of this group, the needs of people throughout the world. Besides God, Hope Ministries and similar organizations truly were the only hope for millions of lost souls.

Now, as he sat on a bench under a tree, he let the British Columbia sunshine pour over his aching heart.

"Mind if I join you?" Rachel Pontelli, who was tall and wore her auburn hair pulled back in a loose ponytail, stood before him and waited for his nod before sitting next to him on the bench. She was beautiful with green eyes and a smooth creamy complexion, but it was a gentle and caring girl-next-door kind of beauty instead of the Hollywood Victoria's Secret version.

"I know what you're going through," she said, putting her hands together in her lap and looking ahead at the plush green expanse of lawn and the towering pine trees. "When I started working as administrative assistant for the chairman of Hope, I thought I'd have to quit. I couldn't bear hearing the stories or seeing the photos or thinking about all the desperate people, especially the children."

He turned to her. "So how did you come to grips with it? I feel like my sermons and everything I've ever done is so shallow and meaningless."

She laughed softly and reached out her hand to touch his arm but then pulled away.

"I felt the same way. I'd had some rough spots in my life, but for the most part, it was like I'd just floated through as a bystander and my whole existence had revolved around what color eye shadow

I should wear or if I'd gained weight or if I should buy straight-legged or boot-cut jeans."

Then she turned on the bench to face him. This time, she did put a hand on his arm. "Did you ever hear the story about the fellow who was walking down the beach and throwing the dying starfish back into the ocean? There were hundreds—thousands—of them. Someone who was watching said to him, 'You're wasting your time. There are hundreds of them. Thousands of them. You can't save them all.' And the man answered back, 'But I can save this one,' and tossed another starfish into the water.

"That's your answer—we can save this one. And that one and that next one. One at a time. We just have to look at one person and one problem at a time."

"You are a very wise woman, Ms. Pontelli," he said.

"You can call me Rachel," she said, laughing. "So tell me about your little town back in Montana. Do you have a horse and wear a cowboy hat? Let me see those shoes. Is that cow dung I see on them?"

"We have all afternoon free. If you'll have lunch with me, I'll tell you all about Danford, Montana."

"Lead the way, McDuff," she said, jumping up from the bench. "This wise woman is starving. By the way, have you ever been to Butchart Gardens?"

"I saw the brochure in my room, but no, I've never been."

"Would you like to visit them? They aren't far away. I know guys aren't usually into gardens, but this, I promise you, is more like the Garden of Eden than a few flower beds mere mortals could create. I promise you've probably never seen anything like it. I need to go there before I leave, and it would be nice if you went with me."

"I can't think of anything I'd rather do," Mike said with total honesty.

Over the past two days, the meetings had been intense, with emotions running high. He knew he had learned more about his fellow board members and Rachel in these hours spent together than he would in years under normal conditions. He couldn't ever remember feeling as drawn to a woman as he did Rachel Pontelli.

After going to their hotel rooms to get jackets and grab Mike's camera, they walked to where Mike's rental car was parked. When she saw the car, Rachel stopped dead in her tracks.

"You rented this?" she asked in surprise and admiration. The red Ford Thunderbird convertible gleamed in the sunlight. Running her hand along the hood and up over the front window, she walked to the passenger window and looked in at the cream-colored leather seats and glistening black dashboard.

"My, my," she crooned softly, "aren't you a beauty."

"I really didn't rent it. It sort of rented me," Mike said sheepishly. "All the other cars were lined up like sardines in a can and were so dull and drab in pale blue or white or tan. This one just looked at me happily and said, 'Pick me! Pick me!' So I did. Now I'm embarrassed, especially after learning about all these poor people in the world."

Rachel looked at him over the roof of the car. "Don't you remember what Jesus said? 'The poor will be with you always?' God wants us to have pleasure and to enjoy life, Mike. He wants to bless us. And this…Wow, what a blessing this is! Hey, can we put the top down?"

Mike grinned like a fifteen-year-old. "Sure! Oh, man, I've been dying to put the top down on this baby since I picked her up. I have to admit that I've never been in a convertible before."

"Me neither," Rachel said, grinning back at him. Five minutes later, they were settled into soft leather seats with a V-8, 280-horse-power engine speeding them toward Butchart Gardens.

"Listen to this," Rachel hollered to Mike as he headed out of Victoria on Blanshard Street. The wind was blowing her reddish hair forward over her eyes, and she used one hand to hold it back. The other hand held a visitor's guide.

"Fifty-five acres of wonderful floral display are open to the public, offering spectacular views from the many paths that meander through the four main gardens. In 1904, Jennie Butchart began to beautify a worked-out quarry site left behind from her husband's pioneering efforts in the manufacture of cement. The family's commitment to horticulture and hospitality spans one hundred years and continues to delight visitors from all over the world. From the exquisite Sunken Garden to the charming Rose Garden, the gracious traditions of the past are still maintained in one of the loveliest corners in the world."

"And get this. 'Each year over 1,000,000 bedding plants in some 700 varieties are used throughout the gardens to ensure uninterrupted bloom from March through October. Close to a million people visit each year, enjoying not only the floral beauty but the entertainment and lighting displays presented each summer and Christmas.'"

"It sounds pretty amazing," Mike said loudly, glancing at her as he maneuvered onto Keating X Road. The city of Victoria was so beautiful with its buildings and flower beds and parks he couldn't imagine anything much more spectacular, especially with the fall colors.

"Have you ever been there before?" he asked Rachel. She hesitated just for a few seconds before answering.

"My first time was as a kid, about ten years old. My little sister and my parents and I took the ferry to Vancouver. I thought Butchart Gardens was the most magical, beautiful place I'd ever seen."

"Was there a second time?"

"Two more times, but maybe I'll tell you about that later," she said. "It's hard to talk through this wind."

"Isn't it great?" he yelled at her loudly. Rachel threw her hands into the air.

"It's wonderful!" she hollered back gleefully.

Suddenly, there was a flurry of red, and she yelped and frantically tried to tame her flying hair.

"My elastic band broke and flew off," she explained as she held the mop tightly with both hands.

"Good!" Mike said. "It's beautiful. It should fly free."

"It's sure going to be a mess by the time we get there, but you asked for it," Rachel said as she removed her hands, and her liberated hair whipped around her head.

When Mike Warren thought there couldn't be anything more beautiful than the city of Victoria, he was wrong. Butchart Gardens were so gorgeous that they summoned forth in him a strong nameless emotion. It wasn't happiness or awe but something else entirely. In some strange way, the beauty of the place made him want to weep.

Rachel reached over and put a hand over his as they looked down from the overlook to the Sunken Garden. "I know," she said. "I felt the same thing the first time I saw this. The raw emotion this place brings out is totally beyond words."

"And to think that this probably looks like the city dump compared to heaven," he said, shaking his head.

Turning so his back rested against the railing, Mike faced Rachel. Her hair, thanks to a folding hairbrush in her purse, now cascaded tamely down her shoulders. She was as beautiful as the gardens, he thought.

"Tell me about the other two times you were here," he asked her. "That is, if you want to, I mean."

She looked at him and smiled and then took a deep breath.

"Well, the first time was with my parents, and the second time was with my husband. We honeymooned here. Vince and me. His name was Vincent Adolfo Edmondo Pontelli, and he was, as you probably guessed, a true Italian. He was handsome with curly black hair and black eyes, and he, my mother always declared, could charm the rattles off of a rattlesnake.

"We stayed at the Fairmont Empress Hotel. You probably saw it—it's the one in Victoria along the water that looks like a huge gorgeous castle. We were so young and in love, and we came over on the ferry from Seattle. We parked our old Ford Fairlane in the parking lot and traipsed in there with our mismatched luggage. I had a plastic grocery bag with my hair dryer and pink rollers in it, and my grandmother insisted I use her old green-and-blue plaid train case. You know, one of those small square suitcase things that hold toiletries? A train case! They probably hadn't seen one of those in a decade or two.

"The concierge was so polite and kind, and I guess he noticed Vince's military haircut because he asked. Vince proudly said he was a private first class and we were on our honeymoon. He, his name was Albert George, was the hotel manager. He listened as a clerk told Vince the most reasonable room would be $159. Vince took out his wallet and carefully started counting out the money. Then the most wonderful thing happened. Albert George said, 'Oh wait a minute,' to the clerk and took over. He told us about a rich fellow who had reason to depart suddenly but had paid for his suite for another week. The rich man, according to Albert George, had declared that it was available to anyone in the military. She shook her head at the memory and started to walk down the path.

"So you got it for free? A suite?" Mike prompted as he settled in beside her and matched her stride.

"Yup. You would be amazed if you saw it. It is gorgeous. We had the whole thing to ourselves. Not only that, but according to Albert George, all of our meals were included. Plus a free tour of Butchart Gardens. It was three days of pure unadulterated bliss and pampering. Two days after that, I was back in Seattle, and he was gone. On his way to Iraq."

"I don't know what to say," Mike admitted as he stopped to face her. "I know you are a widow. If you don't want to talk about it, please don't feel you have to."

She turned and looked at him and shook her head and smiled. "You know, I've never told much of this to anyone, and I don't know why you are so easy for me to be with and to talk to. I will tell you the rest, Mike Warren, but it will be the quick version."

She reached down to pick up a bright-orange blossom on the path and twirled the stem between her fingers as she resumed walking. He stepped in beside her.

"When you are twenty-three, you don't know nearly as much as you do when you're in your thirties. Vince and I both knew there was a risk, but it was part of military life. Maybe if I had been more involved in the military spouse organizations, I would have known. To make a long story short, he was there nine months and died in a roadside explosion two weeks before he was due to come home."

She tucked the flower behind her ear and looked at him.

"I am so sorry," Mike said, gently taking her hand.

"It was a long time ago," she said with a shrug as she squeezed his hand and then let it go. "That chapter of my life was closed many years ago. You never really get over losing someone, but you eventually are able to think of them without it hurting. God has a plan for each of us, and while we don't always understand it, we need to have faith and trust that he knows what he is doing. We surely don't!"

"That's for sure," he said, and they continued walking in silence and letting the gardens envelope them.

After a time, he said, "I don't have much of a history when it comes to a love life, but maybe sometime, I'll tell you about all the women who are after me."

"Oh my, is that bragging I hear from the good pastor?" Rachel asked with a burst of laughter. "Are they chasing you down like the fox after the rabbit?"

"No, it's more like the friends of the fox are out to catch the poor rabbit."

"That sounds very intriguing. I'd love to hear more."

"If you'll go out to dinner with me tonight, I promise to tell you all about it," Mike said.

"Only if it's Dutch treat," Rachel said in acceptance, and then she added, "Come with me. I want to show you something in the rose garden."

The spring roses were gone, of course, and the summer roses. But the hearty autumn roses, before starting their winter slumber, were beautiful to behold, especially with the backdrop of trees and bushes that were clad in all shades of orange and red and fuchsia.

"I can't believe this place," Mike said as he turned in a slow circle and looked around. Somewhere close was the tinkle of tumbling water. He had noticed that everyone visiting the gardens did so in a hushed and quiet and respectful way, as if visiting a cathedral.

"Before we leave, we need to go into the Sunken Garden and then to the Garden Lake," Rachel said as she sat down on a bench. She sat on her hands and gave herself up to the sun, closing her eyes to bask in its warmth. Then she opened her eyes and looked at him.

"The third time I was here," she said with a scrunched-up face and a smile, "and I know you want to hear about the third time, Mr. Nosey…"

"Not nosey," Mike protested, throwing up a hand. "Just very interested in you and your life, pretty Ms. Rachel."

"Pretty, is it?"

"No, not pretty. Beautiful. And I must tell you that, that is the very first time I've called a female—except for my mother and a cat named Petunia when I was a kid—beautiful."

She turned to face him and tucked one leg under the other. "Really?" she asked.

"Mm-hmm. And now I am very embarrassed."

Rachel got up from the bench then and walked to a rose bush and squatted down. Moving the foliage and being careful not to touch a thorn, she fingered a slim brass band at the base. Mike knew by instinct not to disturb her and to be quiet.

After a few minutes, she came back to the bench, and her eyes were glistening with tears.

"I'm sorry, Rachel," Mike said.

"I'm fine," she said, reaching into her jacket pocket and fishing out a Kleenex. Then she took a deep breath.

"Well then...the third time...The third time I visited here was six months after Vince died. He is buried in Seattle, but I felt I needed to come here. I visited Albert George, of course, and I could see right through his rich-person story and see that he had been our benefactor. Turned out, he had just lost a grandson who was in the air force and was killed in a freak airplane crash. Albert arranged for me to buy a yellow rose bush and plant it here in this garden in Vince's name. It is that one, the bush I was looking at. The brass tag at the base has his name and birth date and date of death."

"What a beautiful thing to do for him," Mike said.

"Truthfully, it's been so many years I'm surprised the band is still there. And I'm surprised I walked right to it," she said.

"So, whatever happened to Albert George? Is he still here?" Mike asked.

Rachel shook her head. "Nope. He retired and moved to Arizona. I still get a Christmas card from him. He must be eighty-something by now. I'd love to see him someday, but it probably won't be this side of heaven."

"We should do that—go to Arizona and look him up," Mike said without thinking. Rachel looked at him.

"What?" she asked.

"That really did sound stupid, didn't it?" he asked, rolling his eyes. "We've known each other, what, three days? But I feel like I've known you forever, Rachel. Like you've always been there, just waiting, and I've always been over yonder, just waiting. I'm sorry. That really sounds scary, even to my ears. I apologize. I really am quite a level-headed and ordinary guy."

"The really crazy thing is that I know exactly what you mean," she said. "Somehow, being with you is as comfortable as being in my old orange bathrobe."

"I don't think that's a compliment. Is it really ugly? Your orange bathrobe?"

"You have no idea how ugly it is," she said, grimacing. "My sister made it for me years ago out of bath towels."

"I have an aunt like that," he said, nodding in knowledge, and suddenly, they were off on a campaign to compare flawed and quirky relatives.

Chapter 22

* * *

Anna had a beautiful voice, and she sang in a quartet in grade school. When we had our annual chorus presentations, she and her group usually sang something special. I was in chorus too, but I was more of a backup singer—one of those who droned the background music, making those with real talent shine. Because she liked to sing, we sang a lot on Rice's Hill. She had a clear, beautiful, angelic voice, while mine was a rough alto, so we sang in two-part harmony. Sometimes, we made up Indian songs and chants, and one summer, we practiced singing "America the Beautiful" until we had it perfect. We stood before her parents to present our song and giggled so much we couldn't sing.

* * *

In the back of the Peterman home, at the edge of the yard, Jim Peterman had strung, years before, an old-fashioned white canvas hammock between two pine trees. The front of the hammock faced the back of the house and Sharon Peterman's vegetable garden and gladiola bed. The entrance into the gladiolas, which Sharon lovingly cared for and nurtured, was guarded by four peony bushes, two on either side. Marcy always slipped sideways between them, careful to avoid accidentally picking up one of the hundreds of ants that happily thrived on the plants.

Sometimes, she visited with her mother while she worked in the gladiola garden, and her mother always laughed at her for jumping through the bushes. "They're just ants," she would say. Before she brought a bouquet of peonies into the house, she would put them upside down in a bucket of water for a few minutes to drive the insects out of the blooms.

She explained to Marcy one summer that there was an old wives' tale that the peonies needed the ants to help the buds bloom, but that wasn't the case at all. The ants were drawn to the sweet nectar secreted when the bushes were in the blooming stage. She advised Marcy to just enjoy the unique relationship between the ants and the peonies.

Behind the hammock at the edge of the lawn were acres of untouched Montana land that was owned by the farming family down the road. Most of the land was wooded with pine trees, but beyond that were open fields.

Over the years, there had been herds of cattle housed on the acreage for a short period of time before they were moved to the high pastures. One day, the woods would be quiet, and the next they would awaken to the mooing of cattle, and there they would be, scores of them huddled against the fence and watching the house as if they were at the zoo and the Petermans were the interesting creatures on display.

Marcy hadn't seen them of course, but her grandmother sometimes talked about the two big ancient plow horses—with hooves the size of dinner plates—that spent their final days of retirement on the land. The grand old horses were gentle and loving, and her grandmother fed them apples. When Sharon was a toddler, they worried that she would make her away across the fence and be accidentally mashed by a hoof.

The hammock was a favorite place for Marcy and her brother Ben. There was enough slack in the heavy ropes securing it to the trees that it made a good swing. They also frequently spent summer nights sleeping in the hammock and took great pains to carefully lay out blankets and pillows on it. Marcy slept at one end and Ben at the other, their legs overlapping in the middle. Special nights were the ones where there were night winds. In the quiet of night, the two would fall asleep to the trees creaking and the gentle sway of the hammock.

For Marcy, the hammock was a place to get away from the family and to be by herself. Once, she found a Spanish book on her mother's bookshelf, and she spent hours poring over it, convinced she could learn the language. Another time, her aunt loaned her a very old ten-button accordion that was just the right size for a girl Marcy's age. By summer's end, Marcy could play a dozen tunes.

Marcy sometimes wished she could build a little cabin in the woods next to the house and just live by herself. She and Ben had, over the years, built a multitude of tree forts and special hiding places under the big trees, but she yearned for a place that was private and all hers, something sturdier than a small space created by leaning old boards against the side of the garage and something stouter than a teepee created out of a pole barn.

Since Anna's death, Marcy spent a lot of time in the hammock. Sharon would see her there as she washed dishes at the kitchen sink. Her heart ached for her daughter, but she knew that it was a journey Marcy had to take by herself.

The afternoon the Millers walked down the street to talk to her, Marcy was up in her room. She heard their voices and joined everyone in front of the fireplace in the kitchen, which was Barbara Miller's favorite place in the house.

Marcy sat nearby in a dining room chair and listened to the conversation but, except for answering questions posed specifically to her, didn't talk much.

She was glad to see they were finally handling Anna's death so well. Almost too well, she thought with an inner frown that didn't reach her face. She knew she was needlessly hanging on to her grief and that she needed to let it go, but it was almost a comfort to clutch it tightly and cloak herself in it. She wondered if it was easier for Anna's parents because there were two of them.

Before they left, Barbara reached into her jacket pocket and pulled out a small packet. She handed it to Marcy.

"We were cleaning out the hall closet and found Anna's camera on the shelf," Joe said. "There was some film in it, so we took it in and had it developed. The photos are a couple of years old, but a lot of them are of you and Anna on Rice's Hill. We thought you'd want to have copies of the prints."

Barbara gave Marcy a quick hug. "I can't tell you what a thrill it was to find these, and we are so thankful that you took so many photos of Anna. We'll treasure them always."

Marcy felt her heart surge. She remembered instantly the day the photos were taken. Anna had just gotten the camera, and they took turns photographing each other and taking photos of Kemo and Sabe, the two horses. A few photos were taken with them standing close together and Anna holding the camera out as far as she could.

Marcy hugged the packet to her chest. "She thought she'd lost that camera. We looked everywhere. Can I look at them later?" She didn't want to look at the photos in front of everyone. She knew they'd all be scrutinizing her carefully, watching every emotion that passed across her face.

After they left, Marcy tugged on her tennis shoes and a pulled on a hooded sweatshirt. Then she went through the kitchen on her way to the hammock.

"Can you keep Ben in here for a while," she asked her mother, who was busy rolling out pie dough.

"Sure, sweetie," she said. Then she motioned with a floury hand to the envelope. "You haven't looked at them yet?"

Marcy shook her head. "I'm going to sit in the hammock and go through them. It's quieter out there."

"I understand. If I see Ben headed your way, I'll make him help me with the pies."

"Thanks, Mom."

"You're welcome, sweetie. And you know where I am if you want to talk."

Chapter 23

* * *

From the book about Indians at Anna's house, we learned about creating pine needle baskets. We wanted to make baskets to bring to Rice's Hill. We could keep them, we thought, in the Bone Tree. We gathered the pine needles and went to Anna's house, where we boiled them for a few minutes to soften them. Then we removed the heads and used brightly colored embroidery thread to tie the ends together. Before long, we had several feet of linked pine needles, with colorful knots of thread every six inches, where they were tied together. We coiled as we went, using more thread to fasten one row to the other. It probably wasn't, but we thought our basket was beautiful. We placed it in a big Ziploc bag and put it in the Bone Tree. It would be used for ceremonies.

* * *

Marcy sat for a long time in the hammock, her feet scuffing the ground and the envelope of photographs unopened in her lap. She wanted to look. She was scared to look. Maybe it would be better to just get up and go back into the kitchen and hand the photos to her mother. She'd tell her that it was too soon, that she'd look at them some other time, like maybe in fifty years.

Sounds were different now even though the weather was still mild. The laughter and happy yelling of neighborhood kids across the way didn't seem to be as carefree as it was during the summer months. Even though many of the brilliant gold and red leaves were still on the trees and the lawn was still green, there was a feeling of brittleness in the air. In the slight breeze, aspen leaves seemed to clatter, and dry weeds rustled. The signs were subtle, but they were there. "It's almost time," Mother Nature was saying.

It was getting to be dusk, and Marcy knew that she had to make a decision. Look or take them to her mother for safekeeping.

Marcy never knew when or where sudden feelings of resolve would force a decision. She could go back and forth on something, and suddenly there it would be—a decisive resolution would just jump out of nowhere and take over. This time, she knew it was coming before it actually did. Although she didn't remember doing so, her mind must have gone into a computer-like mode where it weighed the pros and cons of opening the envelope. To hurt or not to hurt. Then taking into consideration Marcy's mental state, it spit the results into her active mind, and there it was—a decision.

The first photo was one of herself, grinning stupidly and crossing her eyes. She remembered when Anna had snapped the photo. It was just after telling Marcy that she was beautiful enough to be a movie star. Marcy chuckled at the photo and the memory. If she ever became a movie star, one of those tabloid papers would pay big money for it.

Other photos were of Anna, but she didn't act silly. Instead, she posed carefully, leaning against a tree one time and another with her face cuddled close to Sabe, the colt. The best was one of her sitting on the ground, her legs crossed, with a piece of grass in her hands. Her head was tilted back, and she was laughing. The sun behind her caused strands of her black hair to gleam. She was surrounded by a halo of sun.

There were photos of Kemo and Sabe and one of Kemo alone that brought tears to Anna's eyes. How she missed the gentle and wonderful horse.

The twenty-four photos marked a point in history and captured forever a blink of time when she and Anna were on Rice's Hill. She pored over them carefully, searching the background for clues to that day before starting again at the first photo. What were they wearing? What had they brought, if anything, to the Bone Tree? She tried to remember, but couldn't.

Two years had made such a difference in the two of them, and she was surprised. They looked so young in the photos. So carefree. So happy.

Marcy slid the photos back into the envelope and went back to the house. Her mother was washing dishes. She looked at Marcy questioningly.

"Do you want to come and sit and look at them with me?" Marcy asked. Sharon pulled her hands from the dishwater and dried them on the towel hanging from the oven handle.

"I would love to look at them with you," she said to her daughter.

Chapter 24

Barbara Miller always thought Thursday nights were special. There was just one day to get through before the blessed relief of the weekend. She and Joe had just one more day with Midas. Mike was due to fly in the next night, and they would pick him up at the airport.

Barbara had gotten home from school promptly and decided to make bread from the black-spotted over-the-hill bunch of bananas on the counter. She had just turned off the mixer when Joe came through the kitchen door.

"What are you making?" he asked, slipping his finger through the batter and sticking his finger in his mouth.

"Get your dirty finger out of there," she scolded. He grinned around his finger then he took it out of his mouth and pulled her into a quick hug.

"You get away. I know your tricks, mister," she said, wriggling out of his arms. She wasn't quick enough to keep him from swiping another fingerful of batter behind her back.

"Mmm…Banana bread," he announced.

"Oh, aren't you just the clever one," she said. "Give the man an A plus."

"How come you're making that?"

"Because they don't make bananas like they used to," she said, bending over to grab four bread pans from deep inside a bottom cupboard. He leaned back and admired her trim rear end.

"Now, they rot before you get a chance to eat them," she continued, taking the stack of pans apart and setting them one by one on the counter and reaching for the pan spray. "You buy them at the store, and ten minutes later, you take them out of the bag, and they already have spots on them. They pick them green and then put them in that nitrogen bath or whatever it is to make them ripen, and I think the things just don't stop. The banana people have speeded up the rotting process. And what are you smiling about?"

"You. You're just so darn cute. Maybe you should start a movement and start carrying "Free the Bananas from Death" signs in front of Polsky's Market," Joe said with mock seriousness.

"You're making fun of me. Don't you have a paper to read or something? And take Midas with you. I've tripped over him at least a dozen times."

At the sound of his name, Midas lifted his massive head and looked from one to the other. He was sprawled out in the middle of the kitchen, dozing contentedly. He put his head back down with a groan and closed his eyes.

All in all, it had been good watching him. He was a loveable brute, and Barbara had fallen in love with him. But he did have his faults. He lost shoes and carried socks in his mouth and loved getting in the garbage. And the hair. Barbara had always wanted a fur coat, and now she had one, along with matching fur pants and fur shirts.

The night before, when she invited Midas into the bathroom while she was taking a bath, he had stood there for a minute watching her lounge in the bubbles, and then he had leaped in on top of her. Her screams made him scramble back out and brought Joe running. It took a half hour to mop up the water, and she had footprints and claw marks on her belly and legs. She couldn't fathom why on earth Midas thought he could just jump in and join her.

Joe had kept up the nightly meetings with Bob Markham, the dog trainer, and he was so impressed with how easy it was to train a dog he was actually considering getting himself a retriever, although he hadn't told his wife.

Before spending time with Bob Markham, Joe had looked on in amazement at dogs that were trained to sit and stay and heel. The day before, he and Barbara had watched as Bob's retriever was sent out into the backyard and, with one sharp blow on a whistle made to sit and then, with hand signals, was moved to the right or left or back to retrieve a round canvas item called a bumper. He and Barb were both surprised that all it took was a bit of work and consistency.

Joe chuckled after Barbara stepped over Midas the third time while getting the banana bread ready for the oven. Her growls were getting louder.

"C'mon, Midas," Joe said, fondling the dog's ears. "We know how to take a hint, don't we, fella? Guys know when they aren't wanted. When they're rejected."

Barbara smiled as the pair walked out of the kitchen. Midas had been a good house guest, and it was going to be hard to let him go. It had been fun having a dog.

An hour later, the smell of fresh baked banana bread filled the house. The loaves were cooling off on a rack on the counter, and Barbara had already washed and put away the bread pans. Now, she was fixing dinner—cube steak hamburgers with thick slices of tomato and cheese in potato buns and served with those great sweet potato French fries she had discovered recently in the freezer at Polsky's. She loved them sprinkled with sea salt.

She could hear Joe on the computer and thought about asking him to set the table but decided to do it herself. She knew he was probably working on his thesis. One of these years, he would complete his master's degree. It was good, she thought, that he was back working on it. It showed that he was starting to pull himself out of the past and choosing to live in the present and consider the future.

After pulling out plates and silverware and setting them on the counter, she decided to make a quick trip to the bathroom. She was rubbing an overabundance of sweet pea-scented hand lotion into her hands when she came back into the kitchen. She stopped in horror at the scene in front of her.

"Oh no! Midas! You miserable brute!" Her hands flew to the sides of her head, leaving streaks of pink cream.

At the sounds of her dismay, Joe hastily left the computer and headed to the kitchen. His eyes flew to Barbara, and at first he thought, because of the matted-down and lotioned hair, that she was undergoing another one of her unfortunate beauty mishaps. Then he looked at Midas and the rest of the scene.

One loaf of banana bread was left untouched on the rack on the counter, but the other three were on the floor, all in varying degrees of demolition. Midas had evidently gotten them to the floor and eaten around the edges of each loaf, rolling them as he went and leaving behind only two cylinders of bread and a lot of crumbs.

Barbara looked at her husband. "If you laugh, you'll be sleeping in the garage." Considering her hair was sticking out at odd angles and she looked slightly demented, it took every bit of willpower and a lot of lip-chewing to keep from laughing. He focused on the dog.

"Midas, you are a bad, bad dog. You come with me," Joe said severely and dragged Midas by the collar to the living room.

"You lay down, and don't you move a muscle, you bad dog," he added loudly, more for Barbara's benefit than the dog's. Throwing his arm around his mouth, he convulsed into silent laughter.

"Bad dog," he said loudly when he finally stopped laughing. Then he flopped Midas's ear back and forth a few times before pulling it gently through his hand. He grinned. "Do you know how many times I've wanted to eat a whole loaf of that stuff?" he whispered. Midas wagged his tail and bared his teeth in what could only be called a canine smile.

"Smile all you want, you're still in trouble," Joe said. "You stay there, you hear? I'm going back in there to help, and you'd better not come back in that kitchen."

Midas smiled again just as the phone rang.

"Can't answer that," Barbara hollered before muttering to herself. "I've got to clean up this mess and scrub the floor. Stupid darned dog."

As she swept up the remains of the feast, she could hear Joe chatting in the background. Then he came through to the kitchen.

"Here, I'll let you talk to her," he said as Barbara vigorously shook her head and mouthed "no." He held the phone out to her. She gave him a hateful look.

"It's Mike," Joe explained to her. "He's wondering how Midas is doing. I told him that he's just been the perfect houseguest and that we might not give him back. I told him that you and Midas seem to have a special bond."

"Give me that phone," she said, snatching it out of his hand. "Okay, Mike, let me tell you about your dog…What? Yeah, well. I'll bet you do miss him. You're right. He is a special dog. That's the truth. He is very special. No, he's fine. No problems at all. We're all getting along just great. Sure, we'll be there. Pick you up at seven."

After hanging up the phone, she looked at Joe and said, "Perfect houseguest, ha! Special bond, double ha!" Then she yelled, "Midas! Get your hairy rump in here."

A few seconds later, Midas loped through the doorway, a drifting of fur fluttering to the ground behind him. "You made this mess, you clean it up," she demanded tossing down the broom and kicking a leftover hunk of banana bread toward the dog. Midas wagged his tail and accepted the punishment with glee.

You couldn't help but love the dog, Barbara thought, watching him excitedly cleaning up the floor. And he was a smart fellow. He had learned to quit jumping and would sit instantly when told. Joe and Barbara had worked with him patiently and vigorously so that they could surprise Mike when he came home the next night. They had even taught him to shake hands, roll over, and a spastic, jerking version of playing dead.

"I think he likes that stuff," Joe said, motioning to Midas as the dog licked his lips and scouted along the floor for any crumbs he might have missed. Barbara snorted and crossed her arms.

Midas's nose led him to the counter where the one untouched loaf remained. By now, Barbara was able to read his body language. As he tensed his muscles to stand up to the counter, the big dog glanced at her. She shook her head.

"You touch that, and you're going straight to the pound," she said. Midas scooted out of the kitchen and into the living room. Barbara turned to her husband.

"Would you care for a slice of banana bread and some tea?" she asked sweetly.

"Sounds great!" he said. "By the way, is that a new hairdo? I like it. Some might think it looks slightly primitive, but I think it looks good on you."

Barbara's hands flew to her hair. "Yuck!" she said as she raced to the bathroom. "What is this stuff? Did that stupid dog do this? Is it dog spit or something?"

Joe just laughed, picking up the loaf of banana bread he tossed in the air a few times before putting it on the cutting board and reaching for a knife.

"I'll get the tea started," he hollered toward the bathroom.

Chapter 25

Barbara got up early the next morning and started water running in the bathtub. She had towels laid out and had found an old bottle of baby shampoo deep in the bathroom closet. She placed it on the counter by the sink. Beside it was a bottle of hair conditioner. Midas pranced around at her feet, getting in the way, before she ordered him to lie down and stay there.

The door opened a crack, and Joe peered in. "What are you doing? It's only eight thirty in the morning, and it's Saturday. Remember Saturday? The sleep-in day?"

"I'm giving this dog a bath," she said, motioning to Midas, who was sprawled out happily on a pile of towels. "He stinks. Besides, Mike is getting back tonight, and I don't want him to think we're bad babysitters."

"How are you going to get him in there?" he asked curiously, motioning to the tub.

"I thought about that. Remember that this is the guy who jumped in on me in this very same bathtub. He likes this tub. I figured I'd just use the k-e-n-n-e-l command when I'm ready. It works when we want him to scoot into his airline k-e-n-n-e-l or when we want him to jump in the backseat of the car.

"You have to spell it?"

"I don't want him jumping in before I'm ready," she said, shaking her head at her husband's ignorance. "He is a very smart dog, Joe."

"Mm-hmm. Well, you two have a jolly good time," he said as he shut the door. Then from down the hall, she heard him holler. "If you need help, call me!"

The water was about a foot deep. Plenty deep enough for her to dip panfuls of it over the dog's head. The water wasn't cold, and it wasn't hot. It was, as Goldilocks would have declared, just right.

"You stay there. Don't you move, buster," Barbara told Midas as she straightened up from the tub and pulled off her clothes and piled them in a corner. They she stepped into her swim suit and pulled the straps over her shoulders. She had a feeling that this was going to be a very soppy ordeal.

Standing by the tub, she squared her shoulders. "Midas, *here*," she said firmly, slapping her hand on her thigh. Midas got up and walked the three steps to her side.

"Kennel!" she said, motioning the tub. He looked at her.

"Kennel, Midas. Kennel!" she said again, dipping her hands in the water and splashing it around a bit. He put his shaggy head into the tub and took a few drinks before raising his head and looking at her. Water dripped from his jowls, and he used his massive tongue to wipe it away. He sat down.

"No, don't sit. *Here*," she said, and he stood up again. Barbara stepped in the tub and said, "Here, Midas. *Here! Kennel!*" The dog wagged his tail and smiled.

"You need some help in there?" Joe hollered from outside the bathroom.

"We're fine," she yelled back. "Don't come in here. He'll lose his focus."

Stepping out of the tub, Barbara thought about her options. "You stay there," she said to Midas, who was standing up and facing the tub.

Straddling his body, she picked up his front quarters and placed them in the tub. Then hunkering down behind him, she used all her strength to shove his rump toward the water. One leg went in and then the other. Standing knee deep in the water, he looked at her sadly. She thought maybe he rolled his eyes.

Barbara stood up and rubbed her arm across her forehead. She was sweating, and she hadn't even started. "Okay then. Good boy. You stay there. Don't get out," she said as she turned her back to him to grab the shampoo and conditioner near the sink.

It was too late to reprimand herself for not putting them next to the tub. At the word *out*, Midas leaped from the tub and ran to the door. He shook one foot at a time and then his whole body, splattering water around the bathroom.

"Get back in there! You stupid dog, get back in that tub!" Barbara dashed between Midas and the door and shoved him toward the bathtub.

"Now get in there!" she ordered, heaving him back into the water.

"There's water coming out from under the door," Joe yelled from the hallway.

"Oh, shut up," Barbara muttered to herself before hollering back. "So clean it up! I'm just a little bit busy here."

Five minutes later, Midas was lathered from tail to toe despite the fact that he kept trying to sit down in the water and she had to use one hand under his belly to keep him standing up.

She didn't realize Midas was planning his escape until she reached for the pan to rinse off the soap. She moved her hand for just a split second, really only a nanosecond, and before she knew what was happening, he had bounded from the tub. He stood in the middle of the room, shaking violently and spraying the entire room with soap and water. The clothes she had so carefully placed in a safe corner when she put on her swimsuit were drenched.

She started to laugh and grabbed a towel to hold in front of her until he stopped shaking.

"For some reason, this isn't much fun, is it, boy?" she said to Midas as she maneuvered him back into the bathtub.

Two latherings, a blob of conditioner, and a thorough rinsing later, they were done. The tub was drained, and she was just about to let Midas out of his forced trauma when the door opened just a peep.

"We have company," Joe said as he stuck his head in. His eyes widened in shock as he surveyed the disastrous bathroom. A half inch of water covered the floor, and the shower curtain was ripped from the rod. A roll of soggy toilet paper trailed through the river next to the toilet, and a basket of silk flowers, once on the counter, floundered on their side on the floor, soaking up soap. Barbara, in her red bathing suit, looked like she'd been through a tornado, her hair hanging and dripping and mascara running down to her chin.

"Company?" she said weakly. Looking behind Joe, she could see Mike Warren. Using one finger, her pastor pushed opened the door, looked stunned for a few seconds, and then howled in laughter. Midas leaped from the tub and almost knocked him over; he was so glad to see his master.

"I got here early. Caught an earlier flight out of Seattle," Mike explained as he hugged his dog. He knew he was getting soaked, but he didn't care. If anyone had asked him, he would have admitted he really missed the brute.

After getting dried off and fixing her face and pulling on jeans and a sweatshirt, Barbara joined Joe and Mike in the living room. Midas, still damp and looking bedraggled from his ordeal, kept his distance from her.

Walking into the kitchen, she fished a giant dog bone out of a bag and returned to the living room. "Forgiveness food," she explained to Mike and Joe.

She sat in a chair and fingered the bone and ignored Midas even though she knew he was watching every move. Finally, he made his decision and loped to her side.

"Oh, does this mean I'm forgiven for being so mean to the nice puppy?" she crooned as she gave him the bone. He wagged his tail and offered up his paw for a shake.

"What's he doing there?" Mike asked.

"Shaking hands," Joe said. "Want to see what else he can do? We have had such fun with this dog." The next few minutes, Mike watched in awe as Midas flawlessly went through his repertoire of tricks. At the end, they all agreed that he was a brilliant canine.

"I wish Anna could have seen that bathroom scene," Joe said, laughing at the memory.

"She'd have been right in there with me," Barbara declared. "Heck, she would have been in the tub with that creature." They all laughed, and Mike noted that God was showing them how to bring Anna into their lives without it hurting so badly.

After some more bantering, Mike told them about Hope Ministries and the meetings and how troubled he was over the plight of Christians in third-world countries. They discussed ways the church could help, including being more active in missions.

Then Barbara looked at him and asked, "What else happened there?"

Mike tried to evade her query and countered it with a statement. "That's about it."

"Oh, really?" she asked. "You've talked nonstop about the meetings, but you haven't talked about the people. Tell us about the people. I have very good female intuition, and I have a feeling you are holding back on us here."

He thought about not enlightening them, but then he shook his head and sighed. "Okay," he admitted. "I met someone. Her name is Rachel Pontelli, and she's thirty-four years old and a widow. No children. Her husband was killed years ago in Iraq. She works with Hope Ministries."

"And…" Barbara said, motioning with her hands that she wanted more information.

"And we hit it off," he said. "She's beautiful and wonderful, and I feel like a teenager. There! That make you feel better, Ms. Snoopy Pants?"

She laughed. "You can run, but you can't hide," she said, reminding him that she could always see right through him. He really was a very transparent man.

"Can I walk a bit?" he said, standing up and pacing back and forth in front of them. Finally, he faced them. "I'm going to be brutally honest here, and I hope you don't laugh at me because I need some advice. Do you think love at first sight is possible?"

"Funny you should ask," Joe said and related their story, about how he and Barbara met and just knew, simply knew. They asked him if Rachel felt the same and were assured that she did.

Long into the night, they discussed strategy. He was, after all, the pastor of a large church and had to answer to a whole congregation of people. It was time to be discreet, but not so discreet that once people found out, they felt betrayed or that he had kept secrets. The best thing to do, they decided, was to bring Rachel to Danford. She could stay with them in their home. They would love to meet her.

Chapter 26

Indian summers are deceiving pranks of nature, tricking people into believing that winter won't come this year, that for once, Mother Nature will forget to throw down her winter cloak and the balmy warm days and the gloriously shrouded trees will continue right on into spring.

Indian summer departed Danford eventually though, leaving residents a bit surprised and unprepared. Now they were seen outside coiling hoses, cutting back rose bushes, and taking down hanging baskets filled with flowers killed overnight by Jack Frost himself.

Lawns would be okay for a while yet, and marigolds always stood their ground until almost the first flutter of snow, but the birches and elms had shed most of their leaves, and flocks of geese and ducks were sending raucous messages of escape across the early November skies.

Joe and Barbara Miller looked up at a flock of departing geese as they walked down the block to visit with Sharon and Jim Peterman and tell them about the Saturday balloon launch.

Barbara huddled deeper into her fleecy hooded jacket.

"Why is it that I always feel like they're smarter than the rest of us," she asked, motioning to the elegant Canada geese winging through the dusk. They were low enough that she could hear their wings sifting through the air. Their honks were plaintive and yet encouraging and tinged with the excitement of resuming their life in another place.

"It must really be nice to have a summer home and a winter home," she continued. "We should do that, become snow birds."

"Sounds great to me," Joe agreed. "But not Arizona. I'd want someplace on a beach. Like Hawaii."

"I love Hawaii. Okay, we're both agreed. Let's add it to the list," Barbara declared.

She and Joe had maintained "the list" since they were first dating. It outlined, in no particular order, things they wanted to do or see or own or conquer. Over the years, many of the items, such as "see the Louvre," "graduate from college," and "visit the Grand Canyon," had been neatly crossed through.

As they walked past the Franklins' house, the ancient poodle Lavender barked at them from her post at the front window, and old Mrs. Franklin appeared and looked through the glass.

"Hello, Mrs. Franklin," Joe hollered at her as she cupped her hands around her plump face and peered at them. Seeing who it was, she quickly made her way to the front door and opened it. Lavender, despite her age, bounded down the steps and pranced around on the sidewalk, happily greeting her neighbors.

"Is that you, Joe Miller?" Mrs. Franklin asked through the early evening gloom. "And Barbara?"

"It's us," he said. "We're just heading down to the Petermans' for a bit."

"Well, they're home," she declared, pulling her tan sweater tight around her thin and bent body and peering down the sidewalk to the Petermans' home to confirm her statement. "Sharon got home a couple of hours ago with the kids, and Jim pulled in around six. They should be done with dinner by now. I have to say, it's nice to see you two out and about."

"Thank you," Barbara said. "It's good to be out and about. It's a beautiful night."

"Yes, it is. Yes, it is," the old lady said, turning to go in and snapping her fingers for Lavender. "Well, God bless you both. I'm still praying for you, you know."

"I know you are, and I can't tell you how much it is appreciated, how much everything you have done for us is appreciated," Barbara said, referring to Mrs. Franklin watering their lawn and flowers for so many weeks.

Kneeling down, Barbara fluffed the old dog and said, "Scoot on home, Lavender." Then she straightened.

"Good night, Mrs. Franklin," she and Joe said in unison.

They walked a few steps before Joe said in a low voice, "How does she do that?"

"Do what?"

"She lives a block and a half from the Petermans' house. How does she know when they get home and when they eat?"

"That's her job," Barbara said, laughing. "We live right next door to her. I'll bet we'd be shocked at what the old gal knows about us!"

They were still chuckling when they climbed the stairs and crossed the massive veranda of the Petermans' home. Barbara was always astounded when she entered this huge edifice. What a magnificent and beautiful old house it was.

* * *

Sharon Peterman had good days and bad days with Marcy. The same with Jim. Some days, he was better with Marcy, and some days, Sharon could more easily get her to open up and talk.

Today had been a bad day for all of them. Settling into middle school would have been enough on its own but dealing with Anna's death and going through puberty added an extra stress to Marcy's life. Frankly, the counselor at school wasn't much help since she had so many students to deal with.

Marcy met frequently with Pastor Mike and that seemed to help more than anything. But still it wasn't enough. Sharon hoped that this visit by the Millers would help. When Barbara had called and told her about their meetings with The Compassionate Friends group, it had seemed like an answer to prayer.

Sharon was just taking a trayful of mini pizzas out of the oven when the doorbell chimed.

"Jim, can you answer the door?" she hollered from the kitchen. "I'm in the middle of something." She waited a second until she heard his footsteps on the burnished oak floor before using a spatula to put the pizzas alongside other hors de oeuvres on a serving tray. Sometimes, she wondered about herself, why did she find it necessary to go to such lengths to entertain?

Joe and Barbara were coming over for a visit and would have been happy with a few Oreos and a pot of coffee. She always had to go the extra mile and a half.

Where other women were happy making a meatloaf and boiled potatoes for guests, she had to have a five-course dinner plus two choices for dessert. It brought her rave reviews, but sometimes, she wished she could just throw on a few hot dogs and heat up a can of beans and call it good.

The happy chatter of voices reached her ears, and she took off her apron and threw it over a kitchen chair just as Barbara came through the kitchen doorway, followed by Jim and Joe.

The kitchen was old-fashioned and big enough to be a small apartment. While there was a formal dining room in the house, the big table in the kitchen held eight, and except for holidays, it was where the family took meals. In addition, there were four comfortable chairs situated around a big brick fireplace, a pair on each side facing each other.

After giving Sharon a quick kiss on the cheek, Barbara scurried to the open fireplace and put her hands out as an offering to the fire gods.

"I knew that's where she'd head," Joe said about his wife as he gave Sharon a hug. "She does love that fireplace, especially on a chilly night like tonight."

"I don't think this could be classified as a fireplace," Barbara said, turning around to warm her backside while still holding her hands behind her to capture the heat. "You could roast a cow in this thing."

"We don't use it much," Jim said. "Just when it's really cold or when our wimpy neighbors come to visit."

Everyone laughed.

"So," Sharon said, "do we want to sit in here or go to the living room?"

"You all can go to the living room if you want," Barbara said, "but I'm sitting right here." And with that, she plopped down in a comfortable chair and scooted it closer to the fireplace. Then she slid off her shoes and held her feet toward the fire.

"I guess this is it then," Jim said, selecting a chair opposite her.

"Yup," Joe said, sitting in the chair next to Barbara.

Sharon laughed. "I thought that would be the choice," she said. "So what can I get you to drink. Soda? Coffee? Hot chocolate?"

Jim got up and got everyone's drinks, while Sharon finished putting things on a nearby countertop. Reaching into a cupboard, she pulled down a stack of mismatched salad plates, and then she opened a drawer and pulled out a handful of forks. Without looking, Barbara knew none of them probably matched.

The first time Barbara saw Sharon's penchant for putting together mismatched items and pulling it off with brilliant success was when they first met. Sharon was reupholstering the dining room chairs and couldn't come to a decision on the fabric. The result was eight chairs with eight different elegant fabrics. It looked stunning in the formal dining room.

When hosting dinner parties, Sharon used beautiful china and silverware, but each setting was individual and unique. It looked a bit like a display in a fancy china store that showed choices for purchase. Again, the result was remarkably effective.

She was the same way with entertaining, coming up with menus that were original and sometimes quirky. It was always exciting to go to a Peterman party just to see what wonderful ideas Sharon had come up with.

"I hate to take you out of your comfort zone, but I have a bunch of hors de oeuvres over here if you'd like to fix a plate," Sharon said to her guests. Joe jumped up. Barbara groaned.

"Oh, sweetie pie husband, I hate to leave my comfortable spot by the fire, but gee, it looks so good," she said imploringly, laying her head back on the chair and gazing at the laden counter and then giving an adoring look at her spouse.

"You just sit there like a spoiled princess, and I'll fix you a plate," Joe said.

"Oh, you *are* a dear boy," she said in a mock southern drawl. Leaning forward, she said under her breath to Sharon, "I knew he would."

"I heard that," Joe said, laughing. "In retaliation, I'm going to tell our friends that you fed me a Vienna sausage sandwich for dinner."

"Oh, pooh," Barbara said. "You love those awful sandwiches."

"So does he," Sharon said, pointing to Jim. "And Spam."

"Good grief, they're twins," Barbara said. "Tasteless twins."

They chatted while they ate, touching on community news, on the status of Jim's Ford dealership, and on the weather. When Sharon felt they were getting close to the subject they were all gathered to discuss, she turned to Jim.

"You want to go get the kids?" she asked him.

"On my way," he said, sliding back his chair and leaving the kitchen.

Passing through living room, he headed up the curving mahogany staircase to the bedrooms. He knew that Marcy and Ben were in the game room and had been embroiled in bitter competition with some sort of video game. Marcy, he knew, would rather be in her room reading or just being alone, but she always seemed to find time to be with her little brother. Over the loud music, he could hear Ben's banter and laughter, and the sound was delightful to him. How heartwarming it was to hear the laughter of his son. He missed Marcy's laughter.

Walking through the door, he could see they had abandoned the car racing game and were now in the middle of the Wii Dance Revolution. He leaned against the door frame and watched. Ben, although awkward and gawky, made his way through the moves before being jeered off the mat. Then it was Marcy's turn. Her moves were flawless and fluid and graceful. The canned background cheered and encouraged as she danced perfectly to the end of the song.

Turning in a smooth circle, she left the mat and went back to her chair. There was no thrill of doing something perfectly, just a sort of relief that it was over.

"I am very impressed, Marcy. You're really good at that," Jim said to her before Ben could say anything. His two offspring turned to him in surprise.

"I didn't know you were there. You watched?" Marcy asked quietly. She was obviously embarrassed.

150

He walked into the room. "I watched both of you. It's obvious where you two got your genes from. Ben, you dance just like your mother. But you," he said turning to Marcy, "you dance like your father. I was quite a dancer in my time."

"You danced?" Despite her resolve not to enjoy the conversation, Marcy couldn't help herself. She had to admit she was shocked. She couldn't imagine her father dancing, except for the slow waltzes she sometimes saw him do with her mother late at night in the living room when she was supposed to be in bed.

"The twist, jitterbug, beatle boogie, hully gully, mashed potato, swing…you name it and I could dance it."

Marcy was puzzled. He wasn't old enough for the twist. "The twist is from the 1960s," she told him. Except for the swing, it was the only other dance she had ever heard of.

"They're all from the sixties," he said. "By the time my generation came along, all the good dances had been taken by the sixties flower children. The dances I learned were American Bandstand stuff my mother taught me. She was actually on American Bandstand once. She met Dick Clark in person, and he told her she did one of the best shimmies he'd ever seen."

"Grandma? Our grandma?" Marcy asked. "The woman who has sleep apnea and varicose veins and has a whole row of prescription bottles on the windowsill?" She was astonished at this revelation.

"Yup, that grandma," Jim said, shaking his head. "Hard to believe, isn't it? I'll have to show you some photos. It'll be a shock."

"Who is Dick Clark, and what is American Bandstand," Ben asked.

It was Jim's turn to be astonished. "You don't know who Dick Clark is? Or American Bandstand? Unbelievable! I can tell we need to have some father-son and father-daughter talks here. But for now, I need you both to come downstairs. We have company."

"Who?" asked Ben before Marcy could ask herself.

"The Millers," Jim told him, and Ben took off running down the hall. Marcy turned to her dad.

"I'm glad they're visiting. That's good," she said quietly, and he nodded.

"Have you ever heard of the dirty dog or the watusi or the continental?" he asked her as they left the game room.

"Are those dances?" she asked.

"Yeah. You want to learn them?"

"I don't know. Maybe someday," Marcy said. She really didn't want to dance or do anything else right now. She just wanted to be left alone.

"I'll bet we can find the dance moves on the Internet," he said thoughtfully. "We should practice up so we can really wow your mom and Ben. That would be fun."

He didn't want to push her into doing something she wasn't ready for, but he couldn't resist grabbing her by the hand and swinging her around.

"So, can I call you 'partner?'" he teased when he let her go.

She just looked at him and shrugged her shoulders.

He was heartened. She hadn't said no.

Chapter 27

After explaining about The Compassionate Friends and why the group was created, the Petermans had a dozen questions. Surprisingly, Ben had the most questions and asked them one after another.

Mostly what he wanted to know was about the other people who attended the meetings and how their loved ones had died. He was obviously fascinated by the subject of death.

Jim and Sharon were upset and thought Ben was being disrespectful to the Millers, but after trying to discreetly rein him in, the Millers assured Jim and Sharon that it was okay. They wanted to answer his questions. They thought it was healthy.

"I think it's good to talk about it," Barbara said. "Heaven knows no one in my family ever talked about death. It was as off the table as the subject of sex."

"Yuck," Ben said. "If you start talking about that stuff, I'm outta here."

Marcy was red to her toes in embarrassment that the word *sex* was brought up, and she prayed they would go back to death, which was more palatable to her.

"So anyway," Joe said, laughing at Marcy's red face, "this Saturday we're having a balloon launch, and we want to know if you all would like to come."

"What's a balloon launch?" Ben asked, his interest now clearly piqued. Something to do with balloons sounded right up his alley.

"Well, basically, we all meet at the park, and we send up balloons in honor of our family members who have died. But not only the balloons. Before we get there, we write letters or notes or poems to them. We each will get a balloon, and once our balloon is filled with helium, we attach our note. Then when all the balloons are ready, we all let them go at the same time," Barbara explained.

"But before we get to that part, someone will say a short prayer, and people will be allowed to talk if they would like," Joe added.

"Wow! That sounds really cool. How many balloons will there be, about a thousand?" Ben asked. He had gotten up from where he sat cross-legged on the floor by now and was standing up and almost jumping in excitement.

"I doubt if there will be a thousand," his dad said, "but maybe fifty or a hundred."

"Maybe a hundred," Barbara confirmed. "I guess a lot of people come out for the launches—not just members of The Compassionate Friends group, but others who have lost a loved one."

"I think the most important part," said Sharon thoughtfully as she looked at Marcy, "is writing the note or poem. It's a sort of a farewell message to someone that you miss so much your heart feels like it is breaking. It's telling them that you miss them horribly but also that you are okay and that you are strong."

Marcy turned her head away and looked into the fire. Sharon took her hand in her own and squeezed it gently. "I think this is good," she said to Marcy. "It will be good to do this, to let these balloons from all of us go up toward heaven. We all know it's just a symbol and a memorial, but it will be good anyway."

Marcy didn't say anything but nodded her head.

"I'm going to see if I can get a red balloon," Ben said. "And right now, I'm going to go up and start my letter to Anna. I've got a whole bunch to tell her. I think I'll use stickers too. Spider stickers. 'Member how scared she was of spiders? She sure didn't like spiders."

Jim reached over and smacked his son on the back end as he ran from the room. He shook his head. "I have a feeling he's not only going to write a letter, but he'll also pack an envelope with a toy car or two and maybe a stuffed animal. I predict he'll never get his balloon off the ground."

"He might need three or four balloons," Sharon said with a chuckle, and then she turned to Barbara. "You said there would be a picnic afterwards. Can I bring anything?"

Joe looked at Barbara, and they both laughed.

"Cookies!" they said in unison. Then Barbara explained. "Do you remember the Lincolns? They were the couple from here in Danford who lost their two kids in a weird car wreck two winters ago. We were all praying for them at church."

Sharon and Jim looked at each other and nodded. "We do remember that," Jim said.

"Through Compassionate Friends, the Lincolns have become mentors and friends to us," Joe said. "They sort of hold the group together, and their mission is to help others deal with the death of a child. Anyway, Rod Lincoln has a cookie fetish."

"It's a joke in the group—his thing for cookies. It doesn't matter the kind or the flavor, the man just loves cookies," Barbara said. "And you, Sharon, are the queen of cookie making. If you could make a couple dozen cookies, it would be more than wonderful."

"She's probably got at least twelve dozen in the freezer right now," Jim told them while looking at his wife with fondness. He knew from the expression on her face that she had already accepted the assignment and the cookbook area of her memory bank was on the fast track to perfect cookie recipes.

"Are you sure a couple dozen are enough? How about six different kinds?" she asked Barbara and Joe.

"Don't you just love this woman?" Barbara said to no one in particular.

Chapter 28

Sometimes when she looked back at the time she spent with Mike Warren at Butchart Gardens and in Victoria, Rachel Pontelli was shocked at the things she told him. She had always been reserved and quiet and discreet—except for Vince, and then only after they had known each other for many months; she had never been this open and at ease with anyone.

She wondered which persona was really hers—the one who hid inside a beautifully crafted shell or the one who was open and sincere and fun. It was a bit fearful to admit, but she truly hoped it was the latter. The upkeep on the shell was darned hard.

The day after their visit to the gardens, Mike left to go back home to Montana. She was slated to stay another day before her group with the Hope Foundation left to go back to Seattle.

Early the morning of Mike's departure, before he left for the airport, she had met him in the hotel restaurant. Maybe it was the early hour or the fact that they both slept fitfully that put things off kilter.

The weather didn't help. Sometime during the night, clouds had settled over Victoria and it had started to rain. Not a heavy thunder of rain, but a plopping gentle rain. Gloomy rain.

The restaurant was painted in bright colors and bedecked with a mass of fake plants and flowers and light-faded prints of nondescript, pointless art. The room was tight, with a parade of waitresses brushing against the booth on their way to the coffee pot, and the overhead fluorescent lights were garish for that hour of the morning. To top it off was the jarring noise from the tile floor, clanking cups and glasses, and silverware.

After a few false starts at conversation, Mike and Rachel carefully studied the menu as they sipped coffee.

Before they needed a refill, a foursome of hung-over Texas dentists, in town for an orthodontics convention, shoved into the booth next to them. After the third ribald joke about dental assistants, Mike was ready to leave, or ask to be moved. Rachel pretended they weren't there and kept her eyes on the menu. She knew enough about men to know she should keep her head down and not invite comments. Her reddish hair tended to invite comments.

Nothing on the menu sounded good to either Mike or Rachel, but by the time the waitress returned, they had made a tentative choice.

The waitress was too cheerful, and her face was made up as if she were headed for a night out on the town. Her blond hair hung in hundreds of frizzy curls, some fat and dangling and others tight as corkscrews. Turquoise eye shadow covered her eyelids, and a bright smear of red lipstick clung in aging desperation to her lips. She wasn't old, and she wasn't young. She was just simply there, with a ring on every finger and big fake pearls at her ears and throat. They knew by looking at her that she favored line dancing to the tango, men in tight jeans rather than a Brooks Brothers suit, country to classical, and a pickup truck to a sedan. She would be right at home with the rowdy dentists.

"You decided?" she asked neither one of them in particular. She snapped her gum once. Twice.

Mike looked at Rachel, indicating that despite the conditions, he would remain a gentleman. She smiled. The waitress had, without even knowing it, bound them together in camaraderie. Do or die, they were in this breakfast thing together.

"I'll have two scrambled eggs, two slices of bacon, a poppy seed muffin, and the fruit dish," Rachel said, closing her menu decisively.

"I'll have the same," Mike said, admiring the fact that Rachel enjoyed food and wasn't one of those pencil-thin women who lived on grape leaves and celery hearts.

"You got it," said the waitress. As she turned to leave, Mike slid out of the booth to follow her.

"I'll be back in a flash," he said to Rachel, who looked at him with curiosity.

After a hurried conversation with the waitress, during which he discreetly handed her some bills, he came back to the table and picked up the white plastic urn of coffee and his mug. He tucked some napkins under his arm.

"Grab your purse and coffee and follow me," he whispered to Rachel, who cocked her head and looked at him quizzically.

"Ahh, you aren't leavin' us, are you, pretty lady?" one of the dentists drawled as she stepped out.

Rachel ignored him and followed Mike as he left the hotel restaurant and walked down a hallway toward the gym and pool. A short way past the pool was a small tiled alcove with a table and four chairs. Tall floor-to-ceiling windows overlooked the hotel's inner courtyard. A fountain was the centerpiece and was surrounded by a small tidy lawn, flower beds, and autumn-decorated trees. A mist obscured the background as, closer, leaves and branches dripped with silver droplets of rain. It was a beautifully peaceful scene.

The alcove was quiet and serene and intimate, and canned hotel music played softly. Mike pulled out a chair for her, and Rachel sat down and put her purse in her lap.

She looked at him questioningly. He shrugged.

"I didn't want our last hours together to be in that loud, obnoxious restaurant and listening to dental jokes," he explained. "Sue—she's our wonderful waitress—will bring our breakfasts to us."

Rachel laughed, and the sound tinkled in charmed delight. "Mr. Warren, you are too much," she said.

Since that morning, they had talked at least once during the day and spent hours on the phone at night. She sometimes wondered if there was enough time left for her to say to him all the things she wanted to say. He felt the same.

One day, she had been particularly busy in the office, mostly because she was compiling reports of their Victoria meeting. She had come home to her apartment on Queen Anne Avenue, taken a long bath, and now she sat by the phone and waited for his call. Despite the fact that he assured her frequently that it was all right for her to call him, she was still old fashioned enough to insist that he do the calling.

The phone rang, and she picked it up before it could ring again. Her heart fluttered.

"I have a dog," he told her without preamble, before she could even say hello.

"Oh?" she said. She smiled. She had decided earlier that day that she had smiled and laughed more in the weeks since meeting him than she had in an entire lifetime before. Sometimes, he got her laughing so hard she had to hold her cheeks together with her fingers to ease their aching.

"I don't know what kind he is, some sort of a concoction that combined fluffy and furry with wrinkled and large. He's yellow like a golden retriever, so I named him Midas. I have to tell you that he's a monster. Well, he *was* a monster, but he's getting better since we're doing some training. He can play dead, but it isn't for long enough to give a person much of a break."

"I guess this is true confessions, is it?" she asked. "Is he mean or something, this dog of yours? Does he bite your church members or chase them over onto the Catholic grounds?"

"Of course he doesn't bite or chase. He's just a big oaf who likes getting in the garbage and swiping food off my plate when I'm not looking. I wanted you to know about him, warn you that unlike me, he has no manners. He's trained, but he has no manners. He can sit, but while he's doing it, he can pass a horrible cloud of gas. He can stay, but after a time, he creeps on his belly to the trash can."

"Hmmm. Well," Rachel said, settling back and tucking her feet under her bathrobe, "anything else you want to tell me about this beast?"

Mike sighed. "He howls at fire sirens, chases old Ms. Phoebe's cat, digs up the flower beds, and belches like a drunken sailor. Plus, he sheds. Continually. Piles and piles of hair. It drifts in the corners."

"What are his good points? Surely there are some good points."

Mike laughed. "Rachel, my girl, those *are* his good points!"

She hooted with laughter that ended with a loud snort. After a bit, she was able to respond.

"Well, hmmm. That is all very interesting. I think I could grow to love your dog. And now that we're confessing about our pets, I have to tell you, Mike, that I have a fish. She's a goldfish, and her name is Joyce," Rachel said.

There was silence on the other end, so she continued, "Unlike your dog, Midas, Joyce has very good manners, and she is a wonderful swimmer. Every morning and evening, I feed her, but before I sprinkle in the food, I say, 'Bon appetit, Joyce,' and she makes a mad dash toward the top of a tank. She's a wonderful little friend."

"You have a goldfish…named…" Mike's voice was so choked with suppressed mirth he couldn't continue.

"Joyce," Rachel said seriously. "Her name is Joyce. Are you laughing? Do I hear you laughing?"

"A wonderful friend? A *goldfish*? You've got to be kidding!" Mike burst into unleashed merriment. Rachel couldn't maintain the charade any longer and howled with him.

"Actually, I *am* kidding," she admitted through gales of glee. "A fish named Joyce. Good grief! You'd believe that?"

"It's kind of scary that you can lie that well," Mike said, and they both started in again.

"Truthfully, the only pet I have is a little garter snake," she said with a chuckle when they had settled down. Mike instantly became sober and attentive, and she could almost envision him jerking to a straight-up position in alarm.

"You're kidding. Rachel, please tell me you are making that up," he said. "I really do not like snakes."

"Aha, I think I've discovered a chink in your armor," she said merrily. "So snakes are your downfall, are they? Well, you can rest easy because I won't knowingly come within four miles of a snake. I can barely look at a photo of one. I guess that's another thing we have in common."

"You had me scared there for a minute. I thought I might have to call the whole thing off."

"The 'whole thing?' What 'whole thing?'" she teased.

"You know. The 'us' thing."

"Oh, that thing. The 'us' thing." Her voice was breathless and quiet. In just a few words, the mood had shifted from easy joking to high alert.

"Rachel, can you come here to Danford this weekend? It's only about an hour and a half flight, and I've already made arrangements for you to stay with friends. The Millers. Joe and Barbara. They're the ones…"

"I know," she broke in distractedly, her voice not totally focused as her mind whirled over his request. "They're the parents of Anna… the little girl who drowned. Why this weekend, Mike? Is there something special happening?"

"Have you ever heard of a balloon launch? Where you let loose a balloon in memory of a loved one?"

"I've never been to one, but I've heard of it," she said. "You can tie messages into the string or put them inside the balloon."

"A bunch of us are going to do balloons in memory of Anna, but that's not the reason I want you to come. I need to see you. It sounds crazy, but I feel like I can't breathe right without you beside me. We've only known each other for such a short time and…Oh, heck, Rachel, I'm a pastoral counselor, and I'd tell anyone coming to me with our story to run for the hills and pray to God for sanity."

"It is crazy," she admitted, "but I know exactly what you are feeling because I feel the same way. Things are just so right when I'm with you. The odd thing is that I act so differently when I'm around you. I feel like I've been set free to just be me, Rachel Pontelli. Do you know what that is like?"

"You said it with one word, 'free.' I think, through our togetherness, we somehow set each other free to be who we are supposed to be. When I look back, it is so easy to see how God has maneuvered this. I feel like I've known you my whole life."

"I know I've known you my whole life," she countered. "God just hadn't revealed you to me yet. Things had to happen in his time, and our experiences had to mold us into the people we are now before he could bring us together. Meeting you at age twenty-three just wouldn't have worked."

"I love you, Rachel Pontelli."

"I love you too, Michael Warren. And yes, I will come to Danford this weekend."

Later, as she lay in bed, Rachel's mind raced in fearful anticipation of the upcoming weekend. To the east of her, in Danford, Montana, Mike was undergoing the same anticipatory torment. *This is crazy*, they both thought, and then they both automatically reached out to God for answers.

Chapter 29

* * *

We had walked to town to buy ice cream cones, and we were walking back when we spotted a half-empty pack of Marlboro cigarettes on the side of the road. We studied it for quite some time, not sure what to do. Anna picked it up finally and smelled the pack and wrinkled her nose. "Pee-yoo," she said. No one in our families smoked, and we had never, either one of us, actually touched a cigarette. Anna handed the pack to me, and I slipped it in my pocket. Was it her idea? Was it mine? I can't remember, but one of us thought that the cigarettes could be used in place of peace pipes. There was great power to be had in smoking a peace pipe. Anna held out the cigarette while I, using the lighter from the Bone Tree, held the flame on the end long enough to get it lit. She went first, blowing into the cigarette. I told her I think you suck in the smoke. She tried and choked and coughed. My turn didn't go much better. The smoke filled my lungs, searing them, and making me instantly ill. We had to lie on the ground until the sickness passed and our heads cleared. We learned it was true. A peace pipe has great power.

* * *

On weekdays, Jim Peterman dropped Marcy off at the front door of Danford Middle School on his way to work at his car dealership. After classes let out in the afternoon, she walked home down the same road she had traveled since first grade. Second Street started on the west side of Danford, came straight through town, and continued east until it was well into the country.

For all of those years, except when one of them was sick, she and Anna had walked home together. Their steps always slowed as they neared their homes, and they invariably ended up standing in front of her house or Anna's house and chatted until their books were too heavy to hold any longer.

Marcy was learning that being a survivor was a very difficult role to maintain. She could feel people watching her, and she didn't understand what they wanted from her. She was a reminder to the whole town of that day in July. They looked at her as if she was a grand wizard who knew the answers and wasn't sharing.

At first, she thought they were thinking, "Why her? Why did that one drown and this one live?" She thought maybe they were judging her worthiness to be alive. Before the accident, she was no more noteworthy than any other young girl going about her business in Danford. Now she felt their gazes when she was in stores. She heard the chatter stop, the laughter die, and the hushed whispering start.

"That's her. Poor thing. That's the girl who was with Anna Miller."

In time, she realized they were just curious, some of them, and that others were deeply sympathetic and heartbroken not only for Anna but also for her, Marcy. They didn't know what to say to her to make things better. She didn't know what to say to herself either, let alone to them.

She thought a lot in her solitude as she walked home from school. Her journal bore out the fact that she was getting better, that she was surviving.

About three quarters of the way home, at the base of the hill where Mr. Knutson's big old house settled on the left-hand side of Second Street, the road forked. The road to the right, Larkspur Lane, took her home. The one straight ahead took her up the hill and at the very top, to the left, was Rice's Hill.

From the bottom of the hill, just before she turned right to go home, Marcy could look up the hill and see where she and Anna had played. She couldn't see the Bone Tree from the road, but she recognized every ponderosa pine and could make out the sloping roof of the old pole shed they used as a teepee.

Even from down here, she could see the break in the snowberry bushes along the barbed wire fence that separated the road from the land. One summer, she and Anna had broken off the bushes at this spot so they could more easily slip through the fence to their private paradise.

She wondered if anyone, this fall, had stripped the snowberry bushes of their fruit and used their feet to pop the berries. Sometimes, she and Anna would gather buckets of the white berries and put them on the ground and wait for a passing car to go by and pop them. It was silly, she now thought, that they never once considered that the sound of the vehicle negated any sound of popping.

There were other children walking this road, of course, but Marcy kept to herself. She sometimes saw Mr. Knutson, who owned Rice's Hill and the pasture with the irrigation ditch and land beyond. She knew he had gone through some trouble with authorities over the ditch, but officials concluded there was no wrongdoing. They were satisfied with his signage, his warnings, and his sturdy fencing. The blame, of course, all of it, rested on the shoulders of Anna and Marcy.

One afternoon, just after school started, Mr. Knutson pulled up in his pickup beside Marcy, and she stopped and turned to him. He turned off the truck, and she could tell he was uncomfortable. She waited. He took off his sunglasses and set them on the dash.

"How are you doing with all this, Marcy?" he finally asked, looking at her. His eyes squinted in the light, and she noticed that despite his craggy face, his eyes were brilliant blue and as clear as a child's.

"I'm okay," she said, nodding and shrugging her shoulders. Then she added, "School started," and wondered why she said that, about school. It didn't really explain anything.

"I talked to your folks, just after…" he said, turning his head and looking straight ahead.

"They told me. It wasn't your fault at all, Mr. Knutson. Anna and me, we shouldn't have gone through your pasture. You had signs."

"It's still hard, isn't it? Wondering what you could have done to make it not happen."

"At first, I felt bad that I didn't save her, but now, I just figure that this is God's business. I expect he knows what he's doing," she told him.

He swung his head and looked at her. "God's business," he said almost to himself. Then he took off his baseball cap and reached up to smooth down his gray hair before putting it back on. She noticed in those few seconds that under the brim of the hat, his skin was pale as milk.

He smiled at her. "You're pretty wise for a kid," he said.

"Not me," she confessed to him. "Pastor Mike and church helped a lot. You could come some Sunday if you wanted. It's at eleven in the morning. You could sit with us."

"I'll think about it," he said, reaching over to turn the key and start his pickup. "You take care, okay?" he said as he pulled away.

A few feet away, he stopped and leaned out of his pickup window. "I want you to know that you can go up play on the hill anytime you want. You have my permission. Just don't go in the pasture," he said. Then he pulled his head back in his truck and rumbled off, a cloud of dust swirling in his wake.

A week later, she was a block away from his house when she spotted him pulling his mail out of the box. She whistled and waved to get his attention. He leaned back and waited for her, sorting through his mail to pass time.

She was breathless by the time she got to him. She grinned as she gulped in air and tried to talk. He smiled and waited.

"The horses…" she said breathlessly. She nodded vigorously to let him know that was what she wanted to know about.

Was it really two whole years ago that she and Anna had spent the summer riding Kemo while young Sabe frolicked and pranced alongside? She thought of Kemo often, and sometimes, she cried more over the loss of this horse than she did over losing Anna. Then she felt guilty and wondered at her callousness.

She sometimes felt that if she could just have a few more days with Kemo, things would be better. She would be instantly healed of all the pain. She ached to bury her face in the horse's smooth brown neck and pull the thick golden mane over her head and feel the strength pour into her.

"So you want to know about the horses that were here a couple years ago? Brandy and Pete?" he asked her.

"We didn't know their names. Anna and I called the mare Kemo, and we called her baby Sabe. You know, like Kemosabe from the *Lone Ranger*. It means trusted friend."

"Good names," Mr. Knutson said, nodding his head. "Better than Brandy and Pete. The horses belonged to my granddaughter. Her folks kept them here that summer while they put in a new fence. They live down by Helena. The colt was sold off, but they still have

Brandy. Lena went off to college, so the horse don't get rode much anymore."

"Do you think she will ever come back here?"

The question was so quiet and pleading Mr. Knutson looked at Marcy closely. He wasn't the brightest of men when it came to dealing with females, but he knew that she was close to tears.

"She meant a lot to you, did she?"

Marcy could only bite her bottom lip and nod. "Umm-hmmm," she said. She was embarrassed to feel her face crumple and tried valiantly to keep any tears from falling. She turned her head so he couldn't see.

"Well, I expect there's not much reason for her to come back here now that the fence is fixed and all," he said gently. He reached out to pat her shoulder but thought better of it.

"Oh," she said in a small sad voice. One word and it made his heart ache for her.

"There's something about a horse that sort of pulls at your heartstrings," he told her then. "I had lots of horses in my day, back when we had cattle to move from the high pastures to the low or vice versa. Some or those horses were pure knotheads, but others, like my Bandit, were smarter than most fellers I knew. I had Bandit for nigh onto twenty years before he passed on. I dearly loved that horse."

They stood in silence and watched as a hay truck rattled by, a sifting of chaff falling off its load as it headed up Rice's Hill. Mr. Knutson scuffed his boot in the fine powdery dirt under his foot.

"Well," he said, "we stand here much longer, we're both gonna be bawling over our horses like a couple of babies."

Marcy smiled wanly. "Thanks, Mr. Knutson. I just wanted to know. If you ever go there, down to Helena, could you get a picture of her for me?"

"I can do that. Next time I'm there, I'll take a whole roll for you."

He watched as she walked away, slump shouldered and hugging her books, headed down Larkspur Lane and home. He shook his head sadly as a memory of old Bandit slid into his brain. He shoved it aside and turned to go to his house.

"Old cowpokes shouldn't be thinking of old horses of the past," he muttered to himself.

Chapter 30

The balloon launch date was nearing, and the only one of the group who didn't have troubles writing an "Anna note" for the balloon launch was Ben. At nine years old, his message was simple: "Dear Anna. We miss you a lot. I got a new game, and Marcy and I play it sometimes. I'm going to put this note in a balloon and send it. I hope it gets to Heven and you find it. Love and XXX, Ben."

Sharon wrote a note for both herself and Jim, and it was simple and loving. Marcy, after a half dozen attempts, finally wrote two pages conveying her agony and her anguish.

Anna's parents, Joe and Barbara, despite both being educated as teachers, had the most difficulty in putting words to their heartache. Joe, after several aborted attempts, declared he didn't want to write a note and said he would simply send up his balloon with his love.

"Are you sure? You don't have anything to say to her?" Barbara found it hard to not criticize and to understand. Of the two, she was the wordiest and had thought that someday when she retired, she would try her hand at writing.

"I have a lot to say to her, and I talk to her all the time," he responded. "I just don't want to write it down. Isn't this whole thing just a little bit pointless? A bunch of bawling people standing in a park and letting balloons loose?"

Her heart swelled with compassion. She went to him and gave him a hug. "You don't have to write anything, but you need to be there for me, okay?" He nodded.

Two nights later, Joe woke up from a deep sleep, and in the hush of early dawn, the words came quickly and easily. He never showed Barbara what he wrote, but she knew he kept a copy in his Bible. Someday, he would share it with her—maybe not for years, but someday.

Barbara decided not to write down her feelings of guilt and anger and grief but chose to focus on Anna and how delighted she must be in heaven, sitting right beside her Jesus. Instead of writing about missing her, Barbara wrote about how glad she was that Anna was free and that she would be forever young and forever happy.

She ended her note with this:

> "I look at the nighttime sky, and I see you there. I look at a flower, and I see your smile in the petals. Everything seems to bring a memory of our Anna. Yesterday, it rained, and I thought of you at three years old and running bare naked through a warm summer shower. I see you in the smile of a baby, I see you in the gentleness of an ancient hand, and I see you, especially I see you, in your father. He is a good man and a loving man, and you inherited his goodness and kindness. You are missed, my dearest Anna, but I am comforted that you are waiting for me. You are helping prepare my place. Someday, in just a blink of time, we will be united. My pain is diminishing, and I sometimes want to cling

to it, to savor the hurt and anguish. But I know that isn't what you would want, so I am setting it free with this balloon, just as I am setting you free."

The notes were all written and were in safe places until they were brought to the balloon launch on Saturday. They were all looking forward to it. They were all dreading it.

Of all the members of the group who planned to launch balloons in Anna's honor, only Pastor Mike had reason to be happy. In just a few short days, he would pick Rachel up at the airport.

He was a nervous wreck. Luckily, he had Barbara and Joe and a few others, like the Petermans and his office staff, in his corner.

He stressed to all of them that Rachel was only a friend. They knew, however, that the fact he was bringing her to Danford was an important step.

His volunteer receptionist, Violet Lemke, who adored going to funerals and weddings, was delighted. Even though he stressed "friend" to her two separate times, he could tell she was already planning the big event and couldn't wait until she got away from the church and could tell the exciting news to her friend, Lillian Dip. Together, he knew, the two of them would effectively get word out around town. The bachelor pastor was flying a Seattle woman to Danford. Gossip didn't get much better than this.

Others didn't take the news of Rachel's visit as well as Violet. Louise Wagner, who was head of the Christian Women's League and did everything but drape her spinster forty-year-old daughter Willie in gift wrap, was dismayed. She had prayed earnestly morning and night that God would make her pastor fall in love with her daughter, her dear Willie.

She wasn't alone in her fervent prayers. Mike knew there were at least a couple dozen others who held out hope for nuptials involving him and a female family member.

Pulling his cell phone out of his pocket, he pushed menu and selected the first number that popped onto the screen. He grinned in anticipation.

She laughed when she answered. No hello, just that warm and vibrant laugh. He loved her laugh.

"I know I'm a pest," he said. "I can't help it. Are you as excited as I am?"

Five minutes later, he was whistling around the office. He had hospital visits that afternoon, and he had to work on his sermon. Somehow, his duties were made easier knowing that Rachel was praying for him.

Chapter 31

* * *

Two boys raided our village one day when we were there, kicking and throwing the rocks that ringed the graves and using a BB gun to shoot randomly at the trees. They were older, probably middle schoolers, and wore black T-shirts with skulls on them. We saw them coming and hid in a corner of the pole barn. I had to hold Anna back when one of them shot a robin out of a tree and then kicked the poor thing as it flapped its wings in hurting despair. We prayed that they wouldn't find the Bone Tree.

* * *

Marcy was putting her books in her locker between classes when she spotted a trio of troublesome classmates coming toward her. She asked God to help her if they started taunting.

School wasn't getting easier, but Marcy had settled into a routine. Some of her former friends had tried valiantly to make her part of their crowd again, but she wasn't interested. In time, they simply left her alone.

Sometimes, one of them would single her out and talk to her about Anna, but they didn't dwell on her. Marcy knew that in time, except for big events like eighth grade graduation and maybe high school graduation, Anna would become less and less a part of their conversations. She thought how strange it was that Anna would remain forever young while the rest of them grew up.

Anything that could have been called good at school seemed to be canceled out by the bad, which was usually brought about by the few that harassed her. Marcy knew she had a good case for bullying had she chosen to go to the school counselor with what she was going through, but she decided to just keep things to herself.

As she watched the giggling trio walking toward her, Marcy didn't know whether to just ignore them or to scramble quickly and get down the hall. She decided to stand her ground. She closed her locker door and turned around and faced her enemies.

One of them started a saucy sashay a few feet away, and Marcy knew the girl was about to spout off something about dead Anna Miller. Before she could say anything, Marcy folded her arms and stepped forward.

"Let's just have this out. I don't know what your problem is and why you think it's your job in life to make me more miserable than I already am," she said loudly. One of them started to say something, and Marcy held up her hand. A few curious onlookers stepped forward to listen.

"My friend Anna died on July 21. She was your friend too. We had a lot of fun together. All of you and me and Anna. We went to parties and had sleepovers. It was an accident. No one was at fault except for a whole bunch of rain that flooded the irrigation ditch. I didn't push her. She slipped on the bank and fell in. I couldn't save her. I tried. I jumped in and tried to save her, but she was gone.

"See the scars on my hands?" she continued, holding up her palms so everyone could see the white jagged marks on them. "That's from hanging on to the culvert. All of you went to the memorial service, and so did I, and so did most of the rest of you. We all cried over losing our friend Anna.

"And then something happened. Somehow, I became the center of taunts and jeers and hateful notes in my locker. Some of you started mocking my grief over Anna and even saying awful things about Anna herself. I let it go all this time. Maybe because I felt like I deserved it because I couldn't save her. I did everything I could, but I couldn't save her. Maybe because I felt guilty because I lived and she died. But no more. Today, it ends. If you want to talk to me, it will be with courtesy and politeness and respect. And you will no longer betray the memory of my friend, Anna."

With that, Marcy turned and walked down the hall toward the door. Behind her, a few people started applauding, and someone yelled, "Way to go, Marcy." She didn't have energy or desire to look back.

Marcy walked out of the school building, down the sidewalk, and headed down Second Street with purpose. Today was the day. She had put it off all this time, and today was the day to face everything that was awry in her life. She would go to the irrigation ditch.

Chapter 32

* * *

Anna and I were constantly on the lookout for treasures for the Bone Tree. When we first started adding our offerings we would put anything in and soon had it filled with big pine cones and rocks that, at the time of finding, seemed to be priceless jewels. One day Anna decided the Bone Tree wasn't what it was meant to be. We had a meeting and quickly decided to throw away anything that wasn't truly special. Anna joked that our Indian clan was related to the Clan of the Pack Rat as we threw away a bushel of pine cones and plain old ordinary rocks.

* * *

It was a chilly day, but not brutally cold. That would come soon enough. The leaves had long fallen to the ground, and everyone seemed to be just waiting for the onslaught of winter. Marcy hoped it would be a snowy winter. She loved the snow.

Mr. Knutson's pickup rattled toward her and passed by slowly. She waved to him and smiled. He was headed to town, and that was good. It meant he couldn't spot her as she crossed the pasture to the irrigation ditch. Later, if she climbed Rice's Hill, it didn't matter because she had his permission to go there. She had no one's permission to go to the irrigation ditch.

When she got to where she would go through the fence, she scrambled down the ditch and up the other side to the barbed wire, her jeans collecting dust and picking up bits of brush and leaves. Pushing down on the second to the bottom wire with her hands, she swung her left foot to the other side and then skillfully slipped her body through. She had been going through barbed-wire fences since before she was a kindergartner, and no matter how tight the wire, she rarely snagged her clothing.

It was still early enough in the afternoon that she had a few hours before darkness settled in. That would be more than enough time to confront and chase away the ghosts of the past.

She stopped on the other side of the fence and looked around for evidence, some shred of proof that she and Anna had passed through here on July 21. She remembered that Anna had caught her shirt on a barb and looked closely for some red threads. There were none.

She scouted for the small herd of cows that laid claim to the pasture and could see them a long ways away, their heads bowed as they grazed. They probably wouldn't bother her.

She retraced the steps she and Anna had taken, and she thought she could pinpoint—out of a pasture full of them—the thistle that had caused her to stop and pull out stickers. She would never know for sure, of course, but the thistle may have saved her life.

The water in the ditch was low, barely a trickle. Today, no one could fall in and drown. Even before Anna's death, she had thought how odd life was and how quickly Mother Nature could snatch it away. Here one day, buried the next. The first time she thought of it was when one of the salesmen at her dad's dealership skidded out of control one morning after a snow. He hit a telephone pole and died instantly. The roads were dry the day before and dry again three hours after the accident.

The dead weeds, kept low by the cows, crackled under her feet as she made her way along the bank. The mud was dried and hard, and there were many footprints buried deep in it. So many footprints. Usually, she just saw cow hoof prints here, so she knew the imbedded patterns from the bottoms of tennis shoes and boots were probably from the searchers.

She looked carefully for evidence of what happened that day—a slide mark maybe, where Anna went into the water. She also searched for whatever it was that Anna was carrying. The treasure she had for the Bone Tree. Something her grandfather had given to her, she had said.

The day of the accident, Marcy had carried a treasure herself— old strands of pop beads given to her by her mother. They were still in her pocket when she was fished out of the irrigation ditch, and now they were in the bottom of her dresser drawer. She fingered them sometimes and recalled the joy and anticipation she felt that day when she was going to show them to Anna.

She sat on the plank bridge and dangled her feet over the edge. She could feel the weak sun on her shoulders. Ahead, she could see the big culvert she had clung to so desperately that day. It looked no more frightening than the bridge she was sitting on, but she knew that if she put her palms up to the metal edges, the scars would fit perfectly. Odd that she didn't remember much at all about that traumatic ordeal, except for being cold—so very, very cold.

After a time, Marcy examined her feelings and discovered, quite to her surprise, that what she expected to feel wasn't there at all. She wasn't angry or horrified or grief-stricken. Instead, she found it peaceful here, and beautiful. Across the pasture was the meadow and, beyond that, the mountains.

Getting up, Marcy continued to walk along the ditch and eventually came to the bend where they found Anna's body, at least it was where she thought they must have found her. A tangle of debris, the web that may have ensnared Anna's body, was well out of the water.

As she stood looking, a puff of wind fluttered a clump of leaves left on a broken branch, and a bird settled there for a scant second before flying off toward the mountains.

Marcy turned her head to the right and settled her eyes on Rice's Hill and resumed walking. She looked back to make sure the cows hadn't circled behind and that's when she saw the strand of thin leather half buried in the dirt down by the water. Somehow, she knew that this was what Anna had to offer.

She clambered down the hill, crouched down, and carefully pulled on the length of leather lacing, which seemed to be stuck on one end. Looking around for something to dig with, she found a stick and started excavating. Within minutes, she had unearthed the treasure.

It was a perfect agate arrowhead, reddish brown and about two inches long. It had been crisscrossed with copper wire, and a loop was fashioned at the top. The arrowhead had been strung on the leather thong.

"Oh, Anna, it's beautiful," she whispered. "A real arrowhead. No wonder you were so excited to get to the Bone Tree that day."

The arrowhead was caked with dirt. Marcy rubbed most of it off with her fingers and then went to the shallow water, where she squatted and swished it a few times to clean it more thoroughly. She blotted it dry on her shirt.

Marcy raised her arms and pulled the arrowhead over her head and was comforted by the feel of it against her chest. A peace settled over her.

Chapter 33

Rachel Pontelli was amused that the airplane that would take her from Seattle to Montana was so small that passengers didn't gain access through a tunnel-like chute but walked down a flight of metal stairs to the outside tarmac where they were treated to a familiar Seattle drizzle. A hundred steps away the airplane, which she would learn during the pre-flight instructions was a Bombardier Q400, sat waiting. A rolling staircase was in place for passengers to climb and then enter the plane through the side door.

As she worked her way up the stairs with a small cluster of fellow travelers, Rachel suddenly realized that this was more than a simple trip to a chosen destination. It was more than a few days with a friend. She was headed into the unknown. She might be headed straight into her future.

The plane was a new turboprop with high wings and a beautiful white leather interior. It held around sixty-five people, although there were far fewer than that on the flight that morning.

The flight attendant greeting passengers at the doorway was young and pretty and happily welcomed them to Horizon Air. Rachel settled into her window seat and stuffed her paperback novel and a crossword puzzle book into the seat pocket in front of her. Then she watched as the remainder of the passengers entered the plane, each of them peering closely at the seat numbers displayed on metal plates below the overhead bins.

The passengers comprised a cross-section of what she would learn was Montana. Two old men, obviously brothers, wore cowboy hats, scuffed boots, and Western shirts with mother-of-pearl buttons. They didn't look like men of the world, and Rachel wondered what business forced them into the air. She knew they were headed home to Montana. A beautiful Indian woman carrying a toddler and dragging a diaper bag bigger than the child walked past, followed by three couples of varying ages and moods. A rough handsome fellow in brown Carhardt overalls settled into the seat across the aisle. He was soon joined by a well-groomed fellow in an expensive suit who looked like he might have gotten on the wrong airplane by accident.

One of the last passengers to enter the cabin was a beautiful elderly lady with perfectly coiffed white hair, priceless jewelry, and an expensive pantsuit under a costly black wool coat. Rachel knew somehow that this would be her seatmate.

Her name was Katherine O'Malley, she said, introducing herself to Rachel.

"Are you going to Kalispell?" Mrs. O'Malley asked as she placed her purse and a small bag under the seat in front of her and then fastened her seat belt. She was so trim she didn't have to pull on the end to enlarge the belt.

"Actually, my final destination is Danford," Rachel said, fastening her own seat belt. "I thought maybe it would be easier to land in Missoula and drive from there, but I guess Kalispell is closer."

"If you have the time, it is a wonderful drive from Missoula since you drive around Flathead Lake, but Kalispell is much closer," Mrs. O'Malley said. Then her eyes twinkled. "I happen to be going to Danford myself."

"Do you live there?" Rachel asked.

"For about a century now, I think," Katherine said, laughing. "I'm older than the hills. Older than dirt, as one of my neighbors says."

Rachel was about to respond, but the plane had started to move, and the flight attendant was making a quick trip down the aisle to make sure all the overhead bins were fastened securely.

"We can talk later," Mrs. O'Malley said, leaning toward Rachel conspiratorially. "I always take time to read the placard about the airplane I am in, and I always listen to every word the flight attendant says. No one else pays any attention, so I feel it's my duty to know what to do in case we…well, you know…in case there's a mishap."

"You do that? So do I. I always count how many seats to the nearest exit. I read once that most people die after a…mishap… because they forget to unsnap their seat belts. They panic and try and try to get out, and all the time the only thing keeping them pinned down is their seat belt."

"Oh my," Katherine said, her eyes widening.

They both listened with such concentration that the flight attendant addressed her memorized spiel directly to them. No one else on the plane paid her any attention or laughed at her small jokes, and little did they know that there were two fellow passengers who were willing to accept the utmost responsibility for their safety.

Unlike the huge jets that Rachel was used to, this airplane was noisier and bouncier, and they taxied for so long that Rachel wondered if they were going to drive all the way to Montana. After takeoff, it took a few seconds for the pilot to adjust the props to get them in sync, and the plane wallowed and lurched a bit as it climbed. Rachel was happy to learn that this airplane, being smaller than anything in the jet family, flew closer to the ground, giving her a wonderful view of the wooded areas and intricate waterways along the Sound.

After a time, Katherine fished in her purse for a pair of reading glasses, pulled down the tray ahead of her, and settled in to read a book. Before she opened the cover, Rachel asked the elderly woman if she would tell her when they were over Montana.

A few chapters, a small bag of pretzels, and a bottle of water later, Katherine, after looking at her watch a few times, finally announced that they were definitely in Montana territory. Rachel turned to flash her a grin and then continued to keep her face to the window. Montana. This was Mike Warren's country. She had never been here before—never set foot in the state.

Montana. Open land, majestic mountains, buffalo, beauty unequaled…She knew part of the state, the east side, was prairie and grain fields and that the west side, partitioned off by the Continental Divide, was mountainous. The northwest corner, where Mike lived in Danford, was beautiful with jagged peaks, tree-studded hills, and sprawling expanses of lush farmland. He had talked about his little town and his state at great lengths. He was intensely in love with this place called Montana.

Mike, she knew, came from a long line of Montanans. His great-grandfathers on both sides of the family had come to Big Sky Country in the 1880s. The Warrens, who had a huge ranch close to Great Falls, still had a stronghold in the state. The Grenfels, on his mother's side, were of more modest means. They had settled along the Milk River and were down to just a few sections.

"Are you visiting family?" Katherine asked after a bit, closing her book and smoothing the cover with her age-wrinkled hand. The diamonds in her rings glinted in the overhead light. Rachel moved her face away from the window to answer.

"No, I've never been to Montana. I'm visiting a friend. He and I met a while back when he attended a series of meetings put on by Hope Ministries. I work for them and, well, we just became very good friends. He asked that I come to Danford this weekend for a visit."

"It sounds as if you really hit it off," Katherine said with a smile. "I have heard of Hope Ministries, of course, and have actually contributed to it quite regularly. As a Christian, I believe in missions."

"Oh, you're a fellow Christian. Then you go to church in Danford?" Rachel asked with a smile and gave her complete attention to the elderly woman. She took a drink of her bottled water as she waited for Katherine to answer.

"Every Sunday. I attend Danford Baptist Church and have for years, although I have to admit I do sneak into other churches at times. I don't believe we're going to have all Catholics or all Baptists in heaven, so I figured I need to get to know my fellow believers."

Rachel took a deep breath. "So have you ever heard of Danford Worship Center?"

"Oh, of course!" Katherine said, laughing. "Danford is only about 6,000 people. It would be hard to hide a church, especially one of that size. It's probably the fastest growing church in the area, and people drive from forty miles away to attend services. I've been there a few times, and I must say it is very much different than my Baptist church, which can be too traditional at times. I loved it. The message was terrific and very thought-provoking, and the music was outstanding. It is a wonderful church. Is your friend a member there?"

"Actually, he's the pastor," Rachel said, ducking her head and crunching her face.

"Mike? You're going to visit Pastor Mike?" Katherine sat back in her seat and laughed gaily. "Oh, my," she said, shaking her head and holding her hand to her chest.

"He's really nice," Rachel said defensively.

"Oh, that wasn't why I was laughing," Katherine said, wiping the corner of her eyes. She fussed with her rings, straightening a big diamond band that had turned sideways. Then she looked at Rachel, and her eyes were probing.

"I hate to be nosey, but I'm going to just come out and ask you a question. If you want to answer, that's fine, but you don't have to. Do you have feelings for Mike Warren?"

Rachel could feel her face reddening. "Yes," she said. "Yes I do."

"Well, that's good," Katherine said, settling back in relief, "because he is a fine young man, and I'd hate to see him hurt."

In a split second, Rachel realized why God had arranged for her and Katherine O'Malley to be seatmates. She decided that this person, who obviously knew Mike, was the one who could see things clearly.

"Can I talk to you about it?" Rachel asked.

"Well, of course," Katherine said. Her eyes were warm and gentle, and Rachel knew instinctively that she could trust her.

"You're going to think this is crazy, but we met each other just a few weeks ago at a big meeting that Hope Ministries had in Victoria, British Columbia. Hope has asked Mike to serve on the board, and it was the first time he had attended one of our meetings. We got to know each other because I am the assistant to the director of the organization. It sounds crazy, but it was as if we were meant to be, that God just put us together. We have talked about it for hours. We talk about it every night. Except for my mother and father, I don't have anyone else I can ask for advice. I need a second opinion. I've always thought love at first sight was a bit of a fantasy, but I truly do love Mike, and he feels the same.

"We're in a real quandary," Rachel continued. "Especially since he is a pastor and has to answer to all of his church members, and they're going to think we're both crazy. He takes off for four days and suddenly has this strange woman in his life? I don't know whether I should be going to Danford or not, but he begged me, and truthfully, I couldn't go another week without seeing him."

Shaking her head and giving a sigh, Rachel looked at Katherine in embarrassment. "I'm sorry. I just sort of got carried away there."

"Don't be sorry. Sometimes, we are too close to our situations to stand back and see things as others see them," Katherine said thoughtfully. "But let me tell you what I think about love at first sight. I have to believe that God has indeed created love at first sight. All throughout the Bible are examples of almost instantaneous happenings. Look at the disciples who dropped what they were doing and just followed Jesus. Surely that was love at first sight. Everywhere Jesus went things were changed instantly, lives were changed instantly. He didn't court people or lure them to his side or set up a series of conferences. They simply knew they had to follow him or that they had to ask him to change their lives. So I guess that, yes, I absolutely believe in love at first sight."

"My goodness. What a wonderful way to look at it. I wish I could write that all down and tell Mike," Rachel said. She wanted to simply hug this woman with her uncomplicated explanation. Surely Katherine O'Malley had been sent by God to give her some advice and some wisdom. Now she knew for certain that it wasn't an accident that they had been seated together.

"I have to tell you, dear, why I was laughing earlier," Katherine said, leaning closer and snickering. "You see, every old biddy in Danford who has a spinster daughter or an unmarried niece or other relative has her eyes set on marrying them off to poor Mike Warren. The fellow has been chased down by these women since he hit town. I must say he's been a valiant trooper and has been very nice about it all. I heard through the grapevine that in one Sunday alone, he took in five pies, a German chocolate cake—homemade, mind you—and a gallon of home-churned huckleberry ice cream. I'm surprised he doesn't weigh four hundred pounds. He could start a bakery to augment his finances, not that they need augmented."

"He mentioned the parade of spinsters," Rachel said, chuckling at the thought of him carting home all the desserts.

"Be forewarned that many people are going to be mighty disappointed when you show up on the scene. I'm sure some of these mamas have wedding dresses picked out and have figured out the wording for the invitations. There are going to be a lot of bubbles burst when word gets out."

"Now I am scared," Rachel said, running her hand through her long hair.

"A lady should never show when she's nervous or frightened," Katherine advised. "Just be gracious and kind and interested. Make an effort to know their names, and you'll win their hearts. About your situation, as you call it, you need to just trust God. He knows what he's doing. Also, trust your heart. And trust Michael. You can be sure that he has sore knees from praying over this. Finally, if you'll just listen I think you'll discover that God is giving you all your answers."

"You are full of good advice and wisdom. I really do appreciate it, Mrs. O'Malley."

Katherine O'Malley patted her hand. "Please call me Katherine," she said. "I think you and I are going to become good friends. You'll have to make sure that Michael brings you over to visit me before you leave. How long are you going to be in Danford?"

"I leave Wednesday morning."

"Maybe Tuesday, if that works for you both. But wait a minute. Do you have a place to stay? I would love to have you stay with me. I certainly have plenty of room."

"I'm staying with Joe and Barbara Miller. I know Mike and I are going to leave after church Sunday and drive to visit his folks who live near Great Falls. We'll spend the night there and drive back to Danford Monday afternoon."

"It's good you're staying with Joe and Barbara. You'll like them," Katherine said, and then she chuckled and looked at Rachel closely. "So he's taking you to meet the family, is he? This is serious then. I know his relatives through business dealings. They're quite a family."

"I don't like the sounds of that! What do you mean, 'quite a family?'"

"You'll have to find out for yourself! They aren't evil or anything. Just very interesting. I think you'll do fine with them."

Before Rachel could try and pry out any information, the plane started descending.

"Look down, and over there to the right a bit," Katherine said. "It's nestled at the base of the mountain at the end of the lake. That's Danford. That's my Danford."

"There's a lake? It looks absolutely beautiful. Mike didn't tell me there was a lake or that there would be so many trees."

"Oh, there are fields too," Katherine said, laughing. "Danford Lake isn't huge, compared to Flathead Lake, but it's gorgeous. Back in the twenties, my father used to log just outside of Danford, and they floated the logs down the lake and then down the Flathead River to Kalispell."

Rachel, looking across the land to the town of Danford, felt a fluttering start in her belly.

Chapter 34

Rachel knew they would soon be landing at Glacier Park International Airport outside of Kalispell, and her heart raced. The few minutes before the landing were like a speeded-up collection of movie clips: farmland with fields dressed in November brown, old barns and farmhouses, a huddle of black Angus cows, snowcapped mountains, a packed jumble of houses in subdivisions, and, in the distance, forested areas that seemed to go on forever before climbing mountains and disappearing over the other side.

Once the airplane doors were open and passengers made their way down the stairs, Rachel and Katherine walked across the tarmac together. Katherine chatted about Glacier Park and said she hoped Rachel and Mike would find a day they could visit the park.

"It's gorgeous, and I think the Going to the Sun Highway is still open since they haven't had as much snow as usual in the park so far this year. But maybe it is closed. If the road is open, you really shouldn't miss it," Katherine said. Rachel nodded but didn't respond. She was intent on trying to spot Mike through the windows of the terminal.

Katherine knew her new young friend was nervous and excited and terrified. She reached over and linked her arm through that of

Rachel's. "I just want you to know that I will be praying for you both," she said.

"Thanks," Rachel said, and she was shocked at the emotion that surged through her. She was suddenly filled with the desire to cry, but she shoved the feeling away. "And thanks for listening to me blabber. I really needed to talk to someone, and it was so wonderful of God to put you next to me."

"It was. You could have gotten a seat next to them," Katherine said cheerfully and motioned ahead to the two old cowpokes with matching bowed legs who were walking with odd short steps toward the terminal. Rachel had the feeling the two were much more comfortable on horses.

The airport was a hubbub of people, some waiting for passengers from the Horizon flight she and Katherine were on, and others waiting to catch other flights. The airport was small and pretty with glassed-in displays of paintings and Indian artifacts and fringed buckskin clothing. In front of the window was a large sculpture of an eagle with its wings spread regally. Rachel didn't see any of it. She was looking for a familiar, handsome, brown-haired man with an easy smile and a demeanor that invited trust and warmth.

Suddenly, there he was. Right in front of her. He had wondered on the trip to the airport if he should kiss her. He never had. They had held hands and embraced, but their lips had never touched. For some reason, that seemed important—to wait.

"Hey there," he said, breaking out into a large grin.

Rachel laughed. "Hey there back!" she said, and they automatically fell into each other's arms.

Pushing her away from him gently but keeping his hands on her shoulders, he looked at her closely. "It is so good to see you. It's like taking a drink after not having water for weeks." Rachel, her eyes filling with tears, simply nodded. They fell back into each other's arms, and he rocked her gently back and forth.

After a time and holding hands, they had started walking to the baggage area when Rachel spotted Katherine O'Malley. Stepping out ahead, she urged Mike along. "I want you to say hello to someone," she said, pulling on his hand.

Katherine was standing in front of a beautiful painting of a trio of teepees nestled in a grove of aspens. A small brook was in the foreground, and patches of snow covered the ground. Rachel put her hand on the old woman's shoulder and Katherine turned around. She beamed when she saw them.

Then, still smiling, she looked at Mike and shook her head. "You're going to break a lot of hearts and dash a lot of dreams when they meet this one," she said to him.

"Ahh, I take it you two met on the plane and I was the subject of some of your conversations," Mike said with a mock groan and gave Katherine a quick hug. "I hope you gave her some of your wise advice, Katherine, my friend."

"I did indeed. To put it simply, I told her to 'go for it.' Life is too short to waste time worrying about other people. Grab on to happiness when you can, and follow your hearts. If people have problems with you and Rachel and the length of your acquaintance, that's their problem. You'd better hang on to this young lady with both hands, Michael, because she's a keeper."

"You are a wonder, Katherine O'Malley," he said. "I should have headed to O'Malley House for advice the minute I got home from the Hope Ministries meetings."

Then he turned to Rachel. "I know she didn't tell you, but Katherine here lives in one of the largest and grandest mansions in the Northwest. O'Malley House has been in her family for generations. I was hoping we'd have time to go there and visit, and now that you two have met, we have even more reason to visit."

"She didn't tell me where she lived, only saying it was big enough that I could stay there if I wanted to. Katherine and I have sort of set up Tuesday morning for a visit, if that works."

"I think that will be great, but I'll have to consult Violet Lemke, our volunteer vacation planner," Mike said, looking pointedly at Katherine.

"Violet? You told Violet about Rachel?"

"Yup." Mike grinned as Katherine shook her head and grinned back. Rachel was puzzled and looked from one to the other.

"Mike, you might just as well have put an ad in the Danford Daily News and taken out a few spots on the radio station," Katherine said with glee.

"Don't worry. I gave her all sorts of good information about our Rachel here, and showed her pictures. It'll all be good press. I figured it would be better to have Violet and Lillian Dip spread the news rather than just having Rachel show up for church on Sunday."

"Good thinking! Good grief! If I didn't have to be in church for a baptism, I wouldn't miss visiting your church this Sunday for anything."

"We can tell you all about it Tuesday," Rachel said. "If we survive."

Chapter 35

* * *

Over time, we, Pocahontas and Sacajawea, had actually transformed our mock Indian burial grounds into a true place of burial. Dead birds were shrouded carefully in paper towels or scraps of fabric and placed in boxes. Insects, if they became special like the bumblebee that spent the afternoon with us and died before we left for the day, fit perfectly in small jewelry boxes. The boxes were reverently placed in shallow graves. We took turns leading the ceremony, which comprised of a short prayer. Turning a small King James to a page at random, we took turns reading the solemn, highly religious words.

* * *

Danford Cemetery, Marcy had decided over the months, was about the most peaceful place she'd ever been. Despite the fact that below the surface it was a place of bones and decaying flesh, it was very comforting and beautiful. She loved coming here and sitting on Anna's bench next to the big white marble angel that was seated at one end. The angel had her hands together with her palms up, and sometimes, Marcy would bring something to put there—a few flowers or a bundle of leaves when they were in color and once a bright blue marble she had found on the ground. It was gone the next time she visited.

She had come here at least once a week during the summer after Anna's death and had observed the changes as the season slowly ebbed and gave way to autumn. Soon, it would start to snow, and they would be deep in winter.

Marcy knew, of course, that Anna's remains weren't here and were in an urn at the Miller house. It wasn't like she could go to their house and ask if she could talk to Anna even though she knew that they would understand perfectly if she did do that.

This place was just a memorial, but even so, it was a place of centering. Although she'd been to the pasture and irrigation ditch, she couldn't quite make herself go to Rice's Hill and the Bone Tree yet, so the cemetery was the place of Anna.

"So I come here," she explained to Anna out loud one afternoon. "I can talk to you here. It's nice. It's quiet." She smiled slightly as she imagined Anna saying, "That's because everyone's dead."

A familiar flutter in nearby birches caused her to look up and smile sadly. The gray jays were back. The birds had first appeared during Marcy's second visit to the cemetery. They sat in the tree and watched curiously, and when she started to wail, they hopped from branch to branch, maybe in an attempt to take her attention off her grief by their comical actions.

Since then, she always brought along crackers or a piece of bread or other treat in her pocket. The birds, sometimes only one but once three of them, had gotten so tame that if she was really quiet and made slow precise movements, she could feed them by hand.

Everyone she knew called gray jays by their nickname "camp robbers," because the friendly birds were adept at sneaking food and seemed to ferret out people who might have a bite to spare.

"Hey there, pretty birds," she said softly, reaching her hand in her pocket. There were two of them today, and the biggest of the pair cocked his head. Four black glistening eyes watched her closely as she took out a sandwich bag.

"This is a special day," she told the birds as she pulled the zippered end. "And you get to have raisin bread. Plus, I brought some of Mom's cranberry bread."

One of the birds fluttered to the proffered angel hands while the other, more shy, soared to a spot on the ground about ten feet away.

"Oh, you think I'm going to throw it to you, do you, pretty bird? You are so spoiled. Not today. Today, you need to get your treat like this big guy."

Tearing off a piece of raisin bread, she slowly held her hand out to the jay standing on the hands of the angel. The bird alternated watching Marcy and looking at the bread and finally reached out and snatched it and then flew to a branch on the nearest tree.

"What do you think," Marcy said to the other bird, which had, by that time, hopped closer. Bending over, she held out another piece of bread. "Are you a brave fellow?"

Reaching over, she put the bread in the angel hands. "Tell you what. I'll make it easy for you today, but next time, I'm not going to give in." After a time of patient waiting, the camp robber flew easily to the statue and seized the bread.

"Oh, how I wish Anna could see you," she said to the birds. "She would love feeding you. Anna would make you so fat you probably wouldn't be able to fly."

Suddenly, a memory flew into her mind. It had been toward the end of summer, and Kemo and Sabe had learned to run toward them when they climbed through the fence to Rice's Hill. Sometimes, they brought an apple, but sometimes, they just groomed the horses with brushes they had purchased at Danford Feed.

On this day, however, Anna had a large plastic container. For the horses, she said. Inside was a stack of rice cakes, each one smeared with peanut butter.

"Peanut butter? And rice cakes?" Marcy had said. "Shouldn't they eat stuff like hay?"

"They'll love these," Anna said confidently as she held one out to Kemo. Sabe, the colt, pranced to get in place for his treat and greedily accepted the offering when Anna fished another rice cake out of the container.

"You'll make them fat," Marcy declared.

They decided to give each horse one more treat and then stashed the rest in the Bone Tree.

Two days later, when they returned to the Bone Tree, the container was lying on the ground, the lid a few feet away. There wasn't a smear of peanut butter or a crumb of a rice cake left. Despite Anna's sweet cajoling, the horses never did confess.

Marcy was still smiling at the memory when a third jay joined the pair. She had only a small hunk of the cranberry bread left and held it out when the birds suddenly, in a flurry of feathers, flew away as if in fear.

Marcy looked around to see what had startled the gray jays and saw a slight figure of a girl trudging across the graves toward her.

Her heart sank.

Whitney O'Dell. One of her classmates from school. One of those she had aimed her remarks at earlier when she was so distraught.

She prayed a quick prayer, asking God to give her the words and to protect her from hurt. Her face was emotionless as she watched her tormenter get closer.

When she was a few feet away, the girl stopped. She looked at her feet and cleared her throat before looking up. She didn't meet

Marcy's eyes and looked, instead, at the angel as if the stone being would help her get through this.

Marcy could see that she had been crying. She was glad. This girl had been hateful, and she hoped she had cried her eyes out. Going through Anna's death had been difficult enough without this ex-friend causing such discontent and being so cruel and, worse, getting other classmates to join in her cruelty.

"I don't blame you for hating me," the girl said finally, looking straight at Marcy. "I was awful. I was mean." She stopped speaking, and the silence was broken only by the muffled far-away sound of traffic.

Marcy waited, and then she offered up the only word that came to her.

"Why?"

The girl shrugged her shoulders, and her chin quivered. She tried to smile but couldn't make her lips move upward. She was encouraged by the fact that by Marcy's breaking the silence, there was hope that she could forgive her.

"I don't know. Anna died, and then my mom found out she had cancer. I was so afraid she would die, and I watched you go through everything with Anna. Crying and hanging out here and getting so lost in school and everything. I guess I didn't want it to happen to me."

"So your idea of helping me, your idea of being my friend, was to hurt me and tease me and to get everyone else to do that too?"

By now, the girl was crying. "Yes. No. I don't know," she said shrilly. "I just knew that my mom was probably going to die, and I didn't want to do that, to be like you. I didn't want to hurt like you. I didn't want to have to go to her funeral and come up here to talk to her."

Taking a tissue out of her pocket, Marcy offered it to the weeping girl. There was a time when she never carried tissues with her and had laughed at her mother, who always had a mini pack in her purse. Now, since Anna, Marcy always had tissues in her pocket. She wondered how many thousand she had used since Anna's death. She no longer carried Anna's moccasin for fear she would lose it, but she always had tissues.

After a time, Marcy looked at her tormentor with compassion. She might not forget right away, but she knew God would want her to forgive.

"It's okay. I guess you really didn't hate me as much as you hated the fact that I sort of represented death."

"I guess that's it," the girl said through her sniffles. "I didn't understand it myself. I would do something or say something and then hate myself. Everyone hates me now."

"They'll get over it. Is your Mom really sick?"

"She's going to be okay. We found out last week. They did surgery and got it all. But she still has to do the chemo thing."

"I'm glad. It's pretty awful when someone dies," Marcy said.

A few minutes later, the girl left and Marcy was alone. Despite the agonized confession and the subsequent words of forgiveness, Marcy didn't feel overwhelmed by jubilation that all would probably be all right in her school world. Instead, she felt lonelier and more bereft.

One of the gray jays flickered its wings as it flew to the angel's shoulder and cocked its head in greeting.

Marcy, her head down, walked out of the cemetery and didn't even notice.

Chapter 36

The Danford chapter of The Compassionate Friends held two balloon launches a year—one in the spring or early summer and the other in the fall. Besides the balloons, during the May event, attendees also let loose five hundred monarch butterflies as bagpipes played in the background. Some of the butterflies simply floated a few feet and perched, happily opening and closing their wings. Most of the others fluttered away in freedom, their wings flashing orange and black and brown.

The second balloon launch of the year had been scheduled for September. Because of membership schedules and a myriad of other events, it had been pushed back again and again until they declared it had to be done in November. Organizers prayed that the weather would hold.

Barbara had gotten up that morning to find Joe seated at the dining room table. They were both anxious and nervous about the balloon launch. Were they ready for this? To, in a way, give Anna up? To let their daughter go?

"We have to," Barbara said, and Joe looked up from the coffee cup that he held between his hands. He had been peering into it as if it held all the answers to life.

He knew what she meant. They had been married long enough that they frequently read each other's thoughts and could finish each other's sentences.

"Yeah," he said and got up and hugged her close. "But it's so hard. You know?"

"I know." She nodded her head and pulled away to look into his dark eyes.

On their way to the church, Barbara read over her short note to Anna. She didn't ask Joe if he brought his message or even if he was going to send up a balloon. That was his decision, and where she had once declared he had to take part, now she knew that it was his decision and she was in no position to judge or gauge his grief.

Joe and Barbara got to the church fellowship hall early to help set up chairs and tables and get ready for the lunch that would follow the release of the balloons.

Rod and Caroline Lincoln, not surprisingly, were there already and had things well under control. The tables were set up, and Caroline had covered them with autumnal plastic table coverings she had found in a cupboard. She was in the process of adding center-pieces when the Millers came into the big room.

Caroline and Barbara hugged while the men shook hands. Barbara, without asking, started putting round candles into big glass containers and centering them on the tables while Caroline added lengths of silk foliage that had tiny red berries.

"So I figure we can set up the food table over there under the windows," Caroline said. "On the opposite wall, over there, we can put up the table for the photos and mementoes. I brought a gold linen cloth for that table, and I thought we could use the bigger candles that are in the box.

"It will be beautiful," Barbara said quietly. "I hope it is okay, but I brought a collage frame with photos and things like her locked diary and a few other things. Will there be room?"

"Honey, if there isn't, we'll just throw up another table," Caroline said, assuring her.

Rod and Joe dragged in a huge cooler filled with ice and stationed it at the end of the food table. Caroline snickered and Barbara quickly caught on after she looked at the men, who were out of breath from heaving the heavy cooler.

"Memo to Rod and Joe," Caroline said, chuckling. "Put the ice in *after* moving the cooler."

"Oh yeah," Rod said, grinning at her and then straightening and rubbing his back. "Better idea. But maybe a better idea is that next time, we'll put the doilies on the table, and you two can do the ice and pop."

Barbara knew their bantering was meant to put them at ease and to take some of the somberness out of the day. She was grateful for their friendship.

By the time they put the baked beans in a slow oven, got out utensils and paper plates, and did the hundred other things necessary to feed a hundred or more people, it was time to go to the park. They wanted to get there in plenty of time so they could set up and greet people as they came.

Chapter 37

Jim and Sharon Peterman didn't know how to handle going to the balloon launch, and Sharon decided that they should simply sit down with Marcy and ask her. Jim puttered around the kitchen, trying to read the paper and then halfheartedly washing the countertops as they waited for her to come downstairs.

Marcy entered the kitchen quietly and opened the refrigerator door and pulled out the milk. Then she opened a cupboard and took out a box of her favorite cereal.

Sharon surreptitiously watched her daughter, thinking that she had grown over the summer and her hair had gotten lighter from the sun. She was changed, their Marcy, and the funny little girl that she had been was gone. It was sad, Sharon thought, that perhaps by the time she moved beyond the grief of Anna, she might have matured enough to have moved away forever from being a giggly little girl. She seemed older, quieter, and so very sad.

She had gotten counseling, of course, and met weekly with Pastor Mike and also visited sometimes with the counselor at school. They knew she was praying steadfastly because she had always been a child of prayer, even as a preschooler.

There wasn't really anything they could do but offer support and to wait.

It was the waiting that Jim seemed to be unable to accept. As a man, he wanted to fix everything right now. He wanted his daughter back. The giggly one. The one who drove him crazy sometimes. He wanted to take out his mental tool belt and drag out everything he needed to repair and mend the damage so they could get on with life.

Sharon knew it was so hard for this man she loved to be patient and to realize that he couldn't fix everything himself. It killed him to realize that he couldn't fix his own daughter.

Marcy got down her favorite blue bowl and opened the box and poured cereal into the bowl.

"And good morning to you," her mother said. "Do you want toast?"

"Sorry. Good morning. No, this is fine." Taking the bowl and grabbing a spoon from a drawer, she walked to the kitchen table.

"Hey, Marcy," Jim said, looking at his daughter. He and Sharon had been exchanging glances, and her hand motion when Marcy was walking to the table indicated that he was the one who was supposed to talk to her. Inwardly, he groaned. He wasn't good at this stuff.

"Hi, Dad," Marcy said, pulling out a chair and sitting down.

"Your Mom and I have been talking. Joe and Barbara asked us as a family to go to the balloon launch, and we would really like to go. But if you would like to just be there by yourself that will be okay too. We will understand. We can just drop you off, and you can catch a ride home with Barbara and Joe, or you can call us. We will totally understand if you just want to do this yourself."

Marcy looked at him in surprise and then turned to look at her mother. "You don't want to go?"

"Oh no, sweetheart," Sharon said quickly, rushing to the table. "That isn't it at all. We just thought that maybe you'd want to do this alone. Just you and, well, you and Anna."

Marcy glared at her mother with a look that was hard but unemotional. "Mom, there will be fifty or a hundred people there. It won't be just 'me and Anna.' The only reason I'm going at all is to be with Mr. and Mrs. Miller, because it might help them. I don't get it anyway, how people can just let their kids go in a balloon."

Sharon's heart fell. She knew she probably had handled this all wrong. She said gently, "Marcy, you know it's just a symbolic gesture. It's a way for people to channel grief. I've read it is especially effective with children because they can easily associate letting the balloons go with letting people go."

Marcy was silent for a long time. Then she looked at them. "Well, what if you don't want to let them go?" she asked loudly in a choked voice. She pushed away from the table and left the room.

"So do you want us to go with you?" Jim called after her. The exasperation he felt was clear in his tone of voice.

"Do whatever you want. I think Ben wants to go. He's got this whole book written to Anna. He'd be pretty disappointed if he didn't get to send it up in a balloon."

"Well then, I guess we'd better wake him up and start getting ready."

Sharon looked at Jim. She knew the look in his face probably mirrored her own. They had both harbored such great hopes that this balloon launch would be a time of healing. Now, they knew that Marcy wasn't close to letting Anna go and that she was still clinging to her grief. Sharon closed her eyes.

"Dear God, please be with my daughter," she prayed.

Chapter 38

The area where the balloon launch was to take place was isolated from the rest of the park. It wasn't that they didn't want observers; they simply didn't want hordes of people descending upon them thinking that there was some sort of free balloon giveaway. While it was a public event, it was also a very private event for people who were grieving the loss of loved ones and for others who chose to take part.

The Peterman family, with Marcy and Ben following after their parents, made their way across the dried grass toward the pavilion. Although it was sunny and a relatively warm day, it was November, so there were far fewer park visitors than in the summer months, just a few holdouts who weren't accepting the fact that summer was long gone.

Joe and Barbara spotted the Petermans and walked out to meet them. After greetings were concluded, Ben held up a plastic grocery bag.

"Look here," he said, holding it open. Joe and Barbara leaned over and peered inside. "I have a letter I wrote just for Anna and a picture of heaven. I didn't know what heaven would look like, so I just guessed. It has mountains and a river and lots of animals like giraffes and elephants, and birds too.

"Look here," he continued. "This is Jesus, up here in the sky and looking at the animals. I was going to put in snakes and spiders, but I decided not to. Anna was afraid of them, so I didn't draw them in. I was going to put in more stuff for my balloon, but Marcy said it would be too heavy."

Joe ruffled the little boy's hair, while Barbara hugged him to her side. "I know Anna would love all of it, especially the picture of Heaven. I'll bet she wishes she could send us a picture of heaven, don't you think?"

"Oh yeah! Wow! I never thought of that. I wish she could send us a picture," Ben said. Then he turned to give his mom a broad smile.

"How are you, sweetie?" Barbara asked, matching her stride with Marcy's.

"Okay, I guess."

"You don't have to do this if you don't want to, you know. It's supposed to make you feel better, not more sad. If you'd like, you can just watch."

Marcy shrugged her shoulders and lifted her hand to show the small envelope she was holding before letting it drop back to her side. "I have a letter," she said.

"Just remember that this is between you and Anna. Do what your heart wants you to do, okay, sweetie?"

Marcy nodded her head and turned to look toward some children who were playing on swings. She didn't move quickly enough to hide the tears in her eyes from Barbara.

Most of the people from The Compassionate Friends group were there. Some were quiet and somber, while others, who had been to several such events, were at peace.

When Pastor Mike approached them, Marcy had the urge to go to him and hug him. He had been immensely helpful to her over the months, and he was the one person she could really open up to. Then she saw that he had someone with him. He was grinning and was very nervous.

"Hello to the Petermans," Mike said, putting his arm casually around the woman. Marcy had to admit the person with Pastor Mike was beautiful with long silky reddish hair and a figure that looked like it came from one of those fashion magazines. She wore black slacks and a black and white checked wool jacket with a turquoise turtleneck underneath. Silver jewelry was at her ears, wrists, and around her neck. She was much too dressed up for Danford, Montana. Almost everyone else had on jeans.

"Hi, Mike. And you must be Rachel," Sharon said, stepping past Mike and heading straight to Rachel. Then instead of taking Rachel's proffered hand, Sharon gave her a hug. "Mike told us all about you, and we are so happy you came to Danford to visit. We were hoping we could have you over for dinner, but it sounds like Mike has you booked up until you leave."

"He sure does. I think he actually has an itinerary for the next few days," Rachel said, laughing. Her voice, Marcy thought, was beautiful, and her laugh was delightful. And her mother knew all about her, but Marcy sure didn't. No one ever told her anything.

"So what do you think of Danford?" Sharon asked, and suddenly the three women were chatting about the attributes, and downfalls, of Danford.

Pastor Mike looked at Marcy and lifted his shoulders. She looked away. He studied her carefully.

"Marcy," he said, getting her attention, "do you remember the other day in my office when I told you I'd met someone at the Hope Ministries conference and she had become a very good friend and was coming to Danford? Remember, I told you she was going to stay with the Millers?"

Marcy looked at him, and he watched as she suddenly remembered. She looked embarrassed, especially since it was obvious that he knew she was upset and had read her mind. He did that a lot—knowing what she was thinking, sometimes before she had even formulated it for herself.

She felt her face redden, and he shook his head slightly. Suddenly, there was a break in the conversation, and he jumped in.

"This is Rachel," he told Marcy. "And this," he told Rachel, putting his hand on Marcy's shoulder, "is Marcy, the one who helps me with Midas sometimes and who creates the most beautiful posters you have ever seen."

Rachel held out her hand. "I've heard all about you, Marcy," she said warmly and very quietly, in deference to the occasion they were all attending.

When Marcy held out her hand, Rachel grabbed it and nestled it between her own two hands and looked into her eyes. "Mike told me about the time you were riding your bike and crashed into his new pickup. And about the time you and Anna came to church all dressed up as clowns and half the little kids were terrified of you and started running and screaming and crying, *and* about the time he was choking during some sort of potluck and you were the only one to come up and haul off and slug him one."

Even though she was talking barely above a whisper, she said it all with great animation, and by the time she was finished, Marcy was smiling. "He told you all that?"

"He also told me you like to draw and do watercolors. Well, I like to draw, and I'm also a watercolorist. Maybe someday we can get together and do some painting."

"Since Anna, I don't do much anymore, but I would like to do that. I was thinking the other day that I miss painting," Marcy said.

"Then we, my friend, have a date. Maybe we can do some plein aire painting—you know, where you sit outside in the hot sun or rain or snow or sleet and paint the scenery. Maybe you know where there are some nice cows. I'd love to paint some cows."

"I'm not sure they'd like it," Mike joked, and he and Rachel laughed. Marcy didn't understand why they both thought it was so funny. It wasn't that great a joke.

"Well, even though we're early, it looks like we'd better get over there," Jim said, trying to herd the little group toward the large number of people gathered around the pavilion.

"Oh! I'm supposed to be manning the helium," Joe said, taking off ahead of them.

"And I'm doing the prayer," Mike said. He grabbed Rachel's hand, and they joined Joe and hurried toward the others.

"C'mon, Ben," Marcy said to her brother, taking him by the hand.

Chapter 39

* * *

We were looking at the clouds and eating celery with peanut butter I had brought from home. "Do you think we're getting too old for playing that we are Indian princesses?" Anna asked. We talked about it, and then we talked about the grand wedding of one of the older neighborhood girls the week before. We had both been there with our families, and I had been horrified to find myself sobbing uncontrollably, embarrassing myself and causing Anna to burst into tears. Karen was the older sophisticated girl in our neighborhood, and she was leaving us and giving up her freedom for some man. We firmly vowed we would continue being Pocahontas and Sacajawea until we were old enough and had enough money to buy a ranch and raise horses.

* * *

Marcy and her family were surprised at the number and variety of people who were there to launch balloons. Some couples seemed much too young to have lost a child, and others seemed too old. One little boy, whose three-year-old sister had recently died from a seizure, sobbed uncontrollably as his mother attempted to console him. His cries cut through the air and pulled down the blanket of despair and grief that many people had tried so valiantly to push away.

The mother looked haunted, with black bruises under her eyes and lips cemented into a down-turned, contorted grimace. She rocked him and crooned, her voice reaching a keening wail at times. Marcy had to look away.

Oh, God, why am I here? Why am I being forced to remember, to have it all flood back because of one little boy's cries? God, how can I do this? Please help me, Father. Please, just help me.

Sharon, watching the emotions washing over Marcy, took her hand. "We don't have to stay. We can leave right now if you need to."

Marcy shook her head then pushed aside the hair that had fallen onto her face. "I'll be okay," she said, watching as two women from the group quickly made their way to the woman and her small son. "If he can be here, so can I."

Rod Lincoln, with Caroline at this side, did a short welcome speech and tried to change the mood of the gathering. He reminded everyone that there was going to be a picnic-type luncheon in the Baptist Church fellowship hall after the balloons were loosed. Everyone was invited, and they didn't have to bring anything, just their appetites. There would be a table set up, he reminded them, to hold photos and mementoes of their loved ones.

Pastor Mike Warren was next, and he said a short prayer, asking God to be with them and to help ease their sorrow and that they would remember that we are all strangers in this land and our real home is in heaven.

"Father, losing a child has to be the greatest sorrow a parent can endure. Thank you for the blessing of memories and for the blessing of time. For some, those who lost infants, it was just a few breaths of time. For others, it was decades. For all of us, those minutes were precious and irreplaceable, and they help get us through the agony and burden of grief. Father, we thank you that through your sacrifice on the cross, we have the hope and promise of eternal life, and we have the assurance that we will be united once again with those we love. We thank you, Lord, for these cherished deceased family members who carved notches on our hearts and who, today, we honor with these balloons and messages. Thank you, Lord, for giving us comfort and solace on this occasion as we share this day of remembrance. Amen."

After his prayer, everyone stood quietly and hushed as his words sunk in. Then they started moving toward the balloons.

Out of deference to her age, a very old woman with a slight limp was called up to be first in line for a balloon. Joe had several dozen already filled with air and tied off to the back of a folding chair. The balloons were Mylar so they wouldn't pop easily, and they were beautiful. Some were shaped like hearts.

The woman, who wore a long maroon quilted jacket and a hand-knitted cap, carefully selected a blue balloon. Well-versed in the routine, she carried it to a nearby table where Caroline and a few others were set up to staple the messages to the string.

"Caroline, I need you to tie this thing to my hand," the woman said loudly. "Remember last time my balloon got away from me just before the launch and I felt so terrible, like I'd cheated or something. It threw off my whole week, that balloon skipping up into the air like that before it was supposed to."

Caroline laughed softly. "Ms. Gladys, it's because of you that we're tying everyone's balloons to their wrists today. You shouldn't feel bad because you taught us a better way of doing things. By looping them on people's wrists, everyone can relax a little bit and not worry about the balloon getting away before it's supposed to."

Gladys held out her hand so Caroline could loop the balloon, with the message attached, over the frail and spotted wrist.

"Well, I guess that's one way to look at it, I suppose," Ms. Gladys said, as she wandered off. She laughed gaily and bobbed her balloon up and down a few times to test its security.

While some people were in line to select a balloon, or at the table to have help in attaching the message, others were seated at long bolted-down picnic tables in the pavilion and dashing off messages. Barbara and Joe and the Petermans were glad that they had taken the time to write their notes beforehand. Maybe people who did this regularly could come and write a quick message, but they all knew the effort and time it took to write their carefully thought-out notes to Anna.

Marcy held back and stood behind her parents and Ben in the balloon line. Joe had given up his post, filling balloons with helium, and he and Barbara were also in line. Except for Ben, they were quiet now, all of them, as the somberness of the event touched them. Ben, along with a few other youngsters who were able to ignore the crying child, was focused on sending his balloon into the heavens.

Barbara and Joe each selected yellow balloons—the color of sunshine, the color their precious Anna loved when she was a toddler. Barbara punched holes in their notes and tied a length of ribbon to each one. Caroline helped attach the ribboned notes to the balloons. Afterwards, they stood away from the rest, the balloons floating above their heads, and looked at each other. "This is hard, this letting go," they said to each other without words.

Jim and Sharon got their balloons without any mishap, but Ben had trouble choosing a color since, he said, Anna liked all the colors. The man handing out the balloons, noting the bag of notes and drawings Ben had for his balloon, let him pick three—red, blue, and yellow—and tied them together. He walked proudly to Caroline's table.

"Three balloons! My goodness, young man, look at all those wonderful messages and notes for Anna. You are going to need three balloons to get this off the ground," Caroline said.

Ben looked at her curiously. "Did you know Anna?"

"No, but I know her parents, and they have become special friends. And I'll bet I know who you are. I'm thinking your name is Ben Peterman," Caroline said as she helped him staple his messages. Before he galloped off, she warned him not to unloop the string from his wrist until they were all told to release their balloons.

Marcy chose a balloon that was dark pink because she knew Anna, with her black hair and flashing dark eyes, looked especially good in pink. After getting the balloon, she held back, and soon, someone else was ahead of her in Caroline's line.

The small letter in her pocket was damp and limp from being handled so much. She looked at it for a long minute and then walked to a nearby, unoccupied, picnic table. She lowered her head and closed her eyes.

She didn't want to launch a balloon. She wasn't ready.

"I know what you're going through," someone said, and she looked up to see Pastor Mike's friend Rachel standing in front of her. Marcy looked at her skeptically. She was a stranger. She didn't even know Marcy, let alone what she was going through.

"Can I sit down?" Rachel asked, and Marcy nodded. She cringed inside, knowing that there were probably a whole bunch of platitudes that were about to come her way. She could write a book, *The Wonderful World of Platitudes* by Marcy Peterman or maybe *Surviving Grief through Platitudes* by Marcy Peterman.

"They all say that, don't they? 'I know what you're going through,' or 'Just give yourself time and it will get easier,' or 'Just look at the good memories you had.' My personal favorite was, 'We're here for you.' I always wondered what that meant. They were going to take it all on? Or maybe they were going to wash my clothes and comb my hair and lead me by the hand through the day?"

Marcy looked at Rachel in surprise and questioning curiosity.

"My sister," Rachel said. "She was fourteen. I was just a year younger. We were both brats and fought like cats and dogs, yelling awful things, and screaming until Mom was ready to pull her hair out. We were frightful teenagers." Rachel smiled at the memory.

"What happened to her?"

"Cancer. She loved to dance and play tennis and baseball and one day she started limping. Mom couldn't see anything. Within a few days, it was worse and Dad checked. He couldn't see anything, either. It got better, and then came back. She had bone cancer and in a few months she was…she was just *gone*. My beautiful, vibrant, wonderful, funny sister was gone."

Rachel couldn't stop the tears that flooded her eyes even though it had happened so many years before. She looked up to see tears in Marcy's eyes. She shrugged her shoulders, took a deep breath, and continued.

"Then, when I was twenty three, I fell madly in love with a handsome, wonderful man named Vincent Pontelli who was in the air force. We hadn't been married a year when he was killed in Iraq. You never really get over it," Rachel added, looking off into the distance. "You learn to cope, and you learn to go on with your life. But there's always a part of you that's back in the past, that stays behind with that person that you loved so much."

"Does it get easier? Do you ever get so you can go through a whole day without that awfulness coming into your head?" Marcy's voice was hoarse and low.

"I promise you, Marcy, that with God's help, it does get easier. Someday, you will remember Anna and be happy with the memories. You will welcome thinking about her and the times you had together."

Rachel turned and looked at Marcy then reached over and tugged at the balloon and watched as it floated gracefully. She turned back and said, "If you aren't ready, don't send up the balloon. You'll know when it's time to let go, and I have the perfect way for you to do that. I'll leave you my phone number. When you are ready, you call, and I'll tell you how you can finally let Anna go."

"Do you think I can just keep the balloon?"

"Honey, I think you can do anything you want. This day is meant for you, for all of you who are here to remember Anna. And for those of us who are here remembering other loved ones."

Chapter 40

Barbara thought she would always bear the image in her mind of all the balloons going up into the sky. She watched her yellow balloon carefully as it floated with the rest, the red ribbon strings dangling and swaying in the wind. When she lost sight of it, she felt a slight panic and then she spotted it again.

The balloons floated in a tight group, but after a bit, some gained speed while others drifted and floated to the left or right. Surprisingly, her balloon and Joe's stayed side by side, bumping each other occasionally.

In just a short time the balloons were mere specks in the sky, floating endlessly upward beyond the vision of those on the ground. She didn't know she was crying until she saw the tears on Joe's cheeks and touched her hands to her own face.

They held each other, their cheeks touching, as they continued to gaze up into the sky.

All those who were there to honor Anna's memory were thankful for little Ben, who was full of nine-year-old exuberance. His trio of balloons, burdened with the heavy missive for Anna, wallowed in the sky and slowly—far behind the others—made their way upward. He had used a black marker to put a smiley face on each balloon, and long after the others had disappeared, they could see Ben's smiley faces looking down on them.

"Oh, how Anna would have loved your balloons," Barbara told him, turning from Joe to give him a big hug.

"Mine were the very best," he said proudly. Then he noticed Marcy, standing nearby with Rachel and still holding her pink balloon.

"Hey, why didn't you send up your balloon?" he asked.

Sharon walked over to Marcy and put her arm around her shoulder before addressing him.

"She still has to work on her letter to Anna. She'll send up her balloon someday. For now, she just needs to keep it for a while longer." Marcy looked at mother in gratitude.

Mike came over to Rachel and looked at her with compassion. Just as he knew about her deceased husband, he knew the story of her sister's death so many years before. He also knew that this was the first time she had ever taken part in a balloon launch and that it had been difficult for her. He was very thankful that she had taken the time to talk to Marcy.

After conversing for a few minutes, they all walked to their vehicles and headed to the church with all the others. The Petermans and Pastor Mike and Rachel were surprised at how easily they fit in with this diverse group and how easy it was to talk to these people. Maybe it was because they didn't have to hide behind any sort of façade and had learned to face life head-on. They cut through the trivialities of life and went straight for what was important.

The memorial table was difficult to look at. So many youngsters. Some were newborns, and others were teenagers or older. Some were adults. They were all beautiful children of God. It was hard to comprehend that they were all dead. Barbara and Joe had brought a collage frame with a dozen photos of Anna in a variety of poses.

Marcy pored over them, going back again and again to look. Barbara decided they would make copies to give to her.

By the time the day was over, they were all emotionally exhausted, and when Mike and Rachel suggested they go bowling, they all, at first, thought it was a bizarre idea. But after the first few balls, they decided this was just what they needed, to work off some of the emotion of the day.

"I thought you said you knew how to bowl," Rachel teased Mike after his third gutter ball in a row.

"It's you," he declared. "You get me all befuddled! I'm wondering if I can't even bowl, how I'm ever going to preach tomorrow morning."

Rachel looked at him in mock dismay.

"Oh, yeah, I'd forgotten you're the preacher. I suppose that means we have to go to church?"

"Heathen," he said, laughing.

Everyone laughed, but inside they all were wondering the same thing: what would members of Danford Worship Center think of Rachel Pontelli.

Chapter 41

Rachel was quiet as they drove out of Danford after leaving the bowling alley. He knew that she was thinking about the balloon launch and her sister and her deceased husband, Vince.

"I'm proud of you," he told her, reaching over to take her hand. "It takes courage, I think, to write letters to those you loved so deeply and to set them loose to float toward heaven."

"It's funny that it was so hard. But it was good too. Like a release. There will always be a part of me that loves Vince and that time of my life when I was young and everything seemed possible. But Jenny…Sometimes, I can't believe how much I miss her. The night after I met you, I'd have given anything if we could have sat cross-legged on her bed and I could have told her all about you."

"Yeah, she would probably have said, 'Rachel, girl, are you craaazy?'"

"No, she wouldn't have said that. She would have gotten this dreamy look in her eye and said you sounded too good to be true. She always was a little goofy when it came to boys."

"Boys, is it. I'm a boy?"

"Yes, and a very cute one. And I wish, cute boy, that you'd tell me where we are going."

"We, my dear Rachel, are going to my house. You need to meet my mutt."

"I wondered if you were going to introduce us," she said.

"I planned on doing the big introduction thing last night, but it got too late after dinner at Joe and Barbara's. Danford is a small town, and if we'd have gone to my house at eleven at night, someone would have spotted us and started who-knows-what rumor."

"You're right, and I appreciate you being so honest. The most important thing, right now, is to be totally above reproach or gossip."

"Oh, we'll never escape the gossip, but I sure don't want to give them something juicy to chew on," Mike said, laughing.

Mike's house on Danford Lake was spacious and beautiful and obviously extremely expensive. It was an older house with a very tall two-story front, which housed the living room and kitchen. To either side of the middle living area were two wings for bedrooms, a work-out room, office, and other rooms. In the living room, floor-to-ceiling windows faced a huge tile patio and, beyond that, the lake.

Mike acted uncomfortable while showing her the house, and after the tour, they ended up in the living room, where she went from one wall to the next, studying original oil paintings. She recognized most of the names and realized that he had a fortune in artwork. There was another fortune in sculptures, ancient books, antiques, and gorgeous Oriental carpets.

"I think I need to explain something to you, and I don't know quite how to do it," he said. She was immediately alarmed.

"Is it really bad?" she asked, turning quickly to face him. She loved him so much and knew he loved her. She was suddenly terrified that there might be something so amiss that they would have to part ways. She didn't think she could bear it.

"You probably won't think it's really bad. I just need to be honest with you."

"So be honest with me. What's going on, Mike?"

"I'm just going to come right out and to say it, all right?" he said, moving away from her and leaning against a sofa table that was nestled against a white couch facing the lake. He looked at her somberly. "My family is very wealthy. I'm the black sheep who went into the ministry and tried to get away from all the hoopla—the endless parties and the fancy clothes and shallow façade. My grandfather never quite forgave me, and my mother never understood. My grandmother though, she loved the Lord with all her heart, and she encouraged me greatly until she died last year."

"I don't know what to say. You declare you're rich, and instead of being thrilled for you, I feel like should tell you how sorry I am about that."

"You should feel sorry. Money brings with it responsibility and skewed ideas from others and sometimes puts you in situations you don't want to be in. Most people dream of having wealth, but it can be very ugly. It brings out the worst in people."

"But it can also be used for such good," Rachel protested.

"That's true, and that's why I haven't totally turned my back on my inheritance. I have established foundations and quietly do as much good as I can. Most people in the church know about my family as well as my family history because it figures into the history of Montana. But they also know that I live on a pastor's salary. I inherited this house and the contents from my grandmother. What I own myself, I could probably put in the back of my Explorer.

"My grandmother was the light of my life," he continued, "and we spent hours discussing the Bible. She was the one who gave me the courage to follow my calling—to do God's work. I will be forever grateful that God put her in my life and made her a bridge that led from my upbringing to my destiny.

"I wanted you to know," he added, "because you are going to meet my family, and I wanted to warn you ahead of time. They can be...well, sort of overbearing. You will probably like my dad. He's kind and isn't judgmental. My mother can be difficult, and they do have their own world. They tease me about my Explorer. My mother would never have a dog like Midas because he isn't registered and worth $5,000."

"Oh, those poor people," Rachel declared, "to not want a dog like Midas." She flopped on the floor beside the dog and reached over to flip his left ear back and forth. Then she looked at Mike.

"Mike, in my lifetime, I have known all sorts of people. Rich ones, poor ones, ugly ones, beautiful ones. People who were sad, people who were happy, and people who had so many problems you wondered how they got through life. On missions trips, I have seen death and poverty and suffering as well as wealth and extravagance beyond imagination. Through it all, I learned one thing—that God loves all his children and if you remove all of what we have and we stand naked, we are all the same. We all need his love and his forgiveness. I am no more, and no less, than any other person. So I figure that these people are your family, and for that reason alone, I know I will love them."

While listening to her talk, Mike felt his heart swell, and he thanked God for the thousandth time for this woman named Rachel.

"Thank you," he said gruffly, his heart swelling with tenderness.

"You're welcome," she said, and then she looked at him mischievously. "Can I borrow twenty bucks?"

Chapter 42

Midas had decided that Rachel Pontelli was the most wonderful thing to come along since dog biscuits. She, upon meeting him, thought he was the goofiest looking dog she'd ever seen, but she quickly succumbed to his charm and fell madly in love with him.

Mike was thrilled that she liked his dog. It was a big test. He knew she was a cat person, at least that was what she said. Knowing her penchant for gentle teasing, she might be just saying that since she knew he wasn't a cat person.

"I learned a while back that my great-grandmother had over a dozen cats when she was a kid," Rachel told him while sitting on the floor with Midas's head in her lap. She scratched behind his ears and stroked his side. Midas groaned in sheer pleasure.

"She adored them. Every night, they slept with her. Of course, that was during the Depression, and in the winter, the water in the water bucket would freeze solid, and they piled clothes on the bed to keep warm. No wonder she liked her cats."

"I'd take twenty dogs any day," Mike said. "Cats know I don't like them, and that's why they always leap into my lap and purr and nuzzle my neck and do that kneading thing on my chest. They try to win me over. It never works. You don't have a cat, do you, Rachel?"

"Not now. But I'm thinking of getting one. Maybe two, so they can keep each other company. Maybe a male and female so they can have kittens."

"Okay, I have to admit I used to like cats," Mike conceded. "I grew up with cats and dogs and horses, and the cats were always the ones that were there for me. Maybe because Mom wouldn't let the horses in the house and the dogs were usually banned too. That left the cats. My sisters dressed them in doll clothes and pushed them in doll buggies. We brushed them in the dark and watched the sparks shoot from their bodies."

"Well, that's mean."

"They liked it."

"Oh, sure they did."

"Now that I have Midas, I don't think I'd want another cat. It would be hard to have an animal that didn't have that idolization gene, and face it, cats just don't have that quality. Have you ever known a cat that would be content to just sit and gaze at your face or would jump into an ice-laden river to save your sorry soul?"

"You think Midas would jump into a river for you?" Rachel laughed and then added, "Maybe if you had a handful of dog biscuits."

"Okay, think about this. Cats also don't share your hobbies. Have you ever known a cat that would leap into a mucky pond to fetch the duck you just shot or would sit in a freezing goose blind gazing into the predawn dark to search out the first goose of the morning? Try to tell a cat to 'sit' and 'stay.'"

"You shoot geese and ducks?

"Well, no, but I'm trying to make a point. And think about this. I can put Midas's bowl on top of the refrigerator, and he'll never know it's there. There's no place, except under lock and key or in the refrigerator, to place a cat bowl. They can get on top of the chandelier if they want to. No place is safe. Cat people will say this is a sign of intelligence. I think they're just sneaky."

"I have to admit," Rachel said, running her fingers underneath the red collar around Midas's neck, "that dogs are loyal, but cats do bring presents. Pumpkin, the pretty orange cat of my youth, was always bringing me dead mice or birds and expecting high praise for her thoughtfulness. She was a wonderful cat."

Rachel gave Midas a big hug. "But as nice as Pumpkin was, I don't think she was nearly as nice as Midas here. You're just a sweet fellow, aren't you, Midas?"

"Sure, he is," Mike said, "even with the hair all over the house, the commotion, the puddles from the water bowl, and the fact that a guy can't even go to the bathroom without him standing by. He hovers. He watches. If I move, he moves. If I roll over in bed too quickly, he thinks it's time to get up and gallops around the room like he's demented, not even noticing that the clock says 3:00 a.m."

"You sleep with him?"

"What?"

"You sleep with this dog?" Rachel burst into laughter.

Mike looked sheepish. "Well, only when he's depressed or unhappy."

"Depressed or unhappy? This is the most stable and happy being in the room!"

"Hey, I'm pretty happy," he said. "In fact, I'm downright happy. I've never been happier. Midas, move over."

He got down on the floor and sat beside her.

Chapter 43

Mike had, of course, given Rachel a tour of Danford Worship Center the afternoon she arrived in Danford. The church was large for so small a town and beautiful with a big auditorium and a platform that was designed to put on special events, such as Christmas pageants. Three very tall brass crosses, in differing heights, were centered on the back wall, and on either side, there were floor-to-ceiling stained glass windows. The effect was stunning. Rachel could only imagine the beauty of these windows when the sun shone through them.

During their time together in Victoria, he had never given her the sense that he pastored a large church, only that he loved the people in his flock and his ministry to them. She learned that nearly five hundred people were on the church membership rolls, and according to Joe and Barbara Miller, Pastor Mike Warren was much-loved and respected and known for his compassion and caring, and for his good humor and crazy antics.

On Sunday morning, Rachel and the Millers got to church early so that she could be introduced to the office staff. Rachel had dressed carefully, and she was surprised at how nervous she was. She was used to leading meetings with dozens of people and traveling around the world to minister to people in incredibly remote and dangerous places. And here she was, worried about meeting a woman named Violet Lemke and others who worked with Mike on a daily basis as well as an entire congregation that would view her with suspicious and probing eyes.

They had barely gotten through the door when Violet rushed up to greet them. She gave Rachel a big hug, and Rachel was surprised that the small bird-like woman had such strength in her old bony arms.

"Welcome to Danford, my dear," she said as she pulled Rachel away from Barbara and Joe and led her away to meet "the rest of the gang." Rachel allowed herself to be led but turned around and sent Barbara an explicit "help me" look. Barbara grinned and waved, but then she said loudly, "We're right behind you. We'll catch up." Rachel was infinitely grateful for these new friends.

Mike was in his office and apologized for not meeting her at the door. He'd had an emergency counseling session with a church member.

"But I see you're in good hands with Violet," he said, smiling at the older woman and gently removing Rachel from her clutches.

Within minutes, there was a whirlwind of introductions, and Rachel tried valiantly to remember everyone. She amazed people, however, at her ability to remember their names. The night before, Barbara had given her the church directory that contained the names and photos of most of the congregation, and Rachel had spent hours poring over the booklet.

Barbara caught her eye after she was introduced to a family of six and smiled as Rachel said, "Let's see if I get this right," and rattled off everyone's name perfectly. Violet beamed as if she herself had produced this perfect person for her pastor.

Just then, the thunder of footsteps sounded, and Ben ran up to her. His parents, Marcy, and an older gentleman followed.

"It's the Petermans!" Rachel declared and hugged each one in turn. By then, Mike had circled behind her and was gripping the hand of the fellow who was with the family.

"Henry, I am so glad to see you here this morning," he said.

"Marcy, here, asked me to come to church a while back, and I got up this morning and thought, 'Well, why not?' So here I am," Henry Knutson said.

"And he's going to sit with us too," Ben declared. "And maybe come over for lunch afterwards."

"Well, I don't know about that," Henry Knutson said. He was clearly embarrassed.

Sharon came to his rescue. "We would love to have you," she said. "Rachel and Pastor Mike are heading to Great Falls, but Joe and Barbara will be there. It would be wonderful if you could join us."

"Well, maybe," he said as he fingered his battered cap.

Just as they were about to go into the sanctuary, a familiar voice reached Rachel's ears, and she turned to see Katherine O'Malley approaching her.

The two women, both beautiful despite differing ages, hugged. "I thought you might need my moral support," Katherine whispered. "They can get along without me at my church for one Sunday."

"I'm so happy you are here," Rachel said, smiling at the elderly woman. Although she barely knew Katherine O'Malley, it was indeed a comfort to have her beside her.

Rachel felt very protected as they entered the sanctuary. She was surrounded by these people she had met and fallen in love with. When she sat down, it was with Marcy on one side and Katherine on the other.

Most people didn't pay much attention since the word that she was Pastor Mike's special friend hadn't reached every ear. But among the spinster/mama crowd, word had definitely traveled quickly. Some of these women at first were almost hostile underneath their surface politeness. However, within minutes, they warmed up to Rachel when they realized she was kind, gentle, and loved the Lord as much as their pastor. They would have to simply search elsewhere for eligible males. But, oh, Pastor Mike would have been so perfect and would have been such a wonderful addition to their families.

While there were some eyes on her at first, there were many eyes on her when Pastor Mike finished his opening comments and had her stand. He told his congregation who she was, how they met, and that he had invited her to Danford for a few days. He carefully stressed that she was staying with Joe and Barbara.

It was what he didn't say that had everyone watching her throughout the rest of the service. She was obviously very special for him to have invited her to Danford, and then to go off after church to meet his family? My, my…

Despite the fact that someone was always watching her, Rachel was delighted to find the worship service was perfect and just what she wanted—many beautiful praise songs and a couple of old familiar hymns with a modern twist. She felt her heart swell with love for her Lord, and soon, she was in that familiar place where everything else was blocked out, and it was just her and Jesus.

Mike's sermon was wonderful: funny, thought-provoking, insightful, and made her consider the subject of gifts and talents from a different angle. She knew, from hearing him speak, that the words weren't those of Mike Warren but were planted in his heart by the Holy Spirit. If she loved him before, she loved him doubly now that she saw his faith in action and realized how very much he cherished being a servant of God.

During the final hymn, when he walked toward the back of the church to meet his congregation, he stopped along the way and reached for Rachel's hand. When she was by his side, he reached in and asked Katherine to join them.

As Katherine stepped out into the aisle, she smiled conspiratorially at him, letting him know that she thought it was a brilliant move. As the matriarch of Danford, having her blessing would save Mike and Rachel all sorts of grief.

Within a short amount of time, the majority of the flock had filed through, shaking their hands, commenting on the sermon, greeting Katherine O'Malley, and welcoming Rachel to Danford.

Barbara and Joe told Rachel they would see her the next day, after their trip to visit Mike's parents, and Marcy gave her a surprisingly long hug.

Marcy didn't know how to say what was in her heart, but Rachel waited patiently even though there were several old women waiting to chat with her.

"Thank you, for yesterday," Marcy said, shrugging her shoulders and looking at the floor.

Rachel ducked down so she could look in Marcy's face. "You're welcome, for yesterday," she said. "And thank you. It was good for me to talk about things, and I appreciate your listening to me. I think we helped each other."

Marcy looked at her and smiled and nodded her head. "Will I see you before you leave for Seattle?"

"I don't know. Maybe. We get back Monday night, and I fly out Wednesday morning. I'll tell you what. If we get in at a reasonable time, I'll call you, and maybe you can come down to Joe and Barbara's and say good-bye. Will that work?"

Marcy nodded.

Chapter 44

By plan, Rachel had brought her suitcase to Danford Worship Center and placed it in the back of Mike's Explorer. His suitcase was already there, and she was surprised to see that their luggage almost matched. They both had red luggage. For some reason, that fact warmed her heart. She smiled. *Another sign, Lord?*

One of the deacons would tidy up the pews, throw away leftover bulletins and other items left behind, and lock up after everyone left. That left Rachel and Mike free to leave as soon as the receiving line came to an end and there were no more people seeking him out. By 2:00 p.m., they were driving through Danford and were on their way toward Great Falls and his family.

Midas, Joe had declared the day before, would be too rambunctious for his mother, so he was staying with Joe and Barbara. Rachel was sad that the goofy bumpkin dog wasn't making the trip with them.

Exhilarated at being with Mike, and actually taking a road trip with him, put a joyous smile on Rachel's face, but it soon broadened for another reason. She thought she had never seen a more magnificent country. Endless fields nestled against tall mountains, rivers, creeks, and towns with names like Whitefish, Columbia Falls, Coram, and Hungry Horse.

At Mike's suggestion, they took a few minutes and drove to Hungry Horse Dam, and she was enthralled. On one side of the dam was Hungry Horse Reservoir, a huge body of water that washed up against wooded hills and mountains. The other side was a different story.

Peeking quickly over the edge made her half-sick and dizzy and brought a gut-quivering feeling of terror. The base of the curved arch of the dam was hundreds of feet below, and she gripped the thick cement wall tightly. Far below, vehicles parked on a cement apron looked like toys. Next to the vehicles, the released water from the dam was deep blue, and if she looked downstream, there was a small cascade of falls before the river wandered around a corner.

There was a brisk wind on top of the dam, and she was shivering as they dashed back to Mike's vehicle. He started the engine and turned the heat on high. Then he got out and went to the back door and opened it and removed a huge bag. Before they left the parking lot, they went through the giant bag of snacks.

"Good grief, what is this junk?" she asked, peering into the bag.

"Road trip food."

"Also known as heart attack food. Candy bars? Trail mix? Let's see what else. Chips and cheese dip, peanuts, pepperoni sticks. Pork rinds? Are you kidding me? Are you trying to kill us both?"

Grinning at her, Mike offered a weak protest. "There's fruit in there too."

Rachel pushed up the sleeves on her sweater in an exaggerated gesture, flipped back her hair, and leaned forward. "Oh, let me dig a little deeper. Past the jerky and chocolate. Oh, wait, here they are. Grapes. Five or six little green grapes. Whew! And I thought you didn't understand the concept of nutrition." She leaned back in mock relief, and Mike laughed at her.

"There is no such thing as healthy on a road trip. You forget about nutrition on a road trip."

"I guess some people do."

"So, Ms. Rachel, what is your idea of traveling food?"

"Well, it certainly isn't anything like this. In the first place, you forgot the cookies and the pop. And where, pray tell, are the Twinkies?"

Back on the main highway, Mike explained their route. Unfortunately, because of snow in the high country, it wasn't possible to go the scenic way through Glacier Park on the Going to the Sun Highway, so they would stick to Highway 2, the less scenic route. Still, Rachel was delighted with the towering rugged peaks, tumbling creeks, and thick strong trees.

Truthfully, Rachel didn't care if they were driving through a mine field as long as she could be with Mike. The highway climbed higher and higher through the mountains, and they spotted elk and deer. Soon, they were at an altitude where the oxygen-starved aspens were dwarfed and spindly and grotesquely misshapen from the endless wind and bitter cold of winter.

Mike gave a history of the country and Glacier National Park and said that Browning was the next town they would see. It was on the Blackfoot Indian Reservation, and they could eat there if she'd like. There was a little café that had wonderful food, including homemade French fries.

The highway continued to climb, and then suddenly, in what seemed to be a flash of time, they were out of the mountains and on a hill. Mike pulled over as far as he could off the road, and Rachel quickly got out of the car. The wind grabbed her hair and sent it flying, and she threw up her hand to hold it down so it wouldn't whip into her face. Her eyes were filled with wonder.

"I wondered what your reaction would be," Mike said as he came to stand behind her. He put his arms around her middle and pulled her close, not so much to keep her warm but to have her close to him. "It's amazing, isn't it? After being in the mountains for so many miles and suddenly breaking through and seeing this vast and gorgeous prairieland? It's wide open Big Sky country. The Blackfoot Indian Reservation is down there, and Browning, and wild ponies that race with the wind across the grasslands."

He joined her in silence for a few minutes, just looking at the tremendous view in front of them, and then he spoke again. "When I was young, we spent a lot of time on both sides of the divide, lots of time in Flathead Valley, where Dad had business, and then we'd go home to Great Falls. My grandmother was part Indian, at least a few drops of Indian blood in her, and each time we came to this spot, where she could see the wondrously vast prairie spread out before her, she would cry. She would put her hands to her face and bawl. And each time, she'd say through her tears, 'I feel like I'm coming home.' I don't know how many hours we spent in the museum in Browning, soaking up and renewing the culture that seemed to be steeped deep in our bones. For me, it was like coming home too."

"Do we have time to stop there? At the museum?"

"We can on the way back if you'd like. It's a great museum and has wonderful dioramas. When I was a kid, I could stand for hours looking at them and imagining how wonderful it must have been to live that simple lifestyle. They have displays of traditional Indian clothing and artwork and cooking and hunting gear.

"It is called the Museum of the Plains Indians and doesn't just feature the Blackfeet but all the Indians of the plains—the Crow, Cheyenne, Sioux, Arapaho, Chippewa, and all the rest. I've always been fascinated by the Indian culture, and I love the little town of Browning. Like Anna and Marcy, I spent a lot of my childhood pretending I was an Indian."

She broke free and turned to look at him. "Don't you miss it? All this? Living on the prairie?"

He shrugged his shoulders and smiled. "Great Falls is wheat country—endless acres of wheat fields and not so much untouched prairie. But it's still beautiful, and there is still a tremendous history there. Besides, Danford is where God wants me, and I spent a lot of my childhood there. It really doesn't matter where God has me live because I know I'll be contented and peaceful and happy wherever that is."

He reached up and pulled a strand of hair out of her eyes. Then he put his arm around her shoulder to shield her from the bitter wind. They stood there for many minutes looking out on the prairie.

Chapter 45

Even though it was dark when they got there, the first thing Rachel thought when she and Mike drove up to the big house at the Rocking W Ranch was that she was on the set of the old television series *Bonanza*. She expected Joe and Hoss and Ben Cartwright to stride out on the veranda with their spurs clinking and lift their hats to her in greeting.

Instead, a busty matronly woman with a light brown bob and wearing blue jeans with a red-and-white checked shirt tucked into the waistband came out on the veranda. After giving her son a big hug, she took Rachel by the shoulders, looked at her searchingly for a second, and then after seeming to make an instant decision, let her arms drop and held out her hand.

"Rachel?" she asked, as if Mike brought home so many females she wasn't sure which one this one was. Mike put his arm around Rachel protectively. He had misgivings about bringing Rachel to meet his parents, but he knew it had to be done eventually, and the timing had worked out nicely. He had also spent a lot of time in prayer, and he knew God was with them both.

Abby Warren talked a mile a minute about anything and every-thing, but Rachel knew by instinct that beneath the shallow surface, there was a woman who was strong and as smart as a whip as well as manipulative and conniving. Plus, she was a woman who didn't much like the fact that there was any other female besides herself in her son's life.

She apologized that Mike's dad, Davis Warren, wasn't on the porch to meet them but his back was out of whack after tearing up the countryside in his Jeep the day before. She had him on the couch with a hot pad.

They headed inside the house, and somehow, Abby maneuvered them so that Rachel was behind and she and Mike, with her arm around his waist, were ahead. They didn't go two feet before Mike stopped and went back to walk with Rachel. Rachel saw the older woman's shoulders stiffen.

"So I understand you work in a homeless shelter. That must be hard, caring for those poor drunks, and it certainly must not pay well. I'm surprised you can afford decent shoes," Abby said, glancing at Rachel's slender feet before opening the front door.

"Mother, you know very well where she works—with the chairman of Hope Ministries. She makes enough money to provide well for herself. She probably has enough leftover each month to buy a Big Mac. Maybe even French fries," Mike said, looking at Rachel and rolling his eyes.

Rachel could feel the tension, and while she appreciated Mike coming to her defense, she was concerned that he was ruffling his mother's very elegant feathers. She decided to get the conversation back to a less volatile state.

"You have a beautiful home, Mrs. Warren," Rachel said, looking around in admiration as they were taking off their coats in the massive foyer.

"Well, one must live up to one's station and breeding," Abby said. Rachel didn't know how to respond. She looked at Mike, and his eyes twinkled ever so slightly, and suddenly, she was choking back laughter that ended in a loud snort. His shoulders were silently shaking with unspent mirth, and Rachel was horrified that they had both shown such a breach in manners.

Abby wheeled, and her eyes were blazing with anger. "Do you think that's funny, or are you just simple-minded?"

"One more word, Mother, or one more snide remark, and we will be back in the car and headed back to Danford before you can explain to Dad why we left without coming in the house. You owe both of us an apology, and we will give you thirty seconds to deliver or we're gone. I prayed about coming here for two weeks straight, and I finally decided you had the right to meet the woman I love and she had the right to meet you. I am praying that I am doing the right thing coming here."

Rachel started to protest, saying it was all right, but Mike held her tight to his side as he looked at his mother with determination and decision. "Well?"

"Oh, all right. I apologize. There, are you happy?"

"If that's the best you can do, we'll accept it."

While Abby was taking their coats to another room, Mike pulled Rachel into his arms. "My mother can be…well, she can be my mother. Just remember, sweetheart, that we're in this thing together, and I love you. Nothing is going to change that."

Rachel's eyes flooded with gratitude. "Thank you. I love you too, Mike."

Abby returned just as they were breaking the embrace. Her lips tightened, and she simply said, "Humph" and shook her head.

The living room of the Rocking W "Big House," as Rachel termed it in her mind, was what she thought a hunting lodge must look like: huge with a massive rock fireplace and groupings of leather furniture; on the walls were mounts of elk and deer, moose, and a massive buffalo; and carpets on the slate floor were in bright hues and accented the original Western art on the walls.

In a corner of the room, Davis Warren was flat on his back on a long brown leather couch. Before he said a word, Rachel liked him. He looked like a man who'd had to battle his whole life to get what he wanted, and she had the idea that living with his wife was truly the biggest conflict he'd ever faced. He was handsome, with a shock of graying hair and a tan complexion that came from spending time outside. His eyes were like Mike's—twinkling and kind, with laugh lines at the corners.

Rachel begged him not to get up. Instead, she shook his hand warmly and sat on a loveseat that faced him. Mike sat beside her and took her hand. The three of them chatted easily with Abby frequently asking a pointed question that added a jarring note to the conversation.

Rachel knew that Abby Warren was studying her like a scientist with a new specimen in his lab, but surprisingly, she was relaxed and answered her probing questions carefully.

And oh my did she have questions. Dozens of them. And each one was answered thoughtfully and truthfully. *But*, Rachel declared to herself, *if she asks me if I like sex, that's going to go too far.*

"Oh, the pie!" Abby said, leaping to her feet and hurrying to the kitchen, which Rachel thought must be about a block away since the house was so immense. "Michael, come help me," she ordered, and Mike got up to follow her, patting Rachel on the shoulder as he left.

Mike got to his feet and let out a loud breath. "Time for the inquisition," he whispered.

"The housekeeper took that pie out of the oven three hours ago," his father said, shaking his head. "Hang in there, son."

Rachel added a chipper, "Good luck!" even though she knew they would be talking about her and Abby Warren probably wasn't going to be too kind. Mike had said that his parents had protested his going into the ministry, saying that he needed to stay in the family

242

business, and she now appreciated the torment his mother must have caused him.

She was soon to learn that Davis Warren could be as forthright as his wife. She noticed for the first time that his graying hair had been cut perfectly. She imagined he'd probably had the same hair stylist for years. She knew from Mike that he was sharp in business and astute when it came to assessing the future of business.

She talked about the ride over from Danford, and he listened politely. Then he moved himself up to one elbow and looked at her. "Why do you love him?" She looked at him in surprise. Most people would have asked, "*Do* you love him?" which would have been a quick and easy yes.

"How do I love him, let me count the ways," she mused in paraphrase as she pondered his question. She settled back and started to tell him. "That's best explained if I tell you how we met," she said. She talked at length about their time at the Hope Ministries meetings and his horror at the plight of people around the world. She told him about their time at Butchart Gardens and about her first husband and his death.

Then she leaned forward and clasped her hands in front of her. "Have you ever had an experience when something just seems so perfectly right that time itself seems to stand still? When you knew that after that one breath of time, things will never be the same? I had decided that I would never marry again, and I would devote myself to trying to do a little bit of good in the world. But Mike and I are like two magnets who wandered the world until we got close enough to find each other. It's just…right! Helen Keller once said something like, 'The best and most beautiful things in this world cannot be seen or even heard, but must be felt with the heart.'"

She smiled and said sincerely, "Your son is a good man, a kind man, and a man who loves God with all his heart. He is the man I want to grow old with and, if God so chooses to bless us, to have children with."

Rachel could feel her face flaming. "I'm sorry. I can't believe I rattled on so."

Davis leaned over and put out his hand, and she got up from the loveseat and kneeled on the floor and took it in hers. "Don't apologize," he said, holding it tightly. "You answered my question with your heart, and I appreciate your truthfulness. You should never apologize for love."

Neither of them heard Abby Warren and Mike come back into the living room. Mike laughed at the sight. "So you're dumping me for my old man?" he asked in mock seriousness.

"Yup. I think he's pretty wonderful," Rachel said, leaning over to kiss Davis on the cheek, which made him blush.

"If it wasn't for this bum back, I might run away with her," Davis teased his son. Abby, looking on, didn't think any of the exchange was funny. Abby looked as if the tussle in the kitchen had left her the loser, and Rachel was thankful that Mike stood up for her and their love. Still, in her heart, she felt bad for Abby. She hoped that what she had told Davis would reach Abby's ear and she might think more of Mike's choice in a life mate.

Without saying anything, Abby had evidently decided to declare a truce, and the rest of the evening was pleasant and even enjoyable. Rachel learned more about the Rocking W and all the assets under that umbrella as well as the family history and some family exploits. They in turn learned about Rachel's childhood, her first marriage to Vince, and her job at Hope Ministries. Most important of all, they learned that she loved the Lord with all her heart and she was a perfect match for Mike.

Before they went to their separate bedrooms for the night, even Abby had grudgingly and guardedly accepted this new woman into the family.

Chapter 46

* * *

Anna and I were riding on Kemo's back late in the summer, with me hanging on to her waist. Sabe, the colt, was prancing happily alongside. Suddenly, Kemo snorted and sashayed sideways, and we spotted something moving in the grass. Anna was terrified it was a snake even though we'd only seen a few and those had been near the creek.

I slid off the horse and cautiously walked over to see. It was a small squirrel, fully furred-out but not quite the size of an adult. We didn't know how he'd gotten there, unless he'd knocked himself stupid by running into a tree. He was alive but obviously stunned. We were worried he'd be eaten by wild animals, although we had seen nothing more dangerous than a rabbit on Rice's Hill, or that he'd succumb to the weather, although it was in the eighties. We decided to keep him, and I rolled him up in my T-shirt, and we walked home. By the time we got to my house, we had named him Elvis.

My mom peered carefully at the listless little fellow before putting him in a box with a bit of cat food and water. By the next morning, he was fully recovered and trying to escape. Anna and I carried the box and Elvis back to Rice's Hill. Putting it on the ground between us, we lifted up the lid and peered in. Elvis stared at us with his black eyes and then leaped to the top of the box. He stood there looking at us, twitching his whiskers and tail, before streaking off through the grass and zipping up a tree. Even though we knew he deserved to be free, we felt bad. We wanted to keep him.

* * *

Even though it was over a month old, the pink Mylar balloon in Marcy's room was still puffy with helium and seemed to have a life of its own. It always gravitated to a place right above her bed. In the middle of the night, she could see it looking faded gray with the dim residue light in the room and bobbing gently as the sleeping house breathed in and out.

She could put the balloon in the family room, and it would eventually drift down the hall, turn the corner, and float slowly through the doorway to take up its post. She took it downstairs and put it in the formal dining room, and four days later when she got home from school, there it was, hovering gently above her bed.

She wished Anna was still alive so she could talk to her about the possessed balloon because no one else thought it was as strange as she did.

Her father told her that one of the front office girls had gotten a birthday balloon once and the thing wandered all over the building. No one ever moved it; it just sort of crept along and went from office to office and even, one time, out into the shop. Finally, it disappeared; maybe, he said, it followed a customer home. "Mylar balloons are just like that," he said, and he went back to reading his paper.

The balloon was her nemesis. She had dragged the thing home from the balloon launch because she didn't want to set it—and Anna—free. That day, she brought it to her room and whapped it around like a punching bag, half hoping it would explode and she

246

would be free of it. She shook it and slapped it and threw things at it, but it was stronger than her will to break it.

Now it followed her, haunting her in it pinkness. She was sure if she locked it in the closet, it would find a way out, so she just learned to live with it, maybe just like she was learning to live with the absence of Anna.

She knew she had changed over the months. The hellhole of grief had been shoved aside by anger, and now, little by little, she was simply accepting things as they were. That didn't mean she didn't have her moments, but she figured she might always have those. The sickening reality of the brutal death had subsided, and the jagged edges of the memory were softening with time.

All the way around, things were getting better. She had reestablished a good relationship with her family, it was getting close to Christmas break, her grades were picking up, and she was starting to interact again with her classmates.

Marcy knew she was getting close to the time when she would call Rachel Pontelli in Seattle and ask her for the secret of letting go.

She frequently thumbed through the photos Anna's parents had given her, and with her mother's help, she had taken several of them to Wal-Mart and had them enlarged. She and her mom then purchased frames and spent the afternoon putting the photos in mats and hanging them on her wall.

Two of them were her favorites—one of Anna smiling with her head tilted goofily to one side and one of Kemo. The horse didn't look at all matronly in the photo. It was as if she knew she was being photographed. She had posed proudly, with one leg lifted and the foot bent at the first joint. Her beautiful chestnut color was vibrant in the sun and complimented the tail and mane that were the color of newly-threshed wheat.

Sharon Peterman stood in the doorway watching her daughter as she concentrated on her watercolor painting, dipping the brush in the water and dabbing it on a paper towel before putting the brush to paper. She was so intent on her painting she hadn't heard her mother's first greeting.

Sharon waited until Marcy's hand was away from the paper before talking again, this time more loudly.

"So what are you working on, sweetie?" As predicted, Marcy was startled and jumped a full inch from her chair.

"I'm sorry. I didn't mean to scare you. I'm just wondering if I can come in."

"Sure."

"Can I see your painting?"

Marcy moved the water and paints and slid the heavy watercolor paper across the desk. She had done the same painting a half dozen times, but she just couldn't get it to capture what she wanted to. "It isn't very good," she said, shaking her head in frustration.

Sharon considered it carefully. "I think it's very good," she said.

Marcy snorted and rolled her eyes. "That's because you're my mother. You thought my plaster handprint when I was four belonged in a museum."

"I'm still waiting for them to call," Sharon said. "But seriously, Marcy, this is very good. Kemo looks dashing, and you have matched the colors perfectly."

"I just can't seem to get across how alive Kemo was. It's like doing a paint-by-number. All the colors are there in all the right places, but I can't get it to show Kemo's personality. She was a wonderful horse, and on paper, she just looks like any old horse."

Sharon cocked her head and considered Marcy's words. "You really loved that horse, didn't you? You and Anna?"

Marcy nodded her head. "It sounds awful, but sometimes, I cry more over losing Kemo than Anna. Isn't that awful? And Kemo was over two years ago."

"No, that doesn't sound awful. Kemo made that summer magical and exciting. That summer, you and Anna truly were Indian princesses riding the prairie with abandon. Besides, I grew up with horses, so I know all about loving a horse. A person who has had a good horse in his life has been truly blessed."

"That sounds like something Mr. Knutson would say," Marcy giggled. "He had a favorite horse named Bandit."

"A lot of people have favorite horses. Do you remember the name of my favorite horse?"

"Of course. You've told me stories about her since I was old enough to hear the stories. Her name was Cindy, and she was black as midnight."

Sharon pulled up a chair next to Marcy. "Did I tell you about the time we washed her with your grandmother's best shampoo?"

"About a thousand times, but you can tell me again."

Sharon smiled and settled back in her chair and grabbed a soft plush teddy bear off of the floor to hold. She settled it between her crossed arms and her belly and began.

"It was a really hot summer day, and my sister and I got Cindy out of the pasture next to the house and tied her to a fence post. We got the garden hose and got her all wet and then used a whole bottle of Breck shampoo to lather her up. We washed her once then put conditioner all over her and rinsed her off again. Cindy, bless her heart, just stood there and took all our punishment. We spent hours brushing her and braiding her tail and mane with dozens of little braids we tied off with red ribbons. Then we had this bright idea that we could make her really glossy with Vaseline, so my sister ran to the house to grab the jar out of the medicine cabinet. We dipped out handfuls of the stuff and rubbed it on. She was gorgeous. She glistened and gleamed in the light. She looked like she should be in a parade."

Sharon paused for a minute to retie the blue ribbon around the bear's neck.

"And then?" Marcy said teasingly since she'd heard the story so often she knew it by heart.

"And then we walked away just long enough to turn off the hose. We turned around just in time to see that darned horse lie down on the ground and roll over and over through the dirt. She had been so beautiful, but now she was a horrible mess with rocks and sticks and muck sticking to the Vaseline."

Sharon shook her head at the memory. "Silly horse."

"And that was the last summer with Cindy," Marcy said sadly.

Sharon nodded, and her face crumpled. "Yes, it was. The crazy thing was that after having her next to us in the pasture for four years, I'd forgotten Cindy didn't actually belong to us and that a friend of Dad's was using our pasture for her. The guy never came to see her, but he must have been sending money each month for her care."

"I can't believe they did what they did," Marcy said, prompting her mother to end the story.

Sharon pursed her lips and shrugged. "I came home one afternoon, and she was gone. They'd come during the day and picked her up. I never saw her again. And here I am, a grown woman, and if I think about it long enough, I can still bawl like a baby. I figured if I ever became a famous actress, that would be my way to cry during a scene—I'd just have to think about Cindy."

"I do that about Kemo—cry a lot. Not so much now, but I still miss her. I didn't get to say good-bye to Kemo either, just like you didn't get to say good-bye to Cindy."

"I guess every life has some unclosed chapters," Sharon said. "And those chapters can be pretty painful."

Then she got up, carefully placed the teddy bear in the chair, and walked a few steps to give Marcy a hug from behind. "If you ever want to get together and cry over two lost horses, let me know. I'll bring the Kleenex. And afterwards, I'll brew us up a pot of tea."

Chapter 47

Henry Knutson wondered sometimes if Marcy had always been walking to or from school when he drove past or if he just now noticed her more. Several times a week, he'd be in his old pickup headed to town for parts and groceries or something else, and there she would be, hiking to school in the morning when she didn't catch a ride with her dad or trudging home at night, always under a load of books. He's asked her if she wanted a ride numerous times, but she always turned him down, saying she liked to walk. It cleared her head. He didn't ask anymore.

In November, he had totally surprised himself by accepting her offer several weeks before to sit with her family at church. That Sunday morning, he had slowly driven into the church parking lot, turned off his truck engine, and was just about to fire it up and leave when the Petermans pulled in. Marcy spotted him at the end of the row and ran over to him. Before he could protest, she had whipped open the door, seized him by the hand, and was leading them to her smiling family. He felt a bit like the grand prize at the county fair.

He knew the Peterman family, of course, since they'd all lived in the same neck of the woods for decades. He knew Sharon's parents and had even known her grandparents. It had always been an acquaintance-type relationship that comes from everyone knowing everyone else in a small town. It wasn't the sort of relationship where he and the family would get together for meals or do much more than send an annual Christmas card.

That was why Sharon Peterman was surprised when he had called and asked if he could drop in during the lunch hour and talk to them. He knew, as did probably most of the town, that Jim Peterman drove home from the dealership promptly at noon each day to have lunch with Sharon. She told him they'd be delighted to have him and to plan on eating with them.

He drove the three blocks to the Peterman home and turned into the driveway. He tried to remember the last time he'd been in the house and decided it was probably when Ida was still alive and the old folks still lived there…before Sharon inherited the sprawling old house.

Opening the pickup door, he stepped down carefully. His bones ached today, and his back. Old age and the weather, he thought, weren't a friendly pair.

Sharon opened the door before he had a chance to knock.

"Henry, come in. We are so happy to have you join us for lunch." She acted as though she didn't know there must be some sort of ulterior motive. Henry Knutson simply wasn't a man who spent time visiting. She knew he had to have a good reason.

If he had any comments on the way she had decorated the house, he kept them to himself, but she knew he was taking in most of the details. She had spent the past few years returning the old house to its former glory and had gotten rid of most of the avocado green, harvest gold, and orange of earlier decades that had been inflicted on the home.

"So what do you think?" she asked Henry.

He nodded his head in appreciation as he admired the glossy oak flooring in the living room and dining room. "Looks a sight better than that orange shag," he said, chuckling.

"A dirt floor would look better than that orange shag," Sharon declared. "This is what was under it. I can't imagine why they'd cover it up. Come with me into the kitchen. We'll eat at the table in there."

Again, she could tell he had admired the progress she had made in the kitchen. He stood for a minute in front of the fireplace and warmed his hands and then turned his back so that side could welcome the heat.

"If I was a cat and lived here, I know this is right where I'd stay," he said approvingly.

Sharon ushered him to the table, and he sat in one of the old oak chairs. "Jim's just washing up and will be here in a sec," she said. "I hope leftover stew is okay."

For Henry Knutson, who had been a widower for years and thought Spam and potted meat were regular fare, homemade stew sounded like food fit for royalty, especially when he learned it would be served with still-warm homemade bread and apple pie for dessert.

Henry could feel his mouth watering at the smells in the kitchen and could hardly take his eyes off the pie sitting on the countertop long enough to greet Jim. The two men shook hands, and Sharon suggested they sit down while she finished getting things ready.

A few minutes later, she had a crock pot of stew on a hot pad in the middle of the table, thick slices of whole wheat bread next to a bowl of butter, and a pitcher of ice cold milk next to that.

Henry was grateful that Sharon and Jim didn't probe and acted as if he was just an everyday visitor. He was grateful they gave him time to sort out his words. They were easy lunch companions, and the three of them touched on a dozen or two topics, quickly going from one to the other without much of a lull in the conversation. They were the kind of folks, he thought, that made you talk better and with more intelligence. Some folks had a way of doing that. Sometimes, they got you to surprise even yourself.

About halfway through his second bowl of stew, Henry was buttering another piece of bread when there was a break after talking about Danford's undefeated high school football team. He cleared his throat.

"You are probably wonderin' what I phoned you up for and why I wanted to have a few words with you all. I've been thinkin' a lot about Marcy and wonderin' how she's faring these days."

Sharon let Jim answer, knowing that Henry was the sort of man who would like to get his facts from the head of the household, not that he had anything against females; he just liked his straight talk from the man of the family, if there was one. It griped him that two of his daughters had abandoned their marriages without any fight whatsoever and left him without sons-in-law to hang out with during holidays. He missed his sons-in-law. Truth was, if it came to choosing between them and his daughters, he'd have to give it a mighty lot of thought.

Jim wiped his mouth with his napkin and rested his arms on the table. "She's doing very well. It was rough for quite a while, but the last few weeks have been good. She went through the normal phases of grieving, and now she's coming closer to accepting that Anna's dead."

Sharon looked at Jim, and when she caught his eye, he let her continue. "It was very helpful that Joe and Barbara have been going to The Compassionate Friends group and helped us to deal with the grief," she told Henry. "They taught us that there are many phases. Let me see if I can remember them. Shock, denial, bargaining with God to make it change, guilt that it could have been prevented, anger, and depression. We think she's starting in the final stage, which is acceptance and hope. She is starting to understand that she may never be the same but that her life will go on."

A thoughtful look had come across Henry's face as he considered Sharon's words. "I didn't know all that. It sure explains a lot of what I went through when Ida died."

Sharon reached over and put her hand on the old man's arm. "I still can't believe your Ida is gone. Before you leave, I can give you a pamphlet that discusses grief more thoroughly. I know she's been gone for many years now, but it might help you understand what you went through."

Henry nodded his head and took a small bite of his bread. He knew that the gravity of the subject mandated that he not plow headlong into his bowl of stew, as much as he wanted to. "I'm glad Marcy is doing better. I see her on the road, and she looks better now than she did when school first started."

"We all look a lot better now!" Jim said with a chuckle.

"Henry, go ahead and eat. We can still talk about this and eat," Sharon said, grabbing a bowl of raspberry jelly to spread over the melted butter on her fat hunk of bread. It was as if she could read his mind, Henry thought, as he smiled and took up his fork.

"What I'm wondering about is if she ever talks about the horses," he said around a mouthful of potato.

Sharon laughed. "We were just talking about the horses last night. Marcy was all upset over losing Kemo, and I was lamenting the loss of an old horse of my childhood named Cindy. I guess Marcy and I are just cowgirls at heart."

Then she had a thought and got up and pushed away her chair. "Hang on a minute and I'll show you something," she said, leaving the kitchen. "Just chew for a bit, and I'll be right back."

"This chow's so good you only have to tell me once," Henry said, laughing and grabbing for the ladle sticking out of the crock pot.

In a few minutes, Sharon returned with a stack of Marcy's paintings and the photo of Kemo she was working from. She handed them to Henry, and he slowly shuffled through them—six paintings in all. Some were good, but some were better. One, especially, captured the light.

"She keeps trying to capture the horse's personality, her...I guess...vibrancy, and she can't quite get it," Sharon said. "I think they are very good, but she says they just don't show Kemo as she really was. I never saw the horse, except from a distance on the hill, so I don't know."

"I think she sells herself short," Jim said, pushing his plate away so he could rest his arm on the table. "I think they're great paintings."

"I don't know much about paintings, but I like this one especially," Henry said, pointing to one where Marcy had deliberately blurred the background.

Then he looked up. "She probably told you about the horses— what I told her a while back when I stopped and talked to her on the road. The mare's name was Brandy, and my granddaughter named the colt Pete. They belonged to her. They was here just that summer while her folks put up a new fence. They sold the colt, but the mare is still at my daughter's place down by Helena. Lena, my granddaughter, went off to college so she doesn't have any time anymore for the horse."

Then he thought about it a bit and, shaking his head, added, "Don't ride her even when she is home." He couldn't fathom that— having a horse and not being compelled to ride. He had spent his life around horses, and they were his unfailing partners when moving cattle. He never would have dreamed he'd get to a point in life where he didn't have a horse in the corral. He sure missed his old horse, Bandit.

Sharon sat listening with her elbow on the table and her chin in her hand. She couldn't imagine ever getting tired of Cindy. She knew that old Henry was probably thinking about his favorite horse. *What was his name? Bandit?*

"Marcy and Anna called it 'the year of the horses,'" she said, moving her hand and settling it on the table. "And it will always be an important part of Marcy's life—having that summer with the horses. I am so grateful that you allowed the girls to ride them, especially now that…well, you know."

"Actually," Jim broke in, "we're really happy that you allowed them all the time they spent on Rice's Hill, not just the year the horses were there. Did you know they played there all the time? You can't really see the top of the hill from your house."

Henry chuckled as he remembered back many years before when Marcy and Anna were third graders. "I tried to run 'em off a few times, but then there they'd be, right back up there. I spotted them often, galloping around and pretending they was Indians with their headbands and moccasins and all. It reminded me of my youth."

He leaned back in his chair. "I admit I was a bit worried at first when the horses showed up even though I knew the horses wouldn't hurt them. Truth be known, I never once dreamed they'd learn to ride that mare without a bridle or saddle. First time I saw them putting her through her paces by just hanging on to the mane and pulling it this way and that, my jaw dropped. I figured if they could do that, they were going to be okay."

As he talked, Sharon got up and brought the apple pie and three plates to the table. Henry's eyes stayed on the pie as he continued. "I was a bit worried about what would happen if they got hurt up there, but they had so much fun I couldn't bear to keep them off the land. If there'd been more kids up there, it might have made a difference, but it was always just Marcy and Anna. I figured if they got hurt and I got sued, there was nothing I owned that was as valuable as the memories they were gathering."

Sharon had put down the spatula as he finished, and she shook her head. "It's almost as if God paved the way for you to allow those memories," she said softly. "We will be forever grateful, and I know the Millers feel the same."

Jim had been silent through most of the exchange, and he knew that his wife was about to get a bit emotional. "Are you going to put some ice cream with that pie?" he asked.

Sharon laughed, knowing full well his intentions. "Well, of course! Henry, would you like some vanilla ice cream on your apple pie?"

"Does it come any other way?" he asked, smiling in anticipation. "I swear I haven't eaten like this since Ida died."

"Then we need to have you join us more often," Sharon said, and Jim agreed.

Ten minutes later, Jim stood up and glanced at his watch. It was about time to get back to the office. He had already taken more than his normal hour for lunch. Sharon was putting the remainder of the stew, bread, and apple pie into containers for Henry. They still weren't quite sure why Henry came. Maybe it was just a simple yearning to know how Marcy was faring.

Henry stood too and leaned with his back against his chair. "Well, the thing of it is," he said to them, "I'm going to Helena this weekend, and I figure if it's okay with you, I'll see if I can buy that mare. For Marcy."

He stopped and waited for their reaction.

Sharon stared at Jim, and they automatically walked toward each other. Together, they faced Henry. Sharon put her fist to her mouth. Jim put his arm around her waist.

"Do you think they'll sell her?" Jim asked quietly. His voice sounded hollow. He knew as well as he knew anything that this horse could bring about Marcy's recovery.

"Oh, my gosh," Sharon said. She could feel her body sort of slumping, and before Henry could answer, she moved away from Jim.

"We all need to sit," she said, moving back to her chair and falling into it heavily. Henry and Jim also returned to their places.

"I never once thought it would be possible to get her back," Sharon said, shaking her head. "I am just sick that we didn't think of it. Jim, why didn't we think of it? Why didn't we even ask?"

"It hasn't happened yet," Jim reminded her. "And you know that all things work in God's time. Not ours. So, Henry, do you think they'll sell her?"

"Actually," Henry said sheepishly, running his hand over his balding head, "I already asked. I talked to Lena, my granddaughter, last week, and she said she could sure use the money for college. She said to ask her mother, and I did. She said she was tired of feeding a horse that no one ever rode. I figure if it's okay with you, we can bring Kemo on back here, and she can go right back to the hill."

"Oh!" Sharon said, dragging the word out into a moan. She stared at Henry, and tears filled her eyes. Then she put her head down on her hands and wept without shame. All the feelings she'd ever had about her lost Cindy seemed to flood over her, and she couldn't stop bawling. Through her cries, she heard Jim's blowing his nose and heard odd noises from Henry also. Jim tucked a napkin into a crevice between her face and her hands.

Finally, she lifted her head. "I don't know what to say," she sobbed.

"I guess just a yes or no will do," Henry said.

Chapter 48

In light of what was happening, Jim decided that work was just going to have to wait. He knew he had a sales meeting at 1:30 p.m., and he made a quick call to the front office at the dealership telling them to cancel. No, he didn't know when he'd be in.

They had a lot of plans to make—he and Sharon and Henry—and it didn't matter if it meant missing two days of work.

Henry decided to get the awkward part over with quickly. He knew he wouldn't be able to totally hoodwink Jim and Sharon, but he wanted to give it a try. "She don't cost much, far as horses go, since they got her on trade or something. Fact is, she's really cheap and is a downright bargain considering she's a right fit mare. Plus, she comes with all the tack. I figure $500 should cover it."

Jim was incredulous. "Five hundred dollars? That can't be right, Henry. That's way too cheap. I don't know much about horses, but I know that horse is worth thousands. I'm not a car salesman for nothing. Wait a minute here. Are you paying the difference?"

"Might be, but that's my business, and it's something I'm doing for Marcy. And in memory of Anna. I think a lot of that little girl of yours. I learned something from the pastor the other Sunday about blessings. He said it's not good to take someone's blessing away from them. And this is my blessing to give."

"You have given us such a gift. You'll never know," Sharon said. She grabbed another napkin and blew her nose.

"If it's okay with you, I'll throw in some riding tips, and I'll teach her how to feed and groom her horse. I'm headed to Helena this weekend to pick up the tack, so's I can work on any repairs and get it ready," Henry said. He was pleased that it went so well.

They would never know the price he was paying for this horse. They would never know that his selfish daughter fussed until he had to beg and, finally, tell the story of Anna and Marcy. It took a lot of talking to soften her heart, but she finally came through. She wasn't soft enough, however, to give him a break on the price. He'd already transferred the money into her account and was comforted that there was no way she could back out. He'd scoot down there this weekend unannounced and pick up everything that came with the horse. That would keep her from selling any of it off. He'd already gotten a list from Lena as to what came with the mare, and his going down there might prevent her from selling any of it. He didn't want any squabbles with his daughter.

As far as her price, he'd paid it without much of a fight. Didn't even flinch. He figured he'd win in the end through his last will and testament. She wasn't too smart, that one, he'd thought at the time he paid her off. He smiled inside.

Jim reached over and put his hand over Sharon's. "I think this may be the catalyst that truly heals Marcy—to have Kemo back," he said, looking at Henry Knutson. "She dearly loved that horse. We didn't know how much until lately."

"We hear her at night crying sometimes, and we know it's for both Anna and the horse," Sharon said.

"I figure they need to be together, her and that mare," Henry said, using his thumb to wipe under his eyes. "I've been thinkin' that for a long time now, that horse is as lonely as she is, moping around in that little corral."

"So when can we tell Marcy? How do we get the horse here? Oh dear, where do we keep her?" Sharon asked.

"Been thinkin' about all that too. Christmas isn't far off, and it would make a right nice present. As far as a place to stay, as I said, she can just go right back up there on the hill. I'm thinkin' maybe Jim here can help me do a bit of work in the barn to make it a little more comfortable. It isn't a total mess but could use some clean-up. Then I figured Jim and me could hook up the horse trailer and just ride on down to Helena and load her up and bring her on home."

"I'd be more than willing to help get the barn ready, but I'm thinking it might be good for Marcy to help. It would do her a lot of good to just work hard hauling hay and cleaning floors and whatever else needs done to get ready. Isn't there a place we could board Kemo for a few days until we got it ready? That way, we could give her the horse for Christmas and spend the rest of the vacation getting the barn ready."

"I know!" Sharon said. "Two ladies in my Bible study have horses, and one of them lives in an apartment in town and boards her horse at a stable outside of town. I can call her. But we need to keep it secret."

"She does love secrets," Jim said to Henry and motioning with his thumb toward Sharon.

"My head is all in a muddle with all of this," Sharon said. "I can't believe it. Can you imagine the look on her face when we show her Kemo?"

She turned to Henry. "Henry, if you aren't going to be with any of your family for Christmas, you have to promise you will be here with us. Promise?"

"I don't have much planned at all," he admitted. "And I can't think of a place I'd rather be. I'd be right proud to be a part of this here Christmas present."

"I think you're the biggest part of this Christmas present," Jim said. "What do you say I follow you home right now and we look at that old barn and see what needs to be done. It would be good to have a plan."

Ten minutes later, they were on their way—Henry Knutson rattling slowly down the road in his beloved old beat up truck and Jim Peterman right behind him in a brand new Ford F-150 Eddie Bauer edition pickup.

After watching them until they were no longer in sight, Sharon grabbed the Kleenex box and an afghan and curled up in her favorite chair to finish up her crying. Afterwards, she would make a cup of tea.

Chapter 49

Barbara was walking aimlessly through Polsky's Market and pondering what to get Joe for Christmas when she stopped in the produce aisle. Christmas was just a little over a week away, and she didn't have a good idea in her head. They knew it was going to be a rough time and had decided, at first, that they would go on a cruise. Somehow, though, it didn't seem like something as joyous as a cruise was the answer to muddling through the season.

They had contemplated not putting up a tree but decided, just before Thanksgiving, that they had to follow tradition. Anna would have been appalled if she'd known they were considering scrapping the tree and everything else that went with Christmas. So Joe had hauled everything inside and put together the artificial tree. Later, Sharon sent him back out with the unopened boxes of animated Santas and wreaths and some of the other decorations she normally put up. Then, at the last minute, she had him drag them back in. She was determined, she told him as she plugged in the train that wound around the tree base, to have a merry Christmas. She would be merry if it killed her, she announced.

Now she didn't know what to do for his gifts. She'd already gotten him the normal small items—books, an expensive pen to replace the one he lost, a few shirts—but she needed that one special gift.

She also had all of Anna's presents to consider. She'd gotten her six or eight things just after Christmas last year and picked up a couple more small items in early summer. They were all wrapped and high on a shelf in her closet and the list of what they were tucked away in a dresser drawer. She had so far just ignored them. She had prayed about them once, asking God to tell her what to do with them, and there wasn't a clear answer. She just didn't feel led to do anything with them, so there they sat, gathering dust and reminding her.

Barbara loved Polsky's Market, which was an old-fashioned place with shelves overflowing with everything under the sun. Although there was a Wal-Mart just outside of town, most old-timers in Danford shopped at Polsky's.

At the rate she was going, she told herself, she'd be there until the place closed. Her list had only half the items marked off, and she seemed to be daydreaming her way through the store. She couldn't even seem to make a decision on a head of lettuce.

"Are you going to choose one of those or just stay here all day playing with them?" Mike asked her, laughing. "You've picked up each one of those at least twice. You're wearing them out, turning them into used lettuce. Old Mr. Polsky's going to come over here and make you buy them all."

Barbara turned and laughed. "I'm befuddled, or maybe it's muddled. Whatever it is, I can't seem to make up my mind about anything. So I'm playing with the lettuce."

"Want me to help you choose?" he said, picking one up at random and tossing it in the air a few times before dumping it unceremoniously in her cart. "There. One head of lettuce. Mark it off your list."

"But how do you know that is the right one. Did you check for blight? Or rot? Did it have a fever?"

"It's just lettuce. Lettuce is lettuce."

"Unless it's Romaine, or Bibb, or Boston or arugula or butter. And then you have your watercress and Swiss chard…"

"Stop! No wonder you're muddled and befuddled. You have too much lettuce in your brain. As far as I'm concerned, this iceberg that comes in such a nice tidy little wad is the only kind there is. As a bachelor, I also know that this one lasts twice as long as those frilly types. They turn brown and slime up in no time."

Barbara looked at him in mock horror. "Iceberg lettuce? Does Rachel know you're so uncultivated and unsophisticated?"

"No, and don't tell her," Mike said, laughing.

"Speaking of Rachel," Barbara said as she pushed her cart toward the cereal aisle, "is she coming for Christmas?"

Mike kept pace and grabbed a box of granola as they went by. He tucked it under his arm. "I asked her and had even thought I might see if she could stay with you again, but we both prayed about it and decided she needed to be with her folks. Because of all the pre-Christmas happenings in church, I can't get there much for Christmas, but I'll fly in late Christmas Eve and spend four days. I'll have just enough time after the Christmas Eve candle lighting service to catch the flight."

"Where do Rachel's folks live?

"Not far from Seattle actually. In Lacey. Rachel will pick me up at the airport, and I'll spend the first night with her folks. I have a buddy from seminary who has a church in Lacey, and after that first night, I'll stay with him and his family."

"I'm glad you'll be together."

"*You* are! I was thinking yesterday I need to get stock in AT&T."

Barbara stopped as a thought crossed her mind. "So if you're leaving, does that mean we get to watch the clown dog?"

Mike grinned. "I thought you'd never ask. I told Midas he might spend Christmas with you, and he hasn't stopped wagging his tail. He's packed up his Christmas stocking and his new shampoo, and he's all set."

"He won't be needing the shampoo. I doubt if we'll ever go through that fiasco again. The dog washing business has ended. Closed down. Kaput."

"Aww. But it was so much fun. You know it was."

"Joe is still laughing about that mess. It wasn't that much fun at the time, but now that I look back, it really was. But don't tell Joe I said that."

Mike laughed. "Well, I should be going. I just came in for some aspirin. Despite my introducing Rachel to the whole church, there are some mamas who aren't giving up. Edith Yorkle brought her niece by yesterday. She's very sweet and charming."

Barbara stopped dead in her tracks, looked at him with shock, and then leaned forward. "Cynthia Yorkle? She's over fifty years old! She taught me piano lessons when I was a kid, and she was old then."

"She's still very sweet and charming, and any man would be proud to have her as a wife."

"But you already have yours picked out," Barbara said, nodding her head to indicate she wanted confirmation.

Mike didn't let her down, and his twinkling eyes confirmed it before he opened his mouth. He knew he could tell Barbara as well as Joe his plans and they wouldn't go any further. They were his best friends, and he trusted them implicitly.

"Yes, ma'am," he said with a lopsided grin, "I already have mine picked out."

"So might a 'curious George' type person ask 'when'?"

"I'll tell you, but you have to keep it to yourself. We'll decide on a date over the holidays. Probably this summer. July maybe. We will have known each other eight months. Do you think that's too soon? I have to be really careful."

"If people think it's too soon, that's their business," Barbara said, moving the cart slowly and looking at him. "One of the most valuable lessons I've learned through losing Anna is that life is intangible. You need to grab it and hold on with both hands. You need to value and treasure each minute God gives you. If it was me, I'd marry her over Christmas and bring her on back here."

Mike groaned at her last sentence. "If you said that one more time, I'd convince myself it was coming from God, and I'd do it," he declared. "But I owe a lot to my church, and they deserve better than that—their pastor sneaking off and eloping."

Barbara sighed and nodded her head. "You're right, of course."

"Now I really do need to get out of here," Mike said, looking at his watch. Then he pitched the box of granola in her cart. "You need to try this. You'll like it."

"Gee, thanks," she said to his retreating back. Then she said, "Hey, Mike." He turned around. "I just want to thank you for letting us keep Midas over Christmas. It will help. It's really hard, you know?"

"I know," he said, walking back to her and putting a hand on her shoulder. He looked at her with great compassion. "I figured it would be good for you to have him there. I know this is going to be very difficult for you and Jim, but you'll get through it. You're strong, and you have a wonderful Savior who is right there to help you through the rough patches."

"I know. I don't know how people would go through this without him." She shook her head.

He had turned to leave again when something crossed his mind. "Speaking of Christmas, I forgot to ask. Have you talked about Christmas with Jim and Sharon?"

She smiled. She knew he was fishing and also knew exactly what he was fishing for. "You mean Marcy's Christmas present?"

"Yeah, her biiig Christmas present," he said, spreading his arms wide.

"Sharon and Jim came over that night after Henry Knutson visited them. We all bawled together. What a wonderful man he is. Joe's going to help Jim and Henry and Marcy clean out the barn and get it ready. They've asked if we'd come over in the afternoon and go with them when they take her to see her present."

"They asked me too, and I sure wish I was going to be there for it," he said. "There is one little girl who is going to be very blessed this Christmas."

"I think we are all going to be blessed this Christmas. God is so good," Barbara said.

"Yes, he is, and now I'm really late!" Mike said, sprinting down the aisle.

"I'll take pictures," she yelled after him, and he raised his arm high to indicate he'd heard her.

Chapter 50

* * *

One day in the middle of summer, we had packed a lunch to spend the day on Rice's Hill. That was the summer of the horses, so we wrapped two carrots in plastic wrap and added them to the bag—one for Kemo and one for Sabe, the colt. We never visited the hill without a treat for the horses.

The screen door on Anna's back door had slapped shut, and we were racing to our bikes when Mrs. Miller yelled at us to hold up.

She teased us, saying, "So you two Indian princesses thought you could sneak out of here without saying farewell or good-bye? Then she handed us each a small wrapped package. The gifts were in plain white tissue paper, but we knew they must be special because Mrs. Miller's eyes were bright with excitement.

She said she had ordered them and it had taken them forever to get here. We tore off the paper. Inside were headbands, beaded in intricate patterns on leather with elastic in back to hold them on. Besides the broad, beaded band, each one had dangling beads hanging from the sides, which tapered to shorter beads in the front. They were gorgeous. Anna's had a lot of blue, which made her black hair look even more *beautiful, and mine had a background of red, which looked good on my blond hair.*

At first, we just stared. Then Anna squealed, and I started in too. We both danced around on the grass like fools. It was a perfect gift, and I didn't even know how to tell her how special it was and how wonderful it was she got it for me. I hugged her though, and I think she knew.

* * *

Marcy knew that something was up. Christmas was just a few days away, and there was too much whispering between her parents. Besides, she couldn't deny that there was a feeling of hushed excitement in the house. It was almost tangible, this feeling of anticipation, and she knew it all emanated from her parents.

She knew Ben didn't know what the secret was because he would have spilled it by now. They all knew not to tell Ben anything private. He didn't mean to betray a trust but went quietly from person to person, making them promise not to tell and then relating the secret with relish. Everyone knew that everyone else knew. There were no secrets with Ben.

Besides, she had grilled him, and he didn't know a thing. He had even, he admitted, done a little bit of sneaking around in their mother's closet. "Underwear and socks," he said, rolling his eyes. "She always has to get us underwear and socks."

Marcy was curious, but she really didn't care what the secret was. Another fancy video game system probably or maybe a trip. It would be just like her parents to think they could cure her by taking her on a trip to Disneyland or something.

Give the girl a few rides on a roller coaster and let her hug Goofy and Cinderella, and voila, she'd be cured of all grief forevermore. Life would be blissful and happy ever after.

Well, she just wouldn't go. She'd rather stay here and mope than go to some stupid place like Disneyland. She and the pink balloon that was still wandering around the house would just stay in Danford, and the rest of them could go off and laugh it up.

The Compassionate Friends meeting a few weeks before that she had gone to with Joe and Barbara had explained a lot about Christmas and how hard it was going to be. Christmases and birthdays and all holidays and special days.

They handed out a piece of paper that had all sorts of tips on getting through the holiday. The main tip was that it was okay to have a good time and enjoy yourself. Even though it was hard to celebrate when you were missing someone, the speaker said, it was important to relax and laugh and have a good time. It did not mean you didn't miss that person or loved that person any less.

The speaker said that it was a time to be selfish and to do things for yourself that you enjoyed, like walking on the beach or having a massage or listening to music or hanging out with friends.

Marcy thought this was a stupid tip. It was December, so walking on the beach at Danford Lake wouldn't be much fun. Sure, it would take your mind off your grief because you'd be thinking about your frozen nose and feet. She was too young for a massage, she already listened to music all the time, and as far as hanging out with friends, she'd rather hang out by herself.

The final tip the speaker offered was to allow yourself to be sad and to maybe write the person a letter or visit a favorite spot you shared or to share memories.

It was a comfort to Marcy to know she was already doing many of those things. She had written several letters to Anna after writing the one that was supposed to go up in the pink balloon. They were all in a bundle in the bottom of her jewelry box with the wrinkled and worn balloon letter on top. Someday, she would send that letter, she thought.

As far as visiting favorite places, she did spend time with Joe and Barbara, and sometimes, she asked if she could sit in Anna's room.

The room was still the same, pretty much anyway. At first, Barbara kept it exactly as it was the day Anna drowned. But then Rachel came, and she tidied it up and put away a lot of things. The last time Marcy was in the room, they had moved in a treadmill. Slowly, it seemed, bits and pieces of Anna were eroding away.

At the end of The Compassionate Friends meeting, Rod and Caroline handed them all Christmas ornaments. They were a beautiful red and had an anonymous poem on them.

First Christmas with Jesus

Please love and keep each other,
As my Father said to do,
For I can't count the blessings
Or love he has for each of you.
So have a Merry Christmas
And wipe away that tear,
Remember I'm spending Christmas
With Jesus Christ this year.

Christmas with Jesus Christ—that's where Anna was this Christmas, with Jesus! The thought made Marcy close her eyes and try to imagine. The thought made her smile. She probably had him pretending he was an Indian chief and galloping around heaven on an imaginary horse. No, probably in heaven, they had real horses.

Marcy had tried to take part in Christmas, and she had learned that if she tried she would be blessed. Her mom and dad cajoled her to help decorate the tree, and she grumbled but grudgingly started hanging ornaments. Within ten minutes, they were deep in memories and stories and laughing. She had even laughed a little. Afterwards, when the lights were turned off and the tree lights colored everything in the room, they sat on the floor in front of the tree drinking hot chocolate and eating cookies.

A quietness had filled her soul, and she puzzled over it. She felt contented and peaceful. She felt happy, almost.

Feelings were fleeting. She learned that if she forced herself to do things, like helping decorate cookies, she would eventually get into the swing of it and have fun. But then something would happen or a random thought would flash through her mind, and she'd be back to hanging on to her grief.

The year before, she had sent out her first Christmas cards, and when her mother handed her the short list a few weeks before, she realized that she would have to cross off Anna's name. Right there between her grandparents and her aunt was Anna. She choked on a wad of instant anguish, and her first impulse was to dash to her room. Instead, she asked God to give her a good thought. Instantly, it came into her head that she should simply write "family" after Anna. Anna's family. She would send a card to Joe and Barbara Miller.

Disneyland or a Mexican cruise. She hoped that wasn't the big gift that had her parents whispering and tittering in the corner. They were also hugging too much, snuggling in the kitchen and kissing and patting each other on the shoulder and holding hands on the couch when they watched television.

Oh no! The thought seared through her brain. Suddenly, Marcy knew what it must be. The big gift. Her mother was pregnant! It had to be. That was why they were acting so goofy. She was having a baby.

She didn't know what to do with the idea. Was it good? A baby? But how could that be. Her father had, had that thing done that time a few years ago, and she remembered it distinctly. After leaving the clinic, he had gone out and played golf all day. Then he spent the next two days groaning in bed, and her mother called him "El Toro." Marcy never understood that part.

Ben wandered by her room. "Ben!" she hollered at him. He turned and came back to where Marcy was at her desk. He had Gary, his pet gerbil, in his hands, and Gary was intent on escaping, racing up his arm, stopping and racing back down to his hands. Marcy didn't know how her brother could be so attached to a rodent.

"You wanna hold him?" he asked his sister. Gary, by now, was sitting on his hind legs in Ben's little-boy-grungy palms. His tiny paws hung in begging pose, and she had to admit the creature was sort of cute, even with his beady black eyes.

"Nah. I'm really not into rats," she said.

"Gary's not a rat. He's a gerbil. He won't bite."

"How come you named him Gary anyway?"

"You know that *Far Side* book Dad sometimes takes to the bathroom and Mom keeps taking out? That guy who writes those cartoons in there is named Gary Larson. I like his cartoons, and I just think it's a good name for a gerbil. He has one cartoon with a gerbil in it."

"I guess Gary's as good as any other name," Marcy said with a shrug. "Ben, are you sure you don't know anything about a Christmas present? They're up to something. I just know it."

"You keep asking me that. I don't know anything. I promise."

"Well, keep your ears open, and I'll do the same. If either one of us hears anything, we'll let the other one know, okay?"

"Maybe it's four-wheelers or a speedboat," Ben said excitedly.

"Hmm. Never thought about that," Marcy said. "Maybe it is something like that, something that we can do as a family."

But somehow she knew it wasn't.

Chapter 51

Henry Knutson's daughter, Claudia, had been shocked to see him pull into her driveway late Saturday afternoon, and she fussed and fluttered, picking up stray newspapers and everyday clutter as he made his way to a recliner.

"You could have called and given me some warning," she rebuked after giving him a perfunctory hug.

"I did, Claud," he protested. He knew being called Claud riled her. Her friends knew her as Dee.

"I don't think you did."

"Cross my heart. Around ten in the morning. You weren't home." Truthfully, he had waited until he was sure she was out of the house.

"You could have left a message."

"You know I don't talk on no answering machine."

"So why are you here?" she asked, getting straight to the point. It wasn't like her to beat around the bush or go through any social niceties, just like she wouldn't ask how he was. If she knew how much money he had in the bank through investments, she'd probably be a lot nicer, he thought to himself.

"Figured I'd come down and check and see if that mare was worth the small fortune you demanded for her. Wouldn't want to haul down the trailer in a couple weeks and then find out she's lame or something. Plus, I'll pick up the tack while I'm here."

He could see she was kicking herself for not trying to sell off some of it sooner. He didn't know she'd already put an ad in the paper—to start Sunday—selling one of the saddles and extra bridles and gear.

Henry patted his shirt pocket, which, along with a pen, held a slip of paper. "Got the list right here."

"What list?"

"Lena's list of what comes with the mare. I have to admit that horse comes with more tack than a Barbie doll comes with clothes. But considerin' what I paid for her, I guess she should come with a lot of accessories."

Claudia was at a loss for words, so she just looked at him. He could tell she was fuming inside. It used to bother him that his daughter was so uncaring and cold, and could be as mean and unfriendly as a hungry rattlesnake.

He'd come to accept it though, and now he almost thought it was humorous. He had to admit that he tried to goad her.

The odd thing was that this time, he was getting no enjoyment out of it. He felt sorry for her. Looking at her, he figured she was probably as lonely as he was. And she had sure done some things to screw up her life.

Pastor Mike's sermons must be hitting home, he thought ruefully, to have him thinking of words like "compassion" and "forgiveness" when looking at his firstborn.

Still, he didn't trust her.

"You remember that Vern Smith down the road from here? Has that boarding stable and tack shop?"

Claudia was puzzled and frowned. "Well, sure. Everyone who has a horse knows Vern. Why?"

"He's coming this afternoon and picking up the mare. Going to take him to his place and get her groomed and shod."

"He's going to take her today?"

Henry looked at his watch. "'Bout an hour or two from now."

Oddly enough, Henry understood the look of dismay that crossed his daughter's face. She never rode the horse and begrudged every day she had to clomp out to the corral and feed it, but she would miss the soft nickering and the horse's presence in the corral. It would look so desolate and empty without her. Her daughter was gone, her husband had left her, and now the only other live thing besides her was leaving. She never cried, but now she was near tears.

"You always love something more when you're about to lose it," Henry said to her to show he understood. "That corral will look right empty without that horse prettying it up. But she doesn't have much of a life here. With Marcy Peterman, she will be loved and appreciated."

"I love and appreciate her," Claudia protested.

"I know you do, but you have a busy life, and there's no room in it for a horse."

He knew full well she didn't have a full life and her nights, after spending the day clerking at Safeway, were spent watching television. A big event for Claudia was going to Bingo on Friday nights.

A while later, after she fixed him a tuna sandwich and he gulped down a cup of coffee, they went out to the shed. It took half the back end of his truck to hold all the gear. He didn't take out the list. It would have only caused hard feelings and looked like he thought she was trying to swindle him. Not that he'd put it past her, but his heart was softening toward her. A month ago, he would have marked everything off the list.

"You sure some of this stuff doesn't stay?" he asked her. He was surprised to hear the words coming out of his mouth.

"No, everything was bought over the years to go with Brandy," Claudia said sadly.

She ran her hands over the horn of a show saddle that had been under a blanket in the corner. "Remember when Lena and Brandy would carry the flag at the start of each rodeo?"

"Sure do. I was so proud I could have popped the buttons right off my shirt."

"No, Dad, that was from all the hot dogs you ate at the rodeo," she teased. For some reason, the teasing melted his heart. For an instant, just a flick of time, he saw Claudia as she had been as a little girl. He was heartened to know that there was still that part of her. Maybe, he thought, part of her misery and coldness came from him. He had to admit he hadn't been the perfect father.

Just maybe, he thought, this whole deal with Marcy was killing her inside—his talking about this little girl as if she was the greatest thing to happen in his life in twenty years.

"It's a good thing you're doing here," he told her. "A kind thing. You've never even met Marcy, but if you did, you'd like her. I think she needs this horse. And I think this horse needs her."

Claudia nodded her head and turned to grab two bridles off the wall.

"Dee, I've been thinkin', we need to spend more time together. You're sitting down here in Helena all by yourself, and me, I'm up there in Danford all by myself. Lena, she's off to college and too busy for either one of us...We need to spend time together."

It didn't escape her that he had called her by her preferred name and just that little gesture made a difference in her heart. She looked at him and smiled a wan little smile. "I think that would be good."

"Life's too short to not be with people we love," he said. "So I tell you what. Let's do something fun. Anything you want. My treat, and dang the cost. Europe? A cruise to Alaska? Las Vegas? Disneyland? You decide. This will be your Christmas present. The only catch is we have to do it soon. I am seventy-five years old, you know."

He wondered why he had waited so long to give her something big enough to make her eyes sparkle. She really was a pretty woman, if you did something to take away that frown and bitter look about her mouth.

Suddenly, he ached inside, knowing that he had abandoned both of his daughters. If they turned out badly and had problems, he was probably the root cause for most of them. *You are a hard man, Henry Knutson*, he said to himself. *May God forgive you for the hurt you've caused your children.* He was instantly comforted with the thought that he had time left in his life to change things.

His plan had been to drive back home, but he decided to spend the night. He could tell his daughter was glad he changed his plans. Claudia had spent some time alone with the horse before Vern came to pick her up, and he could tell it was hard for her. She cried a little in her bedroom and then came out, and they talked late into the night.

The next morning, they chatted in the kitchen over coffee, and he told her he had been thinking and maybe the three of them should go on the trip—Henry and his two daughters. He thought it wouldn't be fair to leave Sara Sue out, so maybe they should ask her too. He asked what she, Claudia, or Dee, thought. Dee was thrilled.

A bit later, she walked him out to his truck and stood shivering in the cold as he checked the latches on the canopy and started it up. Then he pulled her into his arms and held her tight. When was the last time he had hugged her? He couldn't remember. "You're a good daughter, Dee," he said. "You and Sara Sue decide soon where we're going, okay? The cost don't matter none. I can afford it. Soon's I get home, I'm going to get out my suitcase."

She hugged him tighter. "I love you, Dad," she said.

"And I love you, too," he said, and then he released her and gave her a little push. "Scoot on back to the house. You're going to freeze out here!"

She scampered back to the house, and on the front porch, she turned around to see he was watching to make sure she got safely inside.

"Bye, Daddy!" she hollered. *Daddy*. His heart swelled.

The trip back home was uneventful. As soon as he got home, Henry did what he said he would do and pulled down his suitcase from the attic and rubbed the dust off it.

He had also spent hours cleaning and sorting the tack that came with Kemo. There were two saddles and a pack saddle. One was a regular working saddle that he figured Marcy could clean.

The other was one of the prettiest saddles he had ever seen. It was a show saddle with intricate tooling in the leather. The color was a rich reddish brown, and the Cheyenne roll at the top of the cantle, which was basically the back rest, had decorative silver trim. There were also were four silver buttons, two on either side, which held the long saddle strings. The latigo holder and horn were also trimmed in silver. The leather was intricately tooled.

The silver had been tarnished and the leather dull, but now it all gleamed after days of applying silver polish, neatsfoot oil, saddle soap and beeswax. The process of restoring the saddle made him so contented he wondered if there was a market for cleaning saddles and repairing tack. Also, it was strange, but for some reason all the work had seemed to be good for his aching hands.

Chapter 52

Rachel Pontelli knew that her parents, Tim and Christine Fulton, would love Mike Warren, and she was counting the days—only four left—until she would drive to the Sea-Tac Airport in Seattle to pick him up. Although her parents didn't live far away—only a few hours—she didn't see them as often as she should. Work kept her too busy, and they didn't like driving in Seattle traffic, which was always, no matter what time of day or night, pretty brutal.

Compared to Mike's family, hers was humble. Her folks still lived in the four-bedroom two-bath ranch she grew up in. Although it had increased in value tremendously since it was on a few acres, it was nothing compared to the big house at the Rocking W Ranch. And the few acres her folks possessed were laughable compared to the sections owned by the Warrens.

Still, she knew that her mother was richer than Abby Warren. Her mother was also more peaceful, more content, and a lot happier than Abby Warren. She wondered how they would get along when they eventually met.

Mike's dad and hers, she knew, would get along well. They both liked to hunt and fish and were true men's men. She knew they'd get on the subject of pheasant or deer hunting, and they'd become fast friends. It was interesting that even though the wealth in the family came from Davis Warren's side of the family, it didn't seem to matter much to him. Rachel thought he would probably be happy living in a mobile home as long as he had enough land to stretch his legs. To Abby, the wealth and the status were everything.

Rachel was outside on her lunch break, sitting on a bench and peeling an orange, when her cell phone rang. It was chilly in Seattle, but not too cold for her daily walk, and she was heated up from the fast pace she had kept. To cool down, she had thrown open her coat, removed her leather gloves, and loosened the red scarf at her neck. If people thought it odd she was sitting on a bench eating an orange in the dead of winter, she really didn't care.

She fished the ringing phone out of the pocket of her jacket, checked the displayed name quickly, and pushed the answer button.

"Hey there, you," she answered, and she smiled when he tried to disguise his voice.

"Is this Ms. Rachel Pontelli?"

"It is. Might I ask who's calling?"

"You might. Claus is the name. S. Claus at your service."

"And what can I do for you, Mr. S. Claus?"

"I'll be delivering your gift in about one hundred and five hours, and I wondered if you are prepared for it. It is a magnificent gift, I might add."

"Magnificent, is it? Are you sure you aren't mistaken? I believe I ordered the grab bag special that comes with a set of Ginsu knives."

"Hmmm. Let me check here. Nope. Says right here on the form, one handsome, charming, magnificent male. No Ginsu knives. But it comes with a dog."

"A dog? That sounds like a much better deal than the knives. I'll take that one, the one with the dog. Actually, can you bring just the dog?"

They both laughed. "Are you really bringing Midas?"

"Nope. Sorry about that. I know you'd love to see him again, but I think he'll be good therapy for Joe and Barb, so he'll go back to them again. I told her I was sending shampoo with him. If we hadn't been in Polsky's, she might have hit me."

Rachel's after-walk hot spell was subsiding, and she pulled her coat tighter and pulled the scarf back around her neck. She could see her breath in the crisp air. "I can't believe we're down to days here instead of weeks," she said. "Part of me wishes I could be there and see your church all decorated for Christmas and see the Christmas pageant and the play and all that."

"You can see that next year. This year, it's important that I see where you grew up and meet your parents."

"They're excited. I know Mom's been baking for weeks, and Dad's probably cleaned the garage. When he's excited about anything, he cleans the garage."

"They sound like great people."

"They are. You'll like them. I promise. My mother is sweet and kind, and Dad is a loveable guy who is full of good advice. They're both into helping others and are all involved at the food bank, in all sorts of church ministries, and have even gone to Mexico to help build a church."

"A lot different from my family," Mike said, and she could hear the sad tone in his voice.

"Your family is wonderful in its own way. I dearly love your dad, and he and my father would be best buds if they ever met. Your mother will come around. Right now, she feels a little threatened with her little boy chasing after some strange woman. I have been praying for her a lot, and I think that deep down, she's a sad little girl who didn't have a great childhood. It would be easy to take up with the enemy and condemn her for some of the things she said to us while we were there, but I think we should love her all the more because of them. She needs our prayers and our love."

"Excuse me, but I am the pastor here," Mike said jokingly, and then he sobered. "You are very wise, Rachel, and you are making me see my mother in a new light. Sometimes, I think I'm too close to my family to figure them out. Maybe someday you can explain my sisters to me!"

"Oh dear, I keep forgetting that someday I will probably have to be grilled by them too."

"So, where are you right now?" Mike asked. "I keep hearing people and traffic."

Rachel laughed, and he smiled. He loved her laugh. "I'm sitting on a bench not far from my office. I just took a walk, and I was just sitting here in the dead of winter eating an orange when some goofball pretending he was Santa called and harassed me."

"You must be freezing. According to Weather.com, it's only thirty-something in Seattle today."

"Oh, that's what's wrong with my hands," she said. "I can't move my fingers. I wondered what was causing that."

"You'd better get back to work. I'll call you tonight. Oh, and remind me to tell you about Marcy."

"Is it bad?"

"No, it's really wonderful, and you'll have to ponder what that means the rest of the day! I love you, Rachel Pontelli."

"Same to you Santa. Toodles."

Rachel tucked her phone back into her pocket and scuttled back to her office. Heat! She needed heat. She was freezing to death. She would think about Marcy later, when she had her hands wrapped around a hot mug of spiced cider.

*　*　*

After finishing his conversation and plopping the phone back in its receiver, Pastor Mike leaned back in his office chair and put his hands behind his head. He could never remember being so contented so…happy. He was sitting there grinning when Violet rounded the corner and entered the room.

"You look like the Cheshire cat," she said to him. "If you smile any broader, you're going to stretch your lips out of shape."

Pastor Mike considered the tiny woman before him. Violet Lemke was barely taller than his desk, and if you stripped her down and took off her orthopedic shoes, she probably didn't weigh more than ninety pounds. Her purse was almost bigger than she was. She was on his unpaid staff—those faithful volunteers who he would be lost without. They were the backbone of the church, these women who cooked and cleaned and headed this project and that. They kept things humming smoothly. He had, in the past, gotten involved in their petty squabbles, but now he just let things run their course.

Violet helped his secretary in the office, and he enjoyed having her around. Sometimes, it seemed as if she was there more than Margaret, who got paid to be there. He knew she didn't need the job, and she had her social security and pension from her deceased husband and she was at least seventy-five years old, but he asked her once if she wanted paid.

"If I got paid, I'd have to come here and then it would be a job," she'd told him. "Right now, it's something I love doing, puttering around the office and folding bulletins and newsletters and doing a thousand other things. Besides, if I got paid, I wouldn't be free to tell you when you mess up, would I?"

"I somehow think that wouldn't stop you," he had told her, and she had chortled in agreement.

"I have a feeling that wasn't the head of the deacons on the phone," she said now, lifting one eyebrow. "Next time you talk to her, tell her I got that recipe for chicken enchiladas she wanted."

"I'll do that, if I remember."

Just then, there was a commotion down the hall, and his heart sank. He'd put Midas in one of the rooms near the front entrance and told him to sit and stay. And then he had forgotten all about him.

"Get down you brute. Get off me! *Off.*"

Pastor Mike brought his chair forward with a thud and whipped out of it and was out of his office door before it quit shaking. Violet was right behind him.

Agnes Skinner was being accosted by Midas, who had his full length against her pulpy body and was licking her face. Her back was to the wall, and a hotdog was raised high in one hand with her purse hanging from the other. Her hair was all askew, and she had mustard and ketchup on one cheek.

During the friendly attack, her green stretch pants had somehow slipped down, revealing a large white quivering belly.

Pastor Mike instantly ran to the tussling duo and pulled down his dog and placed him into a heeling position. Midas licked his lips and eyed the hot dog up over Agnes's head.

Agnes was furious. "That miserable mutt. Look what he did. Just look!"

Pastor Mike looked and couldn't see anything.

"What'd he do?" asked Violet, who was staying well away from the fracas.

"Dorcas and I brought in two hotdogs for Pastor Mike. Those New York hotdogs from the vendor downtown that I know he loves. That…that *brute* stole one. That ugly miserable dog should be in the pound. Whose dog is that anyway?"

Pastor Mike looked at Violet, who shrugged her shoulders. "It isn't my dog," she said.

"It's my ugly brute," Pastor Mike admitted, still trying to keep Midas from leaping after the second hotdog.

Agnes pulled up her pants, straightened her shirt, and smoothed her hair with her free hand, causing her red vinyl purse to dangle under her armpit. Then she smiled, revealing big brown coffee-stained teeth. "Oh," she said. "Well, I guess he isn't so bad then, if he's your dog," and she reached over to pat Midas on the head.

Unfortunately, in bending over, she also brought her hand down, and before Pastor Mike could react, Midas had jumped a full six feet straight up into the air and swiped the hotdog and swallowed it on the way down. One gulp on the way to the ground and it was gone.

Agnes was shocked.

"You probably shouldn't have been teasing him with that hotdog," Violet said. "Waving it in his face like that. Waved it my face, and I'd probably have snatched it right out of your hand, too."

Agnes pursed her lips and wrinkled her face and looked at her hand in disgust. She emitted a small cry.

Pastor Mike immediately reacted. "Are you all right? Midas didn't accidentally bite you when he was taking the hotdog, did he?" His voice was filled with concern.

"Bite me? No. It's dog spit! *Dog slime!* Ohhhh. Yuck. Dorcas, hand me a handkerchief. Dorcas?"

"She isn't here. Haven't seen her," Violet said, looking at Agnes like she was getting a little senile in her old age. Everyone at the Senior Center knew Dorcas lived in Spokane.

"Oh that girl…" Agnes said, holding her hand straight out as if it had a huge hunk of something totally vile sitting on top of it. She headed down the hall, hollering for Dorcas.

Violet leaned into Pastor Mike. "Girl? Agnes has been claiming Dorcas is forty-three for at least four years." She and Mike, with him holding Midas in a death grip, followed Agnes down the hall.

Dorcas had evidently decided to just sit in solitude until the hullabaloo died down and she felt it was safe to come out. They found her in a conference room, perched straight as a stick at the edge of a chair, with her hands folded carefully in her lap.

Upon seeing her mother, she moved her hands, cracked open her black vinyl handbag, and extracted a handkerchief, which she snapped twice in the air before handing it over.

"Now that you've delivered your hotdogs, I think we are free to leave, aren't we, *Mother*?" she asked, looking straight at her mother and ignoring Violet and Pastor Mike and the dog. She was obviously not happy about being there.

Before Agnes could answer, Violet plowed past Pastor Mike, swerved around Agnes, and held out her hand. "Dorcas, I haven't seen you in ages, not since you moved to Washington. I'll bet you're here for Christmas, right?"

"Hey, Violet," Dorcas said primly, looking away from her mother and touching Violet's hand briefly. If she was surprised to see Violet in the church she didn't display it. "It's good to see you. I'll be here for a few days."

Then she sent her mother a scathing look. "I gave up going to a weaver's convention with friends because Mother here declared she was almost bedridden and needed my help in making funeral arrangements. Obviously, that was just a little bit exaggerated."

Violet laughed as Agnes turned a deep purple. "You look pretty healthy to me, Agnes," she said. "And I know from bowling last week that you can still throw a pretty mean ball."

Agnes puffed up to her true bulk and lifted her chin. Pastor Mike noticed that there was an abundance of thick wiry hair underneath, and he jerked back when he realized he had moved his head forward to better see.

"I needed her here," Agnes whined. "And it was the only way I knew how. I thought it was important that she, well, that she meet some of my new friends in Danford as well as my new pastor."

Pastor Mike groaned inside. Agnes Skinner was a fairly new member. He didn't know that she too had a spinster daughter. What was it with these people? Did they grow them in the closet under sunlamps?

"Let's cut the crap, Mother," Dorcas said as she got up from the chair. Pastor Mike noticed that she had a good shape and a nice haircut. All in all, she was a lot more attractive than most of the females he'd seen on display.

She walked straight toward Pastor Mike, and he felt his eyes widening. He tried to hide his alarm.

"So you must be Dorcas," he said, holding out his hand.

"And you must be Pastor Mike Warren," she said sweetly, ignoring it. "Should I tell you what I know about you? You are in your mid-thirties and, oh so sad, a bachelor. You live in a huge fabulous house on the lake that you inherited from your grandmother. You need a wife. And my mother, evidently, needs me to be married off."

Then she stepped away and turned in a quick circle before confronting him again. "And let me tell you about me. Despite what my mother says, I am fifty-one years old, which makes her, despite what she says, a ripe old seventy-six. I weigh 179 pounds, and you might have noticed that I have thick ankles. I've heard that in the medical world thick ankles are referred to as "gankles." I am free, and if you want to marry me, just call my mother and let her know. I can meet you at the court house."

That said, Dorcas Skinner picked up her purse and headed toward the doorway where Pastor Mike and Violet stood in stunned silence. Midas was panting but didn't seem overly alarmed. He had his eye on Agnes who, he thought, might have another hotdog up her sleeve.

As Dorcas strode past Pastor Mike, she stopped and looked at him. "Oh yes, would you like to see my teeth?" she asked as she opened her mouth wide and leaned close to his face. He pulled back and bumped his head on the door frame.

"Mother, I will be in the car," she said firmly. "You are either right behind me, or you are walking home." Two steps later, she turned back around and planted a big kiss on Pastor Mike's cheek. Before she stomped off down the hallway, she whispered, "Sorry, Pastor" into his ear.

Agnes was sputtering, and for once, Violet didn't know what to say. She and Pastor Mike moved aside as Agnes jogged quickly down the hall, her purse swinging and her fat behind jiggling.

"Good Lord," Violet said, looking at her pastor.

"Shall we pray?" he responded.

Chapter 53

A lot of people who weren't members of the church attended the Annual Christmas Eve Candle Lighting Service at Danford Worship Center. It was a magical time, and even Marcy had to admit she was enjoying herself.

There was a small skit, and Ben had the part of a talking donkey that was in the manger the night Jesus was born. He brayed at the top of his lungs when the Virgin Mary lifted her newborn son for the wise men to see. Marcy sunk down in her seat as everyone in the audience laughed. The laughter must have encouraged the donkey because he brayed again even louder until Mary frowned and told him loudly to shut up. Unfortunately, this caused her to lose her grip on the baby who fell to the floor. Without missing a beat, Mary picked him up by the leg and smacked the dust off by whapping him on the side of her bathrobe, which caused the angel on the roof of the stable to giggle.

"Oh, good Lord," Jim said softly, and Sharon poked him in the ribs. Off stage, Mrs. Johnson was thanking God that they didn't use the newborn Smith baby instead of the doll.

The applause and whistles after the skit were loud enough that they would have pleased members of a rock band in concert.

Afterwards, they sang a lot of Christmas carols, and then someone read a poem about Christmas.

At the end, they lighted their candles, one candle to the next and to the next until they were all glowing. One of the deacons turned off the lights, and the crowd was hushed and expectant. Faces above the candles glowed, and there was a feeling of total peace in the sanctuary. The worship leader began singing "Silent Night," and everyone joined in. As she did each year, her mother cried. Looking around, Marcy noticed that most of the women were crying. Barbara was holding Joe's arm with all her might, and the tears were streaming. The Millers, of course, had good reason to bawl.

They all trooped out of the church to find a good two inches of new snow on the ground and covering their vehicles. More was coming down—big fat snowflakes that fell lazily from the sky and landed on their heads and shoulders. As a group, all the kids ran into the parking lot and picked up handfuls of snow and tossed it in the air and at each other. Then en masse, they raised their faces to the heavens and opened their mouths to catch snowflakes on their tongues. New snow for Christmas. It was a true blessing.

Marcy missed Anna. She and Anna had sat together at the candle lighting service since they were kindergartners. Most times, they were in the plays or helping serve cookies and punch. She wondered if there would ever be a day, one full day, when she didn't miss Anna.

Pastor Mike came bounding out of the church and chased some of the boys with a snowball. Then he sprinted over to where Marcy's family was chatting with Mr. Knutson and the Millers. His cheeks were red from the cold, and his eyes danced in merriment.

"I'm off," he told them. "The deacons are going to lock up and one of them is driving me to the airport. I'm all packed and ready to go."

He shook hands with the men and hugged the women. Then he turned back and hugged Joe and Jim and shook Henry's hand again.

"Thank you all for everything. And wish me luck," he said. Marcy didn't know what that meant, but all the adults were beaming.

Then he turned to Marcy and bent over and put the palms of his hands on her cheeks. They were cold but made her feel cozy inside. "And you, my sweet Marcy, you have a wonderful Christmas. I know it's been hard, and I am so very proud of you. God will bless your faithfulness to him."

Before she could answer, he was off and running to the side parking lot, where his ride was waiting. "God bless you everyone!" he hollered as he slipped inside the car. They all waved as he left.

Chapter 54

Mr. Knutson and the Millers and some of their other friends were coming to the Petermans for hot chocolate and cookies, and Marcy was glad. Maybe she could get a few hints as to what was happening. She still hadn't solved the mystery, although she knew something really, really *big* was happening. Despite giving Ben all sorts of rewards for his sleuthing abilities, he hadn't been able to unearth a single clue.

If she kept her mouth shut and her ears open, maybe someone would slip. She had a feeling that this Christmas present—whatever it was—involved more than just her family. She thought Joe and Barbara might know something too. Twice, she had caught her mother on the phone to Barbara when her mother had hurriedly, and not very smoothly, changed the subject.

Ben got them to sing Jingle Bells all the way home, and they were in a merry mood by the time they stomped up the veranda into the living room.

"Take those boots off and put them away," Sharon scolded as Ben took off across the foyer. He turned an about-face and tossed them off his feet where they landed in a corner.

"Is that where they go?" she asked.

Ben groaned and leaned forward and let his arms go limber like a baboon's as he walked over to pick them up and put them in a closet.

Marcy never had to be told about her boots or coat or mittens. She was tidy to a fault. Ben, on the other hand, was a slob. His mother had to almost undress him herself to get him in the tub, but once he was in, he could play for hours. The ring he left behind could win an award if there was an award for such a thing. It didn't make a lick of sense to Marcy. Ben could dig in the dirt and fish out angleworms and eat an apple at the same time. The soap in the bathroom soap dish had to have the boy-mud rinsed off after Ben used it. His hair was never combed, his sneakers tied, and it was a household challenge to get him to brush his teeth.

But Marcy had to admit, these all-boy characteristics of him were what made him so adorable. Sometimes, anyway.

Within a few minutes, the house was buzzing with a multitude of conversations. It was a tradition, the Christmas Eve after-church gathering, and each year a few more people came. None of them stayed long, and Marcy knew that, as always, Joe and Barbara would be the last to leave. They would stay to help clean up.

Marcy skulked after her parents, listening in on one conversation after the other. She paid particular attention when Sharon was chatting with a woman from church who was about to give birth and was, in fact, overdue. The woman was huge, and Marcy couldn't believe there was just one baby in there. She wouldn't be surprised if any minute now the woman gave a piercing cry, fell to the floor, and started moaning. Her husband would then start yelling for someone to start boiling water.

Finally, Marcy gave up listening and poured a glass of punch and sat at the kitchen table. That was where Barbara found her.

"Hey, Marcy, why aren't you up playing with the rest of the gang? I just checked, and they're having a great time playing games."

"Nah. I'd rather stay down here," Marcy said glumly. She picked up a cookie and looked at it before putting it back down. Crumbs scattered on the table.

Barbara took a chair beside her. "I know," she said. "It's really hard, isn't it? This first Christmas without her?"

Marcy turned and looked at her. "That too, but it isn't all that," she said. "I really miss Anna, and it was hard at church since we always sit together. But this is something else."

"Do you want to talk about it?"

Marcy lifted her shoulders and then dropped them. Barbara waited and prayed that no one would come into the kitchen for a few minutes. It was obvious that something was on Marcy's mind.

"If I ask you something, can you answer me?" Marcy asked mysteriously.

"I guess it depends on what the question is," Barbara said. "Try me. I'll be as honest as I can."

"Okay. My parents are up to something, and I don't know what. They're acting all strange. They're hugging and giggling in the corners, and they quit when I come in the room. Ben can't find out anything. I know that you and Mr. Miller know about it because she keeps acting funny when I walk by and she's on the phone with you. She changes the subject. At first, I thought they were taking us to Disneyland or on a cruise or something, but we would have already left by now. So there's only one thing left."

"And that is…" Barbara prompted. She hoped with all her heart that Marcy hadn't found out. It would be hard on her folks as well as Mr. Knutson if she knew about Kemo, let alone her and Joe. They were all so excited about this horse they could hardly stand it.

Marcy looked at her and lifted her chin to gather some bravery. Finally, she just blurted it out, "Is my mom pregnant?"

Barbara sat in shock for a full twenty seconds before she started laughing. Then she reached over and pulled Marcy into a huge hug. "No, sweetheart, your mom isn't pregnant."

Then she had a thought and let her go. "Does that make you sad? Would you like to have a baby sister or brother?"

"At first, it was kind of gross, but then I got used to it. I think it would be nice to have a baby."

Then she had a thought, and she looked at Barbara curiously. "Do you think you will ever have another baby?"

Barbara was surprised that the tables had turned and now she was the one being questioned. "No, I can't ever have another baby," she said sadly. "Anna was our miracle child, and after her, I had to have surgery. There aren't any babies in our future. Now we have just you and Ben and all the other special kids we love."

"I didn't know. I'm sorry. I asked Anna once, and she didn't know why she didn't have a brother or a sister."

It seemed strange to Barbara that Anna and Marcy had discussed this. "Did she want one?" she asked.

"Well, sometimes, but then we'd get around Ben, and she'd change her mind."

They both laughed. Then Marcy shook her head. "I guess that was a stupid idea, that Mom was pregnant. I didn't think she could be because Dad had that thing done, but then I thought maybe she was. Nothing else made any sense. So can you tell me what the big surprise is?"

Barbara laughed. "Sorry, Charlie. Nice try. You will have to wait until tomorrow. I will tell you this. You will like it."

Marcy threw her hands up in the air melodramatically "That's all? That's the only hint I get?"

"That's all I'm going to say. My lips are sealed," Barbara said, and she turned and left the kitchen. A few minutes later, she noticed out of the corner of her eye that Marcy was sprinting up the stairs to be with the other youngsters.

Chapter 55

The baggage area at the Sea-Tac Airport outside of Seattle is huge with a multitude of carousels for incoming luggage and streams of people coming and going. Rachel positioned herself near the escalator and watched for Mike. Her eyes ached from watching.

Finally she saw him and watched in amusement as his eyes scanned the crowd, looking for her. Using the advantage of the height of the escalator, he scanned quickly, knowing that in just seconds he'd be on ground level and it would be more difficult to find her in the Christmas crowd.

Halfway down, he spotted her, and his face lit up in delight. She grinned and waved and threw him a kiss. Then they were in each other's arms, and it felt, to both of them, as if they'd come home. They had been adrift, and now they were back in safe harbor.

Mike was surprised at the sheer number of people in the airport. It was late Christmas Eve, and he would have thought they'd be safely at their destinations by now. Rachel explained that some of the flights to go back east had been cancelled due to weather, and the whole airport, she imagined, was full of stranded people.

"You're lucky this is where you get off," she told him. "You're lucky I don't live in Toledo."

"Toledo? Holy Toledo? I can't imagine going steady with a gal from Holy Toledo."

She burst into laughter. "Going steady? I didn't think anyone used that term anymore. Do I get your class ring to wear on a chain around my neck? Do I get to wear your letter sweater?"

"You seem to know an awful lot about going steady," he chided her. "I'd give you my class ring but I lost it and the only thing I lettered in was being a goofball in study hall."

"I didn't know they had a letter for that. I learned about going steady from my mother."

"Really?" he said in mock surprise. "I learned about going steady from my mother, too. She called me last week and asked if you and I were going steady. It was the craziest thing I'd ever heard. Going steady. Good grief, we're both way over the hill."

"I wouldn't call us 'way over,'" she protested.

Before he could come up with a brilliant answer, her cell phone chimed, and she pulled it from her purse. Mike knew from Rachel's answer it was Marcy.

"Is everything all right?" Mike whispered with concern, and Rachel nodded and gave him a thumbs-up sign. Then she said, "Just a sec, Marcy," and turned to Mike.

"She needs to talk to me. Why don't you grab your suitcase, and I'll meet you back here in a few minutes?"

Mike watched as she walked off, headed to somewhere, anywhere, that was private enough to carry on a conversation. He wondered what was happening that would make Marcy call. It was late. Nearly ten o'clock.

He missed his suitcase the first time around since it seemed like there were about 10,000 that looked just like it. He had a friend who always tied lengths of brightly colored engineer's tape on the handle. Mike had always thought it looked sort of stupid, but now, he wished he'd been smart enough to look stupid too. He wondered how many people got to where they were going and discovered they had the wrong suitcase. Opened it up and there was a whole bunch of size-twenty-two muumuus and thong underwear. And you were a guy. And pity the poor size-twenty-two who got who-knows-who's suitcase.

He reached over to snatch it off the moving carousel just as a whole herd of people pulled up behind him. Inching his way through the crowd and dragging his bag by the handle, he went back to their appointed spot and waited. He was glad to see Rachel on her way toward him.

"Is she okay?"

"She's wonderful," Rachel said. "Remember the whole balloon launch thing and I told her that when the time was right to call me and I would tell her how to let Anna go? Well, at midnight tonight, she is going to let the balloon go and let Anna go. She wanted me to tell her how."

Mike beamed. "She's growing up, our little Marcy," he said. "God is really doing some work in healing her. In healing all of us, especially Joe and Barbara. Anna's death was horrible, but when you look back you can see what good has come of it. Henry is coming to church and some of the girls from her school. People are more loving and kind. And this is just the start. God can always take something bad, or tragic, and make something good out of it."

"At midnight, we need to pray for her," Rachel said. She and Mike had prayed together frequently. She found that praying together was incredibly intimate. She and Vince had enjoyed a wonderful sex life, but praying with Mike was infinitely more intimate.

"She also asked," Rachel continued, "if I knew anything about the big present, she's getting tomorrow. I lied and told her I knew a little. I lied!"

"You can confess to me later, my child," he teased. "But it really wasn't a lie. It was hedging. If you'd told her yes, you'd still be on the phone with her trying to worm it out of you."

"Don't you wish we could be there tomorrow?" Rachel asked, tucking her arm into his as they walked toward the parking garage.

"I'd rather be with you," he said.

"I wonder how they'll do it," Rachel said wonderingly.

"I'm sure they've been planning all week," Mike said, laughing.

Chapter 56

* * *

We were playing at Slate Creek, sitting on the edge of the wide plank bridge and dangling our naked feet over the edge. There were always cow pies in the middle of the bridge, but the edges were safe for clean-sitting. Well, except for a bit of Montana dirt. We had found a patch of tiny wild strawberries and filled our hands and were eating them. Sometimes, when we played Indians, we imagined living off the land. I told Anna that if we were true Indians, we would starve to death. She laughed and said we would have to shoot a buffalo. That would feed us.

Just then, old Bessie came plodding up to the bridge, her huge udders hanging almost to the ground. Behind her were the other milk cows: Oreo, Daisy, Lulu, and Snickers. Two of them, including Bessie, were brown Guernseys, and the other three were black-and-white spotted Holsteins. The plank edges we were sitting on lifted with their weight as they stepped on them, and the sound of clomping hooves brought smiles to our faces. We scrambled to our feet, and one after the other, they stopped so we could scratch their foreheads. We loved the cows.

The cows belonged to the people at the top of the hill, and they were heading home to be fed and milked. This knowledge was what sent us racing to put on our tennis shoes.

"The cows heading home means it's five o'clock, and I was supposed to be home by four," Anna yelped. "Oh, man, am I in trouble! My mom hates me to be late."

"Dang it," I said in response. I couldn't get my shoe on, and I knew I was in trouble too. We raced up the hill past the plodding cows and pulled our bikes out of the ditch and pedaled as fast as we could. Time, once again, had gotten away from us.

* * *

Marcy didn't need to set her alarm clock to wake up. She just knew she would. God would wake her up. At midnight, she would go outside and let the balloon go. She would let Anna go.

The pink Mylar balloon, still almost as perky as it was when she got it at the balloon launch event, was ready to go. She had to admit she would miss the balloon and the way it floated from here to there in the house and always ended up in Marcy's room right above her bed. It was like having a constant friend.

After reading through her note again, she carefully attached it to the string. She wondered if she would always remember the words. *"I will always love you, Anna, and no matter what happens in my life, you will always be my best friend. I hope someday I can remember you without feeling sad, that someday I can think of you and laugh instead of cry, and that someday I won't feel so empty and lost and hollow inside. I really don't want to let you go, but I know I have to. I miss you so much. Marcy."*

She moaned softly and wiped her tears and gathered her courage. She was ready to let it go. She was growing up, and things were changing. She could no longer keep one foot in real life and the other in the past—one foot in living and the other in grieving.

She would never forget Anna. Anna would always be a part of her life, and this wasn't abandoning those memories or the parts of her that had been molded by Anna. This was simply letting go of the grief and no longer letting it control her life or her actions.

Of course, she would have bouts of crying and depression and times when she would brood, but she didn't want them to be her whole life. God didn't want her to suffer; he wanted her to be happy and fulfilled and to go about the business of helping others. How could she help others if she was a mess herself?

A few minutes before midnight, she pulled on socks and tugged a sweatshirt over her pajama top. Then she sat on her bed and looked at the balloon. Was she really ready to do this?

Taking the string of the balloon, she walked out of her bedroom and crept down the stairs. Minutes later, she had pulled on her boots and put on her coat and hat and mittens. She opened the door and walked out onto the porch.

She gasped. It was like being in a fairyland. Everything was blanketed in white, and it was the kind of snow that sparkles like diamonds. As far as she could see, there were glittering diamonds.

Some of their neighbors had left on their Christmas lights, and the lights, now covered with snow, shone muted and soft and enhanced the beauty of the night.

The neighborhood was hushed in sleep. There were no sounds of traffic or wind or rustling tree branches or dogs barking. Simply total silence.

Marcy stepped off the porch and walked down to the sidewalk. The balloon bobbed happily behind her. The snow was up to the sides of her boots, and she looked back to see her tracks. The thought flashed through her mind that back there was her past and ahead—

perfect and untouched—was the future. She was at the crossroads, and she could turn around and go back or she could move forward.

She moved forward.

She went past the end of the sidewalk to the middle of the street, where there was more space. She shut her eyes and prayed aloud, asking for God's guidance, and his help.

"Lord, you know how hard this is for me. Please be with me and give me strength and courage. I know we aren't supposed to ask for signs, but please, Lord, can you give me a sign soon that everything will be all right? I still sometimes feel like I'm a mess inside. Thank you for your love for me, and thank you for loving Anna. Please tell her hi for me and tell her I miss her. Oh, God, help me do this. Help me let this balloon go."

She turned her face upward. The sky was black and scattered with twinkling stars. It was if God's hand had spilled them out against the magnificence of the night sky so that they could mirror the glitter of the snow. Overhead, the balloon was perfectly still. The note glowed palely against the shadow of night.

Marcy looked at the balloon for a few seconds, and then she raised her hand. The string jerked when the balloon floated upward enough to snap it taut. Then, just like that, she opened her fist. The pink balloon seemed to hover for a scant second, and then it floated away, straight up, higher and higher and higher until she could no longer see it.

Afterwards, she put her head down and closed her eyes. Then she mentally took one of Anna's hands and placed it in the hand of someone she loved with all her heart. As she did it, she envisioned each of them—Anna so beautiful and full of life, and he, the giver and taker of that life.

The words she spoke were aloud. "Anna, tonight, I have taken your hand and placed it in the hand of Jesus. I am releasing you to him so that you can fly, Anna, and so that I, down here, can also fly. I will always love you, and I am letting you go."

By the end, her words were choked and strangled, but she said them, and she meant them. She sat in the middle of the road and prayed and let the love of the Lord wash over her and give her comfort and peace.

Chapter 57

The Christmas Eve snow in Danford continued to fall through most of the night. At 4:00 a.m., when Sharon got up to put the Santa presents under the tree, she peeked outside to see a beautiful world of white. There were at least six inches of new pristine white snow. No tire tracks on the road had obliterated its beauty, and it looked like a long river of white. Her eyes traveled to the sidewalk, and she noticed footprints going to the end, out into the road, and then coming back. They had partly filled with new snow, but they were definitely tracks. It didn't make any sense, but she was too tired to think about it much.

The sidewalk would need shoveled, and she knew Jim would be out there as soon as he got up. He liked shoveling the sidewalk. She'd ask him to study the footprints and see if he could figure it out.

It had been difficult to think of something to get Ben that would equal what Marcy was getting, and they had finally settled on tickets to a Seahawk's football game in Seattle. Jim and Ben would fly together—just the two of them—and make a weekend of it. The hotel they had reservations for had an indoor water park, and she knew Ben would be ecstatic.

She also realized that there was another horse in their future. Jim had talked to her about it and told her he was buying her one in the spring. She needed, he told her firmly, to replace Cindy. She had cried, of course, and agreed. She was already casually looking in the paper and online.

For almost a week, phone calls and e-mails had been flying. Sharon was amazed at the work that was going into presenting Marcy with this horse. She could have planned a trip to New York in less time.

Jim had brought home a van from work, and the plan was that they would all pile into it and go pick up her gift. Marcy already knew that Joe and Barbara were coming over for Christmas, and they had, just yesterday, told the kids that Mr. Knutson was also spending the day with them.

Marcy wouldn't be suspicious about Joe and Barbara because they frequently did things with them. But Sharon thought she might wonder about Henry Knutson coming over even though he had become closer to the family in recent weeks and sat with them at church. She had already explained to Marcy and Ben that poor Mr. Knutson didn't have anywhere else to go for Christmas and was spending the day with them so they expected him to be there along with the Millers. So maybe it wouldn't be a problem at all.

She crept through the dark house back to bed even though she knew she'd be lucky to get in another two hours before Ben came bounding into the room. The year before, which still caused her to cringe when she thought about it, he had streaked downstairs at three thirty in the morning to see what Santa had brought him. He was so excited he didn't even think and called his best friend on the phone. When his friend's father answered groggily, Ben asked if Ian was there and then rattled off everything that he'd gotten in his stocking and told all about his train set.

Ian's father said, "Ben, do you know what time it is?" Then as the story went with retelling, there was a long pause, and Ben said "Oh!" and hung up.

Marcy heard her mother get up and sneak down the hall. She also heard her come back up the stairs to her bedroom. She thought about going downstairs but decided not to. She knew it was right down there, right there under the tree. She'd given up trying to guess what it was. She just wished it was over. Then again, the anticipation was delicious.

Ben had them up by seven, and within minutes Sharon had coffee brewing, muffins and cherry turnovers on a tray, milk in a pitcher, and eggs scrambling. They could, she told Ben, wait for five minutes before opening their presents so she could fix a quick breakfast. He grumbled, but as much as his head wanted the presents, his stomach wanted food and was telling him that this wasn't a bad idea. They all pitched in, getting down plates, getting silverware, pouring milk, and dishing up food when the eggs were done.

The night before, they had read the story of Jesus out of the chapter of Luke and talked about the meaning of Christmas. Sharon knew her children knew the real reason for Christmas, and she wasn't one of those Christian parents who condemned the whole thing about Santa Claus. She figured he was like inviting a clown to a birthday party. Everyone liked the clown, but they all knew who they were honoring and what the real reason for the party was.

They carried their plates and drinks and settled in the living room close to the tree. Jim and Sharon sat together on the couch, Marcy was in a matching chair, and Ben was on the floor, as close to the pile gifts he could get.

As was tradition, after they were all passed out, they opened gifts from youngest to oldest so everyone could enjoy seeing what the others received. For all of them—well, except maybe Ben—the most pleasurable part of opening presents was to see the reactions.

They went slowly this year and took a few breaks to reload plates or refresh coffee mugs. Ben loved his tickets to the Seahawks game and jumped up and down when they told him about the impending trip. It was, he declared over and over, the best present ever.

Marcy still didn't know what her "best present ever" was. After all the gifts were opened, she knew there was something more. While her mother sat smiling, her dad explained that she would have to wait until afternoon.

"But everyone will be here then. The Millers and Mr. Knutson. Can't I see it in private?" She was thoroughly puzzled.

"It isn't here in the house," Sharon said. "We have to go pick it up. Since they'll already be here, we'll just take everyone with us. We'll go right after dinner, around four."

Marcy looked at her watch. "Well, that's not so long away," she said. "And it will be fun to have the Millers and Mr. Knutson. Well, maybe. What if it's something embarrassing like ear piercing or something? I wouldn't want a whole crowd there watching me get my ears pierced."

"You know it's not getting your ears pierced," her mother said. "You aren't sixteen. When you're sixteen, you can get your ears pierced." Marcy thought that was lame, but they'd had this battle many times, and she wasn't going to ruin Christmas by taking up her sword again.

"I promise you it isn't something that is embarrassing," Jim said. "And now we need to open another present because I can tell you're about to start begging us to tell you what it is."

"I think it's a boyfriend," Ben teased. "She really wants one of those." Jim and Sharon both opened their mouths to speak, but before they could Marcy butted in.

"I know, not until I'm sixteen," she said, rolling her eyes. Then she laughed. "But that's a great idea, Benny!"

Just after noon, Joe and Barbara knocked on the door, and not long after that, Henry Knutson arrived in his old truck. Sharon hugged him close and then stood back.

"Henry, you smell wonderful. What is that? Old Spice? I love that smell. My Grampa used to wear Old Spice."

He turned furiously red. Then he reached down and picked up what he'd placed on the veranda floor to knock on the door. It was huge and wrapped in green florist's paper.

Sharon took it from him and set it on a nearby table and pulled off the paper, revealing a beautiful Christmas centerpiece with roses and carnations, cedar branches, silver balls, and a myriad of other things. It was gorgeous, and she and Barbara were both delighted. Barbara quickly removed the silk flower arrangement Sharon had already placed on the table, and Sharon put down the one Henry brought.

She and Barbara stood back. "Perfect," Sharon said, and Barbara agreed.

By three o'clock, everyone was groaning from eating so much food, and they still had dessert to go. Barbara declared it was the best turkey she had ever eaten, and Sharon told her she thought it was because this year she had purchased a fresh turkey instead of one was frozen.

That sent the two women off on a deep conversation about turkeys and dressing recipes. The men, in the living room, were discussing engines and football and fishing. Ben was playing with his new toys, and Marcy was wondering what was taking the clock so long to travel from one minute to the next.

After the kitchen was tidied, and they had taken a vote and decided they would eat dessert after getting Marcy's present, Sharon declared it was about time to leave.

Marcy was excited, but she felt sort of silly that all this attention was being given to her. She was thankful that they didn't remind her over and over again about how wonderful it was going to be and asking if she was excited. Instead, the adults chatted about this and that and everything else as they made their way out of Danford and to a small side road. Marcy, by now, was thoroughly bewildered.

The road went through farmland, and soon, they came to an intersection, and Jim took a left. A quarter of a mile later, he turned down a long driveway. The sign said, "Rocky Mountain Stables."

And suddenly she knew.

This was their big gift. They were getting her riding lessons. They all thought that this was her perfect gift. They'd bring her here once a week or maybe every other week on a Saturday afternoon, and she could ride some strange horse around and around a corral. She wanted to cry. She wanted to yell and demand that they just turn around.

And then she looked at them. Her dad, smiling as he drove slowly to the stable, and her mother up front and turning around to laugh with Barbara. Mr. Knutson, sitting next to Joe and both of them looking as if they could hardly wait to show her. Only Ben was still puzzled.

They all loved her, and she knew their hearts were in the right place, and she had to be careful not to say anything cruel. But how could they all be so stupid to think that any old horse could take the place of Kemo. This was as bad as if they brought some strange girl to the house and said, "Here. Here's your new friend to take Anna's place."

Choking down the bitter tears that threatened, she forced herself to smile and act excited. "Is this it?" she asked, and they all nodded like grinning bobble heads. Their smiles were on bright, and she didn't think they could smile any broader. Her mother and Barbara looked tearful over the thought of Marcy getting this wonderful gift.

"Look at all those horses!" Ben exclaimed, and Marcy turned her head to look. There were four or five of them in a clump at the end of a pasture. Maybe these were the ones she would visit every week or so. She tried to summon up some sort of feeling of excitement. It wasn't there.

As they clambered out of the vehicle, the door to the stable opened, and a short scrawny man walked over and shook hands all around. "And you must be Marcy," he said, looking at her. His name was Ivan Percy, and he had the western wear and the bowed legs to prove he knew all about horses. She had to admit his good cheer and friendliness was catching, and she was starting to feel better about the whole thing.

"I'm proud to be a part of your Christmas present," Ivan Percy said as he escorted them into a huge building. Sharon had made it perfectly clear that he was not to say one word, not one word, about the horse they had boarded there the last few days. It was their gift to give, and he'd better not ruin it. She'd told him three times since she'd heard he was a bit of a blabbermouth. She shot him a look, and he backed off and let Jim and Sharon escort her through the door.

It was an indoor riding arena, and it was cavernous. The dirt floor had been churned up by a thousand hoof prints, and it smelled good, like horses, hay, leather, and liniment. There were overhead lights way up near the roof so it wasn't dark. A small room jutted out on the left side and had windows looking out over the arena. Marcy thought this was probably an office and maybe a small store. They led her close to the office and stopped.

"Well, I'll just stay back here and let you tell her," Ivan Percy said, and he moved over to a neat pile of hay bales and sat down.

"We don't want to drag this out any longer," Sharon said, "so we aren't going to make a big to-do over it. Before we tell you about your big present, Barbara and Joe have something for you."

The gift was already there, next to the office door on a chair. They really had planned this out. Marcy knew what it was when Barbara handed the wrapped box to her. Boots. Of course it was boots. She unwrapped it and lifted the lid, and even though the whole horse thing was upsetting, she had to admit the boots were beautiful. She'd always wanted cowboy boots. They were beautiful brown suede with fancywork on the sides. She took one out and lifted it to her nose. It smelled heavenly.

"Your mom told us your size," Barbara said. She and Joe were holding hands, and for some reason, he looked like he was about to jump out of his skin.

"Are you all right, Mr. Miller," Marcy asked him.

"Just excited," he said, beaming and doing a little dance in place.

Marcy thanked the Millers for the boots and gave them a big hug. Barbara and her mother sniffled.

"But wait, that's not all!" Jim said. Maybe Marcy imagined it, but his voice sounded strange.

Then he lifted his voice and hollered, "Okay, we're ready."

Suddenly, it was so quiet. Everyone had stopped talking and had walked up a few steps. They were all looking out into the arena.

Suddenly, there was Henry Knutson. She hadn't even seen him slip away from the group. He had a length of lead rope in his hands, and he was smiling and crying all at the same time. He stumbled a bit and then caught himself and continued, walking out toward the center of the ring, the rope dragging in the dirt behind him. Then he stopped and turned around to look back from where he came.

He clicked his tongue a few times, and then there she was...

Marcy gave a choked sound before emitting a piercing cry. She flew across the arena, sending clods of dirt flying. She threw herself against the horse's shoulder and then hugged her neck, sobbing and wailing over and over again. *Kemo, Kemo, Kemo*. The horse reached down and nuzzled Marcy with her nose, making soft snuffling noises.

They were all crying by now, and Sharon passed out tissues as they walked toward the heart-rending scene in front of them. Henry

Knutson was in bad shape, and Sharon went and put her arm around the old man.

Marcy lifted her face, which was streaked with tears. Her nose was swollen and red, and her eyes were puffy, and her father thought she had never looked more beautiful.

She couldn't talk, except to get a "How did…" out before her face wrinkled up and she started crying again.

"It was Henry," Sharon said in a choked voice. "He got her for you. He did it all."

Marcy walked to him, and he opened his arms, and she stepped in. He held her tight in a bear hug as they both cried.

"You needed that horse, and that horse needed you," he said gruffly. "And it wasn't all me. Your folks here and Joe and Barbara, we all have been workin' on it."

Marcy walked back to Kemo and took the horse's massive head in her hands. Kemo lowered it so that their cheeks touched. The horse nickered softly, and Marcy could feel the horse's warm breath on her neck.

"Can we take her home?" she asked. Her nose sounded stuffy, like she'd jammed it full of cotton balls.

"She's going right back to Rice's Hill," her dad said, and Marcy's face crumpled again, and her eyes refilled with tears.

After hugs all around, Henry saddled the horse, and Marcy rode her around the arena.

"She's a natural," Henry hollered over, pointing out her posture and how she held her hands and legs.

When it was time, it was all she could do to leave Kemo's side, but Ivan Percy assured her he'd take good care of the horse. Through the whole thing, he'd wept like a baby, and he was glad he chose to sit back in the corner so no one would see. He never considered that his eyes and nose would give him away.

Marcy hugged him on the way out and thanked him. And he promised her again he'd take good care of her horse for the next few days.

Her parents told her about Mr. Knutson's offer to keep Kemo at his place, which was just a block from her house.

"But before that, we have a ton of work to do to get the barn ready," Jim Peterman said. "We're all going to pitch in and work on it. We could have done it ahead of time, but we thought you'd want to be involved."

"Can we start right now?" she asked. "We could go home and change clothes and start right now?"

Everyone laughed, and Sharon reminded them that the pies were waiting and, if anyone wanted one, a turkey sandwich. She knew Henry Knutson, for one, would side with her on the decision.

Chapter 58

The next morning, Jim and Joe and Henry Knutson headed to Home Depot to pick up some lumber and new hinges, hooks, and a few other odds and ends.

By ten o'clock, they were all gathered at the barn. Sharon had brought a cotton tablecloth, bottled water, and thermoses of coffee and hot chocolate, and a plastic container of cookies. She figured they'd need to take breaks.

The men had spent some time in the barn, measuring and looking at things structurally, but for the rest of them, it was the first time they had seen it, except from the road.

The barn was old, probably built around 1925, the same time as the house. The red paint was mostly gone, but it was still handsome with silvery weathered wood. It was sturdy and had the typical arched roof and the big door on the second level for putting in and tossing out bales of hay.

The barn was behind the house, facing the road, and Rice's Hill sloped off to the right of it. It was, Sharon thought, beautiful.

They walked in the door, and she and Barbara stood there, while Marcy and Ben scampered ahead. Sharon felt her heart flutter, and she wondered if anyone else here was that excited. There was just something absolutely wonderful about a barn.

"I've always wanted to own a barn," Barbara said quietly and with a bit of wonder in her voice. She and Sharon had walked slowly ahead to the huge open area where the hay and straw were. Except for a layer of age-grayed old straw on the floor, it was empty. Voices echoed in the cavernous room.

They were both looking up at the rafters. In a few places, they could see daylight shining through, and there was a long rope hanging from a beam. A group of startled pigeons took flight from deep in the loft and flew out through an opening near the top beams.

"Me too," Sharon admitted. "Isn't this wonderful?"

"Did you ever sleep in a barn as a kid?"

"Once or twice. A friend lived on a farm, and they had a barn. In the summer, they'd sleep out there."

"My grandparents had one," Barbara said. "They sold their place a few years back and moved to a condo. When Joe and I were first married and visited, we'd always ask to sleep in the barn. Gram thought we were crazy to sleep in that dirty old barn, but I loved it."

"We should ask if we could have a big slumber party here sometime," Sharon said.

"I'm sure he'd let us. That's a great idea," Barbara said with excitement.

They all explored and found that it was a simple structure. The man door, which was the main entrance, opened into a small room with a fairly low ceiling that was for tack and similar items. Inside the room and facing the door, there was a bank of small-paned windows on the right, all of them grungy. Barbara thought they probably had never been cleaned.

Inside the room, an old oak table was in a corner with a few rickety chairs, and there was a workbench with old tools under the row of windows. From there, an open walkway with windows all along it led to four handcrafted plank milking stanchions that were situated behind the tack room. Cribs still held clumps of ancient dusty hay, and a couple of old three-legged milking stools straddled the worn wood. A stack of nestled milk buckets were alongside.

Above the stables and the tack room was an open loft for storage of hay. As Marcy and Ben quickly learned, you could climb the wooden ladder along the wall and cautiously creep on hands and knees onto the loft. They hollered down at everyone from up there, and their movements sent down a sifting of hay and grit.

The loft looked out over the huge area for more hay storage. This part of the barn, which was probably thirty feet high from floor to ceiling, took up three quarters of the building.

The entire place was impressive and very dirty and dusty. Cobwebs laced everything together and formed artistic patterns in the corners of the windows.

Since it was just the day after Christmas, it was chilly, and Henry had stoked up an old pot-bellied stove in front of the tack room that quickly heated the smaller room and the stable area. By turning on an ancient dust-crusted fan, the whole barn would was soon warm.

Barbara and Sharon each grabbed a broom and started sweeping down cobwebs from the walls and ceiling and then started sweeping the tack room. They might as well, they decided, start at the front door.

"Marcy and Ben, you two can wash these windows," Sharon said, calling to them where they were romping in the hay.

The three men were barely visible through the filthy windows as they stood in the snow with their hands in their pockets looking at the old water trough. Sharon and Barbara knew from listening to their husbands that the trough was half full of old water, which was frozen solid.

Soon, the three turned and came back to the barn and stomped the snow off their feet at the door.

"So what's the verdict," Barbara asked.

"Well, Henry here says it needs a floating heater. It has a wire cage, so it won't hurt the horse, and it'll keep the water from freezing. We can run a hose from the house to fill it and toss in the heater, and everything should work fine."

"Sounds like a plan to me," Sharon said as she scooted the table out from the wall to sweep under it. She'd already moved the chairs away.

Henry looked a bit chagrined, and she went over and patted his arm. "Don't worry, Henry," she said, "we won't hang curtains on the windows."

"I was getting a mite worried," he admitted. "What would my old cronies think if I had some frilly lace curtains on the windows?"

"I don't know what the guys would think, but I'd think it might get some of the women at the Senior Center thinking of you in a different light," Barbara said.

"I don't think those old biddies need much encouragement," he said ruefully. "They've been hounding me since Ida died, calling and flirting, making some excuse to get me to come over."

"Imagine being a single guy and having that problem," Jim said to Joe and shaking his head. They all laughed. They really laughed when Joe suggested Henry talk to Pastor Mike about females on the prowl.

They had thought it would take several days to clean up the old barn, but it was going a lot more quickly. The three females had the tack room tidied and cleaned in just a couple of hours, and Jim and Ben had cleaned the stanchions out and swept that floor.

For their part, Henry and Joe had used pitchforks and push brooms to pile all the old loose straw in a corner. It would be moved outside when the weather got a bit nicer.

In a few minutes, the men would back up their pickups to the huge sliding doors and offload straw and hay they'd gotten after they left Home Depot.

Marcy and Ben would be in charge of putting down new straw. All the adults, who had done such chores as kids, knew they'd have a great time pulling off slabs of straw from the tight bales and breaking it up and scattering it.

Before long, the smell of years of dust would be taken over by the sweet smell of straw.

While the men were offloading the bales, Barbara, Sharon, and Marcy left to go back to the house and pick up the lunch basket and bring it back, also to use the bathroom.

"It isn't fair that men can just to go to the nearest tree and stand there and do their business," Sharon remarked.

The others agreed.

Along with the lunch, Sharon grabbed as many pairs of work gloves as she could find. They were all starting to get blisters, and without gloves, the kids would hurt their hands when they put down the clean straw.

By the time they returned to the barn, all the hay and the few bales of extra straw had been offloaded as well as fifty-pound bags of horse chow, oats, and sweet feed, which smelled like molasses. There were also, piled in the tack room, boxes filled with all sorts of items related to owning a horse.

Henry said he would spend the next few days going over with Marcy everything in the boxes so she knew what it all was.

"You have a lot of learning to do, young lady," he explained. "It's a lot of work taking care of a horse, and it means feeding and cleaning and grooming every day. It's not like a hamster where you can put in a bunch of food and water and walk off."

He handed her some books he'd picked up on horse care, and she promised to read them. They all knew she would.

"Horses come with their own world of gear and lingo, and it's all stuff you need to learn," Henry told Marcy. "These here, for example, are halters and bits. Hackamores, working, show…You'll need to know how to care for her hooves and how to put ointment on her sores. But we can learn all that over time. Tomorrow, maybe we can put up some hooks and hang this all on the wall. It's good to keep it all in order and in good shape."

He looked embarrassed that he'd talked so long and was thankful that Ben was digging through the boxes and holding up one thing after the other and taking the attention off him.

Of them all, Sharon was the only one who had any idea about horses and even that had faded in time.

"We'll need to buy a saddle, and maybe you can help us pick out one that's good," she said.

Henry smiled. "No need for that. This horse came with enough gear for three horses. She has three saddles, including a pack saddle. Ben, come with me."

Ben scrambled off the table where he was sitting with the boxes and hurried after Henry Knutson. Soon, they came back. Henry was carrying the plain, handsome, dark brown leather working saddle, and Ben was struggling under the pack saddle.

The females instantly went to the leather saddle, while the men checked over the intricacy of the pack saddle with its canvas bags and straps and figuring out how much it could pack.

Marcy ran her hand over the saddle horn and down to the seat. The leather was smooth and taut. It was hard to imagine it was hers. The whole thing was overwhelming.

"It's beautiful," she said softly. Barbara and Sharon agreed.

"It's probably a bit big for you now, but you'll grow into it in no time. It's a dandy saddle," her mother said.

"It's a dandy saddle, but it's a dirty saddle," Henry said. "In the next few days, I'll show you how to clean it and make it look good as new."

"Can I sit in it?" Ben asked. He was dying to try it out for size.

"You have to ask your sister first. And if she says yes, we need to put it on the saddle rack so it isn't damaged. You're light enough. You should be fine sitting on it."

Ben looked at Marcy, and his eyes were dancing.

"Sure, you can sit on it, buddy," she said, ruffling his hair.

Sharon was proud that Marcy was growing up so nicely. A year ago, she would have demanded that she sit in it first; it was her saddle after all.

After they all watched Ben have his turn in the saddle, Henry said, "So do you want to see what I saved for last? The show saddle?"

They all said yes, and he went out to his truck. A few minutes later, he came back and heaved it all out on the table.

"Oh my!" said Sharon, and everyone had similar sentiments.

"Is that real silver?" Joe asked.

Henry looked at it proudly. He wished he'd taken a before photo so they could see the work he'd put into it. "It is. And the bridle has matching silver."

Marcy was dumbstruck, and her eyes were huge. "Oh, wow!" she finally said in a breathless whisper. "Kemo must be beautiful wearing that saddle."

"She is," Henry said. "Lena, my granddaughter, rode her in every rodeo when she was in high school. She carried the American flag."

"Do you think I could ever do that? Ride Kemo and carry the flag?"

"I think you can do anything you want. Kemo is also a great barrel horse. You could learn to barrel race or do calf-roping, or you could just enjoy riding and being with your horse. There's an old saying that there's nothing better than a good horse beneath you and a blue sky above."

"All this is making me want to go out and buy a horse," Joe said to Barbara, and she looked alarmed. Two days before, he had told her about maybe getting a retriever.

After another hour or work in the barn, they all decided they were worn out and it was time to quit. Another few hours and they'd have it completed and they could bring Kemo home. The plan was that the next day, Jim and Marcy and Henry would hook up Henry's old horse trailer and go over and pick her up.

Just as Jim was about to open the barn door so they could all leave, Marcy said, "Um," and everyone turned to look at her.

She shrugged her shoulders, and her eyes filled with tears. She said only two words. "Thank you."

Chapter 59

It had been eight months since Anna's death, and Pastor Mike thanked God daily that he was bringing all of them through it with few scars. He knew, as did all of them, that it was God's grace that carried them. Now, as he sat in his living room and looked out over the lake, he pondered his life and the life of his friends, and they were easily summed up.

Within two months, Marcy had devoured every book she could find on horse care, horse nutrition, and horse riding. Except on the coldest of days, she and Kemo could be seen on Rice's Hill. Sometimes, she rode the horse down the road to her house, edged up to the side porch, and Ben would jump on behind her.

Henry Knutson was enormously proud of his protégé, and he felt perfectly comfortable leaving for three weeks. He and Dee and Sara Sue were going on a week-long cruise to the Bahamas, and they would also spend a couple of weeks in Florida. He couldn't say it was a vacation he would choose, but he knew he'd have a good time.

Jim and Sharon were happy and were very grateful that God had brought their Marcy back to them whole and happy. They knew she still had bad days, but she bounced right back after them. They just left her alone to work things out. Mike knew that the Petermans were closer now, the four of them, than they had been before. Their family was strong and secure.

As far as Ben, he was happy just being Ben. It didn't take much to turn his world upside down, and he had a ton of friends.

Joe and Barbara Miller. How dear these people were to him. They were the brother and sister he wanted and didn't get. They supported him unconditionally, and he felt free with them. He had discovered over the years that a pastor's life was a lonely life, and he was ever grateful that God had provided these treasured friends.

They talked about Anna often, and he knew they still struggled and their lives seemed empty. It was hard to be a family one day and be reduced to a couple the next. He prayed that God would help them deal with not having a child to nurture, and he knew that they also spent a great deal of time in prayer and asking for God's guidance and his peace. They had recently discussed taking in foster children.

He and Rachel? Mike and Rachel? Didn't that sound good, he thought to himself: Mike and Rachel.

His four days with Rachel and her family had been delightful. He had decided to stay there instead of with his friend since Rachel's parents had a big suitable house, big enough to forestall any sense of impropriety. He fell in love with her parents, and oddly, he felt as if he belonged there, much more than he felt he belonged with his own parents. That, to him, was infinitely sad.

As usual, when he sat daydreaming, his thoughts returned to giving her the ring. He hoped he would never forget the look on her face.

It was the day after Christmas, and Rachel and her mother had ducked out for a couple of hours to buy a few groceries. Mike had to chuckle inside when they announced they were headed to the store. He had been asking God to give him some time alone with Tim Fulton.

Tim was putting monofilament line on a new open-faced Daiwa fishing reel he'd gotten for Christmas, and Mike sat across from him and held the plastic spool as Tim wound the line on the reel.

"So are you a fisherman," Tim asked Mike. "I know you are a fisher of men, but do you go for real fish?"

Mike laughed. "I used to. I grew up fishing with my dad, but then I went to college and seminary and sort of drifted away from it."

"What kind of fishing did you do as a kid?"

"Some trolling in a little blue wood boat we had, but mostly fly fishing. Montana has great fishing spots, and I think Dad and I hit most of them when I was a kid."

"Too bad you got away from it. Fishing is a good way for a man to just get out there and enjoy life."

"I don't think I even realized it until I saw your tackle box and started digging around in it. I've been wondering all day what happened to all my old fishing gear. I hope Mom didn't throw it out because I think it would be good to take up my fly rod again."

"You should, but be warned. Rachel is a terrific fisherman… fisherwoman…fisherperson. Heck, I don't know. She can just catch fish!" They both laughed.

There was a lull in the conversation as Tim checked the tension on the bail, and then he placed the reel on top of his tackle box and sat back in his chair. Mike leaned forward in his. They looked at each other.

Mike cleared his voice and started to talk and then cleared his voice again and looked at his feet. He didn't see the smile flash across Tim's face.

"Sir," he said, and he could feel his face flame. He felt like a fifteen-year-old asking a girl to the prom. He stood up, and Tim's eyes followed him.

"The thing of it is, sir, Rachel and I love each other. I know we've only known each other since September, but we are both old enough to know that this is a forever type of love. I can't imagine life without her, and I know she feels the same. We have both prayed for weeks asking God's guidance, and we feel certain that he is showing us the path he wants us to take."

He paused to catch his breath and then sat down again in his chair. He looked at Tim boldly and just blurted it out. "I would like to ask your permission to ask Rachel to marry me." There. He'd said it. He leaned back in the chair.

Tim's eyes twinkled. "She came into the bedroom this morning. She told me that if you asked my permission and I said no, she would never forgive me. Then her mother told me that she would not only never forgive me, she might kill me. So in order to preserve my health and safety, I am obliged to say yes."

"Thank you, Mr. Fulton," Mike said, relieved. "I will do everything in my power to make her happy."

"And you will make her happy," the older man said. "I know you've only known each other for a short time, but I also know that I've never seen her more content. You are perfectly suited for each other. May I ask what you have in mind for a wedding date?"

"Mid-summer, probably. We will have known each other eight months. A lot depends on the congregation at my church. I have to be very careful not to cause hard feelings."

"That's understandable, and I think it's very wise of you to consider all of the members of your church. This is probably pretty unprecedented, a pastor getting married. Usually, they come that way."

They talked more, and Mike laughed as he listened to stories of Rachel as a child and a teenager. Before long, they heard the car pull up into the driveway, and Rachel and her mother banged into the kitchen.

The rest of the day was a blur, but he remembered that night. They had gone for a drive and then stopped at a tiny little Italian restaurant for dinner. It was dark and cozy and soft romantic music played in the background. He couldn't have handpicked a more perfect place. The waitress, as if on cue, gave them a small table in a corner that was flanked with greenery. A candle flickered on the table and mirrored the flickering in his heart. A wall next to the table gave them a view of a small courtyard that was festooned with twinkling white Christmas lights. He was amazed at how perfect the setting was. He knew it wasn't a coincidence. God was at work.

They ordered and chatted and laughed through dinner. Then they lingered over coffee and dessert. Finally, Mike knew it was time.

He slipped his hand in his pocket and pulled out a ring box. Then he stood to his feet and walked to her and got down on one knee. He placed the box on the floor and reached up and took both of her hands in his.

"Rachel," he said, looking into her eyes. "I love you with all my heart, and I want to spend my life with you. Will you stand beside me and follow God wherever he leads us? Will you marry me?"

She couldn't speak. She just nodded her head, causing the tears to spill from her eyes down her cheeks. Then she laughed. "Yes!" she said very loudly, causing heads to turn their way. Then she lowered her voice and bent toward him somberly. "Yes, I will marry you, Michael Allen Warren. And yes, I will follow God wherever he leads us."

He picked up the old blue velvet ring box from the floor and lifted up the high-curved top. Nestled in the white satin was wedding set that had been his grandmother's and his great-grandmother's. Crafted by Tiffany's in 1919, the engagement ring consisted of three large diamonds surrounded by sapphires and, beyond those, smaller diamonds. A matching wedding band rested beside it.

The beauty of the rings took her breath away, and when he slipped the engagement ring on her ring finger, it fit perfectly. Mike wasn't surprised.

They had both been in a state of high excitement all the way home, talking about wedding dates, attendants, which church, and all the rest when she suddenly gave a small yelp.

"What?" he had asked in alarm.

"I don't think I can marry you," she exclaimed. "If I marry you, that means I'd be a pastor's wife, and I can't play the piano, and believe me, you don't want me to sing."

"But can you make a casserole?"

"Yes, I can make a mean casserole."

"That's qualification enough," he told her.

Chapter 60

The phone brought him out of his reverie, and when he answered it, he realized he was smiling. He must look like a goofball as he wandered around Danford, smiling all the time. They'd start to wonder if he was losing it.

It was Jamie York, who headed up the countywide counseling and adoption agency. Pastor Mike knew her since he was on the board of the group and also helped with counseling. He was surprised she was calling this time of night; it was well after work hours.

Ten minutes later, he was on his way to her office, where he would meet with several other people about an emergency case.

Jamie and two of the agency's social workers were already there and seated in front of a long scratched and stained wood table in the large conference room.

Jamie stood as he entered the door and walked to him. She held out her hand. "Thank you so much for coming," she said. "We have a sort of a big mess here, and we thought it would be great if you could share it."

"Sounds delightful," Pastor Mike said, smiling. Before taking his seat, he shook hands with the others at the table—Mason Tippett and Angela Birdsall.

Jamie slid three photos in front of him. They were beautiful children. The oldest girl had dark brown hair and was missing a front tooth. She showed it off with a big smile. The younger girl's hair was a little lighter, and he could tell she was laughing about something. She held a doll in her arms. The baby looked startled in the photo and had his mouth open in a perfect circle.

Reaching over and touching the photos one by one, Jamie said, "The oldest girl is Emily, and she's six. This is four-year-old Bevin, and the little boy just turned two. His name is Daniel."

"They're cute. So what's the story?" Pastor Mike asked.

"We've been working with their mother, Sherry Greenhaw, for months. She has cancer…had cancer. She died a few days ago. She had gone into remission and was doing fine, and then her health just collapsed, and within days, she was gone."

"There isn't family the kids can go to?"

Mason cleared his throat and answered. "There is no one except a great aunt. She has the kids now, but it isn't safe there. She is in her late seventies and suffers from diabetes. Her eyesight is failing, and there is a chance she will lose a leg. She really can't manage raising three children."

"We really don't want to throw them into the foster care system because they probably wouldn't be allowed to stay together," Angela added.

"There's no one else?" Pastor Mike asked.

"No one. Sherry was a widow. Her husband was killed in a car accident just after little Danny was born. She had struggled horribly since then and had come in many times for counseling. She had just gotten on her feet when she learned she had cancer. Her parents are dead, and her husband also had no family. We've searched far and wide and questioned her thoroughly, and except for an alcoholic great uncle she hasn't seen in decades, there is no one. She wasn't even sure the uncle was alive."

"We brought you in," Jamie continued, "because we are hoping and praying that you know a couple in your church that could take in these youngsters. They're good kids. Polite and smart. They're having a rough time right now, of course, but in the right home, they'll do well."

"We're looking for a couple that would consider adopting them instead of just providing foster care," Mason said. "These kids deserve a permanent loving home."

"All kids deserve a permanent loving home," Angela said ruefully. They all nodded their heads in agreement.

He didn't need to run the church membership roll through his mind to know who was a perfect fit for these children. God had plopped the names into his head long before Jamie even asked if he knew someone, anyone.

"When do you need to have someone to take them," he asked. He tried to stay calm, but inside, he was bursting with excitement.

"We need to work quickly. The old aunt, as sweet as she is and as much as she'd love to keep them, simply can't. We aren't exaggerating when we say it isn't a safe environment for them. I'd say three days at the most. Sooner would be better."

"What about doing the home study, background study, financial check, and all the rest that is required?"

"We're ready to rush all of that through," Jamie said. "And that aspect of it is one of the reasons we invited you in to discuss this with us. You have the biggest church in the area, and you know your congregation—their faults and their attributes and the skeletons in the closet. We're networking here, and we're hoping that you can help us find the perfect home."

"I think I know a couple," Pastor Mike said. "I'll drop by and talk to them tonight. They might flat-out say no, but they would be perfect. Give me until tomorrow. If they don't like the idea, we can go from there."

They all stood up, and Pastor Mike gestured to the photos. "Can I borrow those until tomorrow?" he asked.

"Sure. We have other copies. You can keep them," Jamie said. Then she turned to Mason and Angela. "See? I knew he'd be able to come up with something."

"It isn't done yet," Pastor Mike said with a small laugh as he tucked the photos into his jacket pocket.

Walking out of the building with Jamie, he hesitated and then turned to her. "Did she go to church? The mother?"

"No, she didn't. But if you are asking if she was saved, yes, she was. I got to know Sherry very well over the past couple of years, and she definitely knew her Jesus. And her kids also know him."

As he drove back to Danford, he talked to God and prayed. He had learned that it was possible to multitask with God and that it was truly possible to "pray without ceasing" as you went about your day.

"God, you continue to shock and amaze me. Father, I know that all things happen for a reason and that you have plans for us that are grander than we can imagine. If it is your will that these orphaned children are to be placed in the home you have put on my heart, I know that you have already softened their hearts and set everything in motion. I just pray, Lord, that your will is done and that everyone involved follows your leading. Father, please be with these three children and give them comfort and peace and the assurance that they truly aren't alone in the world when they have you."

Chapter 61

It was after 9:00 p.m., and the lights were still on in the living room. Mike had decided on the drive that even if they weren't, he would pound on the door until Barbara or Joe came to open it.

He had made a quick call to Rachel on his cell phone, asking her to pray. He didn't give her many details, and she knew only that it involved orphaned children and the Millers. She assured him she would get down on her knees and pray until he telephoned her back. He knew she would.

Mike bounded up the steps, taking two at a time, and rang the doorbell and, at the same time, knocked. Within a few minutes, Joe opened the door, and he knew instantly it wasn't really one of those "just passing by and thought I'd drop in" visits Mike was famous for.

For some reason, his heart pounded in anticipation. He had a feeling it wasn't bad news—Mike's face didn't convey that—but it was something important. Maybe, he thought, some calamity at church like a deacon in trouble or the music minister quit. He scrapped that thought. No. It was something else.

"Barbara!" he called as he invited Mike in the house. The two men, long past handshakes, grabbed each other by the arm in greeting.

Barbara was in sweatpants and a sweatshirt that came close to matching what her husband was wearing. She had washed her face clean of makeup, and she looked young and pure. Her hair was disheveled, and he thought it looked good on her, a little bit of a wild look.

"Is everything okay?" she asked. Barbara never beat around the bush and was always forthright.

Mike ran his hands through his hair and let out a deep breath he didn't even realize he was holding. "Yes. No! That depends."

"I like a man who is sure of himself," she said, laughing, and then she sobered. "No one has died or is sick, are they?"

"I could say yes, but that would even confuse you more. We need to talk."

They sat in the living room, and it flashed through Mike's mind one other time when they sat in these very chairs—the day Joe, roiling in grief after the death of Anna, had kept Marcy captive. How things had changed since then. Were they about to change again? It comforted him to know that Jamie York and Rachel were both praying.

"Let me tell you about Sherry Greenhaw. No, you don't know her, and she's never gone to our church. She lives near Missoula. Lived near Missoula. Her husband died a couple of years ago in a car accident, and not long after, she was diagnosed with cancer. She was doing well and was back working for an insurance firm, and her doctors thought everything was going to be fine. And then the cancer returned with a vengeance, and she was dead in a matter of days."

"Oh, that's just so sad," Barbara said, her eyes filled with compassion.

"The sad part," Mike said, "is that she has three children." He fished in his pocket and pulled out the photos and walked over to where they were sitting on the couch. He handed over the first.

"This is Emily, and she's six and just started first grade. I love her toothless smile."

He handed over the second photo. "This is four-year-old Bevin. As you can see, she's quite attached to her doll."

Barbara and Joe were still looking at the first two photos when he handed them the photo of the two-year-old. "And this is Baby Daniel."

"Oh, look, Joe. He's just adorable. They're all just adorable."

"This one in the middle looks like she could be quite a character," he said, smiling and looking more closely at the photo. "She doesn't look like Anna, but she sure looks like she could have that same mischievous character."

Barbara leaned over and looked at the photo again. "You're right. She does look like a little character."

"Well," said Joe, still hanging on to the photo of Bevin, "whatever you feel the church should do, you can count on us. Even if the mother wasn't a member, we should help with funeral finances, and we sure need to be praying for the children."

"Are they going to live with family members?" Barbara asked. She had taken the photo from Joe and had them all on her lap. Mike noticed she and Joe could barely take their eyes off the photos.

He leaned forward in his chair and put his hands together between his knees. "That's the problem," he said. "There is no family. Sherry's husband had no family, and she had no one except for a very sickly and aged great aunt who is unable to care for them. They are with her now, but it isn't a good situation."

Barbara knew what Mike was going to say next, and so did Joe.

"They're up for adoption," he said, and he looked at their faces closely.

Barbara's hand flew to her mouth, and Joe automatically reached over to take her other hand. She held on to it so tightly her knuckles turned white.

"All three of them?" Joe asked quietly.

"Even the baby?" Barbara asked, and then she realized what stupid questions she and Joe had just asked. They were just saying anything that popped in their minds.

Mike nodded his head. "I just met with Jamie York and a couple of social workers from the counseling and adoption agency. They called me in thinking that I might know a perfect couple or family that would want to adopt them. They're prepared to rush through all the necessary background checks and other paperwork."

Joe and Barbara sat quietly and waited for the rest.

"God immediately brought you two into my mind. You know how it is when you just know that it's coming from him and it's perfect? That's what I feel about this. You two are perfect. You have enough love to share with a hundred children, and you both have the training to deal with any problems and hurts. And you know what it is to lose someone you love with all your heart, so you would know how to deal with the grief these children will go through."

He stopped and waited for them to speak. Joe spoke first, while Barbara went into the kitchen to grab a tissue. She blew her nose and wiped her eyes on the way back into the room.

"As you know," Joe said, "we've been praying for a long time that God show us the path he wanted us to take. We had decided a few weeks ago to get into the foster care program and picked up an application and talked to them. We love kids, we have a big old house, we have enough income, and we have a lot of love to give. It just seems so empty in here without the laughter of a child."

Barbara sat down next to him and took his hand. "Joe and I have discussed being foster care parents at length, and we wanted to make sure that our motives were pure and we weren't just willing to get a child to replace Anna. We wanted to know that we were taking in a child because of the child's needs, not ours. We have prayed and prayed seeking God's wisdom and his guidance and asked him to open the doors for us."

Mike decided to be forthright. "Do you realize the sacrifice it would be if you took them?" he asked. "Three kids you have never seen before? Jamie says they are wonderful children, kind and polite, but they will also be damaged children who are grieving for their mother. It would also mean taking care of a toddler, and changing your lives to wrap around their lives."

"I'll tell you what," he continued. "I've given you a lot to think about tonight. They would like the children to be in a new home as soon as possible—Jamie said a few days—but if you need more time than that, they can probably go into emergency foster care until you decide. And if you say no, that is fine. Everyone will understand, and they will find them a good home. The most important thing is that this has to be God's decision, and you have to be comfortable that it is his plan and not yours. And especially not mine. Otherwise, it would mean heartache for all of us. So don't give me an answer tonight. Just call me tomorrow, and if you still haven't decided, we can just go slowly from there."

"Can we keep the photos?" Barbara asked.

"Sure. I'm sorry I don't know more than what I told you tonight about these kids, but if you have questions, we can call Jamie tomorrow. And if you need to meet them before you decide, I'm sure that's fine too. I apologize that they can't give you more time."

A short time later, Mike headed home. He wasn't a block from the Miller's house when he called Rachel on his cell phone and told her the whole story. They both admitted Joe and Barbara would be perfect parents for the Greenhaw children, and Rachel said she said she would continue to pray.

Hours later, at just a little after three in the morning, the phone next to his bed rang, and he answered it before the ring had finished.

It was Joe, and he was laughing. "We knew you were still awake," he said. "And I'll bet you're praying. Well, you can go to sleep now. Barbara and I just wanted you to know that the answer is absolutely yes. We would love to have Emily and Bevin and Daniel as our children." His voice broke when he spoke their names, and Mike felt his own heart swell with emotion.

"I can only think how Anna would rejoice at your decision," Mike said gruffly. "God bless you both. I want you to know you won't be in this alone. Sharon and Jim and their two kids and Rachel and I will be right there with you."

Joe hung up the phone and turned to Barbara. "I can't believe this," he said.

"Isn't it funny how life is?" she agreed. "We both got up this morning and went to work and came home, and everything was fine and organized. Then, in a matter of seconds, our lives are turned topsy-turvy."

"It only seems that way," Joe said thoughtfully. "If you look at it a long way back, it all started eons ago. The current history is that Sherry Greenhaw fell in love, had three children, lost her husband and then died, leaving them orphans without anyone to care for them. We grew up and fell in love and had Anna, and we lost her, and here we are—they need us, and we need them—all these souls coming together at this crossroads of life. When you ponder things like this, you can't help but know that there is a God and that he takes incredible care of us and he loves us beyond our imaginations."

"I don't mean this to sound awful," Barbara said, "but have you ever considered the amazing things God has done through Anna's death? People's lives have changed. People's lives have become better. Her death has touched countless people and made them better."

"And have you considered that we have just two or three days to get ready for our children—Emily, Bevin, and Daniel?"

Barbara fell against him in shock and started listing the things that needed to be done.

Joe laughed. "I think if God has put this whole plan together, he will take care of the details," he said. Hand in hand, they finally went up the stairs to bed and hoped they could sleep.

Chapter 62

The next morning, the Millers took the day off from teaching and met Pastor Mike at the church. Together, the three of them drove to the agency to meet with Jamie York and the other social workers. They were carefully holding back any feelings of elation and celebration until this step was taken, and they had been cleared by the authorities to adopt the three children.

They were confident nothing would be amiss. As teachers, they'd had to undergo numerous background checks and had been fingerprinted several times. They also had plenty of money in the bank, and their house was more than adequate. They had four bedrooms, but not enough beds. That was a minor problem.

However, there was something that could be a problem. It had been just a little over eight months since Anna's death. The authorities might feel that it was too soon.

Mike assured Joe and Barbara that he had talked at length to the people at the adoption agency and had explained his relationship with the Millers. Without going into the details, he assured Jamie and the others that he was confident that the Miller's decision wasn't based on losing Anna but was based on wanting to parent Emily, Bevin, and Daniel. He said that their journey through grief had been manifested appropriately and normally. He also told everyone involved that God was at work here and told them about Joe and Barbara's decision to take in foster children. Evidently, he said, God had other plans.

Joe had given Jamie York a list of references over the phone early that morning, both personal and professional, and it was clear from the phone messages that morning that every reference had been called. Everyone had called the Miller home, wanting to know what was happening.

They also learned the principals in their schools had attested to Joe and Barbara's stability and their ability to relate to children. It did help that they were well-known and respected teachers.

Mike led the way to the conference room he had been in the night before and made Joe and Barbara comfortable before going to find Jamie in her office. He met her coming down the hall.

"We saw you pull in," Jamie said, reaching out to shake Pastor Mike's hand. She was followed by Mason and Angela, the two social workers.

The four of them went into the conference room, and Mike introduced everyone. Joe and Barbara sat expectantly but visibly relaxed once Jamie started talking. Pastor Mike had learned over the years that Jamie had a way of bringing peace and comfort into any room.

She smiled serenely as she regarded Joe and Barbara. They were an attractive couple, trim and fit, and she could tell they were intelligent and kind. Joe was handsome with thick black hair, and Barbara was beautiful with light brown hair and friendly brown eyes. They looked like the kind of people who could take on a dozen kids and not bat an eye.

After a bit of idle "how are you" trivia, Jamie decided to cut right to the chase. There was no time to waste pussyfooting around the issue. These children needed a new home as soon as possible.

She looked at the couple sitting in front of her and said bluntly, "So tell me why you want to adopt the three Greenhaw children?"

Then she sat back and waited.

Joe and Barbara knew they would be asked this question, and they were prepared. They spoke straight from the heart and talked in depth about Anna's death and what they had told Mike the night before. They spoke candidly and truthfully and openly.

If Jamie was pleased with their answer, she didn't say. She asked if the others had questions, and Mason Tippet lifted his hand slightly off the table to indicate he did. They all looked at him.

"I'm going to honest here and just ask if you want these children to replace your daughter who drowned."

Barbara answered, "No child could ever replace Anna," she said. "Just as no woman could ever replace Sherry Greenhaw. Anna will always be our child and have a special place in our hearts, just as Sherry will always be their mother and have a special place in their hearts. But I would hope that, given time, I could become their mother. And that Joe could become their father. They must so miss having a father. All children are special and individual, and none of them are replaceable."

Mason nodded when she finished and then turned to Joe for his answer.

"I have thought about these children a lot since last night," Joe said. "And I have thought about how amazing it is that we have been asked to consider adopting them. Out of all the people in the area who would do anything to have these three beautiful children, we were asked. God paved the way, and I think I know one reason why. I can't tell you the horror of losing a child and the horrendous time of grief a parent goes through. I pray none of you has to ever go through it. But because of that loss and because of that grief, both Barbara and I know exactly how these youngsters feel at losing their mother. I think we have a lot to offer them. Not only love and parenting for the rest of their lives, but compassion and understanding for what they're going through now."

Barbara leaned forward. "I don't know if any of you are Christians, but if you are, you will understand when I say that this is God's plan. This is bigger than all of us. Joe and I want to bring these children home and make them ours. Forevermore."

After saying that, she sat back and regretted every word. For some people, the mention of God and his plan would bring about a swift and unchanging answer of no.

Jamie stood to her feet and motioned to her two coworkers to follow her. She said they would return in a few minutes and to make themselves at home.

Mike and Joe and Barbara sat in silence.

"Do you think I blew it with the 'God's plan' statement?" Barbara asked miserably.

Mike patted her arm reassuringly. "No. If it truly is God's plan, you could have told them that you planned on pretending the kids were pet hurdy-gurdy monkeys and were going to take them to the park to collect money in tin cups and it would have passed inspection. If this is God's plan, it will happen. Pray and have faith!"

"Thanks, Mike," she said. She turned to look at Joe and saw that his eyes were closed in prayer. Oh, how she loved this man of hers.

* * *

After about fifteen minutes, Jamie York and Mason Tippet came back into the room. Both were smiling as they took their seats. Barbara wondered if it was to ease the pain of being rejected.

"You'll see Angela again in a few minutes," Jamie said. "First of all, I want to tell you that it is obvious that God truly was involved in this whole thing. I have never seen anything come together like this has, and it is a true miracle. Adoption clearances take months, and this came to pass in a matter of hours. Everything was already in place, which is remarkable—your most recent background checks were recent enough to be viable, your financial check cleared in minutes rather than weeks, and you were just fingerprinted for the foster care application. That usually takes forever, but not in your case. It took less than two days. No one in this business will believe that this all happened this quickly. It is beyond a doubt a miracle."

She shook her head in wonder.

"Does this mean we get them?" Joe asked. He still wasn't sure what all her words meant. He wasn't sure he even comprehended any of them. His head was buzzing.

"Yes!" she said in delight. "It means you get them!"

Joe and Barbara were instantly their feet and in each other's arms. Mike also jumped up and placed his arms around both of them.

Mason and Jamie watched with broad smiles on their faces. They loved the happy part of their jobs—fulfilling people's hopes and watching their dreams come true.

The three of them were still hanging on to each other and wiping up tears when Jamie brought them back down to earth. "We still need to do the home study, but Pastor Mike here has described your house, and we are sure it will be fine. You will want to make sure you have a carbon monoxide detector and enough smoke detectors. You said you had picked up paperwork for a foster care application, and all that information will be helpful in telling you what you need to do."

Barbara's mind was swirling in a dozen different directions as they sat back down. "We need to buy beds and a crib. Does Daniel need a crib? And Emily and Bevin? Do they want to be in the same room?"

Jamie smiled at her. "Do you want to ask them?" she asked Barbara and then turned her eyes to Joe.

"Are they here?" he asked.

She nodded her head. "With Angela. Just in the other room. Do you want to meet your children?"

Barbara was about to race out of the room but then reached for her purse and pulled out a mirror. Taking a tissue out of her pocket, she wiped away the smeared mascara and then smoothed her hair.

She squared her shoulders and walked to Joe. They both grinned and looked at Mike and then nodded to Jamie. "We're ready."

Then she had a thought. "Can Mike come with us?"

Jamie nodded her head, and Pastor Mike joined the trio.

The room down the hall was a big playroom, filled with toys and a mini trampoline and small tables and chairs. The walls were painted bright colors, and there were many framed paintings and drawings.

Barbara and Joe entered first. Pastor Mike, Mason, and Jamie followed, and the three of them leaned against a wall, well out of the way.

Angela was sitting with the oldest child, Emily, and they were putting together a *Sesame Street* puzzle. Emily was slim with long dark hair. Bevin, who had lighter curly hair, had her doll in a buggy and was pushing it. Little Daniel, who was wearing a pair of baggy little jeans and a striped T-shirt, stood in the middle of the room doing nothing, just standing there with his thumb in his mouth.

Angela stood to greet them and led them first to Emily.

"Emily, remember I told you about the Millers? Joe and Barbara? Well, this is them. They'll be taking you home to live with them day after tomorrow."

Emily looked at them without emotion, just resigned acceptance.

"Hi," she said shyly.

While Angela moved to the back of the room to stand with the others, Joe and Barbara sat on the tiny chairs to be at Emily's level.

"Hi, Emily," Barbara said quietly. "You have beautiful hair. I want you to know that we are so happy, Joe and I, that we get to take you all home with us to be our family. We think you will like it there. Do you want me to tell you about it?"

Emily shrugged her shoulders. "I guess," she said.

"Well, we have a big house with a big backyard. We have a cat, but we've been thinking about a dog since we babysit a dog named Midas and we think he's a lot of fun. Joe and I are both teachers. I teach at the elementary school, and he teaches in the high school."

"Do you have kids?"

"Nope. We used to have a daughter. Her name was Anna. But she lives in heaven now."

"That's where my mom lives too. In heaven."

"I know. I think that is very sad. You must miss her a lot."

Emily just nodded her head. Then she looked curiously at Joe, who hadn't opened his mouth.

"You have a hole in your mouth," he said solemnly. "Did someone steal your tooth?"

She burst into giggles. "No, silly, it fell out."

"Just fell out? Just like that? You should use better glue."

"No. It's supposed to fall out, silly. Then you get a new one."

"Oh, I remember now. And the tooth fairy comes and all that."

"I got a dollar," she whispered. "I still have it. I keep it under my pillow, which is right where the tooth fairy put it."

"Maybe you could buy a new tooth," Joe whispered back.

"I think you're funny," Emily said.

"Sometimes, he's just a big old goofball," Barbara said. Joe crossed his eyes at her.

Bevin had joined the group by then, followed by Daniel.

Without saying a word, Daniel walked over to Barbara, looked into her eyes for a second, and then lifted his leg to crawl into her lap.

She pulled him up and hugged him close. He smelled wonderful, like powder and baby shampoo. "Hey, baby," she crooned into his ear.

Bevin reached into the buggy and pulled out her doll by the arm. She walked over and stood beside Mike. Since he was sitting on the tiny chair, she was almost to his shoulder.

"My mom's in heaven. Like Emily said," she said somberly to him. She pulled her doll up to her chest.

"I heard that," Joe said.

"She takes that doll everywhere she goes," Emily said. "Even to the bathroom."

"I used to have a doll I took everywhere too," Barbara told her. "I left her at the store once and didn't realize it until I went to bed. I cried so much my mom called the store owner and had him open the store so we could get it."

"Was he mad?"

"Let's say he wasn't happy. But he had a little girl who had a favorite doll, so he understood. We doll people have to stick together, don't we, Bevin?"

"See, Emily? It's okay to carry a doll."

"Not when you get to school though. When you get to school, they make you leave it home."

Bevin thought about that a while. Then she declared. "I don't think I want school. I'll stay home with Baby Danny."

Within a few minutes, Bevin was in Joe's lap, and Emily had scooted closer to him so that their legs touched. Daniel had fallen asleep in Barbara's arms. The sight of the children snuggled close to him made her heart ache with longing to take them home.

They only had an hour together before the children would be taken back to the great-aunt. All too soon, the time was up. Jamie stepped forward and pointed to the clock on the wall.

"I guess it's time for you to go back to your aunt," Barbara said to Bevin and Emily.

Emily frowned. "We could go to your house tomorrow instead of day after tomorrow. We could. We just have some clothes and stuff."

Barbara looked at Jamie questioningly.

"We can talk about it before you leave," she said.

Joe turned Bevin a little in his lap so she was looking at him. Then he looked at Emily. "Do you think you would want to live with us? To be our children?"

Bevin nodded her head eagerly and smiled.

Emily frowned. "What we want," she said, "is for our mom to come back so we can be with her. But that can't happen, so we might as well go with you."

Then she shrugged off the gloom and pointed at Joe and grinned, revealing the hole where a tooth should be. "He's funny," she said. "My daddy was funny too, and he teased me. He could be our new dad."

Bevin pointed to Barbara. "And she could be our new mom," she said.

Chapter 63

Twenty minutes later, the children had departed with Angela, and the rest of them were discussing what needed to be done to take the children the next day. Barbara decided that she needed to take an emergency leave of absence from work and also start the paperwork in motion to quit teaching. She was only working part days now anyway and had enjoyed the freedom. The children, she and Joe had decided the night before, deserved a mother who stayed home.

Jamie said she could come that evening to do the home inspection, and Barbara said that was fine as long as she didn't mind the mess they'd have getting ready. That would be all that was required on their end. The final adoption paperwork, including the court decree, would take more time, but, she joked, considering what God had done so far, they could expect it to be done by the next day. They all laughed.

"As far as the agency, everything's pretty much done," Mike said. "So my suggestion is that we call the Petermans and maybe even Henry Knutson and get your house kid-ready."

Barbara laughed. "I called Sharon this morning, and I wouldn't be a bit surprised if she wasn't over there already, cleaning up and getting ready. She said that we could count on all of them to pitch in."

"Mike, if you don't have anything the rest of the day, I could use some help in moving furniture. Barbara and I have a sort of a plan. I'll need to go to the furniture store and buy a couple of new beds and a crib. Maybe Henry can come over and help us put everything together."

"I'm all yours," Mike told him. "You just give me directions and watch me go. I can call Henry as soon as we leave here."

Before they left the parking lot, they had a game plan. Now they just needed to set it all in action.

Barbara's words proved to be prophetic. She and Joe got home to find Sharon scrubbing the kitchen floors. The whole house was vacuumed, dusted, and smelled wonderful.

"I have never in my life enjoyed doing housework more than I am loving doing this for you," she told Barbara and Joe. She hugged Barbara then quickly pulled away. "Don't get too close. I'm sweating like a stevedore."

"So, Daddy," she said, looking at Joe, "are you ready for this? Diapers and getting up in the middle of the night and chicken pox?"

Joe looked at Barbara. "Diapers?" he asked. "Does Daniel still wear diapers?"

Sharon and Barbara laughed. "Honey, I'm sure he still wears diapers, at least part of the time," Barbara said. Then she turned to Sharon.

"Let me show you the photos of our children," she said. "Doesn't that sound wonderful? *Our children.*"

"I've been bawling since you called this morning," Sharon admitted. "I called Jim, and he came home, and we both bawled. I can't wait to tell Ben and Marcy. This is absolutely wonderful. Not only for the kids, but for you."

Barbara opened her purse and took out the photos of Emily, Bevin, and Daniel.

"Omigosh. They're beautiful," Sharon said in a hushed voice. "So beautiful. You are so blessed to get them."

"They will never replace Anna," Barbara said.

"I know that, and everyone else will know that," Sharon said, looking at her. "No one could ever replace Anna. Have you decided on their rooms yet?"

"Joe and I think we have it figured out, but if you have ideas, let us know."

"We'll need to get some beds and a crib. Mike will be here in a minute to pick me up, and we'll go shopping. He was going to call Henry and see if he could come over this afternoon and help us put them together."

"A crib," Sharon said, shaking her head and cringing. "I remember when Jim put one of those together. It took three days at least. My suggestion would be to go to that new place over on Pine that sells maternity clothes and used baby items. Buy one already put together. I guess they have great things in there."

"Maybe you and I should go get the crib, and the guys can pick up a couple of beds for the girls. We're going to put Anna's bed in the garage since it's full-sized, and we'll need the extra space. Two twins will work better. We should have time to stop by Penney's and pick up some bedding."

"Sounds like a plan," Joe said. "So let me get this straight. You two will get bedding for the girls and a crib. Mike and I are getting two twin beds for the girls."

Barbara grinned at him. She was so excited she wanted to just jump and down and squeal. "Right! And then we'll all meet here and get everything put together and finish cleaning."

"When are you getting the kids?" Sharon asked Barbara.

"It was supposed to be day after tomorrow, but they seem to want to come tomorrow. That's why all the crazy stuff. I called school, and I'm taking a leave of absence, and Joe's taking the next couple of days off. We'll need to get Emily registered, and we both want to be home to get them settled."

"How long will you take off?" Sharon asked.

Barbara looked at her and cocked her head and smiled and lifted her brows. "Forever. I'm going to quit teaching. As you know, I was only doing half-days anyway. These kids need me. And I need them."

"Smart woman. It'll be great to have another stay-at-home mom in the neighborhood."

Mike was pulling in the driveway just as Barbara and Sharon were climbing in Barbara's car, and he backed out so they could leave. As they pulled into the road, Sharon chuckled and pulled down the vanity mirror. She looked at herself and patted down her hair.

"I don't think I've ever gone shopping looking like this," she admitted. "I'm a mess!"

"Do we care? Look at me? Tear stains running down to my chin. They might talk for a few days, but when word gets out, they'll think we looked pretty good, considering."

"I figure it'll be around town by nightfall. The two beds and the crib will do it. Mike's busting his buttons over this, and he'll tell everyone in the furniture store, and we, of course, will have to explain to the ladies at the baby store."

The rest of the afternoon was filled with happy banter as the men moved furniture and put beds together. Barbara had to laugh when Mike and Henry and Joe came home with not only two beds with little-girl white headboards but also had matching dressers and a gorgeous area rug. She couldn't fault their taste.

The room, when they put the bedspread on the bare beds, was beautiful. A room any little girl would want. But Barbara had to admit that there wasn't much left that was Anna's, just the pictures on the walls and some things in the closet. She would cry over that tonight.

Henry turned out to be a godsend when it came to cleaning out the smallest bedroom, which would be for Baby Danny. Without being told, he just seemed to know where all the stuff that had gathered over the years should go. Some went into the garage, some outside to storage, and some he asked permission to just throw out.

They were just moving dressers around when Ben came in. Sharon had left a note for both he and Marcy, telling them to come to the Millers' when they got home from school.

"What's everyone doing?" he said, looking around the bedroom.

"Well," Sharon said, "come with me, and I'll tell you." They went to the kitchen, and she showed him the photos and explained about the children's mother and said that Joe and Barbara were adopting them. Emily, Bevin, and Daniel would be there children."

"Cool!" he said. "We need more kids in the neighborhood." Then he spotted the cookies on the counter. "Can I have a cookie?"

Sharon prayed that it would be that easy with Marcy. But she knew it wouldn't be.

Chapter 64

* * *

When we were nine, Galen Dotson asked Anna to marry him. She told her mother, and her mother told her she was silly, and I was glad. But he still walked with her at recess. I was mad and sat on the swing by myself. I didn't want to share her with a stupid boy. Besides, I told her, Galen Dotson? Yuck. He let daddy longlegs spiders crawl on his tongue and played in dog-do with a stick. Besides, we had agreed, there would be no boys allowed. I said he could never, ever, come to the hill. Plus, she could never tell him about the Bone Tree. She wasn't happy, but two days later, she saw him pick his nose, and that was that. We were back to being best friends.

* * *

When Marcy got home, she spotted the note on the kitchen counter. It was where their mother always left notes if she wasn't going to be there when they got home from school. It was for her and Ben and told them to come down the Millers' house. "Something exciting is happening," it said with a whole row of exclamation marks.

Marcy snorted. Knowing her mother, it was a new recipe or maybe they'd gotten a new couch. She put her books upstairs on her desk, changed into a pair of jeans and a sweatshirt, and ran down the front steps to get her bike.

She loved being back on her bike after the winter, and April was a wonderful month when the land was coming back to life. Everything smelled so good—the mud, the ripening earth, the puddle water, and especially, the pavement when it rained.

But there would be no rain today. It was a beautiful day, and there were a few hours left before it would start to get dark. Spring was her favorite time of year. Well, maybe except for autumn, when the leaves smelled so good. She was, she had decided a long time ago, a person who liked smells.

Henry Knutson's pickup was pulled in the driveway and so was Pastor Mike's. Glancing at the window, she saw her father walk through the living room. She frowned. What was going on? He should be at work.

Ben came bounding out of the house when he spotted her. He was yelling at the top of his lungs. "They're getting kids! The Millers are getting kids! Three of them. Even a baby!" He was jumping up and down.

"What kids?" she asked, slipping off her bike seat and walking up the sidewalk. She was totally at a loss as to what he was talking about.

"Little kids," he said. "Plus a baby! Talk to Mom, and she can tell you."

Marcy was leaning her bike against a tree when she spotted Anna's bed in the garage. The headboard, with all its little cubbies, was upside down. The smiley face sticker Anna had put on it was frowning. Her heart plummeted. What was going on here? It couldn't be good.

She had been praying so much and about everything, but this time, it just slipped her mind to ask God to be with her.

Without bothering to knock, she went in the front door and stood in the foyer. Her mother and Barbara Miller were scrubbing down a crib in the middle of the living room. The mattress was leaned up against the couch, and a mobile with ponies was tangled up on a chair.

They were laughing. They didn't see her.

She stood there watching, and just then, her dad and Joe came in through the back door carrying a mattress and headed toward the stairs. They were laughing too and teasing each other about which one had the heavy end.

Before they started up the stairs, Henry Knutson hollered down from somewhere deep on the second floor. "Will someone have Ben bring me up the screwdriver set? It should be on the kitchen counter!" Ben scrambled from where he was about to jump on to the baby mattress and headed to the kitchen.

Just then, her mother saw her. "Marcy!" she said then leaped to her feet. "Come out to the porch with me, out of this chaos, and I'll tell you what's going on." She wiped her hands on her pant legs to dry them off and then walked to her and put her arm around her. "You won't believe what's happened," she said.

They sat on the porch swing. Her mother looked at her with bright eyes and absolute excitement. "I don't know where to start," she said, clapping her hands together.

"They moved Anna's bed out of her room. It's in the garage. Just shoved in the garage." She hadn't known she was angry and upset until she said the words.

Sharon instantly knew what she was feeling and was filled with compassion. "I know," she said. Her voice was quieter now. Calm. "Last night, Pastor Mike got a call from an adoption agency. There were three little kids whose mother died of cancer a few days ago.

They have no relatives except one, and she can't take care of them. They asked Pastor Mike if he knew a family that would adopt them."

She stopped in order to let that sink in.

"And he thought the Millers?" Marcy asked.

"He thought the Millers. He knew they had been thinking of becoming foster parents, and he knows that they have great capacity to love and care for a child, even for three children. So he asked them, and they prayed about it, and in the middle of the night, they decided it was something God wanted them to do."

"But they moved Anna's bed," Marcy said. She didn't know, in light of this whole thing, why she kept coming back to Anna's bed.

"There are two little girls, ages four and six, and they will be in Anna's room. The baby, whose name is Daniel, will be in the smaller room."

"When will they come?"

"Tomorrow. Tomorrow afternoon. That's why we're all here. The agency will do a home study this afternoon, so we're cleaning house, and all the men are putting together the beds."

"Oh," Marcy said. Her voice sounded so small, so young.

"I think I know what you are going through," Sharon told her daughter. "It probably seems to you like bits and pieces of Anna are disappearing one by one. But you have to consider how she would feel about this. Don't you think she would want her folks to take these little kids who have no one in the world?"

"I guess," Marcy said grudgingly. She kicked her feet together. Hard.

Sharon felt herself suddenly becoming angry. "Joe and Barbara deserve to be happy. Just as you deserve to be happy. They are thrilled they get these children. They wanted to have a dozen kids and couldn't. If you say one thing or do one thing to ruin this for them, it will be despicable. Now I expect you to come in there, ask what you can do to help, and pitch in and act a little more grown up."

Marcy just stared at her and got to her feet.

Before her mother could say anything else, a station wagon pulled up, and Caroline and Rod Lincoln and their son Michael scrambled out of the car.

Caroline was almost running to greet Sharon. "We heard! It's all over town! We couldn't stay away, and we're here to do anything we can do to get ready for these children," she said.

Within seconds, Sharon was telling them the whole story as they walked toward the house. No one noticed Marcy grab her bike and slip away.

Chapter 65

Pastor Mike and Henry Knutson were sitting in the middle of Anna's room and howling with laughter as they took apart a do-it-yourself bookcase for the third time. "It shouldn't be this hard. The thing only has about a dozen pieces. Maybe we *should* read those directions," Henry said, grabbing them from behind him. Shaking the folded paper, it fluttered to a length of about four feet.

"The directions are taller than the bookcase!" Mike declared.

"If you can't get it put together, I'm sure Barbara and I can figure it out," Sharon teased them from the doorway. Then she asked, "Have you seen Marcy?"

They hadn't. "Did you lose her?" Mike asked, laughing. The smile faded as he saw a frown come across her face.

"She came over after school and saw Anna's bed in the garage and then learned about the Greenhaw children. She's upset. We were talking, and then Caroline and Rod drove up, and when I turned back around, she was gone. She probably went back home."

"Do you want me to talk to her?"

"I tried, and I have to admit I got angry. I understand what she's going through, but she has to realize how good this is for Barbara and Joe. And these kids."

"She and I have gotten pretty close during our counseling sessions. If you and Jim don't mind, I can walk down to your house and talk to her."

"Would you? That would be really good. Maybe you can help her."

"Will she answer the door?"

"Check the hammock behind the house first. That's where she sometimes goes when she's troubled."

He found her there, swinging slowly and dragging her feet in the dirt. He stepped on to the seat of a nearby picnic table and sat on the top, resting his feet on the seat. She looked at him, and he could tell she'd been crying.

"You want to talk about it?" he said.

"How can they do that? Just throw her bed in the garage like it doesn't mean anything. And get these new kids like she didn't mean anything."

"You know that's not fair. Can you honestly say that any child can ever replace Anna to them, or that any friend you might have can ever replace Anna to you?"

"Well, no. It's just that everyone is so happy. They probably have her room all torn up, and nothing in there is like it used to be anymore."

"They did have to put in two beds, and they bought two dressers for that room. Anna's big dresser was moved to the baby's new room, but they kept up the pictures and the posters. I can't tell you they will stay there forever, but they're there for now. I'll bet if you ask, you can have them if they decide to take them down."

"I just don't want things to change."

"Life is full of change. Nothing ever stays the same."

"It just seems so wrong for them to be happy."

"Does it seem wrong for you to be happy?"

"Sometimes. I guess I feel guilty when I'm happy."

"Do you think that's what Anna would want?"

"No. She'd hate it that everyone is depressed all the time, or even part of the time."

"What do you think she'd tell you if she were here?"

Marcy gave a small laugh. "She'd say I was a big baby. She'd tell me I should do what I can to make these little kids feel loved and wanted." She shrugged her shoulders. "Because that's what she would do. She would turn them into a project."

Pastor Mike laughed. "You are so right. They would be a big project."

He changed the subject and said cautiously, "I know you let the balloon go, and Rachel told me what she told you about releasing Anna. Did that help?"

"Yes. And I'm okay most of the time, and I think I really have let her go. I thought I was doing fine, but then this happened. Maybe it's because she's not sharing in all of it."

"It is absolutely normal for you to have setbacks, especially when something as big as this happens. This is traumatic to you, and I think Joe and Barbara are also having a hard time. It *is* possible to be happy and sad at the same time."

He waited for her to say something, and when she didn't he continued. "Let me tell you something, Marcy. I want you to think about it carefully. I don't believe God does anything without a plan. And I don't believe that there is anything that happens that can't be turned around to bring glory to him. Just consider what has happened since Anna died. Can you tell me some of the good things that have come about because God chose to bring her home?"

"I got Kemo back," she said, giving a small smile. "And Henry Knutson is going to church. And he's going on a fabulous cruise with his daughters. And I guess all of us are different, and we are nicer to each other."

"I can think of a few more things," he told her. "You helped your friend at school deal with her mother's cancer scare, and you and the Millers have learned compassion and understanding and you help people at The Compassionate Friends meetings. And now, three little orphans are going to have a good home with kind and loving parents."

He reached in his pocket and took out an envelope. "Here, I want you to see these," he said, handing them to her one at a time. "This is Emily, and she's six. This is Bevin, and she's four. The baby with the goofy look is Danny. He's two."

Marcy took the photos and studied them carefully. "How did their mom die?"

"Cancer. Last week, she was alive, and this week she's gone, and these poor youngsters don't have anyone except an old aunt who is too sick to care for them. It would be very sad if they went into foster homes and were separated. It truly is God's will that they go to the Millers. Someday, I'll tell you the amazing details of this whole thing. It truly is a miracle."

"I guess Anna would want that. She always wanted brothers and sisters. She didn't want to hurt her parents, so she didn't talk to them about it much. But she always wanted them."

"And now she will have them."

"I guess I can go back and help," she said, and then she shrugged her shoulders. "Maybe they would let me babysit sometime. Do you think?"

"I think you can count on it," Pastor Mike said, reaching for her hand to pull her out of the hammock. "And if you know anything about changing diapers from the children you babysit now, the Millers could use your help. They don't remember a thing about it."

Marcy giggled.

Chapter 66

By the time Jamie York got to the Miller house at just a little after 7:00 p.m., everything was in place. Everyone had gone, and Joe and Barbara were sitting in the living room drinking iced tea with lemon. No one, upon entering the house, would have comprehended the total turmoil that it had been in just a few hours before.

Joe and Barbara showed her around the house, and Jamie took notes. They showed her the backyard, which still had Anna's big wooden swing set, and boasted a fort and a rock wall. Joe had spent weeks building it and just didn't have the heart to sell it. Now he knew why. It was just like the Christmas presents for Anna that were in the closet. Now Barbara knew why they were supposed to be there.

Jamie appreciated the beauty of the big old house with its high ceilings and large rooms. And she was happily impressed when she saw what they had done in the rooms for the children.

Emily and Bevin's room had already been painted a pale gold, and the new beds with white headboards and matching dressers were perfect. Above the beds were decorative wooden letters that spelled out *Emily* and *Bevin*. Between the two beds was a small white bookcase, and on the beds were matching bedspreads with yellow and pink and blue butterflies. Barbara told her she was shocked when she and Sharon had returned from Penney's to find that the men had picked up an area rug at the furniture store that also had butterflies. Jamie just laughed, shook her head, and said, "God again."

It was a beautiful room for little girls, and somehow, even though there was such a small amount of time, they had managed to buy toys, a doll buggy for Bevin, and a small table and chairs for the corner. Joe said there were many toys that had belonged to Anna that were in storage and they would get them out soon.

"Look in the drawers and closet," Barbara said. Jamie pulled open drawers and doors to find stacks of new carefully folded clothes for both girls. "Caroline and Rod Lincoln. Friends of ours. They brought it all. And wait until you see what they brought for Danny."

The nursery had pale green walls, and they had decorated the entire room in a horse theme. Framed childlike pictures of horses were on the walls, the bedding for the crib had cute little horses, and in the corner was a handmade rocking horse that Joe's father had made when Anna was born. As in the other room, the dresser was full of baby clothes.

"It's just adorable," Jamie said. "I can't believe you did everything so fast."

"We want to do more, but we want the girls to help," Joe said. "We think it will be good for them to do the finishing touches on their room."

"So are you ready?" she asked them.

Barbara looked at Joe. "I don't think we've ever been more ready for anything," she said. "With Anna, we were terrified, but she taught us well. This time around, we're just excited."

Jamie said she would bring the children to the house the next morning. She had informed Emily's kindergarten teacher she wouldn't be returning, and she was happy to learn that Barbara had enrolled her in the school where she had taught for years.

"The teacher she will have is the best there is," Barbara said.

"Do you know what time you'll bring them?" Joe asked. "Not that I'm anxious or anything." He pretended to chew voraciously on his fingertips.

"How about just before lunch. They can eat here, and that will give them time with their great-aunt. By the way, I am so thankful that you took time to visit with her. I know she is very grateful that you want to keep her in their lives. She does love those kids, and I know she's devastated she can't care for them."

"She's their only living relative, and it's important to her and to the children that they keep in touch with her. She'll be welcome here anytime, and we will make sure we make regular visits to her and that we keep in phone contact," Barbara said.

After Jamie left, they went from room to room to room, making sure everything was perfect. Barbara was coming out of Danny's bedroom when she noticed Joe on his tiptoes digging through a stack of Anna's old books, which were on the top shelf in the closet.

"What are you looking for?" she asked.

He pulled a book out of the pile and turned to her. "This!" he said, and he turned the book around so she could see. It was Anna's well-worn copy of *The Perfect Nest.*

"Do we have to?" Barbara said, laughing. It was the book that Anna demanded to hear over and over and over.

"Maybe they won't like it much as Anna did," he said. "Maybe Bevin and Danny will choose a book that is really horrible, and we'll wish they'd taken to this one."

"You have a point," she said, reaching for the book and thumbing through it.

Then she looked at Joe, and her eyes were twinkling. "Wouldn't it be funny if Anna was here and she had to read this thing a zillion times in a month?"

By nine o'clock, there was nothing else they could do, and they were too antsy to watch television or read. After looking at her watch again, Barbara laughed aloud, and Joe asked what was so funny. "It's a good thing we don't have to pay to look at a clock or a watch or we'd be broke," she said. "I can't believe how slowly time is going."

"Do you think we'll be okay?" Joe asked. "Aren't you just a little bit nervous?"

"No, actually, I'm not," Barbara answered after thinking about it a bit. "Actually, I'm a *lot* nervous!"

"It might be hard, the first few weeks. But we'll be all right. It will just take time," Joe said.

"We've sure got time," Barbara said. "We have the rest of our lives."

Chapter 67

By eleven o'clock the next morning, Joe was pacing in front of the big living room window. He had already mowed the front lawn, swept the porch, and carried out the garbage. Barbara was busy in the kitchen. She had decided the girls and she and Joe would make little individual pizzas. It would keep the kids busy, and it might be fun. It was either a great idea or a really bad idea.

The night before, she had called three women from church who had toddlers to ask them what to expect with the baby. She and Joe had studied late into the night a book about childcare. It was a little overwhelming. Finally, Barbara had closed the cover and tossed it on kitchen table.

"This is crazy," she said. "I think we just need to rely on God and our instincts."

"You mean fly by the seat of our pants?" he asked.

"We are two adults, and they are three little kids. How hard can this be anyway?"

He picked up the book and held it up. "This hard!" he said.

Just before noon, Jamie pulled into the driveway, and she'd barely come to a stop when Joe and Barbara raced down the porch stairs and were opening car doors. Barbara helped Emily and Bevin, while Joe unbuckled Danny from his car seat and grabbed his diaper bag. The baby looked at him and smiled, displaying a group of perfectly white teeth. Drool ran down his chin.

"Hey, Emily," he said, turning around as he picked up Daniel. "I think I found your tooth. Daniel has it!"

She laughed.

Bevin settled her doll in her arms, and then Barbara took each girl by the hand, and they went toward the house. Bevin was jumping up and down all the way to the front steps, but they noticed that Emily was taking in every detail. Her eyes lingered on the flowerbed in the front of the house.

"My mom liked flowers," she said. "We had all kinds."

Barbara veered off the sidewalk and steered them to the front flower beds, which were overflowing with petunias, zinnias, geraniums, lobelia, and dozens of other flowers. She picked two big pansies and tucked one behind Emily's ear and one behind Bevin's. "Did you help in the garden?" Barbara asked.

"Mmm-hmm," Emily said, nodding and bending over to smell a yellow rose. "It smells good," she said.

"I love the roses," Barbara said. "And the geraniums. Well, and the nasturtiums and the daisies. And I guess I can't really leave out the Johnny jump-ups or the daffodils in the spring. And what would the pansies say if I left them out?"

"They would be very sad," Bevin said.

"Bevin, do you like digging in the dirt?

"Sometimes. I like the hose part."

Joe laughed. "Well, it sounds like the garden is going to be well taken care of. But what about me? Doesn't anyone care about me? I'm starving!"

Jamie York broke in and told them that she was going to leave. She thought it would be better if Joe and Barbara just handled things on their own. If they needed anything—anything—just call her cell phone.

She gave Barbara and Joe a hug, and then leaning over, she hugged and kissed the girls and whispered something in their ears. Then she went over to Danny and shook his foot.

"Good-bye, sweet baby," she said. They watched as she walked back to her car, and they all waved as she pulled away from the house. She waved back.

Joe looked at Barbara with an "Oh lord, we are on our own" look, and she flashed him a big fake look of terror before laughing.

They had decided to keep the radio on so it wouldn't be too quiet in the house. They had pondered whether they should have gifts waiting but decided not to. The girls especially would be overwhelmed enough as it was.

Just inside the house, Danny started to wiggle and squirm and then lifted his arms and turned into a tube of Jell-O. Joe barely caught the baby before he slipped all the way to the ground. Joe put him on the floor. They were shocked at how fast he moved. Within seconds, he'd made his way to an end table and was reaching for an antique vase.

"Yikes!" Barbara said, snatching it out of his reach. She put it on the mantle.

Emily shook her head. "Your house isn't baby-proofed," she said reproachfully. "Danny can get really hurt in here. We need to put some of this stuff up." She quickly pointed to things that needed to go: a tipsy floor lamp, knickknacks, a statue on a pedestal, and—just before Danny reached it—a glass of iced tea. Within minutes, the house, which Barbara had so prided herself on, was stripped of anything that might cause injury to a two-year-old.

Baby Danny had by then moved to the fireplace. Barbara looked at Joe, and they moved the wood coffee table in front of it.

"Sometimes, he climbs," Emily said in warning.

The baby raised his little fists and beat on the table over and over and at the same time speaking some sort of foreign language.

Then as they watched, he became perfectly still, and his face turned red.

Bevin went over to the diaper bag and opened it and took out a diaper, diaper wipes, and some ointment. She took them to Joe. "Here," she said.

"You've got to be kidding," he said. The smell had reached his nose by then, and he looked appalled. He looked at Barbara.

"Hey, you're the father," she said. "You might as well get used to it. Take him upstairs to his room, and I'll bet Bevin can give you instructions."

As the threesome climbed the stairs, Emily and Barbara looked at each other and broke into snickers. "It's not a pretty sight," Emily whispered gleefully, wrinkling her nose in disgust. She was glad that she and Barbara were alone, and she was happy that she was asked to help put out all the ingredients for the pizzas.

"We can put the pizza stuff out," Barbara said. "Or do you want to see your room first?"

Emily thought about it. "I guess pizza first. No. Room first."

Barbara put her finger to her lips, indicating that they should sneak. Emily giggled. They crept to the doorway of the nursery.

The baby was on the changing table, and Bevin was on one side giving directions, and Joe was on the other. On his hands were bright yellow rubber utility gloves. He had grabbed a bright blue-and-red striped tie from his closet and wrapped it around his nose. One end was tossed behind his back. The other dangled in front, and Danny had hold of it and was yanking.

Joe had a handful of baby wipes in his hand and was in the process of wiping up the mess on Danny's bottom.

"You missed a spot," Bevin said, pointing.

"Oh, lord," Joe said, tossing the wipes in the garbage can and reaching for another handful. Danny pulled himself up a few inches with the tie, and it came off Joe's nose and went around his neck. It was obvious he was trying not to breathe, mainly from the fact his face was turning purple.

"Ye gods!" he said under his breath.

"You shouldn't swear," Bevin scolded. Then she giggled. "Oh, Daniel, you are a stinky boy," she crooned, tickling his naked feet.

"There," Joe said. "Does that look clean enough?"

Bevin looked. "It looks good. Good job!" she said, handing him a diaper.

Joe put the diaper under Danny and fastened the tabs. Then he stood him up, and the diaper fell down around the baby's knees.

"Don't you dare pee on me," Joe warned, putting the baby back down and refastening the tabs. Then he put his little pants back on him, put on his socks, and lifted him up. He hugged Danny to his chest, and Barbara couldn't remember the last time she'd seen anyone more contented.

"That was pretty good, for a first time," Emily said, and all three of them in the diaper brigade turned to look at the doorway.

"Did you see the whole show?" Joe said.

"Sure did," said Barbara. "You did good. I'm proud of you."

Then she turned to Bevin. "Would you like to see your new room?"

They all went into the girls' bedroom, and Bevin instantly ran downstairs to fetch her doll and put it in the buggy. Then she sat on her bed and bounced. Emily ran her hand over the bedspread and then studied the pictures on the wall.

"Our daughter Anna colored them," Barbara said. "If you'd like, we thought you and Bevin could help pick out other things for your room." Emily nodded her head.

Then Emily turned around and saw her name above her bed. "Look, Bevin," she said, pointing. "There's your name, and there is mine."

"I can spell it," Bevin said to Joe and Barbara. "B.e.v.i.n. Bevin."

"Very good," Joe said.

Emily opened a dresser drawer.

"That's Bevin's dresser, and the one over against the wall is yours," Barbara said.

"Whose clothes are in here?"

"Why, they are your clothes. Some friends of ours brought bags and bags of clothes for all of you. The closet is full too!"

"These clothes are all for us?" Bevin said, squealing and pulling out a sweater from a drawer."

"Yup. Maybe after we eat, we can come back up. And you still need to see the backyard and the swing set and explore the rest of the house."

"I vote we go make pizza," Joe said, lifting Danny into the air and gazing up at him. A slender strand of drool just missed his chin and landed on his shoulder.

"Emily, can you tell me what to feed Danny," Barbara asked as they walked down the hallway. "We bought a bunch of things for him, but I'm not sure what he eats."

"Boy, you sure don't know much about babies," she said, shaking her head.

"I used to," Barbara said. "But I've forgotten most of it. I really think Joe and I need a partner here. Are you interested?"

"Sure! I know all about Daniel. And Bevin too."

The rest of the day, while Daniel took his nap, was spent exploring and playing. Barbara and Joe both laughed uproariously when he brought down the book *The Perfect Nest* and offered to read it to Bevin. Emily and Bevin laughed too without really knowing why.

By nighttime, they were comfortable and had all learned a lot about each other. Barbara gave the girls a bath and put them in new pajamas and then got the baby ready for bed and fixed him a bottle. He was asleep before he finished, and she gently wiped the milk from his lips and kissed his sweet mouth, and she and Joe walked together to put him in his crib.

Joe prayed over their son, and then he pulled Barbara into his arms for just a second before they went back downstairs.

Barbara fixed hot chocolate, and she and Joe and the two girls snuggled on the couch while Joe read two books. They begged for another, but he declared it was time for bed.

After a trip to the bathroom, the girls went into their room and climbed into their beds. Emily held the sheets to her nose. They smelled so good. She felt good and clean and very tired. Joe kneeled beside her, and Barbara kneeled beside Bevin's bed.

They prayed, thanking God for his goodness.

Chapter 68

* * *

It is July 21. One year since Anna died. I wonder sometimes how I got through it. Sometimes, it seems so long ago, and other times, the memories wash over me, and I find myself laughing as if I was right back there again, playing on Rice's Hill or at Slate Creek or in her bedroom or mine or any of a hundred places. So many places. So many memories.

Rachel and Pastor Mike will be married next week, and I will be a bridesmaid. This afternoon, I will show everyone where we played and try to explain how it was—those golden years on Rice's Hill. I will relive the memories, and we will honor Anna today, and we will rejoice. We will rejoice.

Kemo and I were so good together that Grampa Henry said I could open the gate at the left side of the hill. The gate opens to a great meadow and, beyond that, the mountains. Wide open Montana with not a house on it or a road through it. This morning, I pulled down a box from the top shelf in my closet. The moccasins are tight now, but the beaded headband still fits. I placed the arrowhead necklace around my neck and went to get my horse.

I didn't put the saddle on Kemo, just her bridle. We rode through the chill of morning up the hill and crossed the wild grass to the old wooden gate. I slid off Kemo's back and pushed the gate open, and then I went back to her. I love this horse. She nickered softly and pranced daintily with her front feet a few times before settling down. I reached up and scratched her forehead and then slipped off her bridle and put it across the fence.

Kemo hesitated at first when I lifted her mane in my hands and then touched her neck to move her to the right. Then suddenly, she remembered.

I touched my heels to her flanks when we were clear of the gate, and my heart soared as we thundered down the slope and into the meadow. We could smell the sweet clover, wild mint, and Montana dirt and freedom. We were free! I was Sacajawea again, and I was with my beloved Kemo, and we were riding the winds! My heart and soul soared.

* * *

The July sun was warm as the group made their way up Rice's Hill. Joe carried a sleeping Danny, whose head was snugged up against his neck. He held Barbara's hand, and she clung to it tightly. The diaper bag she had slung over her shoulder seemed as natural as the wedding ring on her finger. This was Anna's hill. They were visiting Anna's world, and Marcy was leading them through this journey.

Bevin, Emily, and Ben were running ahead of everyone. The girls stopped often to raise their arms and giggle and twirl in the grass.

The children had been with Joe and Barbara long enough now that they called them Mommy and Daddy. Sometimes, it seemed as if the five of them had been together forever, and maybe, in a way they had. God had been working since the beginning of time, getting things in order and perfecting his plan.

Sharon and Jim brought up the rear. As to be expected, Sharon brought food for a picnic. She carried a heavy bagful of drinks, and Jim lugged a huge picnic basket and carried a king-sized blanket. Sharon had always felt the call to feed everyone she encountered, and no one ever complained about her way of showing them how much she cared.

Rachel and Pastor Mike were to be married in soon, and Marcy had been chosen to be a bridesmaid. Rachel was in Danford to attend a church-wide bridal shower, and the giddy couple had been asked to join the group on the hill, but they said it was better for the two families to be together. Marcy was glad about their decision in a way, but in another way, she wished they would be there. Pastor Mike had taken part of the grieving, and they both had played a major role in the healing. Besides, it would be good if Rachel could know their Anna.

Marcy was sitting on the log, watching the group come up the hill. If she looked beyond them, she could see Slate Creek merrily wending its way through the gully far below, and she could see Second Avenue and the big maples that lined it. She couldn't see Danford, but she knew the little town—her town—was there.

Two hours earlier, she had put Kemo away from the day's ride. They had gone through the meadow and reached the hills and found an old logging trail and rode uphill until they were high enough to see the town of Danford, Danford Lake, and beyond. She could only think how Anna would have loved being here.

When they were riding, Kemo seemed to read her mind and responded to the touch of Marcy's hand and the pulling of her mane as easily and quickly as she did to her bridle. When they were riding it was if they were one, she and this beautiful horse with the big gentle brown eyes. They talked in their own language—Marcy with words and Kemo with head movements and soft snuffling sounds or soft nickers. She had read that when a nicker is softer and quieter than a "hello" nicker, it is usually made by a mare to her foal.

Marcy brought Kemo back to Rice's Hill slowly so that they could enjoy the day and each other. Then she had put the horse away and gone to the part of Rice's Hill she had avoided on her rides—the place she hadn't been since before last July 21. It was still all there and absolutely unchanged: the small area on the hill that held the pole shed, the burial ground, the big log, and most importantly, the Bone Tree.

It had been hard coming here, but she had gone from place to place to place, visiting the past and putting it all together in her head. Now, in just a few minutes, she would start telling her family what that hill had meant to her and Anna.

Looking down the hill, Marcy smiled as she watched Bevin and Emily giggling and frolicking as they made their way. Looking at them made her feel so old. She was barely thirteen, and she felt so ancient sometimes. The other girls in school giggled and carried on, and she didn't understand. Would she ever be normal again? Would she ever get to the point where life wouldn't seem so serious, so achingly vital that she could act crazy and impulsive? Would she ever giggle again? She hoped so.

Emily found a sunflower and handed it to Bevin. Then she changed her mind and slipped the stem through the top buttonhole in Bevin's sundress. She stood back and looked at her handiwork, and Bevin put her head as low as she could to see. Then they were off, chasing and running and squealing.

Marcy had learned to love these two little girls, and Baby Danny was precious. He was walking well now and even running a few steps before he tumbled in a heap. Anna would have so loved these sisters and this little brother.

She looked at her mother and father, trudging up the hill and breathing heavily. They had been so wonderful and so caring and understanding. She owed them a debt she could probably never repay. She listened to her friends at school gripe about their parents, and she couldn't comprehend it. Her parents had helped pull her from a black pit of despair, and she cherished them for the sacrifices they made for her. Her respect ran deep, and her love was all-enveloping.

She was the hostess. She had called them all here for a reason. She was ready, and she knew the calmness and peace in her soul came from God. He of all was the one who deserved the most appreciation from her. She could look back and see that he had either carried her or walked with her the entire past year.

Standing up from where she had been sitting on the log, Marcy stood up to greet her guests. Emily ran up to her and gave her a hug. Bevin, not to be outdone, squeezed her until Marcy declared she couldn't breathe.

Finally, they were all assembled before her. Her parents and Barbara and Joe gave her a hug and then stepped back and looked at her expectantly.

She looked at them boldly. She didn't have the words planned; she just started talking.

"Today, I want to tell you about my best friend, Anna. Maybe by the time we are done today, you will be able to feel the magic of this place as we felt it, and you will learn a little bit about Anna and me and our special friendship and maybe about yourselves."

She asked them to sit while she talked and then she would take them on a tour of the hill and their village. They would visit the burial grounds and the pole barn, which served as their teepee, and she would tell them about the games they played, the time they shared, and the contents of the treasured Bone Tree. She wasn't ready to take out the contents and would ask that they just leave them there—a memorial to childhood. A memorial to Anna and life as it was.

Joe and Barbara sat on the log while Jim and Sharon sat on the blanket with their backs up against it. Baby Danny was still sleeping in Joe's arms, and Bevin and Emily and Ben sat attentively. She wondered if they had been warned.

Taking a deep breath, she began.

"There were once two young girls who were Marcy and Anna in real life but up here—here in this special place—they became Sacajawea and Pocahontas...."

Epilogue

The trip back to the Bone Tree had been planned since the day Marcy held her sleeping newborn daughter in her arms. Actually, it was probably planned before that, back when visions of marriage and children swirled in her head.

The Bone Tree—it was the one thing that was left to make her journey complete. She and her family had been back to Montana nearly once a year since she left for college, and she hadn't once, in all those years, been back to Rice's Hill. Too many memories. Not just of Anna, but of the simple life that they all lived back then. Even with the heartache it was a good life, a peaceful life. The little town of Danford had hugged its residents and enveloped them in a cocoon of goodness and a richness of life that she didn't even realize was special until she moved away. Danford was a paradise, and she hadn't realized it.

How long had Marcy been gone from Danford? Sixteen years? College and marriage and children, in that order, just as she and Anna had planned. Well, that wasn't true. The truth was that they were supposed to have a horse ranch first and then college and marriage and children. Anna would have loved John, her husband, Marcy thought, and the fact that she had become a counselor, working with children who were hurting and suffering. She specialized in art therapy. How much of life was the way it was because of Anna?

She thought it was strange sometimes when she looked in the mirror and saw the wrinkles next to her eyes and the graying of the hair at her temples. She was getting older and Anna would be twelve with black sleek hair and dancing blue eyes forevermore.

So many things had changed, but so many things were still the same. Her parents were approaching sixty and were well and happy and still in the old house. Ben was married to a wonderful woman, and they had twin boys and still lived in Danford. He worked alongside their father at the dealership.

Joe and Barbara and the three children had lived happily ever after, and now Emily and Bevin were in college, and Daniel was going into the air force. A few years after getting the Greenhaw children, the Millers adopted three more.

Pastor Mike was still preaching at Danford Worship Center, and he and Rachel had a houseful of children and a dog that was a direct descendant of Midas. Rachel never did learn to play the piano or sing. They were a delightful couple, and at least twice a year, they took their family onto the mission field to spread the gospel and to ease the suffering of others. Rachel had become a nurse so that she could do more.

Grampa Henry Knutson had died three years before in his sleep. He and his daughters had become very close, and in his will, he gave them a remarkable amount of money. Dee moved into the house at the bottom of Rice's Hill and became an active part of the neighborhood.

His will stipulated that the big meadow went to Marcy as well as Rice's Hill, on the condition that it would never be subdivided and never sold in her lifetime. He had included enough funds to pay property taxes for the next fifty years. Maybe someday, she and John would build a retirement home on Rice's Hill, a humble log house that blended into the land.

Kemo. Dear, wonderful Kemo—the horse that brought her back to life and was a beloved companion and friend all through school and college. Her children had also grown to love the gentle giant and rode her daily. They were all heartbroken when she became ill. Marcy spent four days sitting on the floor beside Kemo in the stall, stroking her neck and crooning, sleeping curled up against her, and praying for her. When the adored mare finally recovered, Marcy stayed in the stall and wept for hours in thanksgiving. John came into the stable, picked his wife up in his arms, and carried her home. They had Kemo another three years before she died a peaceful death one day in early spring.

Now, John and Marcy and their children, Shelby and Matthew, had come to Montana so that Marcy could take Shelby to the Bone Tree. The children had grown up hearing Anna stories, and she was a part of their lives. They knew the story of the small moccasin their mother treasured. It had been long known that when Shelby turned twelve, she and her mother would go to Rice's Hill. Someday, she would bring Matthew, but today was a mother-daughter time, a time for celebrating girlhood and teaching Shelby about the wonder of having best friends.

Marcy had wondered often if the items would still be in the Bone Tree or if maybe curious youngsters had come along sometime over the years and taken out the bones and the rest. She wondered if the secret treasures put there by two young Indian maidens would still be three. Today, they would find out.

It had been raining for days, but today the sun was shining and warming the earth. The sweet smells of summer as she and Shelby walked down Larkspur Lane to the hill were delicious. She could discern wild mint, honeysuckle, fresh mown grass, rain-soaked earth, sweet clover, and even the tangy smell of the cows in the pasture by Slate Creek.

Instead of slipping through the barbed-wire fence, they took the road long the bottom of the hill and opened the gate and slipped in. It was odd, the feeling in her heart, as if she was standing on sacred ground. Out there was the outside world; in here past the gate was magic.

Shelby grabbed her hand, and they hiked up the hill. When they reached the top, Marcy was disoriented for a few minutes until she spotted the log. It seemed so funny that the last time she was here, her parents and Anna's parents were all sitting right there, and she was telling them the story of Anna and their friendship.

"Is this the log?" Shelby asked. Her mother nodded and smiled faintly.

"Can you still walk it?" Shelby challenged, and Marcy looked at her and grinned.

"Watch this," she said, and she jumped up, put her arms out, walked to the end, and then pivoted neatly and returned. Shelby's attempt wasn't nearly as impressive.

"Look here," Marcy said, pointing out the names carved into the top of the log. They were still there and after all these years, readable. Anna. Marcy. Sacajawea. Pocahontas.

Everything seemed so strange—all these things of the past that were still just as she left them.

"Come with me," Marcy said, and she led Shelby through the damp grass to the pole shed, which was in sad shape. Many of the poles had rotted and fallen away, and for some reason, she wanted to cry. She had so wanted everything to be the same. Then she looked again, and she could see vestiges of what it had been.

"This was our make-believe teepee. We worked for days getting it cleaned out, and we piled it with branches and put soft cedar branches on the floor. It smelled wonderful. We would sit in here if it rained, and we would be a little protected. Not much but a little."

They moved to the graveyard, and Marcy knelt down and pulled away some of the weeds to reveal the white rocks that had been placed in squares and circles. Her heart lurched when she pondered that she and Anna had placed them, every one, and they were still there, just where they had put them. No one else had touched them over the years, and they had lain here in wait, just for this day. The transplanted daisies also still thrived.

Her voice was low and husky. "It seems so silly to cry over the graveyard," she said. "Nothing is buried here but a few birds and bumblebees and a beautiful young raven. Remember, the feathers in the old headband? They came from the raven. A gift from the raven."

"Your memories are buried here too," Shelby said. "It must be hard knowing that everything is the same as it was the day Anna died. It is like keeping someone's room exactly as it was. Sort of like a shrine. That's why it makes you want to cry."

"You are very wise for a twelve-year-old," Marcy said to her daughter, and suddenly the words echoed in her mind, and she remembered another time—when Joe Miller, a grieving father—said those very words to her.

They walked around to the left of the hill and went to the far gate that led into the great meadow and the mountains beyond. Shelby knew it well from the stories.

They leaned against the gate, side by side, rested their chins on the top board, and gazed at the beautiful scene before them. The rain had washed the air, and the mountains were clear and seemed so close.

"This is where you and Kemo rode like the wind," Shelby said, gazing out over the beautiful spacious piece of land. "It seems so funny that you own it now. Why have we never come here before? Grampa Henry died a few years ago."

"I don't know. I guess it was just special that you and I did it the year you turned twelve. Silly, maybe. Your dad and I came here after the funeral and walked around. And Dee has let you and Matthew play in the old barn. I guess the meadow was just a part of the hill and I wasn't ready.

Then she turned and smiled. "But I am now. Are you ready to go to the Bone Tree?"

But was she really ready? She knew she'd be heartbroken if it had been vandalized. Maybe it would be better to just leave it be. Maybe it was too much, like digging up a grave and what they discovered would be ugly and hideous and rotted. Maybe her memories weren't even close to reflecting reality.

She had decided that if things were still there, everything that was taken out would be put back in. Maybe someday when she was grown, Shelby could bring her children here and they could look at treasures from the Bone Tree. Maybe her great-grandchildren could do the same.

The broken and hollowed-out stump had fared well over the years. The bark had long since fallen off and disintegrated leaving the sides of the wood smooth and silky and the color of burnished silver. She had never realized that it really was beautiful, the old stump. It was something you would see in photographs—a gnarled remnant of a majestic tree that still oozed dignity and character.

Peering in, Marcy saw the top layer of bones. They were pitted and decayed and had patches of moss growing on them. She hadn't considered that this would be a dirty job, but she didn't hesitate. Reaching in, she pulled them out one by one. Shelby took them and set them on the ground in a row. When there were six, Marcy stopped and straightened. She wiped her hands on her jeans.

"I don't really know where they came from," she told Shelby, smacking her hands together. "But we always seemed to find shiny white bones. Some were long with joints on either end, like cow or deer shin bones, and some were thick joints. Some were just shards.

They were all old and had been cleaned, I suppose, by insects and scavengers."

She leaned over the trunk again and rested her stomach on it while she dug deeper. Suddenly, she gave a cry.

"Look!" she said. The leather thong was dark now, nearly black, and pulled apart under her fingers, but the arrowhead was as beautiful as when she had placed it in the tree, the day she had brought the families here. After everyone had walked back down the hill, she had stood praying. Then she took the arrowhead from around her neck and laid it in the Bone Tree and walked away.

"That's the arrowhead that Anna had that day—the special treasure for the Bone Tree," Shelby exclaimed, holding out her hand. The arrowhead was brownish red and was damp and cold. Copper wiring attached it to the crumbling leather. Testing it with her thumb, she discovered the edges were sharp. She had never held a real arrowhead before and she was entranced as she considered that it had been handcrafted by an Indian over a hundred years—or many thousands of years—before.

Even more entrancing was the fact that the stories that she had heard all her life were coming to life.

There were rocks, some shaped like hearts and others that were of quartz or shiny with mica. Marcy pulled out the deer antler that they had thought was a special offering from above. Now it looked so small and not nearly as majestic.

She took out pieces of tinfoil, but for the most part, the folded pieces of paper inside were unreadable. Too many winters and too many rains had disintegrated any writing on the bits of paper. In one, though, she found two marbles. Yellow and blue cat eyes. They had found them on their way home from school and brought them to the Bone Tree.

In another, they found a tiny red plastic heart, and Marcy was thrilled. Another held a small metal statue of a horse. In a plastic bag was the pine needle basket they had so lovingly made. It was fragile now, and if she had squeezed, it would have crumbled into a million pieces.

One by one, the memories of those days clunked into place like numbers on a slot machine, jiggling a bit until they were settled and clear.

At the bottom, Marcy could see the old piece of red-and-white plastic tablecloth that they had placed on top of the moss that covered the small tin box. She lifted it and then the moss and could see that both had done a remarkable job in preserving the old tin box.

Handing the tablecloth and moss to Shelby, Marcy reached in and lifted out the box gently, reverently. She hugged it to her chest and closed her eyes. She had been so afraid it would be gone. It was still encased in a plastic bag, but she could see through it enough to see that it was in good shape.

The tin box hadn't been the first item they had placed in the tree. The bones were first and then the rocks and special items wrapped in tinfoil. But it had surely been the most special. It was the summer they were nine. They had agreed to cement their friendship by writing secrets: a list of life goals, of people they liked and disliked, and declaring they would be friends forever.

Marcy remembered the day so vividly. "I brought pens and paper and two plastic bags. Anna brought the tin box that was shaped like a heart and enameled with pink flowers."

They had gone to separate areas to write, she told Shelby. Anna sat in the middle of a patch of sunflowers, and Marcy sat on the log. After a time, Anna had declared that she was putting Marcy on the list of people she didn't like. They had laughed when Marcy retorted that she had a whole page written about why she didn't like Anna.

Now here she was, nearly twenty-five years later, and the box looked nearly as good as they day they put it in the Bone Tree. True, there were rust spots, especially around the lid, and the color had faded, but she would recognize it anywhere. They took it to the log and sat down.

"Are you scared to open it?" Shelby asked.

Marcy considered her answer. She pushed out her lower lip and let out a big breath of air. "Sort of," she admitted as she looked down the hill into the gully below. She could see two boys frolicking in Slate Creek.

She turned to Shelby, and her eyes looked worried. "Wouldn't it be awful if Anna really did write that she didn't like me? Even if it was a joke, it would be a terrible thing to read."

"She wouldn't write that," Shelby said, dismissing the suggestion. Deep down though, she realized it was a possibility and how horrible it would be. Maybe this whole expedition wasn't such a good thing after all. Maybe ghosts should just be left alone.

The sun was high by now, and it was getting warm. Bees and ants and other insects were busily going about their business, and a Monarch butterfly fluttered a few times before landing on one of the bones on the ground. Death and life.

The lid wouldn't come off no matter how hard she pulled, so Marcy reached into her jeans pocket and pulled out the old pocket knife. She carefully ran it along the edge and then, using the awl blade, pried off the lid. It popped off, and she barely caught it before it fell to the ground. She placed it on the log beside her.

It was all there and perfectly preserved. On top were their class photos. Anna was beautiful and wore a turquoise sweater, which made her eyes stand out. She was grinning and leaning forward just a little, as if she knew a grand secret and was about to tell. Her black hair was pulled forward to display its length. Marcy and Anna had ongoing battles over who had the longest hair. Now, looking at the photo, Marcy would finally have to admit that Anna had that honor.

Marcy looked solemn in her photo, and her silky blond hair was tied off in twin ponytails on either side of her head. She sat straight and looked into the camera with boldness and just a bit of a twinkle in her eye.

There were cards in there, mostly postcards or note cards their mothers had given them that had nice pictures or paintings. Anna had added a Valentine given to her that year by Billy Blasset. Marcy had been disgusted when she had kissed it. Secretly, she kicked herself that she hadn't thought to bring her own special Valentine that was signed by Ricky Melton.

There was a white plastic rosary that her mother had brought home from a funeral at St. Patrick's Catholic Church and a tiny miniature deck of cards with songbirds on them. A broach with blue glass gems was on the bottom. Anna had purchased it at a flea market for a quarter. They had decided that they needed to have photos in the box, and even though they were stuck together, they were in almost-perfect condition: photos of Anna and her parents laughing in front of the house, of Anna at the ocean the year she was six, and photos of Marcy and her family. There were three photos of the two of them running through the hose. In one, they were running toward the sprinkler, and their heads were turned to look at the camera. It showed their backsides and where their bathing suits had hiked up, revealing rounded bottoms that shone white against their summer-tanned legs.

Finally, they had gone through everything in the tin box. Only the letters remained. Setting aside the box, Marcy placed them in her lap and put her right hand on top of them. They felt smooth. Hers was on top, and the handwriting was simple with big fat letters a nine-year-old would make.

"You don't have to read them now," Shelby said, putting her hand over her mother's. She had been watching her mother and was afraid for her. This was hard on her, bringing up the past like this. She had never known her mother to be so fragile, so brittle. Her emotions were right near the surface.

Marcy looked at her and smiled. "It is so strange to see my handwriting. It looks familiar but at the same time unfamiliar. My goodness! I wrote that when I was not much older than Matthew."

She opened her letter first, unfolding it gently. The paper had to be held down to keep from going back into its folds. It all looked so familiar. She had forgotten she had placed a tiny bluebell inside. It was still there, dry now, and crumbling. It had made an imprint of pale blue on the paper.

Marcy Peterman. 9 years old.

On Rices Hill.

Favorite people are Anna and baby Ben, mommy and daddy, and Grampa and grandma. I like Movies. Bowling. and Playing.

Anna is my best friend. She is Pocoehantas and I am Sakagawia. We are Indian princesses. We will have a horse ranch when we grow up. It will be fun. We will be happy.

I like everybody. Anna is my best friend. I like her best. She is sitting in the sunflowers writing this note for the bone tree.

Love,
Marcy Peterman, aged 9

Marcy laughed and handed the letter to Shelby so she could look at it more closely. "Look at that handwriting," she said.

"And the spelling," Shelby noted. "I can't believe you won the spelling bee when you were ten."

"It was a fluke," her mother said. "All the good spellers were home with the chicken pox."

She was surprised at how rudimentary the letter was. In her mind, they had written grand and extensive missives revealing their darkest secrets and desires—epics of brilliant writing that would be treasured forever. Instead, at least in her case, the letter was simple. But in a way, it did reveal a lot. Her goal at age nine was to simply be happy and to share life with those she loved.

Shelby carefully refolded the letter and watched as her mother picked up Anna's letter. On the outside of the folded letter, Anna had drawn butterflies and ladybugs, and there was a smiling spider in a web in the corner. The spider wore a little hat with a flower sticking out of the top.

"Anna always was an overachiever," Marcy said with a snort.

She unfolded the letter, and a scattering of tiny red glittery hearts tumbled out, followed by a bigger heart that declared "Anna and Marcy, Best Friends Forever."

"Well, that little stinker," Marcy said. "She must have had these hidden in her pocket. No wonder she giggled the whole day. Our plan was that we would come up here the day we graduated from high school and take out the box and laugh over it. She probably thought that was really funny, thinking ahead and imagining how it would be when I opened hers and found all these red hearts."

AJM

My name is Anna Jane Miller. I am 9. I live in Danford Montana.

I love Rice's Hill and the Bone tree and I like playing Indians up here with Marcy. I am Pocohontas and she is Sacajewea and we wear moccasins. Someday we will have horses. Someday when we are rich we will by Rice's Hill from Mr. Knutson and we will live hear on our horse ranch.

Marcy is my best friend. And Marcy, if you read this when we are graduated from school I hope we are still best friends. I hope we never fight.

What I like to do...Swimming at City beach, playing Indians, making cookies, playing at the creek, the funny cows, finding tresures for the Bone tree, going to school, and playing.

What I like about Marcy Peterman...Blond hair, how she laughs, she can draw good, playing with me, how she cares about me. God has made her my best frend. We will be best friends when we are old.

These hearts are for Marcy from Anna. XXX

Love,
Anna Jane Miller, age 9

They didn't say anything, and Marcy carefully picked up all the tiny red hearts that had fallen to the ground and put them in the paper and then folded it gently. "And that's it," she said to Shelby, after wiping the tears from her cheeks. "Like she said, we will be best friends, forever. There will always be a part of me that is still a little girl with a best friend named Anna."

"Will you put it back in the Bone Tree like you planned?" Shelby asked as Marcy put the letters back in the heart-shaped box and replaced the lid.

"I think I will take it down and show it to Barbara and Joe," she said, standing to her feet and hugging it close.

Tomorrow. She would put it back tomorrow.

But not the arrowhead.

She would give Shelby the arrowhead necklace after she had a jeweler put it on a gold chain.

About the Author

 Jan Thacker is a longtime journalist, author, onetime weekly newspaper owner, and columnist with twenty-five years of weekly columns (mostly humor) under her belt. A fourth generation Whitefish, Montanan, in 1976, Jan and her husband, Troy Thacker, decided Northwest Montana was a "beautiful place to starve to death." They packed up their prized possessions (the kids and the new console color TV) and drove to Alaska, where they spent nearly forty years, most of them in North Pole a little town outside of Fairbanks. During their time in Alaska, including eight years living in the bush above the Arctic Circle, she enjoyed endless grand adventures, including learning to fly her own tail-dragger airplane, dog sledding in the Brooks Range, rafting countless rivers, and seeing country few have seen.

Also a business owner and avid artist, she and Troy currently live in Moses Lake, Washington, where they co-own Red Door, a cafe and store, with their daughter and son-in-law. When not working, writing, or painting, Jan devotes her time to cheerleading her daughters, eleven grandkids, and five great-grandkids. A Christian author, she has been married over fifty years and says she is a normal woman who enjoys life, likes to laugh, and vigorously fights the scale and graying hair.